HALF ANGEL, HALF DAUGHTER OF SATAN

From her father Catherine Mayfield inherited her fortune, her sense of honor, her unbending pride. From her mother came her incredible beauty and the fires that burned uncontrollably within her.

In the aristocratic society of old New Orleans, Catherine ruled like a spoiled princess, mocking conventions, violating taboos—until the cunning of one man, and the virile power of another, pulled her off her pedestal . . . and plunged her into a torrent of forbidden love and fearful danger that swept her to the ultimate in desire and degradation—and beyond . . .

LOVE'S WILD ASSAULT

Love is a distant laughter in the spirit.
It is a wild assault that hushes you to your awakening.
It is a new dawn upon the earth,
A day not yet achieved in your eyes or mine,
But already achieved in its own greater heart.

Kahlil Gibran
THE EARTH GODS

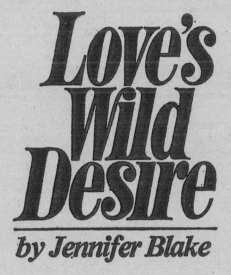

Love's Wild Desire

by Jennifer Blake

POPULAR LIBRARY • NEW YORK

POPULAR LIBRARY EDITION
June, 1977

Copyright © 1977 by Patricia Maxwell

ISBN: 0-445-08616-5

Part I

CHAPTER ONE

The hired carriage clattered over the rutted streets of the Vieux Carré, enveloped in the misty night air. A girl sat inside the carriage next to the window, her face illuminated by the glow of the side lamps. Her visage formed a memorable profile with an imperious loveliness on the high cheekbones and well-defined brows. There was a willful tilt to the pointed chin and only the smallest hint of vulnerability about the finely shaped mouth.

A well-dressed, rakish man sat next to her. "Well, Catherine?" he asked, his voice full of lazy confidence.

"Well, what Marcus Fitzgerald?" the girl cried, swinging around, her amber-brown eyes full of contempt. "What gave you the idea that I would agree to such a suggestion?"

Marcus touched one of the studs in his pleated shirt front in an uneasy gesture. "You needn't sound so outraged."

"Outraged?!" Catherine Mayfield hissed. "If I were a man I would call you out."

A warm, indignant voice came from a darkened corner of the carriage. "*Mais oui*, just so. I have never liked this one, this Fitzgerald. I have warned you, and your *maman* too. He deserves to have his manners mended on the dueling ground!"

5

Catherine sent her chaperone, and nursemaid since childhood, a quelling glance. The middle-aged Negro woman shut her mouth with a snap in a kind of arrogant servility, drawing her ample bulk further into the corner. She had been Catherine's nurse, but she had been the friend and confidant of her mother, Yvonne Mayfield, née Villere, since birth when she was given as a child of three to the newborn as a gift. She had never accepted reprimands from her younger charge with good grace, never given her anything like the allegiance and adoration she gave Catherine's mother.

There was nothing unusual in the presence of the nurse. She was an acceptable duenna. Many women brought their female attendants with them to the balls to tuck up a curl or mend a flounce. It was customary for refreshments to be provided for the maids, coachmen, and valets, making it a social occasion with much dancing and flirtation in the servant quarters also.

Marcus chose to take her censure of her chaperone as a favorable sign. He reached out to place his hand over Catherine's where it lay on the worn leather seat. "Come," he said coaxingly. "Would it be so different from the games you played at the convent or the swimming you did with your two male cousins?"

Catherine jerked her hand away. "Childish pranks, no more than that. That was the summer my father died. I was twelve and a little wild with the pain of loss. My mother was absorbed with her suffering, which is why I was allowed so much freedom. My cousins, those terrible twins, were brats only a little older than myself. They thought it a great lark to half-drown me in the river—but I learned to swim instead." And, she added to herself, to run and swing on the grapevines that grew on the plantation where her mother had gone to hide away in her grief.

"I seem to remember," he went on reflectively, "that you danced barefoot at your first ball—"

"My slippers pinched."

"And then there was the red slippers and ribbons, the *coulour de diable*, which you wore to Holy Communion a

6

year or so ago. That caused quite a few hands to be upraised in horror."

Catherine lifted a white shoulder in a shrug, though a frown drew her brows together. "I was bored." She had been kept in her room for a month over the incident. It had improved neither her conduct nor the relationship between her and her mother.

"All very understandable," Marcus agreed soothingly. "But what explanation have you for enticing your friend Sophia Marie's fiance out into the courtyard at the *soirée* announcing their betrothal? He looked bemused and somewhat silly when he returned to the salon with your fan in his waistcoat pocket."

The girl beside him was silent for so long it seemed she did not intend to answer. At last she said, "It was a stupid wager, one I was extremely sorry I won. It cost me a dear friend."

"Ha!" Marcus pounced on the admission. "A wager! A stupid wager, but one you won. Surely, then, you can understand my feelings?"

"You are asking me to jeopardize everything, name, social standing, and future prospects, while you risk nothing. Why should I do it? What could be more ruinous to a girl's good character than to be seen at a quadroon ball? It would brand her as lost to all honor, besides starting terrible rumors of a touch of *café au lait* in the family. I had as well enter a nunnery, if one would have me, or kill myself, if discovered."

"You exaggerate, but there would be no danger. It's a masquerade ball. And you need stay no more than a moment. I have only to be seen with a white woman on my arm. No one will ever learn her identity. I have here beside me the half-mask for your face, a turban affair for your hair, and this shawl to cover your gown. Only a moment of your time and it is done. What could be the danger?"

Barely glancing at the brilliant garments he indicated, Catherine said, "You must have felt certain I would agree."

He gave her his most attractive smile as he shook his head. "I only hoped."

Catherine felt her lips curving in an unwilling response. Marcus could be attractive when he wanted. He was a well set man of medium height with a distinguished set to his shoulders. He had crisp chestnut hair, audacious hazel eyes, and a countenance saved from being too handsome only by a short Irish nose. He had been one of Catherine's admirers and most persistent suitors since her first appearance in society two years before at the Conde Street ballroom. He had proposed marriage a number of times, but Catherine had just as often refused. Eventually, she would accept him or someone like him. But her mother, whose duty it was to find a suitable husband, was in no hurry to see her wed and producing the children who would make her a grandmother. As a result Catherine had much more freedom in the choosing than many considered either becoming or good for her. Catherine, intent on pleasure, was in no hurry to exchange her present way of life for the dubious advantages of an alliance ring.

Though his surname was Fitzgerald, Marcus came from an old Louisiana family. His grandfather had been an Irish adventurer who came to the country with little more than his sword and his name. But he put both to good use and was rewarded with a grant of land by the Spanish Crown. Following his marriage to a lovely French-Creole woman, he had built on his land a beautiful home of Spanish design which he called Alhambra. His son, Marcus's father, had been more of a gentleman of leisure than an adventurer or empire builder. Marcus' father made big inroads into the estate before his death in a riding accident. Marcus completed the ruin, finally losing the house and unencumbered acreage on the gaming table.

But despite the financial disaster Marcus retained his personal charms. Personable, a good conversationalist and polished dancer, related on his mother's side to most of the best Creole families, he was a favorite with the hostesses of the city. Family background was more important than money. There was many a Creole father who would have been happy to make a place for such a one at his table for the sake of the alliance—and many a daughter who would have been delighted to accept a meagerly filled bridal basket if it was given by such a *parti*. If Catherine suspected that Marcus himself would not be content in any such arrangement, she had nothing positive to base her suspicions upon. He had expensive tastes, he dressed well and kept lodgings in a fashionable street; and, though he did not keep his own carriage, he was creditably mounted when he rode out for an evening along the levee. All this was managed without an obvious income, so far as Catherine could see, though Marcus often spoke with irony of his phenomenal luck at the gaming halls and cockpits since the loss of his ancestral home.

But perhaps fortune was frowning on him once again. He was being extraordinarily insistent tonight. The wager he spoke of must be a large one, with greater than average importance to his purse. In that case the events of this evening must have seemed arranged by *le bon Dieu*. First, Catherine's mother, complaining of the headache, had decided at the last moment to stay home with cologne on her brow, allowing him to escort Catherine and her duenna alone to the theatre and the small subscription ball given afterward for the relief of the orphans of Santo Domingo. Then, there had been her convenient accident. Catherine, with unaccustomed clumsiness, had spilled wine punch down the front of her gown of celestial blue muslin before places were called for the first quadrille. But had it been just a clumsy accident? In the press of the crowd hadn't she felt a slight nudge at her shoulder as she lifted the glass to her lips? The impression, lost in the dismay of the moment, came back with undeniable strength as Catherine surveyed the man beside her through narrowed eyes.

Marcus chose that moment to give a warm chuckle. "Let's not quarrel about it," he said. "If you feel you can't, then you can't. Don't let it trouble you any longer. It's just that I have an ingrained dislike for defaulting on a wager. A matter of pride. Do you understand?"

The devil of it was, Catherine did understand. That same distaste for being bested ran in her veins also. She at once felt more in charity with him, and genuinely regretful that she could not oblige him. A smile forced its way to her lips before she turned back to the window.

Though only March, the night air was warm. As they crossed one of the more noisy, brightly lighted streets, the smells of cooking seafood, brewing coffee, and orange blossoms from the levee came through the open window, mixed with the inevitable smell of offal from the open gutters that lined the street. A pair of seamen, identifiable by their close fitting caps, tarred pigtails, and the sunburned darkness of their skin, stumbled drunkenly down the street singing a lewd ditty at the top of their lungs. Inside of one of the dimly lit barrooms a fight was in progress marked by the sounds of crashing glass and the thud of falling bodies. The "Kaintocks," the Mississippi River boatmen, were at it again. They seemed to thrive on violence and pain, preferring an uproar to peace at any time. Then through the open doorway she saw a woman leaning against the wall with her hands behind her. Her head was thrown back in laughter, exposing her bare throat and the white skin of her breasts above a low cut gown.

With a slight gesture of her hand, she drew Marcus's attention to the woman. "Perhaps a woman like her," she suggested helpfully.

Marcus shook his head. "A *demi-mondaine?* No, she must be a lady."

"With the proper training—" Catherine said, ignoring Dédé's scandalized gasp and compelling gaze.

"The Masquerade ball of the quadroons is tonight— didn't you notice the scarcity of gentlemen at our charity dance? It was stupid of the orphans committee to choose this Thursday. There will not be another quadroon ball for two weeks, and even then there is no guarantee that it will be a fancy dress affair. It is this evening, or not at all." He paused, then went on. "But never mind that. Would you ladies care for a rice cake, since you missed the supper table?"

A *vendeuse*, a mulatto woman in her white tigon and apron, was crying her wares along the banquet. She carried the *calas, tout chaud* in a covered tray on her head,

10

and stopped with a smile and a curtsey to surrender a packet of them to Marcus as the carriage drew in beside her.

It was an effective dismissal of the subject, and Marcus seemed cheerfully resigned to her refusal as he passed on to other topics for the remainder of the drive.

At last the carriage halted before a narrow building with a wrought iron balcony overhanging the street. The house was a strange mixture of English Georgian and Spanish styles. Unlike most of the Creole dwellings that surrounded it, the lower floor of the two story building was in use, and its main doorway, beneath the Adams fanlight in a cobweb design, opened from it out onto the street, rather than on an interior courtyard. This lower portion was of red brick, while the upper half, behind the balcony, was plastered in white. Not an attractive house, it was in essence, a symbol of the marriage between Catherine's father, a New England banker who had come to New Orleans in the last decade of the 18th century to start one of the first banking ventures in the city, and her pleasure-loving Creole mother. Since the death of Edward Mayfield Catherine and her mother had lived in the house alone, against the earnest advice of their Creole relatives and friends who felt they should have a male relative to lend them protection. Yvonnne Mayfield had only laughed, asserting that a half-dozen menservants and four or five maids surely constituted guard enough for any one. But Catherine had often wondered at the wisdom of the arrangement. Large families with numerous aunts, cousins, grandparents, and great-aunts, in addition to brothers and sisters, living under one roof were normal in New Orleans. There would have been much laughter and gaiety, less loneliness for a young girl in such an establishment. There might have been less friction between her mother and herself, less time for her maman to brood upon the passing of the years and the fine lines gathering at the corners of her eyes.

Pitch pine flambeaux burned brightly in their holders at each side of the front door. Their orange light slid over the shining, honey-gold curls piled *à la Grecque* on her

11

head as she accepted the hand Marcus offered to help her alight. She stood to one side while he assisted Dédé, staring up at the unlighted windows of the upstairs bedrooms. Had her mother retired already? It was not like her to seek her bed so early. Standing before the quiet house with its blind, vapid windows, Catherine acknowledged a moment of uneasiness.

Marcus stepped to the carriage perch to speak to the coachman. With Dédé crowding behind her, Catherine moved toward the door, but it remained obstinately closed instead of swinging open as she expected. All doors in the Vieux Carré were locked at night against the marauding bands of drunken "Kaintocks." Their greatest pleasure seemed to be the destruction of property. But there should have been a servant on duty to admit her, regardless of the hour. Casting a puzzled frown at the nurse, she lifted her hand to knock.

"Wait, wait, Mam'zelle Catherine. You might wake your maman. She will not be pleased, especially if she is ill. Let me go to the back. I will let you in."

"What is it? Why is no one about, Dédé?" Catherine asked. The nurse only shook her head, a grim look on her dour face as she turned to walk away.

"Is something wrong?" Marcus asked, strolling up behind her.

"I'm not sure. There are no lights, and the servants have been dismissed—or so it appears."

"Probably a whim of your mother's," Marcus said easily, "but I'll come in with you all the same."

"I'm sure that won't be necessary—" Catherine trailed off. Only a few weeks before Monsieur and Madame Duralde had returned from a soiree to find their home being ransacked by the river ruffians. Having his sword-cane at his side, M'sieur Duralde had attacked the invaders and had been severely beaten for his bravery. He would be lucky if he ever used his right arm again. Furniture and windows had been smashed and priceless heirlooms taken before the constables of the *Garde de Ville* had reached the scene and brought the fury of the "Kaintocks" down on themselves. There were other hazards than the "Kaintocks," other criminals, other dangers. New Orleans had not become known as the most wicked city in the New World for nothing.

The trend of Catherine's thoughts was broken by sounds from within the house indicating the door was being unbarred. As the panel swung open she pushed into the house with Marcus behind her, forcing the nurse to step back.

"My mother—is she all right?"

"Do not disturb yourself, Mam'zelle. I am certain all is well," Dédé said soothingly, shielding the candle in her hand from the draft as Marcus closed the door behind him.

Stripping off her lace dancing mitts and dropping them on a small, mirror-topped table in the entrance hall, Catherine turned to Marcus. "I think I will look in on her, if you will excuse me. You will find a drinkable claret in the salon if you don't mind pouring out for yourself."

These last words were thrown over her shoulder as she moved toward the broad stairs that rose against one wall.

"I'll wait," Marcus agreed, and twirling his beaver hat in his hand, lounged toward the salon.

"No, Mam'zelle Catherine. Allow me," Dédé said, lifting her skirts, in one hand, hurriedly mounting the stairs after Catherine, the candle held high.

"You? Why, Dédé?"

"I—I must—"

"You are keeping something from me. I can feel it," Catherine said, halting to stare at the set expression on her nurse's face. Seeing the perspiration gleaming on her upper lip, a prickle of fear ran down Catherine's spine. She would never forgive herself for leaving her mother alone if anything had happened to her. The two of them disagreed with monotonous regularity on everything from religious observance to fashion, but they were still mother and daughter with the strong blood ties of the Creoles between them.

As she took a deep breath Catherine was aware of Marcus, an interested spectator, standing with his glass in hand in the doorway of the salon below. A part of her mind resented his presence, still she lifted her chin. "Tell me," she demanded.

But Dédé was silent too long. A soft moan laced with a keening edge of desperation came drifting down from the upper hallway.

Catching up her skirts, Catherine raced up the stairs and along the hall.

"No!" Dédé cried, but it was too late. Catherine had thrust open the door of her mother's bedchamber to stand panting in the opening.

It was a moment before the two people struggling among the rumpled bedclothes on the canopied bed were aware of the intrusion. They turned ludicrously empty faces toward the growing light as Dédé drew nearer the doorway with her candle.

A musky perfume hung in the air, overlaid with the smell of warm, perspiring bodies and the sour reek of flat champagne coming from the supper tray left standing at the foot of the bed.

Suddenly Marcus gave a smothered shout of laughter from behind Catherine. The sound seemed to release the two figures locked together on the bed. With an inarticulate cry of rage, Yvonne pushed aside her gaping partner. She rolled off the bed, nearly tearing the willow leaf color mosquito *baire* from its hangings in her haste, snatching up a dressing saque of emerald satin which she clutched to her nakedness as she rose.

"Get out!" she screamed. "You spying, sly little—" Her wild gaze fell on a china carafe standing on the table beside the bed. She picked it up and hurled it at the door, her voice rising in a crescendo of shrill invective, mingling with the shattering sound of glass as the water carafe struck the door, followed by a combing box, a candlestick, and a prayer book.

For an instant Catherine met the wild eyes of the young man cowering in the bed, his aristocratic face stiff with horror and distaste.

"I'm—sorry," she whispered. Swinging around, she ran, blundering with tears rising in her eyes past Marcus, tripping, nearly falling, on her way down the stairs. The

14

scene she had witnessed, with its aura of mindless striving and feverish passion seemed printed on her mind. The excuse, the dismissed servants and darkened house were abruptly explained. It was not that she was unaware of the fundamental needs of men and women or the duties of the connubial couch. She had spent too many years acting as housekeeper under her mother's tutelage, caring for their servants in their quarters across the courtyard at the back of the house, treating them in sickbed and childbed, to pretend to ignorance. Still she had never associated such needs and actions with her widowed mother. It seemed a betrayal of her father's memory, an unnatural adultery. Moreover, the man beside her had been at least twenty years younger than her mother, scarcely older than Catherine herself, and a penniless ne'er-do-well of doubtful breeding, against whom Yvonne Mayfield had warned her daughter several times—

Behind her as she ran Catherine could hear Dédé talking, mouthing soothing phrases as she moved into the bedroom. Let the old nurse calm her mistress, take the brunt of her anger, smooth her outraged sensibilities. It was doubtful anyone else could. Her daughter was not sure she could face her, now—or ever.

The front door yielded easily to her touch. She left it open, swaying in the draft of her passing and the breath of the rising wind.

The freshening breeze was cool on her face as she paused on the sidewalk. She had no idea where to go, knowing only that she could not stay. At a touch on her elbow, she flinched, then turned to face Marcus.

"The carriage is here," he murmured.

Catherine hesitated no more than an instant before she allowed herself to be handed in. Marcus called an order she did not quite catch to the driver, then the carriage shifted as he climbed in and slammed the door behind him. He sank down beside her, the carriage started with a jerk, and they rolled away down the street.

"How could she?" Catherine whispered, and then as her shock moved into an angry disgust she demanded, "How could she?"

"Why not?" Marcus asked in a conversational tone.

"Why not? Because— Because—"

"Because she is your mother? She is a normal woman, attractive in a mature fashion, and not so mature at that. She can hardly be more than forty-one or forty-two, I would imagine, with all the normal appetites to which she is entitled."

"Yes, but with that man."

He shrugged. "Not a prepossessing individual, I'll agree, but so long as both are willing I see no harm. Their only crime is that they were caught, speaking in a social sense, of course."

"You have a strange idea of what is permissible," she said in a cool tone.

"Do I? The most effective weapon society has to keep people in order is ridicule. It stands to reason then that the thing to be avoided at all cost is putting oneself in a—ridiculous—position."

"According to your reasoning, she is still guilty," Catherine said.

"Unfortunately, yes," he agreed. "And her anger and embarrassment were natural reactions."

"Embarrassment?"

"But of course. How could it be otherwise. People are seldom at their most gracious while standing naked before a clothed audience."

"You speak from experience, no doubt," she murmured in a dry tone, a sally she would not have dared at any other time. But somehow this conversation, and the scene that had preceded it, were outside of reality. When he replied to her accusation with a shake of his head and a smile she could not prevent the faint curving of her mouth in response.

"There, that's better," he said quietly.

"You are making excuses for my mother," she said, turning away to stare at the opposite side of the hired vehicle where the cheap brown felt lining was hanging loose above the seat.

His voice held still that timbre of amused tolerance as

16

he agreed. "Reprehensible of me, perhaps, but I rather thought a word of defense was in order."

Was it? Remembering her mother with her plump, white body gleaming in the candlelight and the damp strands of her black hair clinging to her arms and back, it seemed supremely unnecessary. And yet, hadn't there been a hint of shame behind the frustrated anger?

Catherine did not want to think about it. Still, Marcus's calm good sense, though immoral by the standards she had been taught to revere, was having its effect. The incident no longer had the stature of a tragedy.

"I never knew you were so graceless," she told him.

"How can you accuse me, Mademoiselle Catherine, when you have come away without the benefit of a chaperone?"

With a start she looked around the carriage. It was true. For the first time in her life she was completely alone with a man. Turning her head, she gave Marcus a level stare. "Will it make any difference?"

He replied deliberately. "Not to me, but will it to you?"

There was a questioning in his eyes, such a serious overtone that Catherine stopped to wonder if his question held more than its surface meaning. Her presence in the carriage was the direct result of her mother's conduct, but would that affect her own? With unseeing eyes she stared out the carriage window at the closed fronts of shops and their hanging signs, creaking back and forth in the wind. The dusty streets seemed more deserted now, the night darker. The lingering pain of disillusionment moved in Catherine's chest. "It might," she answered her companion recklessly, her earlier suspicions of this man forgotten. "It very well might."

Marcus Fitzgerald was an intelligent man. Leaning forward, he took up the bright garments of turquoise, gold and bronze tissue silk lying on the opposite seat and offered the disguise to Catherine with a quizzical smile.

"Well, then?" he asked.

Such delicacy was disarming in itself. Catherine laughed, a strained sound in the quiet. "By all means. It should be—diverting."

17

Nearly twenty-five years before, in the year 1786, the Spanish Governor, Miro, had decreed that all quadroon women should bind their hair in a kerchief. This kerchief, or tignon, had become the symbol of these beautiful women of mixed blood. They had turned the badge of their class into an article of distinction made of costly and beautiful materials. Though it might have been called a tignon, the kerchief handed Catherine had more in common with a Sultan's turban. Its folds and poufs were sewn into place so that it slipped easily over her hair with the drops of amber on tiny gold chains, adorning the front, perfectly placed on her forehead to draw forth the amber lights in her brown eyes. Swathed in the voluminous folds of the heavy shawl with its gold braiding and dripping fringe, hidden behind a demi-mask of turquoise velvet, Catherine felt safe enough from discovery as she stepped from the carriage before the new St. Philips Theatre. Now that she was committed to the deception, she was able to put aside apprehension, pushing it from her mind along with everything else that had taken place that evening. A kind of gay defiance carried her forward.

Money changed hands and the driver of the carriage agreed to wait. They entered the theatre through wide double doors and mounted a curved staircase toward the sounds of lilting music, quick moving feet, and laughter.

While Marcus paid a small admission fee Catherine stood quietly watching the dancers moving over the floor of the theatre, and the chaperones in the boxes surrounding it. The curiosity of the two crones taking money at the door was obvious. They did not appear to find anything amiss however, and her confidence rose.

A soft-voiced manservant dressed in a bottle green tailcoat with fawn pantaloons offered to take her shawl, but Catherine declined with a small shake of her head. Her simple blue muslin gown with its wine stain would have looked awkwardly out of place among the dazzling toilettes of the quadroons as they moved like an enormous kaleidoscope about her. She was used to pale muslins with white predominating at the gatherings of the *haut monde*. The glittering, shimmering splendor before her was unbe-

18

lievable. No expenditure of talent, time, or money had been spared. Most of the gowns were in the style made popular by Napoleon's Josephine, with a graceful but slender skirt falling from a high waist caught just under the breasts, and a wide, decollcte neckline. But there any resemblance to the fashions worn at the white assembly ended. Gowns of flame silk, topaz satin, sapphire blue velvet and shades of every other jewel color graced the dancers. These creations were trimmed with grosgrain rosettes and fluttering ribbons, loveknots of gold and silver gilt braid, with tassels and fringe and crustings of seed pearls, diamante and embroidery—all with embellished turbans to match. For a single moment Catherine knew herself to be eclipsed, and she felt a wistful envy of such lavish adornment. Then she drew herself up. Simplicity. True elegance depended on simplicity, not on superfluous decoration.

After that first overpowering impression Catherine noticed the women themselves with their skin tones ranging from a pale cream through café au lait to a soft golden bronze, their liquid brown eyes slanting audaciously through the slits of their demimasks. They moved with grace and poise in the arms of their partners. Their partners—

With an abrupt movement Catherine turned away, a warm flush moving over her neck and face. More than one of the gentlemen of the floor was known to her. Few were in costume, many were unmasked. All Creole women lived with the hope that their suitors, or their husbands, were immune to the attraction of the quadroons. It was disquieting to have the identities of those who were not suddenly revealed to her.

She should never have come, she suddenly realized. As Marcus offered his arm she clutched at it, hardly aware of the movement as he drew her closer to his side.

CHAPTER TWO

"Marcus, *mon vieux! Comment ca va?*"

Marcus was slow in turning. The man looked harmless enough to Catherine. Short and portly, his rotund figure was covered by a gray domino.

"Why aren't you masked, my friend?" the newcomer cried. "Behold me! This color is called 'mist of intrigue.' Clever, *n'est ce pas?* I shall start a new vogue."

"Of a certainty," Marcus assured him.

"Come, I did not risk apoplexy rushing across the room in order to talk to you, you know, Marcus. Present me at once to this ravishing creature beside you."

Catherine felt herself stiffen at the familiarity in his tone and the assessing expression in his small, protuberant eyes as they raked over her as if mentally dragging away her clothing.

"There's no need for an introduction," Marcus said, his voice cool. "The lady has been claimed."

"Ah, that's a pity, but then you were always a lucky dog. Still, if I am to converse with her I must call her something. Her name, *mon ami*. Make me free of it since you have all else."

Catherine smothered a gasp as anger welled up inside her. Surely she could not be expected to stand and endure such insults.

Marcus did not move though a frown gathered between his eyes. A moment's consideration convinced Catherine that his was the wisest course. He could hardly make a show of resenting the portly man's manner without attracting undue attention. This man with the testy gleam invading his small eyes was the type to enjoy embroiling them in a loud disagreement. Why he should think he could do so without being called to account was something of a mystery—unless he was involved in this damnable wager and was aware that Marcus could not engage in a public altercation without endangering her reputation. Perhaps the little man was not so harmless after all.

"My name is—Celeste," Catherine said abruptly.

"Celestial indeed," the man murmured as he reached out, grasped her hand, and bore it to his lips. "A veritable star of the heavens—and pale, surely the palest star that has ever graced this ballroom. I, Antoine Robicheaux, would give a great deal to know your bloodlines, *ma chère*. Such a beautifully shaped head, so slender—exquisite."

"If you will excuse us," Marcus said in clipped tones, "Celeste has expressed a wish for a glass of champagne."

"Certainement. The champagne is potable, much better than was served across town this evening." Taking the opportunity of the farewell to salute her fingers once more, he bowed to Catherine. *"Serviteur,* Mademoiselle."

But before they had taken a half dozen steps the man called after them. "Oh, Marcus, you knew Rafe was back in the city, did you not?"

Marcus stopped, standing as if turned to stone, his hazel eyes glittering with green lights. "No, I did not know," he answered harshly.

"No need to fly up in the boughs," Antoine Robicheaux said, his voice fruity with wine and an oddly malicious amusement. "Someone said he was asking after you at the exchange earlier in the afternoon. Some say he took the death of poor little Lulu hard. I'd keep an eye out for him, *mon ami.*"

Marcus did not bother to answer. He shouldered ruthlessly through the crowd, pulling Catherine after him.

There was such a crush before the table supporting the huge silver bowl filled with champagne that they were forced to a standstill. Two white-coated waiters ladled the sparkling wine into flat bowled glasses as fast as they could, but the crystal stems were snatched up almost before they were set down.

"What was that all about?" Catherine asked when she had caught her breath.

"Nothing," Marcus answered without meeting her eyes.

Catherine tilted her head consideringly. "I don't think I liked that man. It seemed like he was trying to warn you—in a frightening sort of way."

"Don't let a toad like that upset you."

"No, of course not," she agreed softly before asking, "And who might Rafe be?"

"A pirate."

At that one savage word Catherine was startled from her mocking curiosity into real interest. "What business could a pirate have with you?"

Marcus smiled with grim humor. "He would like to run a sword through me."

"Could he?" Catherine asked after a moment.

"He thinks he could," Marcus flung over his shoulder as he removed a pair of filled glasses from beneath questing hands. Handing one to Catherine, he looked away over her head, and though he made a pretense of nonchalance, she thought he was searching the crowd. Was he a shade paler beneath the olive of his skin? Catherine watched as he raised his wine glass to his lips, his knuckles white where he gripped the stem.

"Is this pirate such a formidable swordsman then?" she asked.

"He was the best in New Orleans. Two years ago his father was ambushed and murdered by a trio of his own slaves. Rafe tracked them down in the swamp and killed them. There was unrest among the slaves in the area at the time, and quite a few people felt he should have stood trial—at any rate, Governor Claiborne was displeased with him. He banished him from the city until the furor died down."

"He is just now returning?"

Marcus nodded. "He was recognized in Paris, then, after a year or so, he dropped out of sight. About the same time that wily rascal out in the gulf, Lafitte, gained a new right hand man, someone known only as *El Capitan*."

Seeing the direction of his narrative, Catherine said, "Slender evidence, surely."

"Few people forget the face of Rafael Navarro."

No, she had not imagined the bitterness in his voice. "Navarro? That is a distinguished family."

"Oh, certainly. Rafael can play at being a gentleman with the best of us, when it suits him. And that family you speak of is the reason he is back in the city."

"They interceded for him?"

"Oh, I wouldn't say that. I doubt that anyone has that much fondness for him," he ground out. "But he does have a sister dependent upon him—and a plantation going to seed in his absence, reasons enough for allowing him to return now."

"A plantation? I don't think I know it."

"Don't you? It's called Alhambra."

Catherine stared at Marcus in sudden comprehension. Alhambra. The home of the Fitzgeralds, the estate Marcus had lost by gaming. Alhambra, now in the possession of this man, this Rafael Navarro. Though not particularly sporting, it was natural for Marcus to be reluctant to engage in social pleasantries with the man who had taken so much from him. Still, that did not explain his wary attitude. Why this agitation? Did Marcus have something to fear from the meeting? And if so, did it have anything to do with the death of "poor little Lulu"?

Reaching out, Catherine touched the sleeve of Marcus's coat. But before she could form the question he placed his hand over hers, and with new resolution, drew her out of the crowd toward a window embrasure at the far side of the room.

"Darling Catherine," he said as he walked. "I must speak to Antoine on a matter of importance. You will stand here, out of sight, and enjoy your champagne until I return. You will be quite safe. You have only to refuse to speak to anyone until I return, to act shy and frightened. I'm sure you can pretend to that extent if you put your mind to it."

"Wait. Marcus—" she protested, but he was gone, leaving her alone in the embrasure, between the thick panes of glass and the overhanging portieres of gold satin. With an exclamation of annoyance, she watched him

23

wend his way through the gathering until the dancers obscured her view.

Turning her back to the room, she stared out the window sipping at the golden liquid in her glass, ignoring the curious glances of those who strolled past as well as the couples who sought the privacy of her sanctuary. Weariness invaded her mind and she longed to be taken away from this bizarre entertainment. What was she doing here? How had she come to be foolhardy enough to allow herself to be persuaded to begin this masquerade? The gaudy turban that covered her hair pressed against her temples and she could feel a headache beginning to form. Instead of raising her spirits, the champagne seemed to cast them down into her slippers. With a gesture of distaste, she set her glass down upon the low sill.

There was a movement behind her. Swinging around, she cried "Marcus, take me—"

With one hand lifted to hold back the draperies, the man standing in the opening sketched a mocking bow. "I would be delighted if such a thing were possible, Mademoiselle."

A vivid flush rose to Catherine's cheeks and she stepped back, feeling the coolness of the glass panes behind her. The man confronting her was dressed entirely in the dark colors of mourning. Black velvet revers trimmed his tailcoat of dark superfine. Jet studs glittered among the ruching at his shirt front. His waist coat was of silver-gray brocade, and his deep gray pantaloons were strapped beneath half-boots of a brilliant and unrelenting black. There was an arrogant set to his shoulders as he blocked her passage, and though the smile that hovered on his sun-bronzed face held a deliberate attempt to beguile, it did not quite reach the somber depths of his eyes. He awaited her reaction with infinite patience and a total unconcern for anything, or anyone, else.

Catherine, her poise already shaken, felt her composure deserting her under that still, considering, gaze. "I—I thought you were someone else," she said.

"I regret exceedingly that I am not he, but in his ab-

24

sence, perhaps I could prevail upon you to allow me to lead you into the *courante* they are now playing?"

"You are most kind, Monsieur. But I could not do that." Though it was not necessary to offer an explanation, she found herself seeking one. "We—you have not been presented to me."

"That is easily remedied. If you will let me speak to your duenna, I'm certain she will have no objection."

Catherine lowered her lashes, glad of the mask that helped shield her expression as she turned her back to him. "I have no duenna, M'sieur. Please leave me."

She was aware of a strange element in the silence of the man behind her, as though there was something repugnant to him in her answer. "You have a protector then," he said, though it was more of a statement than a question. "You will permit me to say it was most unwise of him to leave you alone?"

"My— He will return at any moment," she informed him, her back stiff.

"Will he?" the man in black asked with a slow thoughtfulness. "Then I will have the pleasure of making his negligence known to him."

"You can't mean that?" she said whirling to face him, alarm coursing through her veins as she pictured the clash between the two men and the attention it would draw.

"It appears someone must mend his manners. I assure you, Mademoiselle, nothing would please me more."

She hesitated drawing her shawl closer around her. "He is a—ferocious swordsman, M'sieur." She had no idea that it was so, but Marcus wore his dress sword, his *colchemarde*, with as much aplomb as any man of her acquaintance.

"Indeed? I am credited with some skill with the weapon myself," he said, letting his fingertips rest on the knob of the sword cane held under his arm.

Something, perhaps a trace of irony in his tone, caught Catherine's attention. She surveyed him through narrowed eyes, particularly the copper hue of his skin where it had been burned by the sun. It was not the skin of a gentleman. What was he then? A man with some skill at swordplay, a man recently returned from sea? Sudden shock ran through her mind. Could he be Navarro?

"M'sieur—" she began, but even as she spoke she had no idea what she intended to say. She felt instinctively that it would be better if Marcus and this man did not meet, but she could see no way to prevent it. Still, would it not be better for them to meet while surrounded by people? That should have a beneficent effect upon their tempers, forcing their quarrel—if quarrel it was—to await a more opportune moment.

"Yes, Mademoiselle?" he asked.

Beneath her mask, Catherine's lips curved in a deliberately provocative smile. "The music still plays—if you will permit a lady to change her mind?"

"Certainly," he agreed with such promptitude that she immediately doubted the wisdom of her decision. And as she laid her hand upon the arm he proferred, she wondered if she had not been manuevered into making precisely the move he wished.

In any case, they never reached the parquet. Before they had moved a half dozen paces she heard Marcus call the name she had given herself.

"Celeste, my love, I did not intend to keep you waiting so long—" he was saying as he came toward her. Then as his gaze went beyond her he faltered. His smile faded and his face assumed the rigidity of a mask as he covered the last few feet that separated them.

There was a difficult pause, then the man in black said in a deceptively mild voice, "So we meet again, Marcus? Have you no words of welcome after all these months?"

"Yes, of course," Marcus inclined his head. "I trust we see you well, Rafael?"

So she had been right. The man at her side was Navarro. Disengaging her arm, she moved closer to Marcus. "Would you take me home?" she asked him in a quiet, matter-of-fact tone.

Marcus murmured an agreement and they had begun to walk when Rafael Navarro spoke.

"Not so quickly my friend. I promised the lady I would take exception to your manners."

"My manners?" Marcus repeated blankly.

A curious smile tugged a corner of the dark man's mouth. "They leave much to be desired," he said, his voice soft.

Marcus paled, but he seemed to have himself under firm control. "Unfortunate," he said. "Perhaps we could discuss my failings at another time. For the moment I find myself compelled to grant the lady's request."

Navarro slanted a wicked black glance at Catherine. "Ferocious," he said in so droll a tone that she had to bite her bottom lip to keep from smiling, though there might have been something of hysteria in her amusement.

But when he turned to Marcus the words of Rafael Navarro rang with such steel that it drew the attention of the couples nearest them. "I object. The—lady—and I were just becoming acquainted."

Marcus looked quickly around at the interested faces about them. As she watched him, Catherine felt a surge of compassion. He was caught squarely between his need to protect her and the necessity of defending what society conceived to be his honor. He could not let the disparaging reference to his prowess pass. In addition, a slight to a woman under his protection must be avenged as quickly, if not more quickly, than a slight to his dearest relative. Failure to rise to the challenge would mean facing the scorn of his contemporaries, but to embroil her in an affair of honor originating at a *Bal du Cordon Bleu* could be disastrous. He needed time to consider. She sought desperately for something that would divert the clash she knew was near, but she could think of nothing that would stand against the cold enmity she felt in the man, Navarro.

The music of the courante played on, but there was a growing murmur of voices around them. *"What is it? Who? What is taking place?"* As the music stilled a harsh voice spoke out in the quiet. "I do believe the black panther is hunting tonight—and it appears he is about to make his kill—"

The arch comment seemed to flick Marcus on the raw, for his hand clenched slowly on the hilt of his dress-sword. Still he made a final effort to dominate the situation. He directed a stiff bow at Navarro, "Come, Celeste," he said.

Reaching out abruptly, Rafael Navarro caught Catherine's wrist. "Perhaps you had better ask Celeste if she still wishes your escort. Most women are jealous of their good name. But if you cannot be induced to fight in the cause of Celeste's honor, perhaps you can be goaded by the remembrance of—Lulu."

That the name meant something to the people gathered in unabashed curiosity around them was obvious from the volume of comment. But Navarro seemed not to hear.

"Perhaps Celeste should be asked if she desires to remain in the care of a man who lived on the bounty of another of her kind for weeks, then deserted her when the assets given her by a previous admirer were gone. Lulu died, Marcus. Did you know? She died in a sleazy crib on the riverfront, dangling from the cord of her dressing gown. She died in shame and despair—and in the hope that her death would prevent me from learning of your perfidy. But I do not give up my own so easily."

Marcus, white to the lips, cried, "You deserted her first, Navarro. You cannot shift your guilt onto my shoulders; I refuse to accept it. But I will stop your vile accusations!"

The man in black bowed, an expression of unsmiling content in his eyes. *"Bien.* Shall we repair to the Garden?"

With an abrupt nod, Marcus turned to Catherine. "Wait for me in the carriage," he said, and with a firm step, followed Navarro from the room.

St. Anthony's Garden, a small, hedge-enclosed area behind the cathedral, had always been a popular dueling ground. It was conveniently located, secluded, and neutral. Catherine bade the driver bring the carriage to a halt in Conde Street, as near the garden as possible. It was perhaps foolish of her to disobey Marcus's instructions but she could not bear the waiting. She could have walked to the rendezvous as the men had done, but the carriage gave her a measure of anonymity, an illusion of safety.

Pulling aside the leather flap at the window, she listened. The only sound that came to her ears was the faint music from a barroom down along the levee, and the soft scuffle of sandaled feet as a robed priest moved beneath the arcade of the Presbyter just behind her. To her left was the bare parade ground of the *Place d'Armes*, its stocks and scaffold casting menacing shadows over the dusty earth. On the right loomed the bulk of the Cathedral of St. Louis with its round, twin towers, and beyond it the massive Government House where oil lamps on smoke blackened chains burned before the doorways. The flaring light gave her courage. She sat for a moment tapping nervous fingers on the window sill, then, with sudden decision, leaned forward to push open the door and step down.

Ignoring the coachman's startled hail, she hurried along the street to the alley between the Cabildo and the Cathedral. This was a favorite passageway to the front doors of the church, and so a few ballast stones had been laid in its mud for the convenience of the worshippers. Catherine picked her way carefully over them, missing her footing only once. Suddenly the sharp, clear ring of steel on steel came through the air, startling her. It grew darker as she penetrated further between the steep rising walls of the buildings. Finally a massed row of shrubbery appeared on her right. Through it she caught the feeble gleam of a lantern.

A few feet more and Catherine halted, teetering on a paving stone. Farther down the hedge a group of men loitered, obviously watching the contest inside the garden. The urge to retrace her steps was strong, but stronger still was the need to know what was happening in that enclosed space. Her future, with Marcus or without him, might depend on the events of this night. Raising her hand, she touched the mask over her eyes. She was disguised still. It was extremely unlikely that she would be recognized. The men ahead, though they lacked the air of gentlemen, were not ruffians either. What harm could befall her? With her head held high, she went forward.

The men, after an instant of surprise, moved back to

29

permit her to pass. At the back of the group there was a muttered comment too low to catch, followed by a laugh, but the man who stood nearest the jokester gave a warning shake of the head and gestured toward the duelist.

It came as something of a shock to Catherine to have the connection between herself and the fighting men made so quickly, but she dismissed it with a mental shrug. It could not be helped. Surely it could not matter.

The clouds which had obscured the moon earlier had passed over. St. Anthony's Garden was bathed in a cool white light. A faint wind, however, still stirred the branches of the hedge and set the flames in the lantern to fluttering so that the shadows of the two men before her danced grotesquely over the ground.

Marcus and Navarro had removed their boots, tailcoats, and cravats. In addition, Navarro had scorned to retain the added protection of his waistcoat, and its gray brocade gleamed also on the pile of clothing tossed, with the sheaths of their swords, on the grass. In their stocking feet, they faced each other, oblivious of their surroundings, intent on inflicting pain upon each other—and, if possible, death.

How long had this clash of arms lasted? Not long surely; and yet, above the scrape and snick of their blades, she could hear the panting rush of heavy breathing. Marcus, his face flushed with anger and exertion, was almost winded already, and a scratch on his cheek dripped sullenly, staining the pristine white of his shirt with blood. By contrast Rafael Navarro appeared to be enjoying himself. A tight smile thinned his strongly molded mouth, and his eyes burned from between narrowed lids with an intent and murderous light. For a moment she thought he was untouched, then she noticed a slash in the fullness of his shirt at the waist. It was not a serious wound for he did not favor it, but there was a wet sheen at the waistband of his pantaloons where blood had soaked into the cloth.

It was a fight to the death, that much was plain. Honor was usually satisfied at the first drawing of blood. Catherine knew little of swordplay. Still she could see that Marcus, whatever he might have been in the beginning, was now on the defensive. He retreated slowly before the tireless blade of Navarro. He parried each thrust, but his ripostes were ineffectual and he seemed unable to initiate an attack himself.

Watching the flashing rapiers Catherine felt her nerves cringe from the final blow. She kept her gaze on the shadows slipping over the grass. Far better to follow them in silhouette. And yet to her heightened imagination the black shadow of Navarro seemed no less deadly, no less satanic, than the man who cast it. It flowed back and forth with feline grace and agility as he stalked Marcus with the sure control of a hunting panther, the nickname she had heard in the ballroom.

But perhaps Marcus's show of weakness was a ruse— for suddenly he lunged. Sparks of fire glittered along the blades as they rasped together, locking at the hilt. Some murmured comment made by Navarro stung Marcus, for he disengaged violently and made a wild feint. There was a flurry of steel, a sudden curse, and Marcus's sword fell from his fingers to stand on its point in the ground before sinking slowly into the grass.

Navarro stepped back while Marcus clutched at his left forearm with red seeping through his fingers.

"Bind your wound," Navarro ordered. "The dew on the grass is slippery enough without adding your blood to it."

Catherine, with one hand pressed to her lips, drew in her breath at that unfeeling comment.

The sound attracted the attention of the dark man. He raised his sword before his face in a flickering fencing salute, his smile sardonic. Then his eyes widened and the black implacable gaze moved slowly, assessingly over her. Catherine felt a shaft of purest apprehension strike through her. She knew a sense of brooding peril allied in some unforeseen fashion to the leashed strength of this man, Navarro.

She glanced quickly away to where Marcus was knotting a handkerchief about his arm, pulling it tight with his

31

teeth. His face was pale when he took up his sword and took his stance at guard.

As their blades engaged again it seemed to Catherine that their passages were more controlled, that Navarro had subdued his style to a deliberate, methodical destruction of Marcus's defenses. Gone was the flashing, careless brilliance of the swordplay. All that remained was a grim struggle for supremacy.

Catherine could see Marcus flagging before her eyes. Then, quicker than the eye could follow, it was over. She saw in horror the glittering tip of Navarro's sword pierce through Marcus's shoulder, protruding for a brief second. red-tipped, from his back. With a cry of pain Marcus fell to his knees, his blade falling from his nerveless fingers to lie hidden in the grass.

Once more Navarro stepped back. "I find myself satisfied at last," he drawled, shaking his ruffled cuffs loose from his wristbands so they fell once more over his hands.

Catherine saw her own disbelief mirrored in the hazel shadows of Marcus's eyes and she knew that he, like herself, had expected this contest to end in death. She wondered if he appreciated the magnanimity of the Spanish Creole's gesture. The wound could so easily have been to the heart.

But Marcus would most certainly not appreciate the knowledge that she had viewed his defeat, or have the patience to hear her sympathy—even if she could find words adequate to express it. Never in her life had she felt such fearful pity as had risen within her, watching her escort so hopelessly outmatched. No, Marcus, proud, jealous of his reputation, would want neither her help nor her pity. Most of all, he would want her gone from the scene of his defeat—if he had ever been aware of her presence.

Turning to the group of men near her she murmured, "His carriage is at the end of this alley, near the doors of the cathedral—if you would be so kind—" When she saw two of the men begin to move forward to help the fallen man, she gathered up her skirts and pulled her shawl closer about her. With one last backward glance, she turned and started back the way she had come. Her footsteps quickened as she went, and an urgency beat up into her brain. She had to reach the carriage. There was no one behind her, and yet she covered the last steps in the unreasoning panic of one who is pursued.

The coachman climbed down to open the door when he saw her coming. The sound of it closing behind her as she took her seat was a comforting one. She took a deep, calming breath, clasping her hands in her lap. Poor Marcus. Had he had the chance at any time of overcoming Navarro?

Casting back in her mind, she went over the scene that had led to the meeting in St. Anthony's Garden. It was a jumbled confusion of impressions. All that remained clear was the taunting voice of the dark man as he manipulated both Marcus and herself, forcing them into the positions that he wanted. It was not only her overstrained nerves which insisted there was something uncanny about this man. She wished fervently that she had never met him. That being denied her, she hoped she never saw him again.

A man's voice outside brought her head around. They had been quick, she thought. Could it be that Marcus had taken worse hurt than she had imagined?

She had leaned toward the door to open it when it swung wide beneath her hand. A sword, coat, and cravat were flung upon the opposite seat. As the carriage jerked to a start, a man swung inside, threw himself upon the cushions beside her, and slammed the door behind him.

Catherine drew back, then froze, staring into the laughing eyes of Rafael Navarro. Holding her gaze, he leaned back against the squabs and stretched out his long legs, crossed his booted feet at the ankles.

"Where is Marcus?" Catherine whispered. "What have you done with him?"

"Done? Nothing. He is patiently awaiting the arrival of my carriage—a much more comfortable vehicle than this, I assure you—to carry him for a visit to the surgeon. But if he had taken my advice he would have run miles to avoid the quack."

"You didn't— He isn't—"

"Dead? I didn't and he isn't." His teeth flashed in the dim interior of the moving carriage. "I will admit the temptation was strong, but when I saw you standing there, as cool and regal as any lady, I bethought myself of a more subtle and damaging revenge. Can you guess what form it will take, Celeste, *ma belle?*"

The mock caressing note in his voice set Catherine's teeth on edge. As she was making up her mind how to answer him, the carriage swung wide to turn into a street which went nowhere near her mother's house. She flicked a glance at the man beside her. He could have no idea of her true identity and station. Where could he be taking her?

Summoning dignity she told him coldly, "We will soon be passing the house of Monsieur Duralde. If you will be so obliging as to set me down there, I can find my way home."

"Can you indeed?" he asked sarcastically. "I am desolate that I am unable to grant your request." There was a slight pause, "Such an action has no part in my plans."

With her hands pressed tightly together in her lap, Catherine assured herself that she had only to give her name and that of her mother to end this farce. But she had no way of knowing what this man would do with such information. Her last wish was to place herself that much in the power of anyone, much less the ruthless man who sat beside her. What revenge might he not plot against Marcus if he knew?

"I must insist," she said, but even she recognized the lack of force in her tone, and was not surprised when he did not answer.

They rode in silence for a length of time, then his voice came through the darkness. "Are you in love with Fitzgerald?"

"What difference does it make?" she asked.

"Are you?"

His tone was soft, but its gentle persistence held an implacable quality which demanded the truth of her. "No, no, I don't think so," she said finally.

"Have I found that rare thing, an honest woman?"

34

At that sarcastic inflection Catherine turned away from him. His relaxed air was a pose, nothing more, she discovered as he reached out and caught her arm. "Stay, *ma belle*. That haughty manner is becoming, but a man easily gets a surfeit. A smile would not come amiss. And if you had a kiss going begging—"

The pressure on her arm slowly increased. She tried to twist it from his grasp but succeeded only in bruising the flesh of her wrist. Gradually she was drawn nearer. His right hand came up to cup the back of her neck and then his lips, warm and gentle, were against her mouth.

For an instant she was still, savoring the sensation with an instinctive curiosity. Then she stiffened in outrage and jerked away, pushing at him with both hands against his chest as she felt his grip slacken. He was only shifting his hold. As Catherine raised a hand to strike him, he caught both wrists and dragged her across his hard form.

"Marcus or me, what is the difference?" he demanded. "You were born a quadroon, reared and trained to make yourself pleasant to a man. What does it matter who the man is, as long as you are cared for?"

"I am not a quadroon," Catherine said, breathlessly aware of the strength of his hands and the firm muscles of his thighs beneath her. His smile flashed once again and she thought his eyes reasted on the whiteness of her shoulders where her shawl had fallen away, behind her on the seat.

"Very well then—octaroon. You are certainly fair enough to deserve that title."

"You don't understand," she panted, shaking her head.

"Are you going to insist that I apply to your mother? That seems unnecessary under the circumstances. At any rate, you can be sure she will have no objections to you accepting my protection—not if she consented to Fitzgerald. And you can stop trembling. I am not an ogre."

"No," she whispered. "Only a panther."

Suddenly he brought her hands down and set her apart from him. "Where did you hear that nonsense—not that it matters. I suppose you heard the rest of it too. How I am acclaimed, or blamed, depending on the narrator—

with tracking down three men and killing them in cold blood? How people enjoy legends!"

"You—you deny it?" she asked, more to continue in the safety of conversation than from real interest.

"No. What would be the purpose?" Releasing her, he leaned back and closed his eyes. As the wheels of the carriage passed over a pothole in the street the coach body shifted and Catherine took advantage of its swaying to move minutely away from him. In that moment, she made an important discovery. There had been the taste of absinthe on his lips. She had caught that same smell more than once on the breath of her dancing partners. Absinthe, the most potent of liquors. He was not inebriated by any means. Still, wasn't his speech just a trifle precise, his movements a shade deliberate? And the splendor of swordplay—did it not have the daredevil exuberance of a man who cared little whether he lived or died? And now? Wasn't his control excessive under what he believed to be the circumstances? Perhaps he had drunk deep earlier in an effort to forget his Lulu. Perhaps it was only now beginning to be felt? How much would it affect him? Enough so that when the carriage slowed again he would be delayed in following if she jumped out and ran? The possibility was worth a try, anything at this point was worth a try.

CHAPTER THREE

Catherine recognized the street as they turned into it. She knew, from listening to the whispered conversations between her mother and her friends, that this section along the old ramparts was where many of the quadroons were housed by their Creole gentlemen. She was not too surprised, therefore, when the carriage began to slow as they neared a small but well-proportioned white house set flush with the street. With her eyes on the shadowy figure of the man beside her, she leaned forward bit by bit until her hand was nearly on the handle of the door.

Abruptly she surged upward, pressing the handle, diving for the door. She tumbled out into the muddy road, falling to her hands and knees. There was no time to worry about bruises. She scrambled to her feet, put her head down, and ran with all the fleet unconcern for appearances of that near forgotten summer when her father had died and she had escaped into a boy's world. Her slippers were left behind in the glutinous mud, but she could not stop.

Before her lay the dark tunnel of an alley. She swerved toward its concealment, her heart beating high in her throat. A cat fled hissing from beneath her feet, and somewhere in the distance there came a muffled shout of alarm. Still she did not pause or look back, not even when she heard the thudding of footfalls over the pounding of the blood in her veins.

Cruel fingers fastened on her shoulder. The puffed sleeve of her gown gave with a soft, rending sound, and she was dragged to a halt, the breath driven from her chest as she was captured in a rib-crushing grip.

A moment later, she felt herself swung high against a hard, muscular chest with bands of steel under her knees and shoulders.

"Little fool," Navarro murmured in her ear in an exultant amusement. "Down there are those who would slit your pretty throat for the trinket you wear on your turban. Think you there is no worse fate than to lie in my arms? You are wrong."

The door of the white house swung open as he approached. A manservant, holding a closed lantern of pierced tin, stepped back as he entered.

"Pay off that bug-eyed fool outside for the use of his horse-drawn wheelbarrow," he flung over his shoulder. Obedient to his command, the servant stepped out into the street, leaving him to ascend the steep, interior stairs in darkness.

He carried her effortlessly, his step on the narrow

37

treads firm and sure, as if he had climbed them a hundred times. Nor did he waver or stumble, making nonsense, or so she thought, of her certainty that he was the worse for drink. How could she have been so fooled? she wondered dazedly. But she must not think of that now. Gone was her last chance of escaping without revealing her name, thereby placing her future and herself in this man's hands.

Distrait laughter bubbled up in her chest and she suppressed it with difficulty. How much more could she be in the hands of Rafael Navarro? No, she must not think of that. In a moment, as soon as she was positive they were out of the hearing of the servant, she would tell him who she was.

There was a closed-in smell of dust-laden hangings and unaired bedding in the upper hall, combined with the lingering musk of a long dead perfume. The mustiness grew stronger as Navarro strode into a bedchamber and kicked the door shut behind him. When he dropped her on an unmade bed, dust rose in a thin cloud, tickling her nose.

With a muttered imprecation, Navarro crossed to the tall windows and flung the jalousies wide, letting in the long, stretching rays of the moon along with the rush of fresh air.

Catherine, raising on one elbow to remove her mask in order to breathe better, went still. She was caught unaware by her first glimpse of a purely masculine beauty as the moonlight poured over the head and shoulders of the dark man. It gleamed on the fine black hair with its disciplined waves, and edged the copper planes of his face with silver, leaving his eyes and the faint indention of his chin in shadow. There grew in the back of her mind an intimation of a greater danger to herself than she had dreamed. The man, turning, moving toward her, seemed less than real, a wild, mythical creature unbound by the rules of the civilized world, capable of giving delight or anguish while feeling neither. She lay for a long moment enthralled, unable to move.

With a strangled cry she twisted away and slid off the bed. A single lithe movement placed him between her and the door, and she stopped, clutching at one of the high posts at the foot of the canopied four-poster.

"Don't be frightened, *petite*," he said, gentleness in the husky timbre of his voice. "This was inevitable from the moment I saw you standing lost and alone, hiding at the window of the ballroom. I am not your Marcus, but who knows? Perhaps in the morning you will be glad it is so."

As he advanced Catherine backed away. "There—there is something I must tell you," she stammered, deeply ashamed of the quavering smallness of her voice as he drew nearer. "My name is not Celeste. It is Catherine. Catherine—"

But she had waited too long. With steady strength he drew her into his arms, smothering her words against her mouth.

"I don't care what your name is," he whispered, his breath warm on her lips. "I don't care who you are, or what you have been. I only know I want you as I have wanted no other woman."

"Marcus—my family—will kill you," she gasped, turning her head.

"You think so?" he asked, a grating and cynical amusement in his soft tone. "It will be many a long day before Marcus raises a sword. As for the others, I have found that a full purse salves most consciences, satisfies most honor."

What more was there to say? When she felt herself lifted, felt the turban sliding from her head, Catherine gave a cry of despair. Still, she fought him there in the smothering softness of the feather bed. She beat at his face with her hands, twisting back and forth, trembling with fear and impotent rage, searching with awakened instinct for some weakness that would allow her to slip from his grasp.

There was none. Her blows made no impression. He did not retaliate, indeed she could not see that he felt them. And, even as she fought, with his weight slowly pressing her down into the feather mattress, using its confining depths to subdue her struggles, she was aware that

39

he could have overcome her resistance much sooner, and more painfully, if he had wished. The knowledge was humiliating, triggering an anger so deep it sent her senses tumbling. This could not happen to her. It could not. It could not.

One arm was imprisoned beneath his body, while with unrelenting strength he forced the other up beside her face. Her head was cradled on his arm, and he caught her wrist with this hand, holding her immobile.

His lips bruised her mouth until she allowed her own to part, than he kissed her with slow pleasure, savoring, tasting. Never had a man touched her lips. This violation of her helplessness seemed degrading beyond anything she could experience.

She was wrong. The flimsy blue muslin tore easily, as did the silk underdress. But her nakedness and the coolness of the night air on her flesh was as nothing compared to the searing heat of his hand moving at will over her body. She writhed with her breath sobbing in her throat as his lips trailed along her chin and down the taut line of her throat. His mouth rested in the valley between her breasts, then moved carressingly over the soft, white curves to the nipples taut, not in passion, but in fear. She shuddered as revulsion, mixed with the shock of pleasure, ran over her. She could not bear it, she thought incoherently, turning her head from side to side. She could not bear it—

The kissing stopped for a moment and he looked at her. "Perhaps kindness is the greatest cruelty," he said. "Let us have an end to it."

He shifted his weight, and for a blinding instant Catherine was sure he intended to free her. Then she felt the smooth bareness of his chest against her breasts. With swift competence, he stripped what remained of the muslin gown from her, gathering her close to him, fitting her to him so that she felt the warm hardness of his body and the urgency of his desire.

"Be calm, my lovely," he murmured against her hair. But such a thing was impossible. She arched away from that burning, swift invasion, her throat closed upon a

40

silent scream, her breath caught achingly in her chest. Dimly, she felt him hesitate, heard his soft *"nom de Dieu"* as the air rushed from his lungs, as though someone had struck him. She did not know the reason. She was more intensely aware of the moment when he released her hands and she could strike out at him, raking his chest with her nails in her agony.

He made no move to stop her. "Very well then, *pauvre petite*, hurt me if you must. For I must—"

As he moved slowly above her, molding her body to the rhythm of his desire, Catherine felt the slippery wetness of blood beneath her hands. Surely she had not—but if she had, she was glad, fiercely glad. Her consciousness of sharp pain faded, to be replaced by a strange and barbaric exultation. They were bound together by shared anguish. As the tension left her, he moved deeper, penetrating remorselessly until he was a part of her, and she of him, their bodies fused, inseparable.

She was scarcely conscious when he eased away from her at last, though even so she tried to move, to get as far away from him as she could as reaction gripped her. This he would not permit. As he pulled her to him once more the warm male smell of him assailed her. She clamped her teeth together against a physical sickness while hot tears rose to her eyes. After a moment the nausea passed, but she could not stop the bitter, silent tears that trickled into her hair.

As her chest lifted with her difficult breathing, Navarro reached across to take up his shirt and push it into her hands, turning her face into his shoulder.

"Weep, *minou*," he said, pressing his lips to the salt tears that wet her temple. "It is your right."

For all his permission, the stinging, helpless tears were no easier. Nor did the soothing movement of his hands on her hair, taking the ivory pins from the tumbled, silken skein, straightening the tangles, bring surcease.

After a time, he grew impatient. "Enough little one. You are a woman, not a child or a hurt kitten. Come,

41

sheath your claws, and let us seek together the little death that leads to sleep."

When she saw his meaning, Catherine tried to protest, but it was no use. She had neither the strength, nor, in truth, the will to fight him anymore. The sweet, tart taste of desire was on his lips, and if there were no fires of passion burning in her veins, there was reflection enough from his to dry her tears and carry her into the realm of dark and thoughtless pleasure, something to remember with wonder before she closed her eyes.

A bright glow beyond her eyelids woke her. She turned her head fretfully to escape the glare, unwilling, yet, to leave the comforting forgetfulness of sleep. She wanted to fling an arm over her eyes, but they were confined against her sides. Odd. She was so tired. Her eyes felt swollen. She ached as if she had been beaten—

As full awareness returned she opened her eyes slowly, her lashes quivering. Her restriction of movement was caused by a quilted coverlet spread over her. It was held down on either side of her by strong, brown arms. A man leaned over her, a man naked to the waist, with his forehead creased in a scowl of angry concentration.

Rafael Navarro. For a full minute Catherine stared into his black eyes, thinking, inconsequently, that they should have been the bright yellow-green eyes of the great swamp panthers. Then a slow, painful flush moved over her, staining her shoulders and neck, blooming in hot embarrassment across her cheekbones. She looked quickly away, hating the weakness that destroyed her composure, hating him with a virulence she dared not let him see.

The dark of night hovered still in the corners of the room out of the reach of the light of the lamp on the commode table beside the bed. The jalousies were closed again over the windows, and the door of an armoire in the corner behind the door sagged open, revealing a folded pile of bedding. From the pre-dawn chill of her flesh beneath the coverlet, Catherine thought it could not have been over her long. What kind of man was this who could

42

force her to accept him one moment and see to her comfort the next?

And what was troubling him now as he studied her in the lamplight, his gaze moving over her as he assessed her features one by one? With a slow movement, he reached out and took up a honeygold curl, letting it drift in iridescent strands from his fingers. It fell on her breast and he smoothed it back into order, laying it carefully across the rosy aureole.

With an abrupt movement that made the mattress sway on its ropes, he released her and got to his feet. "What is your name?" he demanded.

She eyed him warily before she spoke. "Catherine. Catherine Mayfield."

"Your mother?"

"Yvonne Villere Mayfield."

"Your father was Edward, and he had his Merchant's Bank on Royal Street. My God!" He put one hand to his head as if it ached, thrusting his fingers through his hair and around the back of his neck. Wheeling around, he strode with decision to a bell pull hanging to the side of a fireplace mantel of wood painted to look like marble. He tugged viciously at the tasseled rope, then turned to face her, sublimely unconcerned with his lack of clothing, unconscious of the startling contrast between his teak brown chest and the whiteness of his lower body. "Why didn't you tell me?" he demanded.

Catherine stared up into the canopy overhead. "I tried," she said at last without looking at him.

"A feeble attempt when your courage misgave you," he said scathingly. "You had time to recount your life's history before we arrived here, but I don't remember much of importance that passed between us."

His manner touched her on the raw. "Certainly," she exclaimed, her eyes sparkling as she turned back. "You were the image of sympathy, weren't you, as you sat there congratulating yourself on your plan of revenge against Marcus. You could have ruined both Marcus and me by exposing my presence at the masquerade. How could I guess you had a more drastic plan of ruin in mind?" His

43

face tightened, but she did not heed it. "As for my feeble attempt to tell you later, you told me plainly that it would make no difference who or what I was. Nothing would stand between you and—and what you wanted. What choice did I have except to believe you!"

He was quiet for a long, considering moment, his gaze so enigmatic that she knew a sudden unease. The ghost of a smile flickered about his mouth before he shrugged. "No doubt I meant it at the time."

"An attitude I find not at all amusing," she snapped, raising on one elbow.

"Don't you?" he asked. "Then what in hell were you doing at a quadroon ball?"

How could she answer that grim challenge? "It—it was a private matter. I doubt it would interest you."

"You think not? You will find I am extraordinarily interested in the affairs of Marcus Fitzgerald."

"I see no reason why I should satisfy your curiosity."

"I seem to remember that your dashing escort for the evening was less than his usual belligerent self last night. He had, in fact, to be forced into a fight. I wonder why?"

"Because he had no wish to embroil me in your quarrel, of course."

There was nothing to show that he agreed or disagreed. Catherine wished she knew what was going through his mind as he stared at her from his copper mask of a face. "It occurs to me," he said, "that a fight was no part of Marcus's plans for the evening. Perhaps you were involved in those plans. Perhaps I was expected to seek my revenge by removing you from the ballroom—then Marcus, outraged, would arrive on the scene, perhaps with your august parent, in time to save you from being ravished? It would have made me look a fool and a seducer of innocent maidens, would it not? The furor might even be enough to drive me out of New Orleans again."

"How can you think I would consent to such an infamous trick?" she demanded when she had caught her breath.

"You were at the ball, weren't you? And after a pretty show of reluctance you accepted my invitation to dance.

44

Moreover, I am credited with having a measure of affluence. Who knows? If properly repentant at the destruction of your reputation, I might even offer marriage."

Wrath, hot and heedless, boiled in Catherine's chest. She looked about for something to throw at him but there was nothing; no trace of the previous tenant remained, no bottles or boxes, or china ornaments so dear to the feminine heart. She sat up, clutching the quilt to her.

"What makes you think I would accept your condescension?" she cried. "I don't need your money, I have more than a comfortable fortune of my own. As for being at the ballroom, it was nothing more than a wager, a perfectly innocent appearance—or it was, until you came!"

"The ladies I knew before I left the city would not have set their pretty little feet in a quadroon ballroom on fear of death, much less a mere wager," he told her.

"Would they not? Then they must have been poor, spiritless creatures."

"I'm beginning to think so," he agreed, though she could detect no humor in his voice.

"No doubt that is what you prefer," she said scathingly. "Weak, spineless women who can't fend for themselves—like your poor little Lulu—"

He moved toward her so quickly, with such an angry expression, that Catherine recoiled with a gasp, dropping the coverlet. But he did not touch her. At her movement he stopped, bracing one hand on the bedpost.

"You, of course, are strong, able to take care of yourself," he said with a lift of his brow, an eloquent reminder of her helplessness in his arms. "Pity Lulu then, sold at the tender age of fifteen by her mother. She played here in this house for half a year, pathetically relieved to be treated well. When I was forced to leave New Orleans, I left her affairs in the hands of my lawyers. A mistake, but what else could I have done? I made over several properties, and their rentals, here in the city in her name, including this house. But I failed to take into account the trusting gullibility of her youth, and so made no provision against her selling them. Such a thought would never have crossed her mind without the help of a man, a man who

45

also took her jewelry and few other valuables into his safe-keeping. What he told her, I don't know, though I can guess. When she had nothing left to take, he left her."

"Marcus?" she whispered.

"Marcus Fitzgerald. I expect he thought it safe, that no one would notice or care what became of her. He was wrong."

"You are a little late, surely?" She would have liked to discount what he said as a distortion of the truth but there was Marcus's own behavior to consider. There in the ballroom last night he had looked ill at the mention of the girl's name, and he had not denied the accusations made by this man.

"True. I could not be reached even by my lawyers—a friend of mine bought this house in my name when it came on the market, a sentimental gesture, one I appreciate. But I doubt Lulu tried to find me. I had left her behind with little more than a pat on the head. I didn't care enough to take her with me, and she knew it. Too, she had herself been unfaithful and according to her code that should have killed any interest I might have had. So she took to the streets. She was neither as pale nor as beautiful as you, Catherine, but she was fair to look upon, and she had that rare gift, a loving heart that seeks no return. She died, alone, in pain and degradation. She was seventeen."

An apology for her attitude was a weakness she could not afford, even if she could bring herself to make it. She remained stubbornly silent, her clear, brown eyes hard with defiance.

He pushed away from the bedpost, his mouth tight with what she took to be irritation that he had told her so much. Why indeed had he bothered to explain? It was not necessary for her to understand his motives. In the act of turning, he swung back, a frown between his eyes as he stared at her upper body.

Glancing down, Catherine saw the rust-red smears of dried blood that stained her breasts and abdomen. He was in no better shape. Though the stains did not show up as clearly against his copper skin, on close examination, he,

46

too, looked as if he had been subjected to some unspeakable torture. Raw scratches ridged his skin and low on his waist there was the puckered edges of a sword slash several inches long. Catherine drew in her breath in sharp relief as she saw it. She was not wholly responsible for his condition.

"You are hurt," she said, then flushed at the look that sprang to his eyes. To cover her confusion she reached once more for the coverlet, folding her arms over it.

"A scratch," he assured her. "Pure carelessness."

"Or absinthe?" she asked as he put a hand once more to his head. Whatever might have been answered went unspoken, for there came a timid scratching at the door. When Navarro pulled it open, the Negro manservant who had let them in the night before stood outside. The scuffs on his feet, rough cotton nightshirt tucked untidily into his pantaloons, and sleepy look in his eyes indicated that he had been abed when summoned.

"Are you the only servant in the house?" Navarro demanded.

"Yes, *Maître*. The others, they went back to 'Lambra, *Maître*. On the orders of your *ami*, M'sieur Barton." He shrugged. "They were idle all the day, always in trouble. I am here alone now, to watch the house."

Navarro nodded. "Is there any cognac then?"

"Yes, *Maître*, good cognac. Left from the old times."

"Bring a bottle then, and two glasses. And put water on to heat for a bath."

"Yes, *Maître,*" he said again, and bowed, backing out the door without once looking in Catherine's direction, though she had no illusions that he had missed a single detail.

A bath would be welcome, she thought as she watched the dark man close the door. But he had ordered only one, and she had not the slightest intention of asking who it was for.

A log fire had been laid in the fireplace. Taking a spill from a brass holder, Navarro used it to set the kindling ablaze. Only then did he look around for his breeches and pull them on.

47

The dry wood must have been on the firedogs for months, for it caught with a rush, quickly sending the light of its cheerful flames out into the room. The smell of the wood smoke seemed to make her more aware of the coolness, and she shivered a little under the quilt, sullenly envious of Navarro, standing with one elbow on the mantel, in reach of the heat. The silence between them deepened. As her position in the middle of the bed grew strained, Catherine eased backward to lean against the carved headboard, pulling the coverlet up to her chin.

The spitting of the burning wood was loud. From somewhere in the distance came the crowing of a rooster, a melancholy and somehow ridiculous sound in the darkness.

Catherine found after a time that she felt at a disadvantage naked while he was clothed, and a wry appreciation of her mother's feeling earlier brought a grim smile to her mouth. She looked about for her gown, feeling tentatively beneath the coverlet.

"Is this what you're looking for?" he asked, bending to pick the blue muslin and the white underdress up from the floor in one hand, holding them out to her.

"I—yes, thank you," she said, keeping her eyes firmly on the clothes as she took them from him.

When he had turned back to the fire once more, she spread them out around her. She had not expected the muslin to be salvagable and so she was not disappointed. The neck and waist tape of her underdress had been torn from their stitching. A sash of some sort could be divised to go with it, and if it fell open in the back at least modesty would be served. With luck it might be possible to survive this debacle with her reputation intact after all, if she could only make her way home. Some tale, plausible on the surface, could be concocted for the servants. Perhaps she could say she had stayed the night with a girlfriend. The house would be locked so early in the morning, but Dédé would let her in. The Negro nurse would have to be told; she could not hope to hide much from her sharp eyes, even under that garish shawl. Dédé was one of the few people who could be trusted with the

48

secret however. She was more jealous of the good name of her ladics, Catherine and her mother, than they were themselves.

The shawl. What had become of it? The last time she remembered having it was in the carriage. Its loss would make things difficult, but she would surmount this problem also. She must. She would not stay trapped here, to be disposed of at the discretion of Rafael Navarro.

CHAPTER FOUR

The arrival of the cognac provided a welcome diversion. Though Catherine had had wine with her meals all her life, she had never tasted spiritous liquors, such as the brandy. These were ordinarily reserved for men. Still, she had no hesitation in taking the glass Navarro offered her. The burning warmth of it in her mouth was a warning, and she struggled not to cough, but the effort made tears stand in her eyes.

As a restorative the brandy had compelling power. By the time she had emptied the glass, she could feel her spirits rising and the chill leaving her body. She was even emboldened to the extent of taking up their conversation where they had left off.

"Were you?" she asked.

He did not look up from his glass. "Was I what?"

"A trifle—*piqué*—from overindulgence," she answered with a small toasting gesture.

"What difference does it make?"

"None, I suppose," she said at last, but that was not true. While she appreciated the fact that he did not like to admit to a weakness or hide behind it, it did matter. The exact circumstances of what had happened between them inevitably affected how she felt about it. It seemed necessary to know the degree of his responsibility.

What was he thinking of, standing there, brooding like an injured and outcast demon? Were his thoughts of Lulu, that plaintive waif—or did she, herself, have a place in his musings? Did he feel regret for what had happened, or remorse—did he feel anything? She doubted it.

If she was honest she would have to admit he was not totally to blame. That did not in any way alter the dislike she felt or the distaste she had developed for his company.

"Do you think it possible to obtain a carriage for me?" she said suddenly.

"You were thinking of leaving me, Mademoiselle?" Bright mockery sprang into his eyes. "I should be desolate."

"Indeed, I am sorry to distress you. But I must not trespass on your hospitality any longer," she said, exactly matching his sarcasm.

"I am certain a carriage *could* be arranged."

Directness seemed the best policy. "Will you arrange it?"

"May I know your destination?" he asked, still gravely polite.

"Home, of course." She allowed her irritation at the need for an explanation to creep into her tones. "My old nurse will let me in, and I doubt very much that my mother will question my whereabouts."

"An unnatural parent, surely?"

She had no intention of relating the history of the sordid episode that had set the events of the night in train. If, because of it, Yvonne Mayfield would have little interest in her daughter's welfare, it was no concern of his. She must have been more transparent than she realized, however.

"Come, petite," he said coaxingly. "Don't make me resort to subterfuge again to learn what I wish to know."

Catherine stared at him. He could be quite charming when he wished. She was sure that slow smile appealed to some women.

"We quarrelled," she said finally, without grace.

"I begin to see."

Did he? She doubted it, but she would not open her lips to give him the opportunity of drawing more from her.

"It must have been serious to send you out of the house on such a wild escapade—or is this your usual style?"

She sent him a look of pure dislike. "It is likely to become my style if I do not get home quickly," she told him.

"You seem certain it is possible to retrieve your position."

Something in his soft tone sounded a warning. "Yes. Why not?"

"Forgive me, but I have no great confidence in Marcus Fitzgerald's powers of dedeption."

"No," she said, unconsciously agreeing with him. "But you and he are the only ones who know."

"And the coachman?" he suggested quietly.

Catherine felt the blood drain from her face. Of course, the coachman, the free-man-of-color who made his living hiring out his vehicle. He had transported Marcus and herself to the charity *levee*, then to her home, and from there, directly to the St. Philips ballroom. He had known she was white, and she had little hope that he would not make it his business to learn her name. Especially after watching her abduction! Such a juicy bit of *scandale* would not go unreported, the penalty for taking the presence of a servant for granted.

But perhaps all was not so bleak. If the man could be reached in time his silence could be bought.

"I see you had forgotten him," Navarro was saying. "And if you are thinking of offering him an inducement to keep a still tongue, I fear you are too late. He had ample time, while waiting with the other drivers outside the ballroom, to divulge the most damaging portion of your secret a dozen times over. Already news of it is probably circulating through the various servant hierarchies of the city. I'll wager two dozen ladies will be served this tidbit with their *café au lait*."

Catherine had seen the swiftness and accuracy of the

51

servant grapevine too many times to doubt his prediction. Grimly she faced her ruin, then lifted her head. "Then I must not allow my mother to learn of it from another source. If you will be so obliging——" She indicated her clothing with a slight movement of her hand, desiring his removal from the room. She might as well have spared her breath and delicacy. Navarro paid no heed. His absorption was broken only by a scratching once more at the door.

"*Entre.*"

"Your bath, *Maître.*" The manservant bowed himself into the room, carrying the copper hip-bath on his back to the fireplace. Cans of steaming water followed, three of them to half-fill the tub. The man left the door open while he went out, then returned with linen towels draped over his arm and a cake of soap that released the smell of vetiver as he shook it from its oiled paper wrapping.

"A screen," Navarro said absently, as though his mind was far from the order he had given.

Catherine looked at the steam rising from the tub, then down at her hands with their brownish-red stains under the nails and lining the creases of her palms. A bath. No, she must not think of it. She must think only of leaving this house. Now. At once. All might not be as hopeless as Navarro indicated. Something still might be done.

The screen, a bamboo affair, its sections painted with scenes of the countryside in imitation of Fragonard, was set in place. The manservant withdrew. A screen was usually set to protect the bather from drafts, but Navarro stepped forward to pull it into place between the bath and the bed.

Moving to the door, he bowed. "My tribute to your blushes," he said with a gesture at the arrangement. "Well, don't just lie there. Even if you fancy a cold bath, I don't." He pulled the door open. "If the rest of the house is as inhospitable as this room, I doubt I will find much to entertain me. Make the most of your opportunity. It won't last long."

He is enjoying this, Catherine thought incredulously as the panel closed behind him. He was actually enjoying her discomfiture and the intolerable situation they found themselves in. Not the attitude of a man bowed with grief for a former love, but then he had as good as admitted he had not loved the childish quadroon. She had been a plaything easily put aside when she no longer amused him. And then when his toy had been broken, in remorse and guilt he had sought to punish the one who had harmed her.

Suddenly the meaning of his last words was clear. She threw back the coverlet and scrambled from the bed, reaching for her gown and underdress.

The water was hot, but not unbearably so. Its heat had a beneficial effect, soothing away her tiredness and distress. The flickering fire, the scent of vetiver, were invitations to linger. She smoothed the silken water over her arms and breast and down her back until she could feel completely clean again. After a time the warmth of the water seemed to drain her strength away. She could not find the will to rise—until she heard the echo of footsteps along the uncarpeted hallway outside the door.

Navarro was returning! She stood up quickly, sloshing water over on to the floor, reaching for a towel. Its linen length was barely adequate. With her other hand, she stretched up toward her underdress, where she had hung it on top of the screen. She dragged it toward her and the light bamboo piece began to teeter. Instinctively she reached out to catch it as it toppled over upon her. The towel fluttered to the floor. The door opened behind her. Catherine clenched her teeth.

Standing knee deep in water, she righted the screen, and took down her underdress with a dignity composed of three-quarters bravado and one-quarter iron will. She could sense Navarro beside her, but still she did not face him until he said in a low voice, "Your towel, Mademoiselle."

"Thank you," she answered gravely, taking it from him. Tears were close. This last trick fate had played on her seemed the cruelest of all. She met it without flinching, but she thought if he laughed, if he turned it into the ludicrous farce it undoubtedly was, she would want to kill him. But when she at last raised her eyes, he was already turning away.

With trembling fingers, she slipped the underdress over her head then tore a sash from the blue muslin. The ensemble was not very satisfactory. She had never noticed how thin and near transparent the white silk was worn alone. Her hair tumbled down her back and she tried to bring some order to its tangled confusion, but her fingers were no substitute for a comb. She had no idea what had become of her pins. At least the smoked-honey mass of it would fill in the back where the underdress fell open.

When she stepped from behind the screen Navarro gave her one brief glance, then moved to tug at the bell pull. As at a prearranged signal, the manservant entered the room with two more cans of hot water which he tipped into the bath.

Turning her back to the operation, Catherine moved to the window, absently pushing her hair back behind her shoulders. A leaf of the jalousies swung inward beneath her hand as she tried it. She saw that the room opened out onto a gallery under the overhanging roof, a gallery overlooking a small garden enclosed by the solid walls of the buildings on either side. The faint tracery of footpaths and the ghostly shadow of a tiny fountain were visible in the dimness. So much planning, so much caring, she thought. Sighing, she stepped back into the room and closed the jalousies behind her.

The manservant was making the bed with fresh linen sheets. It crossed her mind to protest, but she reconsidered. The man was only seeing to his master's comfort. There was no other significance. Still, she was glad when he finished and took his leave.

She knew from the sounds when Navarro settled into the bath. Safe from his intense, following gaze, she strolled to the commode table where a roll of linen lay beside what appeared to be a small sewing case. Neither had been there before. Gingerly, she touched the bandage linen. She thought of Navarro, wondering if he had told her the truth before. Was Marcus being cared for? What would he think when he heard what had happened to her?

What would he do? Would he accept his share of the responsibility? Would he still wish to marry her? Would any
man? Or would she remain a spinster all her life, an object of scorn and scandalized whispers over the ratafia and
orange flower water. Would she fade away in the back
room of some relative's house, growing old and wrinkled,
a figure to be used to rebuke rebellious daughters? *Look
at Tante Catherine! You want to ruin yourself as she did,
hein?*

She had not realized she was tracing the design on the
sewing case, a lyre entwined with petit-point flowers, until
Navarro spoke behind her.

"It belonged to Lulu, but that need not trouble you. I
assume you can ply your needle as well as she? I would
like you to make a few of your simplest stitches in this
gash in my side."

"I—I couldn't."

"Of course you could."

His dark head was sleek with water, a towel hung
about his neck, and he had donned his breeches once
more. For all that, there was little of the civilized gentleman about him, an impression heightened by his casual
suggestion that she practice her embroidery on him.

"Couldn't you?" he asked, one brow lifted quizzically.

She indicated his side, ignoring his question. "A mere
nothing, I thought you said?"

"Deeper than I first thought," he said, looking past her
shoulder. "I seem to have—irritated it. The bleeding is
becoming bothersome."

That certainly was true. The cut, its crusting of dried
blood washed away, was oozing again, and at this close
range she could see that the waistband of his black
breeches was stiff with blood he had shed earlier. It had
never been as slight a wound as he pretended then, and
she had certainly not helped it. It was this knowledge that
weakened her resolution.

"You should see a surgeon," she told him.

"And have him clap a bleeding cup to me the minute I
come in the door? No, I thank you. Other than that, what
could he do that you and I together could not? I know a

55

little of the trade. And you probably have more skill and experience with a needle than any leech in the city." His gaze moved to her hair, laying like a golden mantle across her shoulders. "Do this for me," he said slowly, "and I will see about finding a comb for you, and after that, I will escort you wherever you wish to go."

The promise of deliverance was enough. "Very well," she agreed through stiff lips. "I will try."

He held the needle in the flame of the whale oil lamp, then dropped it, threaded with embroidery silk, into a glass of cognac, tricks he had learned from a shipboard doctor, he said. Remembering the tale Marcus had told, Catherine would have liked to have asked him the circumstances, but did not quite dare.

Next, he tore a pad from the linen, soaked it in brandy, then gave it into her hand while he lay down across the bed.

"Swab the cut well. If your nails are as lethal as the glances you give me I should be dead of blood poisoning before the sun sets on this new day."

The reminder of what had passed between them strengthened her grip on the cloth. Taking a deep breath, she set to work.

Her enmity did not last long. He was an injured human being. So long as she did not look at him, she could forget who and what he was; she could think of him only as someone who needed her help, and give it in the same manner that she used while caring for their household servants. Dédé made an elixir of her own that Catherine often used. As the fumes of brandy rose to Catherine's head, she realized that Dédé's elixir must be based solidly on spirits also, along with a few herbal infusions. For good measure, she lifted the bottle of cognac sitting nearby, and holding the wound agape with her pad, filled the clean-edged incision.

His skin was resilient and it took a strong, deliberate effort to pierce it. She did it quickly and he made no sound, but she felt his muscles tense as his flesh was torn. She worked quickly, sensing the pain she must be causing. The edges of the wound were slowly drawn together.

When she had finished, perspiration beaded her upper lip and her knees felt weak.

Dropping the needle into the sewing case, she sat down on the foot of the bed. Only then did she look at her patient. He had made no sound, but he was perfectly conscious. A smile lit his eyes in spite of the paleness about his mouth and his hand was steady as he reached out to splash a double measure of cognac into the remaining glass and pass it to her.

Catherine took a small mouthful before handing it back. As she watched him down the rest in a swallow, she gave a shaky laugh. "My old nurse, Dédé, would recommend red wine, for strength."

"Along with beef broth?" he said. "I had a Dédé once."

"You had? What became of her?"

As he struggled to sit upright he answered, "She died."

After a moment Catherine moved to take up the roll of linen. She made a pad to place on the injury. Holding it in place she wondered exactly how she was going to secure it. Navarro got to his feet and raised his arms helpfully. She was forced to move in closer, to wrap the linen strip about his waist beneath his ribs, nearly embracing him each time she passed the roll around behind his back. She could sense his amused gaze on her flushed face but she refused to be drawn.

"So earnest," he said, his warm breath stirring her hair. "Did you know you bite your lip when you concentrate?"

She flicked an upward glance, but did not answer. Her fingers pressed the firm skin of his back, holding the bandage taut, smoothing the material so there would be no irritating wrinkles. As she worked she became aware of ridges on his back. They were long and leathery. She ducked beneath his arm to tie a neat flat knot at his side. She gasped. His back was crisscrossed with a mass of ancient lacerations. The skin had recovered most of its smoothness and the sun had gilded the wounds, but they remained, mute reminders of endured pain.

"Satisfied?" he asked.

"I saw a slave once—like this, but never——"

57

"Never a white man? But then, sweet Catherine, I trust you have seen few white men without their clothes— Forgive me. I made a vow to remain impersonal. It seems I cannot, with you. No, the scars were a gift from my father. He had a penchant for the whip. No doubt you will have heard he killed Mother in that way? It was not his intention, but it is true, all the same."

"You need not explain to me," she said hurriedly.

"Because you think we will never meet again, other than as the most distant of acquaintances? Do not be too sure."

"What do you mean?"

"I have a theory—" he said slowly. "But in case I'm wrong—I will keep it to myself."

Though she had said there was no need for an explanation, she was disappointed when he passed over it. She was also annoyed that he refused to answer her question.

"I am sorry, M'sieur, but I am afraid it will be impossible for us to meet on terms of friendship," she told him evenly.

"I agree. Nothing so pallid. I had the best of intentions, but if you intend to refuse to acknowledge me in the future, perhaps it is time I made the most of my opportunities." There was humor in his voice, but she did not care for the look in his eyes as he came toward her.

"So demure, sweet Catherine. All helpfulness and concern. And completely unaware of the firelight shining through the thin stuff of your gown, or the soft press of your warm curves against me. Such an innocent temptress, such a tempting innocent."

"Please—" she said taking a step backward. "You wouldn't? Not now?"

"Does it matter so much? Now? Is it such a large thing to ask—in remembrance?"

"At least before you did not know—"

"No, I did not know," he interrupted, smiling, giving her words an entirely different meaning.

She knew what the panther's prey felt like now, she thought wildly, as she retreated. She knew that mesmerized fear, the invidious weakness, allied to a strange and frightening willingness to be caught. As that realization struck her, she whirled and ran. Sharp pain drove into her foot before she had taken a second step, and she lurched off balance, falling.

Navarro caught her in a wrenching grasp that made him draw in his breath.

"Your stitches," she cried. "You'll tear them out."

"Not if you will be still," he answered on the ghost of a laugh. He lifted her onto the bed, dropping down beside her.

She twisted away from him, bending her knee to peer at her foot. "I think there is something—"

She had stepped on one of the jet studs that had been stripped from Navarro's shirt when he removed it. A prong that held the stone in place had embedded itself in the skin of her foot, but to her chagrin, it did not even bleed when Navarro plucked it out. He held it up for her inspection, then tossed it carelessly onto the table, soothing away the ache with his thumb.

Catherine felt the impulse to thank him, but gratitude did not seem to be an emotion she should be feeling toward someone with the intentions of the man beside her. But did he have any such intentions after all, she wondered, for he rolled away from her, flinging one hand above his head on the pillow while the other pressed against the bandaging at his side.

She watched him a long, cautious moment. When he did not move, she asked, "Are you all right?"

"I'm not sure," he murmured.

"So it is bleeding again."

He did not answer, only allowing his hand to fall away.

Catherine raised on one elbow, and leaned over him, testing the tightness of the wrapping, searching for the stains of fresh blood, finding nothing.

"I don't see—" she began, and then her face was seized and she was drawn across his body to meet the hard, triumphant pressure of his lips.

"You, my sweet Catherine, could give a man his *coup de foudre*," he whispered against her ear.

59

"Let me go," she hissed, "or you will think a thunder-bolt has struck you indeed!"

"I will let you go—only to remove this nun's habit."

"Never," she cried.

"It is a matter of indifference to me," he said with a faint shrug, "whether you go home with it torn, or whether you go at all—"

"That's blackmail," she said, jerking violently away from the trail of kisses he was blazing across her throat. Instead of winning free, however, she only landed herself on her back with Navarro above her, and the hem of her underdress twisted about her knees.

Navarro placed his hand on her thigh and began slowly to ease the material upward. "I believe you are right," he agreed pensively, his narrowed gaze almost unreadable through the thickness of his lashes.

Catherine stared into his eyes, suspicious of that masked laughter. More in disbelief than outrage she whispered, "How can you?"

"Easily," he answered, and the light was blotted out as his face came down and his mouth covered hers.

The agitated babble of voices was muted by the walls of the closed bedchamber. The two on the bed had only just become aware of the commotion when the door burst open to crash against the wall.

Marcus, his arm in a sling of black silk, entered with rapid steps, and a slightly nonplussed expression as if he had expected to find the door locked.

A female figure in mauve-gray stood in the opening. She surveyed the pair before her with a supercilious gaze from hard, black eyes. "Charming," she drawled. "Dare I suggest that we are quits, my dear daughter?"

The manservant, a grey tinge to his skin, slipped into the room behind Yvonne Mayfield. "I am sorry, *Maître*," he said, lifting trembling hands. "I tried to keep them out, but they would not heed me."

Navarro made an absent gesture of dismissal, then sat up unhurriedly, giving Catherine time to adjust her bodice and push the hem of her gown down. He spoke only after the door eased to behind his servant.

"To what do I owe the honor of this visit?"

Marcus, his gaze taking in the conditions of the room with its signs of shared intimacy, brought his attention to bear with a start. He allowed his mouth to curve in a sneer. "Surely that is obvious—by now."

"Do I detect a question," Navarro asked with a bored expression. "Can it be you are in doubt? That you wish to know if you are too late? The answer is yes, much."

The fists of the other man clenched and he took a step toward the bed, only to be checked by a low, throaty laugh.

"You were always a daresome devil, Rafael. But you must not torture poor Marcus. He has suffered through hell enough this night, as have I. His remorse knows no bounds—or end. Isn't that true, Marcus?"

At this prompting, Marcus turned from Navarro. "Catherine," he said earnestly. "I cannot tell you how much I regret this, how sorry I am that I involved you in something that has brought you such shame and dishonor. I will do everything in my power to help you forget, to make it up to you, somehow. I acknowledge that the fault is mine and mine alone. I want only to spend my life atoning for it, if you will consent to marry me."

Catherine did not know how to answer. Embarrassment at Navarro's frankness had thrown her thoughts into chaos. More than anything else, she wanted to be alone to sort out her feelings, to repossess herself, to think in quiet solitude of what had taken place and what she was going to do about it. But the man in the bed beside her did not give her the chance to even put that much into words.

"Very noble," he said to Marcus in a grating voice. "But then you should be used to taking the women I leave."

Even Yvonne Mayfield gasped at the blatant cruelty of that insinuation. Catherine felt suddenly cold inside. Her sense of recoil was such that she edged away from Navarro where he leaned, apparently at his ease, against the headboard.

"Navarro—before God—" Marcus protested, his gaze going to Catherine's white face.

"You're very protective of a sudden, are you not?" Navarro told him. "It is to be regretted that you did not have a thought to her care and safety earlier. Now, it may be that I have a naturally suspicious nature, but I find your ready sacrifice hard to credit—except, of course, that a rich wife whom you have saved from certain disgrace must be forever grateful. That, I find, makes excellent sense when applied to you, Marcus."

"Are you insinuating that I have offered to marry Catherine for the sake of her fortune?" he demanded, a mottled flush of rage on his cheekbones. "Why, if it was not for this injury I would make you regret those words!"

"By all means. Don't let that prevent you. I never let such a small thing interfere with my pleasure."

"Mon Dieu," Yvonne Mayfield breathed, and moved to stand at the side of the bed near her daughter. "And I was very nearly envying you, my poor Catherine. Take my hand. Come away with us. Pay no heed to this barbarian, this *panthère diable.*"

But Navarro reached out, imprisoning her wrist. "Not so quickly. I believe Catherine will find what I have to say of interest—as might you, Madame, if you care at all for your daughter. They say at the Exchange that Fitzgerald is run off his feet, his creditors sleep before his door, and his note of hand is no longer accepted in the gaming rooms. Doesn't it strike you as strange to find this man arranging an elaborate compromising situation around a girl of wealth? Think of it."

"Don't listen to him," Marcus said in a strained voice. "He bears me a grudge and will do anything to strike back."

Navarro ignored him as if he had not spoken. "Taking advantage of a distraught moment, he persuaded Catherine to attend a quadroon ball with him, but made no provision against a gossiping coachman and little for any of the men known to her who could be expected to penetrate her disguise on close inspection. In fact, there might have been a plan for just such an accident, for some friend of his to 'recognize' her and blurt out her name. The position would have been the same as now, with

Marcus contritely offering his hand in marriage—except for my advent on the scene. But he is prepared to stomach even that for the sake of the riches that will be his as Catherine's husband."

Yvonne Mayfield turned a shrewd look in the direction of the other man. "Can this be true?" she asked. "Clever, and so very plausible, considering my daughter's impetuous nature. I suspect I even contributed my share toward its success, did I not?"

"It's a lie," Marcus said, appealing to Catherine. "It was foolhardy, perhaps, to risk so much, to allow you, Catherine, to risk it also—and I will admit it was stupid of me to overlook the coachman—but it was no more than that. I never foresaw such serious consequences. I did not plan it, please believe me."

Catherine's mother stared at him a long moment, her face, with its hint of soft roundness, unreadable. Her movement, when she turned to Navarro, held a studied grace, but there was a marked absence of her usual sultry undertone when she spoke.

"So far as I can see, it matters little what Marcus intended. The harm has been done, and now we must bend our minds to repairing it. Marcus offers a means to this end. The only one, that presents itself, so far as I can see."

"Do you nurture hopes of a second declaration, my dear Madame?" Navarro asked.

"Tell me they are unfounded and I will hope no more, but I had more faith in your sense of spite than that—" She frowned. "Though if that is your object, I'm afraid I find you maladroit."

"Ah, but I depend upon your support, Madame," said Navarro.

The eyes of the older woman flicked Marcus with veiled contempt. "And you shall have it."

Catherine, listening to the exchange, seeing the glance of understanding that passed between Navarro and her mother, wondered what they were discussing. They seemed to have come to an agreement of some kind. Resentment began to rise inside her.

63

"Catherine," Marcus said, trying to come nearer, blocked by the formidable figure of Yvonne drawn up before him. "Don't let them turn you against me. I have loved you so long, so patiently. Haven't I asked you to be my wife many times before this? I want to care for you, to protect you, and, if tongues wag, to have the right to still them for your sake. Give me that right, Catherine. Say you will be my wife."

It was an affecting speech. If she had never heard Navarro's theory of Marcus's machinations, she would probably have given him the answer he wanted.

"I'm sorry, Marcus," she said, shaking her head. "I have no wish to be wed. And I cannot help but feel that all this—is a little premature."

"You heard," Navarro said beside her. "You have your answer, and so there will be no mistake, I will add this. What I take, I hold. And I protect my own. Though I forget, you need no reminder of that, do you?"

The certainty of his words and the possessive grip on her arm grated on Catherine's nerves. With a quick twist of her wrist, she freed herself and slid from the bed, careless of modesty in her need to get away from the overwhelming presence of Navarro.

"Catherine—" Marcus pleaded.

But she shook her head, pushing her skirts into place as she moved only to halt as the slim, chestnut haired man exploded with laughter.

"You—" he said chokingly, pointing at Navarro. "You marry her? That's carrying vengeance a little far, even for a Spaniard. But I would take care. You go too quickly. First you must obtain the lady's consent."

"A problem that need not concern you. You have had your *congé*. And now you will forgive me if I find your presence a trifle *de trop?*"

There was nothing for Marcus to do but execute his bow and take his leave. He did so with ill grace. They heard his bootheels pounding along the hall and down the stairs until the door slammed behind him.

"Bien," Yvonne Mayfield said. "Good riddance to that one, so it would seem."

"Uncharitable, are you not?" Navarro asked, rising from the bed with a lithe ease, and moving around it to stand leaning against the footboard.

"No more than you," the older woman replied. "But I suppose my disappointment is not as great an excuse?"

"If you are disappointed, it is your own fault," he told her cryptically.

Yvonne sighed. "Yes, I imagine you are right. I did encourage him to dangle after Catherine. We are all of us fools at times."

"If you are referring to me—"

But Catherine's mother shook her head. "No, no. I—will leave you now. I see no sign of a wrap that I would permit Catherine to wear, but my own cloak is downstairs. I will fetch it. Then, if we may command your escort home, we may manage to brush through this affair with a measure of dignity."

Catherine had seldom seen her mother so disspirited or subdued. She watched with a sense of wonder as, with her back straight, Yvonne Mayfield disappeared through the door.

"A perceptive woman, your mother," Navarro said.

Catherine slanted a brief glance in his direction. Did he think she should be grateful that her mother had left her alone with him? She was not. She had nothing to say to him, now, or ever.

When Navarro began to walk toward her, she shied nervously and would have retreated if he had not reached out to restrain her. She resented the hand he placed on her chin, tilting it so that she faced him, but she stood still in his grasp, staring straight ahead.

"There are shadows under your eyes, *ma petite*. You are weary, are you not, too weary to be practical or cold-blooded. Too weary to think straight. Shall I give you the opportunity, the undoubted pleasure of throwing my offer back into my face? It would raise your spirits, I'm sure, to be able to do so. But no, I think not. It would not do to force you to make a stand, one from which it might be hard to negotiate a surrender— No, I will not ask you to marry me, sweet Catherine. Go home. Go home and hate

65

me. It is better than crying. Hate me, and realize finally that the insults I have spoken here in this room forced the truth into the open. They saved you from marriage to a man who would have tricked you into a shameful and loveless alliance for the sake of your fortune. Think, petite, and forgive me. Then sleep."

The touch of his lips was tender on her eyelids. She felt the weight of a cloak wrapped about her shoulders, and her mother's arm around her.

Blindly she moved from the room and down the stairs. And, when she left the house, the fresh air of dawn was cold against the wet tracks of tears down her face.

CHAPTER FIVE

An endless cadence of remorse rang in Catherine's ears. After a time she recognized Dédé's voice coming from a distance, perhaps in the next room.

"Oh my baby, my innocent, my Catherine. I deserted her, Madame. I left her to the hands of that man. Why? *Why* did I not go with her? Why did I not see that she would do something desperate? *Ma petite enfant, ma pauvre jolie petite fille.* I have failed her. I have failed you, Madame Yvonne. I will never forgive myself. The fault is mine. All mine—I will carry the grief of it all through my life. Punish me, Madame."

The nursemaid had put Catherine to bed the night before with all the clucking and scolding of a mother hen recovering a lost chick. Catherine had found neither the strength nor the will to explain what had happened. Morning would be soon enough. Now it seemed morning had come, but her mother had taken the burden of that chore upon herself.

"Forgive me, Dédé," Yvonne answered, her voice

calm, "but I cannot allow you the luxury of accepting all the blame. A portion of it must be mine."

"How can you say so, my madame? You are an angel."

"With slightly tarnished wings. I am aware of my weaknesses, Dédé. I have no need or desire to deny them. We both failed Catherine last night. We cannot fail her again. Something must be done."

"Something indeed, but what, Madame? What?"

It was dim in the room. There was only the faint glow of what appeared to be morning sunlight coming through the closed shutters. The door into the small connecting bedchamber used by Dédé stood open. Catherine stared at it without curiosity, bemused. She understood the conversation in the next room, yet lacked the strength to care what it meant. When the voices ceased, her eyes gently closed, and she slept again.

It was dark when she awakened once more. She turned her head, seeking the window. The outside shutters had been opened, but there was no more than a dim glow of moonlight beyond the Swiss muslin curtains.

At the rustle of the bedclothes, a massive figure rose up beside her. The huskiness of a whisper came in the darkness. "What is it, Mam'zelle?"

"Dédé, is that you? What time is it?"

"It is near midnight, Mam'zelle Catherine. A little more, and you would have slept the clock around twice."

Catherine considered that statement in silence. A board creaked in the floor beneath the woolen carpet and its grass mat padding as Dédé left the slipper chair of sea-green satin beside the bed and moved with a heavy but graceful stride across the room.

There was a clicking sound of a tinder box, and a light bloomed on the dressing table beside the fireplace. The nurse turned with the white china candlestick in her hand.

"How do you feel, *enfant?*"

Feel? How should she feel? "Well enough," she said, struggling to sit up against her pillows. "A bit hungry."

"Hungry? But of course. There will be soup in the kitchen—"

"That will do very well."

"And perhaps a little bread and a small glass of wine, yes?"

"Yes," Catherine said gratefully. But when the nurse had gone she frowned. Had there been disapproval in Dédé's voice? Was it wrong for her to feel hunger when it had been something like twenty-four hours since she had eaten? Was it wrong for her to feel rested, healthy, even vital? If there was a disturbance at the back of her mind, she refused to acknowledge it, just as she refused to pretend to a languishing frailty that did not exist. She had not changed inside. With the morning she would take up her usual activities where she had left off. Perhaps a visit to the modiste for a new gown, something other than muslin. Something vivid, unusual; that was the way she felt.

Accordingly, when Dédé brought her tray, pushed pillows behind her back, and took up the spoon, preparing to feed her, Catherine exclaimed impatiently, "I am not an invalid. Please do not make so much of nothing."

"Certainly, Mam'zelle," Dédé replied, her lips stiff with offense.

Catherine glanced at her through her lashes. "It's not the end of the world," she said softly.

"No, Mam'zelle."

"Do you think I would feel better if I allowed you to cry over me and comfort me?" She sighed. "I must not look back."

"No, Mam'zelle. You are no longer a little girl."

"Exactly," Catherine agreed, and turned her attention to the soup.

Dédé did not move away as she expected, however. "Mam'zelle?"

"Yes?" Catherine looked up as Dédé took a parcel from the voluminous pocket of her stiffly starched apron.

"This came for you, this afternoon. I—Madame and I—thought to return it on your behalf, but perhaps you will wish to accept a gift from that man."

The veiled implication was not lost on Catherine, though she could not quite believe that she had heard it.

She took the parcel into her hands. "From Navarro?" she asked. "How do you know?"

"Your maman thought it best to open it."

"I see," Catherine said. It was a common occurrence for a girl's parents to inspect and censor all gifts and communications to their daughters, and yet she was surprised at the irritation the knowledge aroused in her. Also, the almost imperceptible insolence of Dédé's manner annoyed her so that when she spoke her tone was cool. "It is possible I will keep it. Thank you, Dédé. That will be all."

The soup was a chicken broth delicately flavored with spices and onion, thickened with cream. Still it was an effort to continue spooning it into her mouth until the last drop was gone. Her appetite seemed to have slowly disappeared, along with her feeling of vitality. She ate the crusty, buttered roll, drank the strengthening red wine, and wiped her fingers on the napkin before she turned at last to the silver paper parcel sent by Navarro.

The wrapping was extraordinarily difficult under her nerveless fingers, but in time she exposed a cut glass box topped by a chased silver lid. The lid opened to reveal a set of hairpins fashioned with infinite care from purest gold. Gold hairpins to replace those of ivory, the ivory ones she had lost.

What had she expected? A piece of jewelry valuable enough to spread balm on a guilty conscience? A fan? A book? A bottle of scent? A meaningless nothing? Possibly. But nothing so thoughtful, so carefully chosen, so evocative of their hours together. Did the gift have meaning? Or was it a gesture made as easily as a gentleman's bow in return for a lady's company for the evening?

The questions plagued her, but Catherine had no answers.

The night and the candle Dédé had lit ended together. Though she had gone over every painful detail of what had passed between Navarro and herself she was no nearer to understanding him. Had he ever considered marrying her as Marcus had suggested? Had he decided against it thinking she would refuse him? Would she, if he had given her the privilege? There could be only one answer. Still she would have liked to have heard him ask. Why? The pleasure of denying him? The sense of power, so she could humiliate him, as she had been humiliated? She did not know, and as she watched the candle dying, its light drowning in its own hot wax, she wondered if she ever would.

It was still early when she rang for Dédé, but she could not bear to lie there, alone with her own thoughts a moment longer. A bath would be refreshing, and a toilette *en grande tenue* would do wonders for her morale. She might even use the gold hairpins. After all, she had no others. She called for her maidservant and lay back in anticipation. Dédé, her eyes sullen with disapproval, was just putting the finishing touches to Catherine's hair when her mother entered. The older woman stood transfixed on the threshold at the sight of the glittering pin the nurse held in her hand.

"So," she said as she moved into the room with a measured tread that set her skirts to swinging. "He did make you an offer."

"No, he did not," Catherine answered evenly.

"But his gift. You are accepting it?"

"He owes me at least this much."

A hard expression settled over Yvonne Mayfield's face. "No doubt. But do you wish to put such a value on yourself? That is scarcely the way of a lady."

"And you, of course, always follow the dictates for the conduct of a lady?" Catherine asked gently.

Her mother drew herself up as if she intended to make some blistering retort, then as she met her daughter's eyes, her own gaze wavered. She swung on her heel, moving away aimlessly, to settle in the slipper chair beside the bed.

"You are up and about early. Do you plan to go out?"

Catherine nodded. "I thought I might step around to Madame Estelle's for a new gown. Would you care to come?"

"I may," her mother answered, spreading her skirts of apricot silk about her feet. With her gown she wore a sleeveless spencer of jade green velvet. The combination,

70

though modish, was not a success. The fullness of her breasts strained against the velvet whose heavy cut pile emphasized her charms to the point that she seemed top-heavy, a bit too opulent. Catherine, in contrast, looked ethereal in a gown of palest primrose muslin trimmed with knots of amber ribbon.

"I should have known," Madame Mayfield said after a moment of silence. "Navarro has always been *le plus dangereux des hommes*. It was ridiculous of me to suppose he would allow himself to be caught by an air of innocence. It is a great blow to me." She glanced at Catherine. "And to your chances also, of course."

"Yes. A great blow," Catherine agreed dryly.

Was this to be all then, she wondered? No word of concern, or sympathy; only this detached regard for her future. She looked at her mother in the small oval mirror of the dressing table.

"Caught, Maman? Do you mean you think I was provocative?"

"Weren't you, *chérie?* After all, there must have been some reason for his violent attraction to you. I assure you, the black panther has no need to rape his women. There are many who would be only too willing to share his bed. He must have had some reason for believing you were not indifferent."

"Strive to remember, Maman, that he thought I was a quadroon, and, as such, had no right to be indifferent," Catherine said, her voice steady despite the embarrassment that heated her cheeks.

Her mother waved an impatient hand. "Even so— But you must explain to me exactly what happened. Marcus, when he came for me in the night, was nearly incoherent. And you needn't stare at me so. If you are so immodest as to accept the gift of a man who is supposed to have mistreated you in such a fashion, then surely we can speak plainly together."

Catherine was not outraged, merely abstracted. "Poor Marcus. How did he know where to find us?"

"Deduction, *chérie.* It was some time before Marcus was free of the surgeon's hands and had collected his wits

71

about him. He came to me at once—whether for my protection or for the sake of the countenance I might lend any situation in which we could expect to find you, I leave to your imagination. We went first to the Navarro townhouse, but found it empty except for a few sleepy servants and an insolent and superior valet who had to be dissuaded from coming with us. We visited a number of the places of assignation—if you will pardon the term—but to no avail. Then Marcus remembered the house by the ramparts. I was never more shocked in my life than when I walked into that room. You must, you really must, tell me how you came to be there."

There was an appeal in her mother's voice that had been missing before. Haltingly, staring at her hands pressed together in her lap, Catherine told her what she wished to know.

When she was done her mother said in a brittle voice, "It seems I must shoulder a portion of the blame. I have made a dismal job of being a mother to you, have I not? How very disagreeable it is, to be sure, to have the people who prophesied that it would go badly, our living here alone, turn out to be right. But then, it is much more disagreeable for you, isn't it? I'm sorry, Catherine."

"You think there will be unpleasantness?" She looked up suddenly to find her mother staring at the tips of her emerald satin slippers peeping from beneath her gown.

"Unpleasantness? One can only pray not—and make plans to travel to Paris as soon as the *saison de visites* is over and one may leave the city without being accused of running away."

"As bad as that?"

The older woman's smile was a little too brilliant. "Forgive me, petite. My humor was ill-timed, was it not? No, it may not be as bad as that. It may not be unpleasant at all. We will have to wait and see."

Her mother looked down again with suspicious quickness. Her gaze fell on a piece of fingerwork lying almost hidden beneath the slipper chair. "What is this," she asked as she picked it up.

Catherine felt the start of the nursemaid beside her.

72

"Only some mending—" Dédé began, but even as she spoke an object fell from the folds of material in Madame Mayfield's lap.

Shrieking, she jumped up, letting it tumble with a sodden thud to the floor. It lay there, a smoke-blackened lump of melted wax in the shape of a man, pierced through with a golden hairpin. None of the three needed to be told what the figure represented. It was a conjure image, a juju of deadly intent, designed to exact revenge, possibly even death. And the man it represented was Navarro.

Catherine was the first to move. She scooped up the figure, pushed the pin from it, and squeezed it quickly into a shapeless mass.

"Mam'zelle! Don't!" Dédé cried. "I did it for you!"

But Catherine silenced her with a swift gesture of her hand. "Here," she said, thrusting the ball of wax at the woman. "Take this and destroy it. I don't want you practicing this evil in my name."

Dédé stared at her a long moment. "Yes, Mademoiselle Catherine." She pronounced each syllable of her name clearly, a certain sign that she was deeply offended, even hurt. She curtsied low, and then with majestic dignity moved to the door and let herself out of the room.

When she had gone Catherine's mother rose to her feet. "Bravo, chérie," she said softly. "I applaud the courage of the gesture—but you will forgive me if I find your protective attitude just a little bizarre?"

The interior of the establishment of Madame Estelle was dim, not the best circumstance for preserving the eyesight of the women in her employ, but necessary for the creation of the correct atmosphere of mystery and awe. Scorning the more modern Directoire furnishings, Madame offered her clientele the dubious comfort of gilded Louis-Quinze covered with slippery moire taffeta. There were also certain exotic touches; an Arabic rug, a brass lamp, a Chinese screen, intended to depress the pretensions of what Madame, born and reared in Paris before the terror, considered these provincials. The perfume shelf tucked into a corner flavored the air, as did the smells of dye from the rolls of materials stacked in the workroom at the rear and the hint of camphor used to preserve the precious lengths from the deprecations of moths and mice.

Madame Estelle had favorites among those who patronized her. Yvonne Mayfield found favor because of her independence, so like Madame's own, and for her unerring eye for line, and Catherine for the perfection of her form and her unusual coloring—a challenge and a pleasure after designing clothing for the brunettes who made up the majority of her patrons.

"Bonjour Madame, Mademoiselle. Entre, entre," she called, the black silk encasing her plump form rustling delectably as she moved to greet them. "Mademoiselle Catherine, I was thinking of you only yesterday. A Levantine seaman brought to me twenty ells of the most delightful tissue silk straight from Cathay. I tell you how I came by it in the strictest confidence, *entendu?* But *ravissante, ravissante*—the color, exact to a shade, of Catherine's lovely hair. My heart bleeds that you are not a matron, Mademoiselle. I could make for you a gown glorious beyond dreams."

"Tiens, Estelle," Madame Mayfield said on a laugh. "Have you been trading with smugglers and dishonest seamen again? You will be caught, and then where will you be?"

"Here, chérie—so long as I create gowns of great beauty for the wives of every official from the governor downward."

Madame Mayfield agreed with a laugh.

Catherine was just as happy to have her mother carry the conversation. She thought she had seen a gleam of something like sympathy in the eyes of the modiste. Imagination, of course, but it was disconcerting all the same.

"You are in a hurry? No? Perhaps you will take a *petit noir* with me, and I will display to you this golden cascade of silk. Sit, sit. My assistant will bring our *café* and anything else we require. Now. You might cast a glance at a few sketches I have made, little drawings of ways the silk could best be made up. I see it with the cream pearls such as those you inherited from your Grandmother Villère, Madame Yvonne, to make it acceptable to the conservative. How I tire of these insipid colors, this everlasting white, white, white. I find the manner of dress of these Santo Dominican ladies exciting. Do you not? The Spanish influence, but not to be despised for all that. They are indolent beyond belief, these refugees from that blood soaked island, and pleasure mad, with no idea of how to keep household like true French women, but one must admire the vigor and color of their dress. I see a new trend in this direction. Don't you agree?"

Catherine allowed herself to be carried along on the enthusiasm and spate of words of Madame; to be settled into a chair with a demitasse of black coffee in her hand. She brought her attention to bear long enough to listen to her mother explain the purpose of their errand, and to agree to a maiden's blush pink muslin for her new gown. But she let the rest of the conversation, the discussion of draping and puffing, tucks and inserts and pleats, and braid versus ruching versus ribbon flow around her.

When, later, in the closeness of the fitting cubicle dominated by Madame Estelle's pride, and a major part of her investment, a large mirror in an ornate gold frame, the blush muslin was draped around her, she approved that pale, almost nonexistent pink. Still, she did not object when the gold tissue silk was also shaken out and drawn across her breast and over her shoulder.

"Yes, ravissante," Madame sighed, "but yes, it is a trifle too flamboyant for a *jeune fille.*"

"I expect you are right," Catherine agreed with regret. The feel of the silk under her fingers was a pleasure, and she was not blind to its complementary blending with her hair.

"Pardon, Mademoiselle," Madame Estelle murmured as a bell rang in the shop. "I won't be a moment."

Catherine nodded, and with a smile began to free herself of the lengths of material. She could not resist one last look at the silk, however.

"Catherine, you must have it," a girlish voice cried from the doorway. "The color is you."

The compliment was an obvious attempt at flattery, but Catherine turned to smile at the young woman, an acquaintance from convent school.

"My thanks, Gigi, but I think not."

"Nonsense, Catherine. Surely someone like you would dare to break tradition and set a new fashion!"

Was that suggestion as innocent as the smile that went with it? Or was there a too bright light in Gigi's small eyes? The girl had never been a friend. A year younger, she had always been too aware of her muddy complexion and lank, thin hair that could not be disguised by frizzing or the liberal use of a hot curling iron. The bitter knowledge that she was destined to be a wallflower, left, in the parlance, to "make tapestry" while prettier girls danced at the balls had soured her. She was given to effusive, insincere compliments to girls like Catherine and to attaching herself to them at the balls and soirées in the forlorn hope that some of the gentlemen who must inevitably be disappointed when the music began would feel compelled to ask her to take the floor.

Catherine's fears were confirmed when Gigi sidled into the cubicle after a wary glance into the shop.

"Is it true?" the girl asked, dropping her voice to a whisper. "Is it true what they are saying—that you actually attended a *Bal du Cordon Bleu*, that a duel was fought over you and the victor spirited you away? *Sacre*, Catherine. It is the most thrilling adventure I have ever heard." Gigi spoke with excitement. "Tell me everything. What was it like? What did he do? Did you like it? I would die if such a thing were to happen—and yet you look so normal, so—so untouched. They say the man was Rafael Navarro. Was he as satanic as they say? I heard my older brother tell my father he has gone out of town, leaving you without a thought. The act of a corsair, or a devil, not of a gentleman. Are you sad? How do you feel? You must tell me."

In her excitement Gigi clutched at Catherine's arm. It was with difficulty Catherine refrained from shaking it off

76

and fleeing from the room. Her face was ashen, drained of color by the certain knowledge that her name was on every tongue, her misfortune the topic of so much lascivious imagination.

"I am sorry, Gigi," she said. "I don't know what you mean."

"You mean you won't say!" Gigi cried. "I think you are mean not to tell me, when I so long to know."

"You must excuse me," Catherine insisted, bundling the gold cloth over her arm, edging toward the curtain.

But Gigi did not relax her grip. "Perhaps they are right. Perhaps you did ask for what you got—even enjoyed it. They say you will never marry, not here in New Orleans. Maman expects you to join the demi-monde. And I—I think that may be where you belong!"

She stared at Catherine, her face twisted with frustration.

"Gigi!"

The harsh cry made the girl jump. "Here, Maman!"

"What are you doing? Come away at once. At once, I tell you!"

A woman strongly resembling Gigi, except that her face was frozen into lines of permanent distaste, appeared in the doorway. Without speaking, she stood aside while her daughter scurried out. Her eyes bored into Catherine's with cold contempt, then she followed her daughter. Her grim voice could be heard before the slamming of the shop door cut off the sound. "I told you to have nothing to do with that creature. You will pay for that disobedience when I get you home, my girl, you will pay dearly."

Slowly Catherine turned to stare at her reflection in the mirror. What a terrible woman for a mother. An uncharitable witch. But was her attitude so unusual? Did she not reflect the general attitude of the women of her milieu?

To be condemned without a hearing; to have her name sniggered at or spoken with contempt was not to be borne. They expected her to join the ranks of the women of pleasure, the demi-monde, did they? Well then, they must not be too disappointed. She would show them.

"Madame Estelle?" she called.

77

"Oui, Mademoiselle?" the plump modiste swept aside the curtain. Yvonne Mayfield stood just behind her, her face tight with rage.

Catherine pushed the silk into the black-clad woman's arms. "I will have the gold after all," she said. "I wish something unusual—something flamboyant—something—"

"Something outrageous, ma chérie?" the modiste asked, her fine dark eyes filled with sadness.

"Exactly," Catherine answered.

Her anger lasted until she reached home again. It was not proof, however, against the silence of her room or the softening of Dédé's attitude. She did not cry but the effort of self-control left her spent. For long hours she lay on her bed, without eating, without sleeping, staring at the virginal white canopy above her head with wide, dry eyes.

So Navarro had gone. He had run away, leaving her to face the condemnation alone. He had gone without saying goodby. She had not expected it of him. She had found no joy in his company; certainly she had no wish to marry him. She wanted to be angry with him, and yet she felt only a great emptiness, as if she had lost an ally. What reason had she for feeling this way? None, she thought—and knew herself for a fool.

To Dédé, sympathy was best expressed in service. Accordingly, she put aside her pique and brought soft custards and hot soups, coffee and cool drinks which Catherine barely touched. She treated her like an invalid, bathing and dressing her, brushing her hair for long, soothing hours, and dosing her with an herbal cordial Catherine suspected of containing a touch of something to make her sleep. She did not protest, nor did she forbid the burning of a candle which Dédé claimed would keep at bay the demons who seek to possess the souls of the young. Dédé also closed the shutters against the light, guarding the room as if from intruders, and a dozen times a day she inquired after Catherine's health, in an effort to make up for the lack of inquiries and invitations from those she had considered her friends. Once there had been a dozen billets per day requesting her presence at

78

levées, soirées, balls, and rout parties. Now there was nothing.

The attentions did not help. Catherine sank further and further into a listless apathy. Neither a visit from Marcus nor the arrival of the golden gown the same day could stir her to animation. Marcus she refused to see, so that her mother was forced to entertain him in the *petite salon*. Alone, Catherine stared at the dress with dull, unseeing eyes before turning away.

She was pretending to sleep when her mother entered her bedchamber after Marcus had gone. She knew who it was from her pervasive scent, still she lay without opening her eyes, hoping she would be discouraged and go away.

"Catherine?"

As she felt a hand on her shoulder, gently shaking it, Catherine sighed and opened her eyes.

"Chérie, how long will you go on like this? It has been three days now. You cannot hide here forever."

"Can't I?"

"No. It is enough. I have left it so long because I thought—but never mind that. Marcus has been with me this hour or more. He has shown himself truly repentant, and quite willing, still, to marry you—in spite of the vicious *scandale* that has been made of the incident. You will, I think, be wise to consider accepting him." Her mother seated herself on the side of the bed, staring at her in earnest entreaty.

"Maman—"

"Hear me out, Catherine. He is not the man I would have chosen for you, but it is a respectable alliance. And I expect, once the customary five days following the wedding are over, you will find him an accommodating husband. You will be able to live very much as you wish."

"That will be a comfort, of course."

"You will find it so, when you are older. In a few weeks fresh food for the gossip-mongers will come along. With the blessing of matrimony on your escapade you will see less interest in your affairs."

"Another comfort," Catherine murmured with her eyes closed.

Madame Mayfield arose with a fretful movement that shook the bed. "Very well. Be difficult then. It is no more than I expected. But attend to me. Tonight you will dress yourself in something modest and becoming—*not* that gold creation that was delivered this morning—and you will allow Marcus to escort you to the theatre as he has requested. If you do not, you will regret it all your days. Moreover, if you will not help yourself in this way, you need expect no more sympathy from me. I am at the end of my patience. I begin to wonder if a nunnery in the south of France would not be more comfortable for you than living in this house with me. I understand that in the Carmelite order they value silence and solitude. I do not!"

CHAPTER SIX

The door vibrated in its frame as her mother slammed it behind her. Catherine stared after her. A nunnery. Was it a threat?

She seemed to have three choices. The demi-monde, marriage to Marcus, or to become a nun. Strange. Of the three, the first was most intriguing—the kind of reasoning which had landed her in this intolerable situation, no doubt.

On her mother's orders, a bath was prepared, and Dédé was instructed to wash and dress her hair. A white muslin stripped with apple-green ribbon, and a headdress made of bunched ribbon and small, green-dyed egret plumes was laid out upon the bed.

Catherine submitted to the nursemaid's ministrations. It was easier than arguing. Wrapped in her dressing gown, an extravagance of peacock brocade given to her as a New Year's gift by her mother, she watched with stoic calm as Dédé brushed her hair dry and dressed it à la Helene. With swift, competent hands, the nurse gathered her hair into a soft knot atop her head, from which fell a single thick, shining lock. To relieve the severity she coaxed tendril curls to lie upon Catherine's forehead and before her ears.

"It is not everyone who can wear this style, but you it suits to perfection, *enfant*," Dédé said when she was done. "You are pale, but still *très, très belle*. I must leave you now to see to your maman, but I will be back in a little while to help you into your gown and place your headdress. I will bring one of the red papers from Spain your mother depends on to give her color, no?"

Catherine smiled at her concern. "No, thank you, Dédé. I'm not at all sure that I'm not supposed to look wan and penitent."

The humor was lost on the nurse. A troubled frown drew her brows together. "You must not be bitter against your maman, chérie. She does not mean to hurt you— ever. She is only a woman. She does the best she can. Sometimes it is bad, sometimes good."

"It is good of you to defend her, and I expect you are right. But this is my life she is deciding. I'm the one who will live it. Why can I not decide for myself?"

"But chérie, it is not done so. And for all this time you have lain on your bed as if you would spend your life shut up in here. This cannot be. It is not right; your maman would be wrong to allow it."

"I suppose," Catherine agreed.

The nurse left so quietly it was a moment before Catherine realized she had gone. She got to her feet. Dédé was right. She had done nothing to influence the direction her life was taking. It was not enough to wait, hoping that something would happen to return her to the same comfortable position she had once held. Nothing was going to do that. That fact, as unpalatable as it was, must be faced. Her alternatives were clear. All that remained to be done was to choose among them.

She stared at the white and green gown that had been laid out for her. At last she turned away, moving toward the door.

The upper hall was empty as she crossed it to the stair

81

landing. Below, in the entrance hall, a manservant was on duty, sitting on a small claret velvet covered bench.

He stood up quickly as she appeared at the head of the stairs above him.

"Yes, Mam'zelle?"

"Jules, when M'sieur Fitzgerald arrives you will tell him, please, that I am indisposed."

The news did not delay in reaching Madame Mayfield, but neither protests, threats, nor entreaties would move Catherine to obedience and in the end Madame Mayfield herself went with Marcus to the theatre. The man must not be humiliated further. His sensibilities must be soothed and her daughter's idiosyncrasies explained.

Catherine watched from behind the curtain of one of the small sitting rooms that fronted the house as her mother was handed into the carriage. She wondered if the older woman still had some hope of salvaging something for her stubborn daughter in that quarter. Catherine feared she was doomed to disappointment. Marcus could be an amusing companion, but his betrayal had gone deep. Her decision had not been lightly taken. It was, however, the correct one. She was not sure what she intended to do, but she thought even a convent would be preferable to spending the rest of her life at the side of Marcus Fitzgerald.

The house was quiet, with a feeling of emptiness. There were one or two servants about, including Jules at his front door post, but the others had retired for the night to the servants' quarters at the back of the courtyard. Even Dédé had gone along the arcade from the house to the kitchen beside the servants' wing for her evening meal. The privacy was welcome.

Catherine wandered from the sitting room and along the hall, her dressing gown flowing about her ankles with each step. It was growing cooler she thought, hugging her elbows. Not unusual. It had been a mild spring until now. But did the chill come from the night, or from within? She did not know. She let her mind wander. Paris in the summer. A man, a man much like Navarro, at her side. Or the cloistered walls of a nunnery in France, peaceful, quiet, until broken by the destructive malice of the new regime; the wealthy religious house had come under the censure. There was danger there from overzealous officials.

Still, she could not really imagine herself in those places. She knew too little of them. How was she to make a decision, she asked in despair, when ignorance hid the consequences from her?

In her bedchamber, she flung herself down on the bed with her forearm across her eyes. The smoke from the candle made them sting. She had the beginnings of a headache.

She was almost asleep when a tentative knock sounded on the door. It was a long moment before she could drag her attention back from wherever it had fled.

"Yes?"

"Mam'zelle, there is a gentleman to see you."

A gentleman? Who— But it did not matter. She could not receive a man while alone in the house.

"Make my excuses, Jules," she called in a low voice. "And ask him to call again tomorrow."

"Yes, Mam'zelle."

But, though she knew she had made the only possible decision, curiosity tugged at the back of her mind. On impulse she swung her feet off the bed and stood up. If she hurried she might catch a glimpse of his carriage before it pulled away, or even of the man himself, if he was walking.

She was halfway to the door when a firm knock fell on the panel and it opened. A tall, dark man, dressed in impeccable evening clothes, complete to the ankle-length cloak lined with red silk, stood in the doorway.

"Navarro," she breathed.

"Catherine." He inclined his head in a mocking bow and strolled into the room, pushing the door closed behind him. "It was unkind of you not to receive me."

"You can't come in here," she protested, ignoring his bantering remark.

"But I am in."

Catherine, recovering her wits, drew herself up. "You

83

cannot stay then. You must leave at once. What will the servants think?"

"Not knowing the calibre of your servants, I couldn't begin to guess," he answered, glancing around her bed-chamber with an infuriatingly knowing smile.

"I can," she said, her face frozen with distaste. "And if you have the slightest hint of decency you will spare me this further disgrace."

His smile faded. "Catherine," he said softly, "I have found that the best defense against gratuitous insults is swift retribution. You would do well to remember it."

Alarm fluttered along her nerves, but Catherine refused to be intimidated. "If you do not leave at once I will scream for Jules," she said distinctly.

"If you care at all for the health of your manservant you will not do anything so unwise. I would not like to have to kill him."

The slight touch on the sword cane at his side was enough. She stared at him, her eyes huge in the oval of her face. What choice did she have except to believe him?

She moistened her lips. "What do you want?"

A devil of amusement leaped into his dark eyes. "I came, sweet Catherine, for you."

"What?" she asked, her voice a thread of sound.

"I have come to save you from this vale of shrinking self-pity into which you have cast yourself."

"I don't understand."

"The theatre, chérie. I must beg you to give me the honor of escorting you there."

"I see." She took a deep relieved breath, letting it out slowly. "I regret that I must refuse."

"That is not possible."

"Of course it is," she said, her voice rising. "I don't want to go, therefore I will not."

"It is not so simple," he informed her. "When I saw your mother as she alighted from her carriage tonight, I promised her I would use my persuasive powers to bring you to the theatre. I would not like to destroy her faith in me."

Catherine looked away from that beguiling smile with

an effort. "I am certain you will both recover from the blow."

"Heartless," he said softly. He shrugged. "Your only real choice is how we go."

There was a look of steel determination in his eyes as he moved toward her. Unconsciously Catherine took a step backward.

"You can't force me to go with you. I'm not dressed."

"So I see, but, when the occasion demands it, I have been known to act the ladies' maid."

"I shudder to think of the results." She threw the words at him more in bravado than for effect, her nerves stretched taut by his slow advance.

"Then you would do well not to put me to the trouble," he answered.

A few steps more and she would be trapped in the corner of the room. It appeared that she must concede him the victory. Then her gaze fastened on the key to her room dangling from a ribbon on a hook beside the door.

"Very—very well," she said. "I will go with you—if you will wait for me downstairs."

After a narrow-eyed moment he nodded. "I will give you that much."

He went from the room with a swirl of his cape. Catherine closed the door behind him. She waited until his footsteps had faded, then with trembling fingers she took down the key, put it in the lock, and turned it.

Her sigh of relief was loud in the room. Suddenly weak, she pressed her forehead against the door.

"You disappoint me, Catherine," Navarro said behind her. "I did not expect cowardice."

Catherine whirled around. He stood in the door between her bedchamber and the room where Dédé slept. How had he moved so quietly down the hallway and through that tiny room? For a long moment surprise and a kind of superstitious fear held Catherine mute, then rage swept over her.

"Cowardice?" she cried. "You are the one who ran away. And you can keep on running. Get out!"

"And leave you to face the *canaille* alone? You do intend to face them, don't you? I would have wagered half of what I possess that you would have pinned on a smile and faced that crowd with such aplomb they would have envied you your adventure. That is the secret of the gossip-mongers, you know, a corrosive envy of those who lead eventful lives. But perhaps you haven't the courage. Perhaps you intend to cower here like a frightened rabbit with the hounds after it?"

Goaded by that taunting voice, Catherine cried again, "Get out!"

Swooping down upon the dressing table, she picked up the china candlestick holder and sent it spinning at his head. He ducked, and it shattered into fragments against the wall, the unlit stub of the candle rolling into the middle of the floor. The silver frame holding the miniature of her father was next to hand, and she had drawn back to throw it when she was halted by a memory, the memory of her mother screaming like a harridan, and the crashing of breaking crockery against her bedchamber door. While she hesitated Navarro closed in upon her. He took the frame from her nerveless fingers and stood holding it a moment, analyzing the quality of her stricken silence with a frown.

Abruptly Catherine turned her back on him as tears of pain, rage, remorse, and yes, self-pity rose to her eyes. She would not let him see her cry, she told herself furiously. She would not.

Behind her she heard his soft curse. She glanced covertly into the dressing table mirror to see him standing with the candle stub in his fingers. His eyes were narrow as he rolled the yellowed wax between his fingers, then sniffed at them. Contempt flashed in his eyes to be followed by a puzzled thoughtfulness. Still, he did not speak.

Slipping the stub into his pocket, he turned to the armoire and threw open the doors. He made a satisfied sound in his throat, like a panther purring, Catherine thought viciously.

"The very thing," he said, drawing forth the gold silk gown. "Will you get into it, or must I be your maid?"

86

Turning with a stiff unwillingness, Catherine clutched at her dressing gown, her face mirroring her indecision.

Seeing it, he coaxed. "Come, Catherine, will you leave me to face the lions by myself?"

"I thought they were *canaille*," she said, deliberately making her voice hard as she took the dress he pressed into her hands, a gesture of defeat.

"Whether a rabble or a band of lions depends largely on your own attitude. Which shall it be? Will you play the *grande dame*, or the supplicant?"

Dragging her slipper chair forward as he spoke, Navarro swept his cloak to one side and sat down. The action caused Catherine to lose the thread of their argument.

"What—what are you doing?" she asked.

"Insuring that you do as I ask," he answered with composure.

Her voice when she spoke came out as a whisper. "You are a devil."

"An interesting possibility," he agreed. "It has been pointed out before. Still, if this is Satan's work, it is at least entertaining."

"You will forgive me if I do not agree with you?"

"Certainly," he answered, his eyes narrowing at the irony in her tone. "But I am not a patient man, and I have other duties this evening. It is permissable to arrive after the curtain rises and before the first interval, unthinkable afterward."

"Won't you—turn your head at least?"

A faint smile curved his mouth as he moved his head slowly from side to side. "You are much too wily for that. Moreover, I would deprive myself of a major part of the night's—entertainment."

Annoyance with his insolence and with her own pleading moved in her chest with the aching of unshed tears. She jerked at the sash of her dressing gown as she moved toward the armoire. From its depths she drew out the low-necked underdress which matched the gold silk. She held it in her hands a moment, then with a defiant toss of her head she let the dressing gown slip to the floor. A swift lift of her arms, and the underdress of yellow satin

87

billowed above her head and settled down over her naked form; a hurried search for armholes, a few side hooks fastened, and it was done.

She turned to face him with triumph in her eyes, but saw, instead, the massive form of her nurse in the doorway of the small bedchamber.

"Mam'zelle," Dédé exclaimed in outrage as her horrified gaze moved from the half-dressed girl to Navarro lounging in the chair at the far side of the bed. Quickly she made the sign of the cross followed by the age-old, stiff-fingered gesture against the evil eye.

For one brief moment Navarro looked disconcerted, then he smiled. "The faithful nursemaid, I presume, one who dabbles in a touch of black magic?"

Dédé stepped into the room, ignoring the dark man. "Jules came for me, Mam'zelle. Is there anything—we—may do for you?"

The temptation to see what Navarro would do to oppose Dédé's juggernaut tactics was great but she mastered it.

"If Jules is still outside you may tell him he is not needed. And then you may dress me for the theatre."

"You aren't going with this man?"

Dédé's voice seemed suddenly unbearably dramatic. "You would prefer that we stay here?" she asked with a significant glance about the room. "Of course I am going with M'sieur Navarro."

"But Mam'zelle, you said—"

"That doesn't matter. I wish now to go. At once."

Dédé stared at her firm tone, then decided on a different tack. "Very well, but in the gold? Madame said to me plain that you should wear something young, something modest."

"The gold," Catherine answered, then to avoid Navarro's mocking gaze she searched out a pair of yellow satin slippers to complement her gown.

It was quiet in the room as the nurse stepped out to deliver the message to Jules. Navarro, his gaze on Catherine's slender form, spoke musingly. "I must remember, chérie, that you thrive on opposition."

Catherine had expected to attract attention. She had not expected the neck craning, the open stares, and the whispers that ran over the audience as she entered on Navarro's arm. She tried to remain as unaware as he, but it was not easy. Every eye seemed to be boring into them, every imagination busy with their private moments together.

She had hoped for the blessing of a *loge grille*, the screened box used by ladies who were awaiting childbirth, bereaved families, and men escorting ladies of questionable character. Such pleasant obscurity was denied her. The box she was shown into was the most public of them all, in the center of the lower level, and decked with an eye-catching profusion of flowers.

At least she and Navarro were not to be alone. Marcus and her mother were seated to the right. On the left was a young girl with high-piled hair and a simple white muslin dress, while beside her sat a woman recognizable as a duenna or a poor relation by her high-necked dress of dull black stuff. Behind them was a couple with, surprisingly, the fair skin and hair of Americans.

The first act of the play was drawing to a close and Navarro did not attempt introductions. He seated her in one of the two remaining center seats and took his place beside her.

A French melodrama, *Selico*, the play was offered by a company made up of Santo Domingo refugees to a full house numbering more than seven hundred. Every box in both tiers was occupied and the parquet below was packed to capacity.

The story might have been suspenseful, the actors superb; Catherine didn't notice. Her attention was caught by a window alcove; the alcove where she had the misfortune of meeting Rafael Navarro. The quadroon ball, held in this same theatre only a few nights before, revolved in her mind. If she looked about her she knew she would recognize a number of gentlemen who had been present that night sitting now with their wives and children around them. It was as if she had seen a secret portion of these men's lives, and been a part of it herself.

For the first time since Navarro had burst in upon her, Catherine had time to wonder why he was doing this. Was it a new means of discomfiting Marcus? A diabolical whim? She wished she knew. In the darkened theatre his face was a dim bronze mask. It gave nothing away.

The end of the first act came with appalling quickness. The curtains jerked together with a swish. A lamplighter pulled down the great central chandelier with its crystal lustres and set it ablaze, before moving to the holders between the boxes. The crowd sat up with a collective sigh and much rustling as they began to ply their fans of lace, painted silk, and palmetto. Gentlemen began to stir, preparing to make the first of their visits to the different boxes, a custom which caused the intervals to be favored above the play by the ladies of marriageable age.

Catherine's mother broke the silence within the box.

"A most charming addition to the season's play list, is it not? Light, compared to the usual fare, but entertaining."

She waited until the murmurs of agreement had died away before continuing. "It is a great pity you and Rafael missed the beginning, Catherine, but a few words will suffice to set the scene for you. So your head is better? I am so glad you allowed Rafael to persuade you to come. I was sure you would wish to meet his sister."

"By all means," Navarro said, deftly taking up the conversational ploy before Catherine could answer. "Catherine, may I present to you my sister, Solange, and her companion, Madame Thibeaut. The flowers about us are in Solange's honor. She has just turned eighteen and is making her bow tonight. Until today she has lived quietly in the country at Alhambra. It was for her sake that I deserted you these three days, Catherine, but perhaps you will still be kind and introduce her into your circle of friends here."

"Certainly. How do you do, Solange?" Catherine's smile may have been a shade brilliant in her relief that the flowers were not some peculiar joke at her expense arranged by Navarro; a comment on her emergence from seclusion. Moreover he had given her a plausible excuse for his demands for her company. She could begin to be comfortable again. Couldn't she?

Solange inclined her head, but there was no answering smile on her thin, sallow face. Her jet-black eyes held a wary watchfulness as she sat upright on her chair. The hairstyle she affected was much too sophisticated for her age, and her gown of unrelieved white had the unmistakable look of having been done by a country seamstress.

The woman at her side, Madame Thibeaut, was even less prepossessing. She wore a widow's cap of wilted lace threaded with the black ribbon of her mourning. Her shapeless lips were also colorless, and her face under its coating of rice powder was the jaundiced yellow of the tropics. The irises of her eyes had been faded by a hot sun into a light gray-brown. Against such a drab background the gold of the earrings swinging in her ears seemed strange, unnaturally bright. Whether Solange took her cue from this woman, or the woman from Solange, was impossible to say, but the older woman favored Catherine with only a barely civil nod.

Navarro seemed to expect no more. He turned at once to the couple behind his sister and her companion.

"This, Catherine, is Giles Barton and his sister, Fanny, friends and neighbors of mine when I am in residence at Alhambra."

"And at any other time, I hope," Giles Barton said, getting to his feet to bow over Catherine's hand. He towered above her, a broad-shouldered, blond giant of a man, perhaps a little taller even than Navarro, with frank blue eyes and an open and cordial smile. His large hand was warm, and he held her fingers in a firm grasp, letting them go neither too quickly nor too slowly.

His sister leaned forward. "We are delighted to meet you, Mademoiselle Mayfield. I understand your father was an American; that gives us something in common, doesn't it? I hope you don't mind my brother and I making one of the party? Rafe insisted, and it is so seldom that I am able to persuade Giles to come into the city that I did not like to interfere with the arrangements."

"Not at all, Miss Barton," Catherine answered.

"M'sieur Navarro is free to invite whom he pleases, and, for myself, I believe large parties are more enjoyable." Fanny Barton was nervous, that much was plain to Catherine as she answered. Her words tumbled over themselves, and her face was pale so that the freckles across the bridge of her nose stood out like a sprinkling of gold flecks. The smile that curved her wide mouth was hesitant.

"May I compliment you on your gown?" the woman asked, her gray eyes earnest. "It reminds me of creations worn at home, in Philadelphia. I can't tell you how refreshing it is to see color. So much white is worn here. Lovely, of course, and one conforms because it is so practical and suitable in a warm climate where one must change often and clothing is laundered after every wearing—but still so—so colorless. Your gown stands out like a yellow peony in a bed of white roses."

Catherine had almost forgotten what she was wearing. The memory of its donning before the amused eyes of the man they called Rafe brought the color to her checks. She had to admit however, that the gown was a success. It had a low, round neck which rose in the back to a fluted, upstanding collar like a ruff. The skirt fell from just under the bust to flare in shimmering folds to the floor, spreading out into a small, graceful train. The style was regal yet simple, to enhance the beauty of the rich, golden silk. It provided a magnificent background for the rich lustre of her mother's pearls, necklet, bracelets, and earrings, purloined at the last moment by Dédé to detract from her extraordinary *toilette*.

"You have—land near Alhambra?" Catherine asked. It was easier to continue talking to Fanny Barton than to turn and try to think of some commonplace to exchange with Navarro.

"Yes, we have a plantation a distance of some five or six miles from Alhambra. The house is not as large, nor is the acreage as vast as Rafe's holdings since he added Alhambra to his father's old grant, but it is developing nicely."

"But you would prefer to live in the city?"

Not really. I enjoy its amenities, the shops, and the balls and endless rounds of levées and routs—even Monsieur Gaëtano's Circus. But it's not me." She laughed. "Giles accuses me of enjoying the trip down on the keelboat more than the actual visit. I tire of it all soon enough and long for the peace of home. Not that it is so very peaceful."

"Isn't it? I once spent a summer on a plantation. I was a child at the time, but it seemed to me that the days moved past as slowly as the river at low-water that time of year."

"That's still true enough. The slaves have been troublesome of late, however. The place was stocked with island slaves when Giles bought it five years ago, and of course you know that Negroes from the West Indies are riddled with that terrible black magic they call voodoo. That isn't to mention their inoculation with ideas of rebellion fostered by their knowledge of the Negro kingdom of Haiti with its history of revolution."

Madame Thibeaut nodded, and entered the conversation abruptly. "I could tell you a thing or two about that. We have several of the island Negroes at Alhambra. Murderous brutes, you can tell by looking at them. I should know. My mother and father, my older sister, and my husband were killed on Santo Domingo, that they now call Haiti, in '91. My son died in the open boat in which we were escaping to Cuba. I was lucky to escape alive. So many died."

Her flat, hard voice somehow precluded sympathy. There was a glassy, repellent light in her eyes. Perspiration beaded her upper lip, and as the candlelight slanted across her high, bulging forehead, Catherine saw that the heavy rice powder she wore was meant to fill the scars left by smallpox.

Fanny smiled, saying in the soothing voice of one who has heard the story many times before, "It was terrible for you, I know."

"Terrible? They were demons, fiends from hell. Someone should send an army to kill them all."

"Napoleon tried, and failed," Fanny said softly. "But

93

now you are in the city, perhaps you will find some of your old friends among the new wave of Santo Domingan refugees and those who have left Spanish Cuba because of the fighting between France and Spain."

The older woman showed not the slightest interest in the possibility. She hunched her shoulders in a pettish shrug and turned away.

Solange, with unexpected tact, directed her companion's attention to the parquet beneath them. "Look, Madame, at that droll old man. He looks like the Sun King himself. Who can he be?"

Catherine, following the girl's pointing finger, smiled. The old man Solange had discovered was dressed in the style of a generation before. He wore a curled, powdered wig with a queue, satin knee breeches beneath his brocade frock coat, silk stockings, and silver buckles on his red-heeled shoes. In one hand he carried a ribbon-decked cane and a lace handkerchief, in the other he cradled a small white poodle-dog, while a spider monkey clung precariously to his shoulder.

"That's the Chevalier," Catherine answered her. "He has dressed just as you see him, like a gentleman of the *ancien régime*, for as long as I can remember. As a child he was one of my favorites, probably because he keeps a candy shop. You must pay him a visit while you are here and taste his pralines."

Solange stiffened. "Thank you, no," she said in glacial accents. "I am no longer a child."

Catherine had meant nothing of the kind. She herself often patronized the Chevalier's shop on Chartres Street. But Solange had already turned away with offended dignity, presenting her back to Catherine as she spoke to her companion.

The box had filled rapidly. A number of young men clustered about Yvonne Mayfield while she parried their compliments with a practiced air, treating them with a nice blend of flirtatiousness and maternal indulgence. Navarro had gone to greet a number of his friends, and as Catherine watched he led them forward to be presented to his sister. Even the Bartons were occupied by an American couple, and the clatter of English rose about the soft, rounded syllables of the French tongue in the crowded theatre.

Catherine got to her feet, moving to the rear of the box, unconsciously seeking refuge from the lorgnettes and quizzing glasses flashing in her direction.

"You look *ravissante* tonight, chérie."

Startled at the whisper in her ear, Catherine swung around to face Marcus. Deciding on the instant that the banter of light flirtation was her best protection, she smiled. "Thank you, sir. You are most kind."

"And you are cruel," he accused. "I see no other way to explain your behavior tonight. To let me hope there was a chance for me, then to plead illness, leaving me to escort your mother, was not kind. And then the final humiliation, to sweep in, wearing silk and pearls, on the arm of that damned corsair."

Catherine found his attitude of ill usage irritating. Still, though it had not been her fault, she had to concede that he had not been treated well. He was still a handsome man with his chestnut curls falling over his forehead, his hazel eyes beseeching, and his arm held romantically across his chest in its sling. He did not excite her, but it was pleasant to feel that she was able to control the situation between them.

"I'm sorry, Marcus. I did not mean to hurt you. Indeed, I did not mean to come this evening. But, you see, I had no choice."

"Do you mean Navarro constrained you to come? *Mon Dieu*, but he has been industrious. You cannot know, of course, but since his return to the city last night he has met three men over this business. Antoine Robicheaux last evening. This morning, young Marigny, and also my rattlepated cousin, Bernard, whose only fault was to try to protect our family name."

"—at the expense of the name of the lady involved—" Navarro interjected, his voice low.

He stepped to Catherine's side and taking her chill fingers, placed them on his arm. "This is not a subject which can be of interest to Catherine. The blame in this matter

95

is mine alone—after you, Marcus, naturally. Catherine's only fault has been her alluring loveliness, a fact which I explained to the gentlemen of whom you were speaking. I flatter myself that no one else will doubt it."

Navarro's words were a challenge, one that Marcus declined with a bitter smile and a bow of acquiescence. But as Catherine turned away, obedient to Navarro's guidance, the expression of murderous intent in the other man's eyes sent a shiver of fear over her.

"Cold?" Navarro asked. "I believe I have something that will bring the warmth back to your blood."

Catherine sent him an oblique glance, aware of an undercurrent in his voice that she did not understand. Then she noticed the door of the box opening to admit a liveried servant bearing a tray holding glasses which brimmed with champagne.

When everyone in the box had been served Navarro faced them, his glass held high in one hand, the other gripping Catherine's fingers. Yvonne Mayfield moved to stand beside them.

"Ladies, gentlemen. To the future, and to the young lady who has consented to share mine with me, my future bride, Mademoiselle Catherine Mayfield!"

CHAPTER SEVEN

"I will not marry you, Navarro. I will not!"

Catherine had managed to retain her rage until the play was over and they were alone together in his carriage.

"Chérie?" he said, his voice coming warm out of the darkness beside her. "Do you think you could bring yourself to call me Rafael, now that we are to be man and wife?"

"We are not to be man and wife. I told you, I will not marry you."

"You have a reason, of course, for this stubbornness?"

"Stubbornness?" Catherine cried in a choking voice. "You are the most arrogant, conceited man it has ever been my misfortune to meet. You tell me you will not marry me, you go away for three days, and expect to come back and have me fall into your arms agreeing with any outrageous suggestion you wish to make?"

"It sounds delightful," he sighed. "But no, I rather expected you to be annoyed. As a matter of fact, I expected you to deny every word there in the box, and I had in mind a number of enjoyable ways of stopping your lips. Then you confounded me by saying not a word. I wonder why?"

Catherine flung his shadowy form a look of intense dislike. "I did not want to make a scene—besides, I was watching your sister and her scarecrow of a duenna. They were horrified. There is no other word for it."

"Were they indeed?" he asked. "Did they say so?"

"There was no need. It was the look on their faces, a look of anger and disgust, but more than all, disbelief."

"You must learn, Catherine, not to allow other people's emotions to affect your own. It matters little what they think or want. It is none of their concern."

"And then there was my mother," she went on, unheeding, "looking as if she had been relieved of a great burden: myself, no doubt."

"I think you do her an injustice," he said quietly. "But it makes no difference. I did not ask you to marry me for her peace of mind either."

"Forgive me my poor memory, I'm sure, but I do not recall being asked at all," Catherine said.

"So that is it. You feel cheated of a formal declaration."

The laughter quivering in his voice sent her temper climbing. "No, that is not it! I will not have you marry me out of pity or a sense of duty—or even for the sake of what you consider to be your honor!"

"Take care, sweet Catherine," he said quietly. "My patience is not inexhaustible."

"You need not threaten me. I quite fail to see what

97

other harm you could do me," Catherine cried. "Don't you see? For us to marry now, on such short notice, would be like a public admission that we did indulge in all the reprehensible things people are supposing."

His voice was calm again, even reflective, when he answered. "May I point out that a marriage confers forgiveness for the—ah—previous indulgences and legalizes the later ones?"

"I do not want to be forgiven," Catherine said hotly. "I have done nothing of which I am ashamed."

"Bravo, petite. A fine attitude. But I feel sure that your mother and your friends will feel it is somewhat remiss of you when you take up residence in my house without benefit of the priest's blessing."

Catherine twisted around so quickly that she caught the flash of his teeth as he smiled to himself in the darkness.

"Speak plainly," she said, her voice hard. "What is in your mind?"

"I will spare your blushes, sweet Catherine, and tell you only that you will agree to be my wife this night, or you will be my mistress by morning. One or the other. Decide which. Now."

Navarro's carriage swayed on its springs without a creak or a rattle. The hooves of the matched bays that pulled it made little sound in the dusty street. The blue velvet that hung at the windows and lined the body of the coach deadened the street noises. It was a different kind of journey from the one she had made with this man a few nights before, and yet it was the same. Frighteningly the same.

"I do not love you," she protested.

"No? Then we are of a similar mind on that important question. We will start off even."

"Then why? Why are you doing this?"

"It is simple. I want you. I want you, let us say, as a connoisseur, tasting a fine wine, desires to own the entire vintage."

"Surely you would not want an unwilling woman, as either mistress or wife."

98

"No," he agreed reflectively. "It should be interesting to see how long you remain unwilling."

"You——" she began, then stopped, unable to put her anger and chagrin, her embarrassment, and yes, fear, into words.

"I know. Arrogant, conceited, and probably a great deal more, but you will credit me with being willing to give our child a name, if there is a child."

Catherine stiffened with shock. She opened her mouth to deny the possibility then closed it again. What would she do if it were true?

"Well, Catherine?" he asked after a moment. "Have you nothing to say?"

"I—find your sense of responsibility remarkable."

"No more than that? I would have said fantastic. But time grows short, ma chérie. Which shall it be?"

Catherine remembered with irony her brave preference, not so long ago, for the life of a demi-mondaine. It had seemed a free life at the time, unfettered, without the confining restrictions of propriety; a life she could call her own, at the mercy of none. Now, with it presented to her for the choosing, it seemed merely a life without protection, at the mercy of all. There could be only one answer.

Wearily, she leaned back against the cushions and turned her face away. "I will marry you."

"Rafael," he prompted.

"Rafael," she whispered.

The banns were read in the cathedral the following Sunday. They would be read twice more, and then on the Monday following the final reading the wedding would be performed. Time was a factor in the early date of the wedding. The day after the wedding was *Mardi Gras,* Fat Tuesday, followed by Ash Wednesday, the first of the forty days of the Lenten season, the time of fasting and prayer before Easter. To be wed during Lent was a shabby proceeding at best; everyone would have to forgo the usual feasting and merriment. It was also considered to be unlucky, holding dire possibilities of a parsimonious future. A wedding on a Sunday was "common," according to Madame Mayfield. Monday, on the other hand was fashionable. Monday it was.

Catherine spent the time of waiting gathering her trousseau. It was not too arduous a task. Creole girls spent their young lives hemming and embroidering the household linens and supplies they would need after marriage, the twelve dozen each of sheets, bolster covers, tablecloths, napkins, tablescarves, linen bath towels and cloths and dish cloths, even scrubbing cloths. Carefully copied recipes, curatives, preventives, and cleaning instructions were included along with the nightgowns and peignors made especially for brides by the nuns, beautifully, painstakingly, embroidered in white on white, cream on white.

Outer clothing was not, in itself, a consideration for the trousseau. There would be no wedding trip. Instead there would be the custom of the five days, five interminable days spent imprisoned together by tradition, closeted in her bedchamber without visitors or outside amusements. For some couples it was a blessed privacy after the endless chaperonage of courtship. For Catherine it loomed as a desperate ordeal.

Catherine's one cause for gratitude as the weeks passed, was that it was not necessary for her to be alone with Navarro before the wedding. Solange demanded her brother's escort morning and night as she rushed headlong into a round of frantic shopping and gaiety. Rafael would not often let Catherine cry off from accompanying them. They made an uneasy quartet, with Madame Thibeaut. Occasionally, when Catherine felt she could stand the concerted disapproval of the two women no longer, her mother would join them, charming them into smiles with effortless skill.

Gradually Catherine became used to appearing in public on Rafael's arm. She could not help being aware that they made a striking, even attractive couple. And, if she could not learn to enjoy the stir they made, she at least came to accept it as unavoidable.

The *dejeuner de fiancailles,* or engagement breakfast, could not be called a success. It was a family occasion only, but the Navarro and the Villère families were large ones, and not a single member could be omitted, from great-uncle Prosper to great-niece Tine. As Catherine had penned the notes of invitation and piled them in a basket to be carried around by a servant, she had devoutly hoped that some few would make their excuses. Her hopes were short-lived. The families seemed to feel it was an opportunity for solidarity, and turned out *en masse* to support their beleaguered relatives. The gathering seemed more of a funeral than an engagement, however, and the ritual congratulations extended had the sound of condolences. Yvonne, in particular, received a great deal of sympathy, though there were those who felt she had brought the disgrace upon herself by marrying an *Americain* in the first place.

There was a general feeling on both sides that the gathering was an embarrassment to be gotten through with as quickly as possible. They ate what was put before them, the mushroom omelettes, poached eggs on artichoke hearts, the delicate slices of ham, veal, and breast of chicken, the onion soup and orange sherbet, the currants and nuts, with dispatch. They drank the health of the bride in champagne, and after the presentation of the ring, a large traditional ruby surrounded by diamonds in a flat gold setting, they dutifully admired it. They then took their leave with awful politeness and due attention to precedence.

Catherine, watching the exodus from her post at the doorway, was undecided whether to be amused or hurt at their attitude. Then Rafael leaned close to whisper with a grimace, "To think, all these sour faces must be endured again at the wedding."

Glancing up, she caught the hint of laughter lurking in his eyes, and she smiled. The future might be endurable, after all.

On Friday before the wedding Rafael himself brought the *corbeille de noce*. The modiste, Madame Estelle, prided herself on the tasteful choosing of nuptial baskets, and Catherine had expected to have one of her creations delivered at any time. The basket Rafael placed in

Catherine's arms had much the appearance as Madame Estelle's, but for the weight of it and a gold-gilt ribbon threaded among the white ones decorating the handles at each end of the wicker basket.

Catherine, flattered at his attention to detail and irritated with herself for letting it matter, looked deliberately behind him. "Where is Solange?" she asked.

"I have sent her shopping with Madame Thibeaut. Your mother tells me that after today I may not see you until we walk down the aisle at the cathedral together. I thought it time to dispense with formality and chaperones, in the event there was anything that needed to be discussed."

Slanting him a quick glance beneath her lashes, Catherine answered, "I can think of nothing."

"Nonetheless, I do not think your mother will disturb us. Come," he said, relieving her of the basket, "let us go into the salon."

"They are cleaning the salon in preparation for the wedding supper," she said, apprehension making her blunt. "Will the sitting room suit you?"

They mounted the stairs together. When they entered the small, yellow sitting room with its filtered sunlight, Rafael closed the door behind them.

"Don't look so alarmed, petite. Haven't you noticed? I am on my best behavior."

"Yes," she said with a wary smile. "I have been a most appreciative audience to your self-restraint these last few days."

"Have you? That is encouraging. But perhaps you should open your basket before we carry that subject any further."

The lace handkerchief, fichu, and fan were more or less expected, as was the lace veil, that favorite headpiece of the creole women, worn in place of a bonnet while out of the house. The fine, loosely woven cashmere shawl shot with gold thread was a surprise, as were the bleached white doeskin gloves embroidered in a delicate design of bells and curling ribbon. The most costly gift, however, was in the bottom in several velvet covered boxes. It was

102

parure of topazes enclosed with seed pearls in a flower design, a necklace, earrings, a set of bracelets, and a pair of carefully fashioned hair ornaments that, when fitted together, formed a small, upstanding tiara.

Catherine sat so long, staring at the lovely things spread out around her, each chosen with such care, that Rafael pushed away from where he leaned on the back of the settee with an impatient movement.

"If you do not like any of it you have only to say so," he said.

"No, no. It isn't that," she assured him hastily. "It's just that it is . . . too much. There was no need for such extravagance."

He turned to face her, his mouth set in grim lines. "There was every need. I wished to give these trinkets to you. That is need enough."

"Is it?"

With one of his lightning changes of mood he smiled into her defiant eyes. "Are you thinking I bought them merely to still the tongues of the old cats by a show of magnificence? No. I bought them because they pleased me and I hoped it would give you pleasure to wear them."

"In that case, I accept them, with gratitude."

"I am not sure I believe you," he said, tilting his head to one side, his black eyes bright. "Perhaps you had better show me."

"What do you mean," she asked, nervously picking up the scattered articles, returning them to the basket.

"I mean, my innocent, that I expect at least a kiss for my efforts at the milliners, the modistes, and the jewelers."

Catherine met his gaze squarely. "So that is the reason you wished to see me alone."

"Reason enough for the moment. Here, put that away," he said, moving the basket firmly from her grasp, taking her hand and pulling her into his arms. "Don't be shy," he whispered as he lowered his lips to hers.

Catherine yielded, allowing herself to be pressed close against him because she had doubted him, or so she told herself. It was some time before she stirred and drew away.

"You are most welcome," he said, laughing down at her.

Staring at him, Catherine felt an odd pain move in her chest. By his own admission, this man did not love her. What he felt was no more than an ignoble physical desire. Then what moved her? Was she responding to the same kind of attraction?

Turning abruptly, she moved across the room to stand with her hand on the back of an Egyptian armchair. "You will be happy to know you are not to be a father," she told him without raising her gaze from the carved sphinx beneath her fingers.

He was silent for so long that at last she looked up. When she met his eyes, he asked gently, "That will make me happy?"

"Why not? You have shown no sign of caring for the responsibilities of a family before now."

Rafael took a deep breath. His mouth was set in stern lines and his eyes held an emptiness that was more frightening than anger. His fingers slowly clenched into a fist, then abruptly he turned on his booted heel and left the room.

The impulse to run after him, to call him back, warred with her pride inside her. Pride won, though it was an uneasy victory. Why was she being so difficult about what was in reality a simple thing? It was an exceptional marriage in New Orleans that was contracted for love. Most were arranged affairs, an alliance based sometimes on money, but most often on family prestige and suitability as decided by the parents of the couple. But no, her marriage was not like these calm, rational arrangements. In three days' time she would marry a stranger, an angry stranger. She stood carrying the thought for several minutes before turning her attention back to the seemingly endless preparations.

It was jusk dark when Catherine left the house on her way to the cathedral. Her gown, trimmed with the Villere family's ancient cream lace, glimmered ghost-like in the fading light. The crown of orange blossoms holding the short lace veil upon her hair shone with a waxen perfection that was echoed in her pale, set face.

The Navarro carriage had been put at her disposal. As she entered the vehicle, Dédé, trailing behind her, lifted her skirts clear of the steps. Leaning from inside, her mother caught quickly at her veil, holding it up while she leaned back.

"Don't fuss," Catherine said in a sharp tone. "Please—"

She lowered her voice at the hurt expression on Dédé's face. Madame Mayfield made soothing noises that grated on her heightened sensibilities. She clenched her hands in her lap. With all her being she concentrated on getting through the next few hours.

A light rain had fallen during the afternoon. The sky was still overcast, bringing an early darkness. The atmosphere was damp and oppressive. Catherine shivered a little in her nervous state, wishing for the shawl her mother had banned because it would spoil the lines of her gown.

The area around the Place d'Armes was lined with carriages of all descriptions, from curricles and phaetons to pony carts. There were even a few sedan chairs with their bearers standing near them, relics of Parisian days, used mostly by the elderly or when the streets were made impassable to carriages by heavy rain.

To Catherine there was an overpowering scent of horseflesh and the dank wetness of the nearby river, but her mother, stepping out as they drew up before the cathedral, exclaimed in delight.

"The entire world smells like a wedding. It's the wild oranges blooming on the levee, of course, but isn't it a marvelous effect?"

Smiling foolishly at that inane remark, Catherine felt herself swept forward through the crowd clustered about the doorway. She saw the Cathedral's Swiss guard in their medieval uniforms of red, gold, and blue as they marched to meet her, felt her hand taken in a warm grasp, and knew with a sinking of her heart that Rafael Navarro stood beside her. She could not bring herself to look at him.

Candle flames flickered in her wide eyes as she walked toward the altar at the head of the procession of Villere and Navarro relatives. Stumbling once on an uneven stone in the floor, she felt at once the supporting grasp on her arm. Did she acknowledge Rafael's assistance? She was not certain. Her faint smile might have been only an echo of the expression on the face of the priest who awaited them. She repeated her vows in a small voice. Rafael's seemed deep and unnaturally grave. The coldness of the double alliance ring slid over her finger. Rafael helped her push his into place. Sonorously, the blessing rolled over their bowed heads. The quill moved with a loud rasping over the register as she signed her maiden name for the last time. There was the endless wait while the more than thirty near relatives signed the register also. And it was over.

Their carriage waited still before the cathedral steps, its body gleaming wetly in the lantern light with the rain that had begun to fall once more. Thunder rumbled as she and her new husband left the church, but above its roar came the sweet lilt of violins. It was a band of gypsy street musicians standing ankle deep in the mud before the carriage, hoping to earn a few pennies with their music.

Taking in the situation at a glance, Rafael drew out his purse and tossed it to the coachman. He handed Catherine into the carriage and they sat, smiling without speaking, while the largess was being distributed. Catherine approved of the action but the sudden stillness made her uncomfortable. She flicked a glance at Rafael, then looked away, staring out into the parade ground of the Place d'Armes.

There was a pale blur out there in the darkness. Then in a flash of lightning she saw a man. He was a petty criminal, sitting in the wrist and ankle stocks with his accusing placard before him. His hands hung blue and lifeless from their holes. His chin was propped on the board that confined him. With the rain running in rivulets down his unprotected face, he stared straight ahead, uncaring of the pageant being enacted in front of him.

The carriage began to move and Catherine faced forward, but she thought the expression of hopeless misery on that pale countenance would remain with her for the rest of her days.

"Un repas de Lucullus."

The phrase was repeated again and again as the wedding guests gathered about the long table set for their enjoyment in the great room made by throwing open the doors between the dining room, the petit salon, and the grand salon. Upon the tablecloth reposed the Villere dinner service with place settings for a hundred people. In the place of honor, the center, stood the *pièce montée*, an enormous nougat confection. It faithfully represented the Palace of Alhambra, complete with the Gate of the Pomegranates, the Court of the Myrtles, and the Court of the Lions with its colonnade and tiny fountain supported by twelve desert lions.

Due to the large number of guests and enormous variety of the dishes, the meal was not served in courses, but was spread upon the groaning board in all its abundance, a feast of Lucullus indeed. At one end sat a great roast of beef, at the other a whole suckling pig, the *cochon de lait,* its outer skin crisp, the inner flesh succulent. Tureens of soups, green turtle, *court bouillon,* and that creole *bouillabaisse* called gumbo, sat at intervals, interspersed with bowls of steaming rice. Platters of boiled shrimp, seasoned oysters on the half-shell, trays of *vol-au-vents* filled with oyster stew, crawfish, and snipe's tongues, lined the side. An enormous turtle shell filled with buttered turtle and crabmeat crowded a dish of *coq au vin. Filet de boeuf* with mushrooms jostled the *daube glace* and duck liver pâté. Sideboards were ranged down the walls. On one side there were desserts of every description, cakes, tortes, pies, puddings, meringues, jellies, cremes, and candies; while on the other, beverages were being poured, from hot chickory coffee to champagne. Servants stood behind every chair, ready at a moment's notice to serve whatever took a guest's fancy.

In a corner a trio of musicians played classical airs upon a violin, a French horn, and a harpsicord. The long table and its burden would be removed and there would be dancing after the bride and groom had taken their leave. Surely, Catherine thought, so much food and entertainment would serve its purpose and she and her new husband would be left alone in peace without the embarrassment of a charivari.

The sight of so much rich food, the smell of it, mixed with heavy perfumes and the smoky fumes of the many candles that lighted the room, sent Catherine's senses reeling. She pushed at the food without appetite. All she could force down the tightness of her throat was a few swallows of champagne. She played with her wine glass, watching the shining bubbles rising to the surface, intensely aware of the man beside her. His brooding gaze was fixed upon the opposite wall. What was he thinking? Had he noticed that Marcus was one of the company; that he was practicing his gallantries upon Solange Navarro, selecting choice tidbits for her, and whispering such blandishments in her ear that her rather plain face glowed with something near prettiness? Did he see the sidelong glances cast at him by the other women, especially Fanny Barton, who, when she looked at Rafael and herself, had an expression of such resolute bravery in her soft gray eyes that it was like pain?

Giles Barton, seated beside his sister, caught Catherine's eyes. His arm was draped protectively across the back of Fanny's chair, but leaning forward he took up his glass and raised it to her, sending her a smile that was, somehow, totally approving. In acceptance of the toast Catherine smiled, encouraged.

Finally the feasting ended. With moans of repletion the guests left their chairs, turning their backs on the spilled gravy, broken meats, and scattered crumbs. Catherine, intercepting a look from her mother, knew it was time for her to take her leave of the company. With a fatalistic calm, she turned to Rafael, but there was no need to explain. He took her hand and raised it to his lips with a gallant air, watched by half the room. As she turned to leave there was a general stir while all pretended they had not noticed her departure, did not realize that she was going to her room to be undressed by her mother and nurse and left in bed to await her husband.

Holding her head high, Catherine crossed to the door. How much better it would be if the bride and groom could leave together, perhaps even leave the scene of the celebration for another, quieter place. It would serve to relieve this dark-age preoccupation of the guests with the intimacy of the newly wedded pair.

In her blind distress, she did not see Marcus until he stepped into her path at the foot of the stairs.

"Catherine," he whispered. "I had to speak to you."

"Let me pass." Catherine, after one brief glance, looked away from the entreaty in his eyes.

"Tell me you are happy and I will go."

"Please, someone will see ―"

"You cannot tell me, can you? For you are as unhappy as I. I knew it tonight as I watched you go through this farce of a wedding. It isn't too late. Come away with me now. We will find happiness together, somewhere, somehow."

Catherine reached out to place her hand on the newel post beside her. "You must be mad," she whispered.

"Yes. Mad with love for you. Crazed from watching you marry another man. I could not stand it in there another moment. I had to see you, to ask you―"

"I'm sorry, Marcus," she cut across his impassioned plea. "Truly―I am sorry. But you must see I could never do what you are asking. My future was decided when I agreed to marry Rafael. I could not go back on my word now."

His mouth curved into a bitter smile. "Why, Catherine? Pride, honor? Words. Words to shackle the spirit. Words to bind us as slaves to duty."

"Perhaps," she agreed gently, stepping around him, continuing up the stairs. "But, sometimes, it is all we have to cling to."

"All right," he called after her in an intense voice of barely controlled rage. "So he has won again. But in the end the victory will be mine. Mine, do you hear? And the savoring of it will be sweet."

Catherine's mother caught up with her in the hallway.

"Was that Marcus I heard talking to you?" Catherine nodded without speaking. "I thought I recognized his voice. I hope he did not upset you."

Catherine, feeling the trembling weakness of reaction in her knees, walked on. What good would it do to explain, she thought wearily. "No," she said, her voice even. "He did not upset me."

CHAPTER EIGHT

The mosquito *baire* draped back on either side of the bed was of lace handmade in France. Catherine, lying back against the pillows in her low-necked gown, reached out to finger it, wondering at the industry of the servants. Neither it, nor the bridal *ciel-de-lit,* or tester, above her had been in place when she had left the house for the cathedral. The tester was also edged with wide, cream-colored *dentelle valencienne,* while the shirred silk underneath was attached at the center by a gold ring held in the hands of four flying cupids. It was a lovely thing, as fashionable as the bridal veil it resembled, but Catherine rather doubted that Rafael would appreciate it.

Dédé had left one of her candles, made with her own hands, on the dressing table to the left of the bed. It burned with a furious light, a wavering nimbus about the flame. To Catherine, it seemed even more strongly scented with vetiver than usual, but she did not like to complain. The nurse had been tireless in her efforts, brushing her hair, curling it and spreading the burnished tresses out upon the pillow. She had tucked her in, twitching at the coverlet of drawn-work, smoothing away every suspicion of a wrinkle. Catherine, unbearably irritated by the fussing, had been very near dismissing her when Madame Mayfield, with infinite tact, had drawn her from the room.

All Catherine had to do now was wait. Wait for the man she had married.

How would she feel, she wondered, staring at the sightless cupids above her, if she did not know what lay in store for her in the hours ahead? Would innocence have been a protection against this fearful anticipation, or would it have worsened it? Should she, perhaps, be grateful to Rafael Navarro? A strange idea.

But if she could not thank him for her position, at least she could not fault him. He was a man, and had done no more than behave as one. He had taken her, but, discovering his mistake, he had assumed the responsibility for it. Whatever his reasons, whatever his methods, he had made the *amende honorable*.

She could hear the rain falling on the roof above and the patter of it as it was blown against the window. That poor man in the stocks. She hoped they had carried him inside by now.

Her gaze fell to the alliance ring weighting her finger. On impulse she slipped it off and gently worked the two interlocking halves apart. The engraving was there, just as it should be. *R. S. N. and C. D. M., March 13, 1810.* Rafael Sabastian Navarro and Catherine Denise Mayfield. They had both been baptised with several other Christian names, but these initials were enough.

Catherine closed her eyes, replacing her rings by touch. The initials had a dismaying tendency to run together. All those toasts. Two glasses,—or was it three?—of champagne on an empty stomach. The sound of the rain was relaxing. She found her lips moving in a wry smile. It would serve her laggard groom well if he found his bride asleep.

When Catherine awoke Rafael stood over her with his hands on her shoulders. She stared up at him, her amber eyes wide, the pupils dilated, a smile trembling on her lips. His expression did not lighten. The grip on her shoulders grew tighter.

111

"What is it?" she whispered, her voice slow, with a husky timbre.

"Hasheesh and mandragora," he answered. "This room reeks of it—the dried herbs that serve to keep the masses of Asia content with their lot." He looked down at her. "Are you content with yours now, sweet Catherine?"

"I don't know," she said. "I don't know what you mean."

He let her go abruptly. She watched through a drifting haze, as he moved to the dressing table and took up the half burned candle. Turning to the window, he tore the curtains aside, shoved up the sash, and sent the smoking taper spinning out into the darkness.

The rain-wet wind pushed into the room, billowing the curtains like sails. It ruffled Rafael's dark hair across his forehead as he swung around and began to advance upon her. Her heart beginning to pound, Catherine levered herself upon one elbow. When he reached out toward her, a swooping shadow in the darkness, she flinched away, but his strong fingers only curled around the bedclothes, flinging them back.

"What is it?" she cried, belatedly reaching after the coverlet, drawing her feet up beneath her long gown.

He did not answer. Instead he leaned forward and scooped her from her lace enshrinement into his arms. Setting her on her feet before the open window, he sighed.

"This is hardly the way I imagined it, my sweet, but then, what does it matter, one way, or another?" Before she could guess his intention, he bent to catch the hem of her gown and strip it up, off over her head.

Catherine gasped as the cool, rain-wet night air struck her warm body, so that her skin prickled with goose-flesh. Angry words crowded into her mind as she stared at her gown, a white patch on the floor. But before she could speak she realized that this incomprehensible stranger had the right to treat her in this manner if he wished.

"Why," she whispered, dropping her arms to stand gracefully before him. "Why?"

He reached out to touch her arms, smoothing the

112

raised flesh with his warm palms. "I have no need for a zombie woman in my bed. Whatever there is between us, Catherine, whether desire or repulsion, love or hate, let it at least be real."

She could not understand the censure in his tone. She knew nothing of the hasheesh and mandragora of which he spoke. Or did she? Dédé's candle. As her brain cleared, there ran through it the memory of Rafael picking up the stub of her candle on the night they attended the theatre, and of him sniffing it. The smell of the candles was familiar to her, a smell she associated with childhood illnesses, the sickroom, and times of emotional upheavals. Dédé's candles against demons. Neither she nor her mother had ever considered them harmful. They were a part of Dédé's medicine. Whatever they contained, Catherine knew they were intended to help her.

And hadn't they? Even now her nakedness, here before Rafael in the dim room, brought her no aching embarrassment. She was not afraid of him, she was only aware of him as a warm, breathing presence beside her in the darkness. There was a sensation of pain in her throat as she stared at the white blur of his shirtfront. The pressure of his fingers on her arms slowly tightened. Her breasts brushed the rough material of his coat. And then she was crushed against him.

She gave a small, convulsive shiver as she felt the enveloping heat of his body, and unconsciously, she moved closer. Tangling his fingers in her hair, he dragged her head back and his lips captured hers. Catherine knew a moment of hesitation, then with an ancient feminine wisdom, she yielded to him the right to plunder her body at will.

The folds of his clothing, the buttons and shirt studs, pressed into her. Conscious of them in a dark recess of her mind, she longed, with an intensity that amazed her, for the feel of his bare chest against her.

His lips moved to the tender, moist corner of her mouth. "If you are bewitched," he whispered, "the results are a lovely magic. You are in my blood, a golden heat, a tender flame."

113

The lazy humor of his voice held a beguilement of its own. Catherine laughed, a low, enchanted sound in her throat, as she felt herself lifted high and placed upon the linen sheets of the bed. She watched with bemused interest as he undressed, a shadowy, quick-moving form.

When he sank down beside her, she started to roll away to make room, but he caught her shoulder. Brushing his warm lips over its rounded contour, he turned her to him, pressing her to the hard length of his body, flattening her breasts against his chest. Her hair was beneath him. She could not move, nor did she want to. There was a singing exhilaration in her veins, a rising excitement that seemed to mingle with the sound of the rain falling beyond the window. She spread her fingers over his back, feeling the faint ridges of his scars and the play of the muscles under the palm of her hand as he caressed the curve of her hip. From deep inside there came a longing to offer recompense for the pain of his punishment, a need to erase the hurt he had endured. She moved against him experimentally.

She was snared in the sudden, tender assault of his response that rolled her to her back. His knee was between her thighs, the scorching heat of his hands awakening her to her own potential for desire. She felt a growing need, a consuming fire that was, somehow, humiliating. Her eyelids fluttered shut. She felt herself receding, becoming less than herself, a creature that trembled and panted, moving in obedience to the whims of the man holding her. It was a sinister enchantment, a thundering in the blood, a rape of the senses that left her lying scarcely conscious, bereft of tears.

Lightning tore the wild night sky across, and through the rent poured a torrent of rain. It swept, wind-blown, into the room, wetting the thin curtains at the window, puddling on the floor. The noise roused Catherine after a long while. She turned her head, then gathered herself to get up.

"Lie still," her husband said, pinning her to the bed.

"The floor—"

"—Can wait. There are other things you should concern yourself with."

"Such as?" she whispered, aware of the gentle insistence of his hand smoothing the blue-veined fullness of her breast where it shuddered delicately above the beating of her heart.

"The different guises of love between a man and a woman."

"Love?"

"Passion, then. It can lead to distress—or repletion; to exhaustion—or contentment."

"You talk in riddles."

"I know." He gathered her closer. "Some things are better shown. That will be my pleasure."

"Alà vous café."

At the familiar greeting, Catherine slowly opened her eyes then closed them again quickly. Outside the mosquito *baire* the room was bright with the glitter of sunlight on wet surfaces. The smell of the coffee Dédé carried was welcome, but she was in no hurry to partake of it. She seemed weighted to the bed, wrapped in a cocoon of delicious warmth.

"Mam'zelle!" Dédé cried, making a clucking sound of horrified disapproval against her teeth. Sliding the tray upon the washstand, she hurried around the bed. "How could you Mam'zelle? You will be sick. You know it is fatal to breathe the deadly fumes of the night air. And the floor, *Mon Dieu,* so wet. What your maman will say when I tell her I cannot imagine."

But the nurse had only drawn aside the curtains when a command rang out, "Leave it!"

The harsh voice, so close to her ear, made Catherine jump. The nurse stopped, her eyes widening with surprise. Then a mulish look moved over her face. "But M'sieur—" she began.

"I said leave it," Rafael repeated. Releasing Catherine slowly, he raised himself on one elbow. "And in the future you will not enter this room unless you are called, and even then you will knock and wait for permission. If

115

we want coffee we will ring for it. If we want food, clothing, a bath, or service of any other description we will ring for that also. I understand that the room connected to this one is yours. You will remove your belongings immediately."

"But M'sieur, I have slept there these nineteen years."

"You sleep there no longer. You may return to the servants' wing or find other quarters in the house. I care not which. But you will no longer have access to this room —or to my wife. You overstepped your authority and abused the trust placed in you when you dosed her with your poisonous concoctions that sapped her strength and will. You will not do so again."

"Who will arrange the hair of my *bébé* and assist her when she dresses?"

"I foresee no great need of either service," he said deliberately. "If the need should arise, I will do so."

Dédé drew herself up. "As you say, M'sieur."

When the door had closed behind the nurse, Catherine turned her head on the pillow, a troubled expression in her eyes though she did not quite look at the man beside her.

"You have wounded her feelings. Now she will sulk for hours."

"So long as she leaves us undisturbed. I have no liking for interruptions," he said, leaning over to place his lips, warm and firm, on the frown between her brows.

"Interruptions? Of what?"

"Of this, my sweet innocent," he whispered, his lips moving down her cheek to find her mouth, his hand moving over her, making her aware of their nakedness beneath the coverlet.

It was Mardi Gras. Occasionally a shout from the street penetrated to the fastness of the room, as the young men of New Orleans celebrated the last day of merriment before the lean days of Lent in a fashion brought with their ancestors from the south of France. Riding up and down the streets hidden behind the anonymity of dominos and masks, they flirted with the ladies arrayed on the balconies. The women did not mask but derived great enjoy-

116

ment from flirting with the masked riders and tossing down small favors of flowers, dainty handkerchiefs, and the like.

The aspect of their room, overlooking the back court, made it impossible for Catherine and Rafael to watch the spectacle, however. Hearing a particularly noisy group pass the house Catherine sighed, thinking of other years, then she dismissed it as unimportant.

Rafael, beside her, looked up from his newssheet, *Le Moniteur de la Louisiane*. "Poor chérie," he mocked. "Bored already?"

"Excruciatingly," Catherine replied in a dull and plaintive tone which she hoped would disguise the content she felt.

Rolling over, she lifted the plate containing the crumbs of their breakfast croissants from its resting place on his chest. She placed it on the tray between them, then with a show of housewifely concern for the safety of the china, she leaned to place the tray on the floor. It was a long reach from the high mattress. The sight of the tray sitting there was an unpleasant reminder of another tray beside another bed, the supper tray that night weeks ago. It was odd how things had turned out. Was it mere coincidence, or an equalizing celestial justice that had placed her in much the same situation for which she had condemned her mother?

A warm hand closed over the elbow of her balancing arm. "Don't fall," Rafael said lazily. "I refuse to be held responsible for any more bruises."

"Bruises?" she asked, searching her mind for something he might have done to cause a bruise.

"You look so fragile," he said, transferring his hand to her neck, smoothing his thumb over her collarbone as she settled back beside him, "as if I could crush you with one hand, and yet, I realize it isn't so. Did you know there is a pearl sheen to your skin?"

"Certainly," Catherine said, veiling her eyes, striving for a light tone despite the pulse throbbing in her throat. Why did she allow him to affect her like this? Why couldn't she remain indifferent under his touch? It was as if he held her body in thrall, subject to his desire. Did he realize that?

"The conceit of women," he murmured, and gave her an abrupt, hard kiss. Grasping the sheet, he pulled it over her, tucking it tightly across her breasts. "There. Stay like that," he said. "Or you may find yourself flat on your back for the next five days."

Catherine was uncertain whether to feel relieved or annoyed. She watched him as he turned his attention back to his newssheet.

"What is so interesting," she asked at last.

He glanced at her, a smile behind his eyes. "Politics."

"Such as?"

"In Spain they are breaking the grip of the French. The bands of insurrectionists are coming down out of the mountains to help the British harry the enemy. One thing about the Spanish, they never accept defeat. Nearer to home, the question of statehood for the Territory of Louisiana is being debated again. There are still a few who believe we should wait for a better offer, perhaps from Spain or England."

"Will statehood come?"

"Given the importance of the Mississippi River and the port of New Orleans to the western lands now opening to settlement, it must. Not this year, perhaps, or even the next, but it will come eventually."

"I don't imagine things will change too much, not as drastically as when the Spanish dons left."

"Not outwardly, no. But it will bring a stability that is important to the growth of any country, and it will give us a voice in the policies that most nearly affect us."

Catherine nodded her comprehension.

"What else did the *Moniteur* think worth relating?" she asked after a long moment.

"This should be of interest." You knew Napoleon finally rid himself of his Josephine in January? He is now casting about for a new wife and empress. There is some speculation that he will have the daughter of the Czar of Russia. Others claim that he aspires to join the old nobility by allying himself with the niece of Marie Antoinette, Marie Louise of the Hapsburg house of Austria."

"Poor Josephine," Catherine said.

"Undoubtedly, but from past indications I expect she will be able to support her spirits tolerably well. She did while Napoleon was in Egypt. In addition, Napoleon has given her their country home, *Malmaison,* and a promise to meet her not inconsiderable expenses."

"You saw them while you were in Paris?"

"I was presented, yes."

"What did you think of them?" she asked curiously.

"Napoleon is the kind of man you love—or hate. He has an air, a bearing, which you can either tolerate— or not. Josephine is charming, a witty and intelligent woman, but past her prime. She made an admirable empress, but not, unfortunately, a good wife."

"Because she failed to give her husband a child?" she asked, then wished she had not, for the subject had been a sensitive one between them.

Rafael did not appear to notice her discomfiture. "That was a part of it," he agreed. "Josephine was also unfaithful, undutiful, and a little stupid. She refused to join him in his travels outside the country, and she failed to recognize his worth until he was in a position to place a crown upon her head. A man expects more than that."

Was there a warning tone in his voice? If so, she did not care for it. Catherine turned away, a thoughtful look in her eyes. A peignoir of embroidered muslin lay on the slipper chair beside the bed. It was not meant to be worn without its matching gown, but she had no idea where that was. Sliding from the bed, she looped the mosquito *baire* back, then took up the peignoir. It was better than nothing but still so transparent she did not trouble to tie the ribbon fastening under the bust.

Moving aimlessly about the room, she took up a hairbrush from the dressing table, then using it to remove the tangles in her hair, stepped to the window. She pushed aside the curtains and looked out. Below, the court bustled with the usual midday servant activities. Small servant girls stirred purifying alum into the great jars of

119

drinking water brought daily from the river. Older girls plucked chickens for dinner under the supervision of an ancient crone. A woman shook a dust mop of rags, filling the air with a cloud of dust, before re-entering the house with the slam of a door. The scene was so familiar Catherine hardly saw it.

"Rafael?" she said tentatively.

He tossed the newssheet to the floor and stretched, lying back with his hands beneath his head watching her from behind the barrier of his thick, dark lashes. Catherine knew she had his attention, but she could not bring herself to look at him.

"Would you—would you really have made me your mistress?"

Narrowing his eyes, he surveyed her, moving from her small white feet upward over the softly rounded curves clearly visible through the diaphanous peignoir and the long, shining mass of her hair between her shoulders. His gaze rested on the oval of her face with the color slowly deepening on her cheekbones. The hint of a smile tugged at the corner of his mouth.

"But of course, ma chérie," he answered finally.

Slowly Catherine's fingers clenched on the hairbrush. The man behind her seemed suddenly alien to her, an intruder in her life, her home, and her bed; a cruel man who had fought other men and left them bleeding on the field in her name. What was she doing enclosed here in this room with him? How had he gained the right to look at her with that possessive gleam in his eyes? It did not seem real, not even when he left the bed, and taking the brush from her, began to draw it gently through the honey-gold strands of her hair.

Somehow the hours passed, turning into days. By silent mutual consent they avoided controversial subjects. The confinement was too close, their relationship too new to make disagreement anything but intensely uncomfortable.

Catherine thought for a time that Dédé did not intend to obey Rafael's command to clear her room, but toward the afternoon of the first day they heard her moving about inside. When Rafael strode through and dropped the bolt across the other door after the nurse had gone, Catherine considered his satisfaction excessive. But even she, just beginning to understand the constant but unpredictable nature of a man's desire, acknowledged relief that they could not be disturbed. She was more grateful when she saw his intention of using that small extra room as a bathing and dressing room. His forethought made their situation that much more bearable.

For Catherine there was little hope of anything approaching privacy, however. Often, when she was in her bath, Rafael would come to stand leaning against the doorjamb, watching her with frank enjoyment. At times he would talk to her, at others he derived his amusement from her attempts to appear unmoved by his scrutiny.

Once, to distract him, Catherine asked, "What will we do, when this is over? Will we stay in town, or will you be a gentleman-farmer? Have you decided?"

"Which would you prefer?"

She glanced up, surprised to be consulted. "I don't mind either way." She squeezed water from the cloth in her hand so that it ran over her drawn up knees. "New Orleans is—New Orleans—and I love it. Still it is rather thin of company after Easter. Spring and summer bring the fevers to town, while the country is at its best then. I have always rather envied those who could divide their time between the two."

"You have no objection, then, to leaving for Alhambra as soon as possible—after the next two days?"

"My trousseau is packed. I had as well go to Alhambra as any other place."

"You amaze me. I have been strapping my brain for a fortnight for a means of persuading you to come, short of kidnapping."

"You mean you would cavil at that?" she marveled. "Now you disappoint me."

He paid no heed to her provocation. "Alhambra has been neglected," he told her seriously. "The overseer I had depended upon in my absence was worse than incompetent; he was a thief. He had been there for years, a holdover from Fitzgerald's time, and, to give him his due,

121

might have been a good man so long as he was answerable to someone beside a woman or a group of careless lawyers. As it was, I had to dismiss him when I was there to collect Solange. The crops have been mismanaged, the fields are in a terrible state. There has been no return of the nutrients to the soil. The livestock has been allowed to inbreed, running wild in the swamp. The slaves have been brutalized, kept on short ration, and hired out as laborers to other planters, the payment for which went into the overseer's pocket. If anything is to be salvaged, it must be done quickly."

"As bad as that?" she murmured.

"My own lands, which march beside the Alhambra acres, are in little better case. The land always suffers from an absentee owner."

"Your other plantation, does it have a name?"

"My mother called it Serenity," he said bleakly.

"Serenity," Catherine repeated. "I like that."

"Do you? It has always seemed a macabre jest to me. When I go back and look at the old house with its *bousillage* of mud and moss and deer hair falling from between the timbers, and its cypress roof rotting down about the ears of the old Negress who cares for it, it feels anything but serene to me."

"Because of the deaths of your parents?" she asked without looking at him, conscious of the daring of the question.

"Yes. Are you curious?" His black eyes regarded her narrowly. "My mother was a quiet, timid woman. Her marriage to my father had been arranged by their families and it was not a happy one. She was terrified of him. Also, she was not well. A bout of fever as a child had left her heart weak. But to be perfectly honest, it was hard to sympathize with her. She complained incessantly and dosed herself with every quack nostrum, powder, and elixir she could lay hands on. Her illness was used as both a weapon, and an excuse to avoid the things she had no wish to do, which, without being too specific, accounts for the difference in age between Solange and myself." He was quiet a moment. "I can remember the wearing

122

megrims, tears, and turmoil caused by her pregnancy with Solange. I can understand, now, my father's frustration and cutting impatience, still, there was no excuse for what he did. A month before time for the delivery, he brought a quadroon into the house, ostensibly as a maid for my mother, but in reality as his mistress."

The bath water was losing its heat, but Catherine made no move to interrupt his narrative. She watched the play of emotions across his face, absorbed. He spoke in a reflective tone laced with irony. It seemed he did not mind having her know these personal agonies of his parents, that telling of them served to clear his own mind.

"It was a difficult labor. In the last stages, the midwife gave her laudanum for the pain. She made the mistake of leaving the bottle sitting beside the accouchement bed. My mother took an overdose. There was no way to tell whether it was deliberate or accidental. Either was feasible. But people placed the blame on my father's shoulders and he accepted it."

What could she say? The man she had married would scorn a facile sympathy. How bitter his father must have been—and how easy it was to blame him for the whole. There was much left untold still, the scars that marked Rafael, and his father's murder.

Rafael pushed away from the frame of the door, moving to the copper bath and dropping to one knee beside it. "Don't look so distressed, chérie. It took place eighteen years ago, not yesterday. A dusty tragedy now, curling at the edges like parchment." He smiled. "Of course, if you wished to comfort me I would not refuse."

"You'll get—wet," she said with a catch in her voice as he plunged his hand into the water.

"Not," he answered gently, "if I take off my clothes. I can't remember why I bothered to dress in the first place."

"You were tired of lying in bed, and you were cool without clothing," she reminded him quickly, catching his hand as it moved downward over the flat, smooth skin of her abdomen.

He looked up, trapping her amber gaze with his bright

123

black eyes. His lips curved in a slow smile. "You know, I find I am no longer tired—and not at all cool."

"Aren't you?" she whispered.

A soft laugh was his only reply as he let his gaze travel over her to the hair coiled on top of her head. With his left hand, he began to probe the soft roll, plucking out the pins so that its heavy weight loosened and slid down her back, falling nearly to the floor outside the tub.

Her attention caught momentarily by the gold glitter of the pins he had dropped one by one to the floor, Catherine said, "I never thanked you for your gift, did I?"

"These?" He weighed one in his hand with a judicious expression. "No, I don't believe you did. Would you like to?"

Her lips quivered as she tried not to laugh, but it was no use. "Oh, Rafael," she said. "Does everything lead to this?"

"This?" he asked, and lifted her wet and dripping from the water to lie in his arms.

She nodded, unable to speak for his lips against hers.

"Everything of importance," he answered as he carried her to bed.

The Angelus bell two days later marked the end of their confinement. They would emerge to have dinner with her mother that evening. While they were downstairs Dédé would pack what was left of their belongings, and with the dawn they would start the trip to Alhambra.

Why it should be so Catherine could not imagine, but the cathedral bell seemed to have a doleful ring.

The sky outside darkened with relentless swiftness as she stood watching the gray pigeons wheeling against the sky, preparing to roost.

Surely she was not sorry that their five days were over? She was heartily sick of the lack of exercise, of eating from a tray or makeshift table, of the surveillance and having to keep a constant guard on her tongue. Yet in that time there had been no outside problems, no decisions to make. For all her fears and reservations beforehand, these days had been a time of fragile peace between Rafael and herself.

In the room behind her Rafael was struggling into his coat. From his muttered curses, Catherine thought he was missing the services of his valet. Knowing that it often took a valet and two footmen to insert some gentlemen into their perfectly tailored coats, she had offered her help but it had been declined in definite terms. Was it a surfeit of her company that made him short with her, or was he also affected by the problems which faced them? Either way, she felt that he had set her at a distance. The difficulty which she represented had been conquered, his revenge against Marcus was complete, and already he was turning his attention to other obstacles.

You are being ridiculous, she scolded herself; fretting needlessly, all because Rafael had discarded his loverlike attitude to return to conventional behavior. It was not all imagination, however, for when she walked to the dressing table and took up the brush to bring some kind of order to her hair, he watched for a long, unmoving moment, then stepped to the head of the bed to ring for Dédé. When she came, he let the nurse in and quietly left the room.

CHAPTER NINE

The wide curve of the river had an opalescent sheen in the pre-dawn light. Swollen with the spring run-off from the vast reaches of the Louisiana Territory, the Mississippi rode high up on its levee. To Catherine, standing on the earthen embankment among her boxes and bundles, it seemed there were boats as far as she could see, the flood water raising them well above the ground level of the city behind her. Directly before her was tied one of the aristocrats of the river, a huge keelboat; the boat that would carry them on the thirty-five mile journey upriver. Further upstream were stretches of flatboats, known to rivermen as "arks." A half-dozen sailing ships of as many different nationalities were anchored out in the deeper channel. Smaller crafts swung from their mooring lines or were pulled up on the bank, among them birch bark canoes, pirogues made of hollowed tree trunks, and skiffs known as "mackinaws." There was a ferry, and a boat with oars in its locks and a small, furled sail, looking suspiciously like a New England dinghy. There was even a scow with a center treadmill to which an ox could be harnessed to provide the power.

Shivering a little, Catherine drew her cloak close about her as protection from the cool wind blowing off the water. Behind her the city lay wrapped in darkness except for the flicker of a street lamp here and there which had not yet burned out. Nothing stirred at this hour. It was unnaturally quiet. Even the voices of the men loading the big keelboat were subdued. It would be some time before the sun would rise to warm the air and dispel the mist that hung like a gauze veil in the tops of the trees across the river. Perhaps it would serve also to dispel this apathy that gripped her.

"Catherine! Why are you standing there? Come aboard. My maid will soon have coffee ready."

Fanny Barton stepped from the cargo box of the boat, a welcoming smile on her wide mouth. Attracted by his sister's call, Giles appeared around the side of the box in time to steady the gangplank and give Catherine his hand as she jumped down to the deck.

"I don't know what Rafe was thinking of, leaving you standing about," he said with a grin. "He would have felt foolish if we had left you behind. I believe he is seeing to Solange and Madame Thibeaut, making sure the new finery doesn't get water-marked."

Fanny supported him. "Yes, I heard the commotion," she said. There was such an odd tone in her voice that Catherine suspected the other girl had deliberately come to rescue her. A moment later she dismissed the idea as unlikely. No doubt the gesture stemmed only from a natural hospitality and innate good manners.

"These are your boxes?" Giles indicated the things left

126

on the levee. At her nod, he dispatched a pair of menservants to bring them on board. Catherine pointed out the bandbox she wanted with her in the cabin, then watched, bemused, as the blond giant who was to be her neighbor casually directed that the rest be taken to her husband to be stowed away.

"Thank you," she said, turning to face the pair with a resolute dignity. "You are very kind."

Giles smiled down at her. "I would like to take the credit," he said frankly. "But I was joking about leaving you behind. Actually, Rafe asked me to look after you. His sister kept him longer than he expected. Solange has never liked traveling by boat. It makes her fretful—and a bit—"

"The word you are looking for, brother dear, is irritating," Fanny said. "Forgive me if that sounds uncharitable, it happens to be the truth. Solange is demanding, quarrelsome; and before we are a boatlength away from the levee, she will be complaining of sea sickness and making certain we all share her discomfort."

"You may have guessed," Giles said, a gleam in his clear blue eyes that belied his grave tone, "that Fanny and Solange do not get along."

"Because I am not affected by the airs she assumes to create interest, and because I have the temerity to feel sorry for her for the loneliness that makes such affectation necessary?" Fanny demanded.

"Your outspoken habit has nothing to do with it," Giles murmured.

"Hardly anything," his sister temporized with a wry smile. "But enough. When I talked to your mother earlier in the week, Catherine, I understood that your maid would travel with you to Alhambra. Has she been delayed?"

"No," Catherine answered, her smile fading. "She isn't coming."

When her mother had suggested that Dédé go with her in the capacity of a personal maid, Catherine had not been enthusiastic. It was only after Rafael had flatly refused to allow the woman to come that she began to realize how alone she would be in her new husband's house. She had tried to make him understand her feelings. He had remained adamant. If she had to have the services of a maid, he would choose one for her when they reached the plantation, but he would not have that sullen sorceress in his house.

"Never mind," Fanny said. "She would have been company for my woman, but it will mean more room in the cabin for the rest of the ladies."

"You said you spoke to my mother earlier?" Catherine questioned the other girl with apparent carelessness.

"The day after the wedding, I think it was. I needed some idea of how much prepared food to lay in for the journey."

So as early as that Rafael had intended to leave for the plantation. His pretense of consulting her had been no more than that, a pretense. How agreeable for him to find her so accommodating. If she had not been, he might have had another opportunity of exerting his new authority. If she had rebelled he might even have had to resort to force, kidnapping, as he had jested. Nothing was beyond him.

His gaze resting with concern on her pale face, Giles said, "Perhaps you would like to lie down in the cabin. I'm sorry to drag you from your bed before dawn, but we needed to make an early start. I don't like to be on the river after dark."

"No indeed," Fanny agreed with a realistic shudder. "Not if it can be helped. Just be glad you didn't have to sleep on the boat last night, as I did. Even with twenty men and Giles around me, I did not feel safe. Some of the gangs of river pirates, you know, number thirty or forty of the most vicious, bloodthirsty men imaginable, animals who thrive on mangling, mutilating, and gouging out each other's eyes for the sheer pleasure of the fight. You can imagine what they do to their victims."

"You haven't given her a chance to answer me," Giles reminded his sister pointedly.

Fanny glanced at Catherine, "Don't let me frighten you. I'm sure we shall be quite safe. Are you tired?"

128

From the cabin came the sound of a feminine voice raised in petulant anger. There seemed little chance of rest in that vicinity. Catherine hastily disclaimed all intention of trying to recapture sleep.

"Good," Fanny exclaimed. "Then you can stay and keep me company. We can sit here upon the cargo roof and get acquainted while we drink our coffee. I think I see it coming now."

The keelboat was some fourteen feet wide and fifty long with a shallow draft of less than five feet. The cargo box, one end of which had been cleared as a cabin for the women, took up the center with a narrow boardwalk on either side of it, and a small expanse of cleared deck fore and aft. The walkways were cluttered with poles half as long as the boat, ten on each side. Crowding the aft deck was the crew, Negroes in rough osnaburg, who squatted, their backs to the gunwale, nursing cups of hot coffee laced with rum. On the forward deck was a windlass arrangement which, Fanny explained, was used to steady the boat through rapids and swift water and pull it off of sandbars.

As they watched, Rafael left the cargo box and joined Giles at the windlass. They pored over an unrolled chart spread out over its base, the dark head contrasting sharply with the blond.

Catherine looked away clasping her hands tightly about her coffee cup, absorbing the grateful warmth. To express her indifference, she asked the first thing which came into her mind.

"What time shall we make landfall at Alhambra?"

"Giles hopes to be home by dark. Rafe, when he came to fetch us nearly a month ago, made the trip in just under fifteen hours. My brother, in the friendliest spirit possible, naturally, is determined to better his record. Rafe had his own boat and an experienced crew. Giles does not. Those men back there are new hands he bought recently to replace those we have lost; we had a bad winter this year with a lot of pneumonia and ague, and then we have had a rash of runaways. But men are men and, to

129

Giles, using the slaves will make winning more satisfactory."

"This boat is your brother's then?"

"Yes. He bought it from a merchant who brought it, loaded with goods, down from Louisville. I would like for him to keep it. I could fit it out with curtains, cushions, paint and gilt trim, so that our trips to New Orleans could be made in comfort. Giles says it sounds like Cleopatra's barge to him. He intends to break it up for the lumber. I expect he will turn it into a blacksmith's shop, or some such thing."

There was a shouted order. One of the men jumped to the levee, threw the gangplank to a waiting deckhand, loosened the mooring rope, and scrambled back on board.

"I expect we had better move," Fanny said, jumping down from the box as the men began to clatter the poles at their feet and take their places at the sides. They made their way to the bow. Standing out of the way, they watched the operation as the boat began to move.

Twenty men, ten per side, thrust their poles into the water until they reached bottom, placed their shoulders in the crotch at the top of the poles, and, straining against them, walked toward the stern. As the men at the end of each row reached the limit of the walkway, they turned smartly and ran back over the top of the cargo box to the bow, to begin again, in this manner, walking the boat upstream.

Slowly the dark skyline of New Orleans, the sloping slate roofs, the flat balustered top of the Cabildo, and the rounded twin towers of the Cathedral, slid away behind them. With her gloved hand resting lightly on the gunwale and her face immobile, Catherine watched until it was out of sight.

By sunrise most signs of civilization were behind them. Hours passed between the sightings of cleared lands or smoking chimneys pointing upward among the trees dripping with gray Spanish moss. Seagulls followed them a long distance up the river. In the quiet water of small tributaries they saw wood ducks and mallards paddling near the banks. Blue cranes and brown pelicans passed often overhead. In the swampy areas the trees were white with nesting egrets. Their plaintive screeching had an unearthly ring over the silent forest that bounded the river on either side. Turtles slid quietly into the water at their approach, and now and again a majestic white crane would rise on heavy, sun-silvered wings to flap away over the tops of the trees.

Due to the high water they were able to "bushwhack" the boat at times, pulling it along close to the bank by grasping the bushes and small trees at the edge of the water. In the middle of the morning a cold repast of ham or chicken between biscuits and rolls, washed down with quantities of hot coffee made over the brazier in the ladies cabin, was eaten. As the sun climbed high overhead, sweat began to pour from the men from their exertions. They discarded their shirts. Those who had shoes had removed them long before, and the men poled with a will in breeches and barefeet, sometimes breaking into a low and melodious working chanty which helped them to pull in unison.

There was an older man among the slaves. Catherine, noticing the fine weave of his linen, thought he had been a houseservant, and as such, unused to such strenuous labor. She was watching when he began to falter. When he fell to his knees she started forward in concern, but Rafael was before her. Catching the man's pole before it could be lost in the sucking current, he supported him with an arm about his shoulders. In a moment order had been restored. The man was laid on the deck at the rear with a canvas awning for shade and Fanny's maid to cosset him.

Tossing a careless challenge to Giles over his shoulder, Rafael took up the extra pole. Giles, after an instant's hesitation, sent a man on the opposite side to rest in the shade while he took up pole and challenge with a grin. Both men exhorted their crews to greater efforts in an attempt to make the other man's side of the boat yaw toward the shore. They were soon stripped to the waist, straining, laughing, and calling insults in their high spirited rivalry.

Fanny flicked Catherine a look of almost maternal amusement. Catherine barely smiled in return. Watching the play of supple muscles beneath the scourged skin of Rafael's back gave her a peculiar feeling near the heart. The sight of the thin red line, all that remained of the sword cut she had closed for him with her best embroidery stitches, evoked memories she would as soon forget.

"It's getting rather warm—don't you think?" she said, stripping off her gloves and fanning herself with them.

"I do indeed," Fanny said, her tone brisk after a swift glance at Catherine. "You are getting pink across your cheeks and the top of your nose. I'm so freckled already it doesn't matter, but it would be a shame to burn such lovely skin. Solange should be over the worst of her sickness by now, if you would like to go inside."

"Yes, I would like that," she agreed, and swung away without glancing again in Rafael's direction.

The dimness of the cabin, with its one small window, was a relief after the glare of the water outside. It was overheated from the sun and the brazier in one corner, and somewhat stuffy, but that could be endured. In the tiny enclosed space there was little head room. Bunks had been arranged one above the other on each wall, with a pallet of piled quilts in the corner for the maid. Testing the thinness of the rustling cornshuck mattress that covered the ropes of the bunk, Catherine thought she would gladly exchange places with the servant.

Solange lay on the bottom bunk before the window. A damp cloth lay folded across her forehead, and a vial of smelling salts was clutched in her hand. Madame Thibeaut sat at her feet, pushing a flashing needle in and out of the minute piece of petit point she held in her hand.

"I knew our solitude was too wonderful to last," the younger girl said in fainting accents as she turned her face from the door.

Catherine thought she could see the decision to humor Solange forming in the American girl's expressive face.

132

"How are you?" Fanny asked cheerfully. "Is there anything Catherine and I can do to help you?"

"Yes," Solange answered, her voice muffled. "Go away."

"Very amusing," Fanny returned. "We don't intend to be broiled for the sake of your ill-temper, however."

"Ill-temper!" Solange flounced over in the bed, staring at them with black, accusing eyes in her pale face. "I am suffering from *mal de mer*," she said viciously, "and a sickness of the soul from knowing that my brother was tricked into marriage by this—this scheming *intrigueuse!*"

"Chérie—" Madame Thibeaut cautioned, but Solange would not listen to her.

"I will not be quiet. I have held my tongue these long weeks for my brother's sake, because he asked me to befriend this creature. I will do so no longer."

Catherine's face went blank at hearing herself described as an adventuress. It was a term so foreign to her habit of regarding herself that she could not quite absorb its meaning.

"Solange," Fanny began, "you don't know what you are saying."

Catherine shook her head. "Let her go on. Your brother told you that I tricked him into marriage?"

Solange glanced at her companion as if for support. "Everyone knows it," she said defiantly. "From the moment of our arrival, New Orleans talked of little else. Your unprincipled conduct, your brazen effrontery in attending a quadroon ball was on every tongue."

"Was it?" Catherine asked softly.

"Yes, it was. And it is my belief that what happened was exactly what you wished to happen. You found a gentleman ready to be taken in by your odd attraction, and when the affair had gone too far to be mended, you used his honor as a weapon to induce him to marry you."

"That isn't true," Catherine whispered.

"Isn't it? Why else should Rafael decide to marry you immediately on his return to the city? Why else did he drag me from my home, except to add countenance and

133

respectability to you and your aging *femme fatale* of a mother—"

"That will do," Catherine said, something so menacing in her quiet voice that Solange fell silent, though her eyes still flashed with a hate-filled resentment.

Catherine went on. "I misdoubt that anything I have ever done, or dreamed of doing, could be altered one jot or tittle by the addition of your countenance, Solange. As for my mother, we will not speak of her, now or ever— for you, I think, are more vulnerable than I in that relationship. My marriage concerns no one but my husband and myself. If he is satisfied, then I am afraid you will have to be also."

"Yes, and I will have to stand by and see you break his heart, and cast it aside the way you cast aside that of Marcus Fitzgerald."

"I don't believe—" Catherine began, at a loss for the meaning of the triumph that had blossomed on the sallow face of the girl before her.

"Do you not? Marcus told me of the way you behaved, of how you enslaved him with your beauty and honeyed, empty promises, until he would do anything you asked. He told me of how you used him to find better game, then cast him aside, crushed by your treachery. Would it distress you to learn that he was able to find comfort in my presence? It is a simple pleasure, but one he never knew with you. By his own word, a pleasure which would not pall over a lifetime. He intends to pay a long visit to relatives on his mother's side, the Trepagniers, who live not ten miles from Alhambra. Can you guess the purpose of the visit? He intends to pay me court. You may even have the edifying experience of seeing his heart completely cured of your evil spell by my influence. How will it feel, Catherine, to be forced to extend to us your felicitations?"

Catherine smiled, a wry twist of the lips that brought a baffled look to Solange's black eyes. "I will extend my felicitations, and most willingly, if you have indeed captured the interest of Marcus Fitzgerald."

It was impossible to remain in the cabin after that exchange of words. Stepping out into the sunlight, Catherine remembered the small window above the girl's bunk, and wondered how much of her tirade had been heard by the men. Not that any of it could come as a surprise. But she would have liked some sign from Rafael, even if only a smile, to show that he did not condone his sister's attack, that he supported her defense. There was nothing.

It was with intense gratitude that she heard Fanny Barton call to her brother that she could not abide the closeness of the box and must have an awning erected. Did Giles look a little conscious as he turned toward them? She could not tell. The impression passed, however, as he complained good-naturedly about the demands of a sister, and the lack of reward for service.

When they were seated under the canvas shelter, Catherine turned to the other girl to thank her. "You are tolerant, considering what you must have heard of my conduct."

Fanny waved a deprecating hand. "Don't let Solange upset you. She tends to exaggerate in her jealousy. She is not a happy person at the best of times."

"Isn't she?"

"She has been left alone for too much these past years. She is, in consequence, insecure. In my opinion it was not well done to leave her in the sole care of a companion, especially such a one as Madame in there. Still, it could not be helped. People are prone to avoid those who are connected with tragedy. Regrettable, but there it is. I did my best to befriend her, but she developed a childish passion for Giles. She would ride out to meet him in the fields, following him about like a kitten wanting to be petted, and making endless excuses to be alone with him. It eventually proved too much of an embarrassment to him, and an encouragement to her, to continue."

"By tragedy, you mean her mother's death?" Catherine asked, unwilling to comment on a situation that must have been awkward for all involved.

"And that of her father. It did not help to have her only brother banished with the name murderer ringing in his ears. I hesitate to interfere, but I think it is important

135

that you try to understand Rafael's feelings for his sister. Not that I am any kind of an authority on them, of course," she disclaimed hastily.

"Yes, go on."

"It is my belief that he is hampered in his dealings with her by the guilt he suffers for his unintentional neglect. He is inclined to make excuses for her, to be indulgent, even lenient. A mistake, I think, but I am hardly an impartial judge. I am conscious of annoyance with the child, even when she commands my sympathy the most. There, I don't want to prejudice you. It is possible that when you arrive at Alhambra, and she recovers from her illness, you will be as close as sisters."

"It seems unlikely," Catherine said dryly. "Solange disliked me the moment she met me."

"Hardly surprising. You are only what? a year or two at the most, older than she? Yet you have had easy access to the life she craves. You are more attractive than she could ever hope to be. You have had numerous suitors. Why, for all that I could be a bit green-eyed myself! In addition, you have married her only brother."

"It seems there is more than that to her antipathy."

"Don't let it distress you. I will agree that Solange is difficult, but, as I keep reminding myself, much of the reason lies in the peculiar deaths of her parents."

"I wonder—" Catherine stopped, then went on resolutely. "I wonder if you would tell me about her father. I have heard something of it, but I do not understand it, and I would not like to question Rafael. The incident is obviously still painful to him."

Fanny nodded. "I will tell you what I can, but it will not be much. Men, you know, do not talk to females of this sort of thing. Giles is a superior brother, but he has the same maddening reticence on unpleasant subjects as other gentlemen."

They exchanged a smile and Fanny went on. "Rafael's father blamed himself for the death of his wife. You know—"

"Yes, I have been told of her."

"Well, his disposition had not been good to start with

136

but after her suicide it grew worse. He began to drink heavily and the drink gradually destroyed his reason. He could not stand the sight of Solange. The poor child was banished to the nursery, while he was in the house, long after she was old enough to leave it. But it was his son who received the brunt of his drunken anger. He could stand not the least hint of opposition. Any questioning of his orders or interference with his methods made him reach for his whip. The plantation began to fall apart. It is not astonishing that as soon as he was old enough and strong enough to oppose him, Rafael went his own wild way. The slaves, of course, could not escape so easily. Their only recourse was a secret rebellion, slack work, idleness unless watched constantly, petty thievery, neglect of farm animals and tools. Some of these slaves had been present on Santo Domingo during the uprising there and were familiar with a military type organization. These were—and still are—particularly dangerous. The quiet revolt enraged Rafael's father. His answer was an increase in discipline. It was after the whipping of one of the Santo Domingo slaves that open rebellion came. The man and tow of his friends slipped away into the swamp. A week or so later the older M'sieur Navarro was returning along the swamp road on horseback when he was attacked, dragged from his saddle, and beaten to death."

"How terrible," Catherine breathed.

"Yes. Insurrection. One of the most terrible things possible in a slave community. Rafe found the body. Like all young men of his age, he knew the swamp well from hunting in its depths. He sent his valet who was with him for help, and started after the murderers alone. The search party quartered the swamp all that night. At daybreak they found Rafe. He informed them they were no longer needed. What had to be done, was done."

Catherine had known her husband was a ruthless man, but even told in Fanny's soft voice, there seemed a cold-blooded air to this exploit. When she said as much, the American girl defended him.

"There were those who did not understand, a vocal minority who looked at it as you do. Others, Giles among

137

them, felt his action had averted a full scale uprising. So you see, it was not cold-blooded, Catherine, but just. Rafe is always a just man, whatever the cost."

Catherine looked away from Fanny's earnest gray eyes. Ahead the river rushed towards them in its spring spate. Limbs torn from trees and uprooted trunks were borne upon the current as effortlessly as the tattered leaves and bits of bark that dotted the surface. Catherine now knew she had not been mistaken that night at her wedding supper. When Fanny spoke of Rafael there was an expression in her face, a timbre in her voice, which— No, she was being fanciful. What she saw was no more than a guileless affection for her brother's friend. Fanny Barton could not be judged by the same standard she would use with a Creole girl. Their ways of looking at life, at men and courtship were not the same, any more than their customs or religion were the same.

The bright sunlight was not kind to the other girl. In its reflected glare she appeared older than Catherine had thought on first acquaintance, perhaps in her middle twenties. Fine lines radiated from her eyes, and there were the indentations of a smile on either side of her mouth.

To make up for her uncharitable imaginings, Catherine smiled warmly. "Thank you for telling me. Perhaps I can impose on you further by asking you what I can expect to find at Alhambra? What will the house be like? And the grounds?" Because she thought it might sound odd that Rafael had not told her these things she added, "Men are hopeless for details of this sort."

Fanny's face cleared as if she, too, were glad of the change of subject. "You are aware that Ali, Rafe's *valet de chambre,* was sent ahead to prepare for your arrival? Ali is more than just a valet. He has been friend, secretary, fellow-adventurer, and general factotum to Rafael for years. With him in charge you should not have to worry too much about the conditions you will find at Alhambra. The house? It's a typical West Indies planter's style with heavy shutters and deep galleries to protect against sun and rain, and a raised basement with the main living quarters on the second floor to escape flood waters. Alhambra's special feature is the central courtyard which must have suggested the name to the original owner. The bedrooms overlook the area, which has a strong Spanish influence with a wrought iron staircase they say was imported from Madrid, and a fountain. You will not be disappointed, I hope, that the stone basin is supported by only four lions instead of a dozen?"

Catherine shook her head at that whimsey. "You make it sound fairly large."

"Larger than most. There are ten main rooms upstairs, all opening into each other for the free circulation of air. The grand and petit salons, a study, and a lady's sitting room-cum-entrance hall are on the front, then the bedroom wings, three rooms per side form right angles around the courtyard. I expect you are used to this style, but when I first came here I thought it ugly and secretive, a terrible, closed in way of building a house. In New England we have steep roofs, to help keep the snow from collecting, and very little overhang, so the sun can warm the rooms. But I quickly learned the benefits of the galleries for outdoor living at Cypress Bend."

"Cypress Bend is the name of your house?"

Fanny agreed. "It is built back on a rise near a large curve in the river and, like Alhambra, in a grove of oak and cypress trees. The only thing we have changed is the kitchen. It burned last year, a separate building, of course, so the house was not damaged. But Giles could not resist improving the premises by importing brick, red New England brick, and using them for a safer building. I must confess it looks odd to me behind the plastered house."

They chatted on in this style, carefully skirting the personal, through the afternoon. Occasionally Catherine thought she detected a hint of reserve in the other girl's manner, but after her friendliness and consideration she could hardly quarrel with such a small thing. During the day the number of men poling had slowly decreased until at any given time there were only fourteen men on their feet while the others rested. They were all exhausted; you could tell by their gray faces and the vacant look in their eyes, though the liquid strength they found in the rum barrel might have contributed to the latter. Food had been kept ready for the asking, but toward sundown Fanny rose saying she needed to supervise the evening meal.

"Can I help?" Catherine asked, getting to her feet.

"No, no, I have my maid for that. It's mostly a matter of finding the special fried fruit tarts I had made up for this time of day, a little something to put heart back into us all. We still have a fair way to go. Besides, there just isn't room in there for more than two women to stir about."

Catherine accepted her dismissal without further protest. Having learned something of Fanny, she suspected their hostess felt it was time she inquired after the other women also.

This morning she had looked back toward New Orleans. The time for that was over. Keeping well out of the way, she moved to the bow of the boat to stand beside the windlass, facing forward with her hand resting on the capstan.

It had been an uneventful trip for the most part. They had nearly capsized once in the effort to miss a giant sawyer, an uprooted tree, bearing down upon them. Still, they had avoided the sandbars and taken no wrong turnings. Two or three flatboats or rafts had passed them, headed downriver, one with a long cabin complete with smoking chimney upon it. Another time they had seen a canoe, piled high with fur pelts, paddled by an Indian and his woman who had stared at them from flat, incurious faces as they drifted past.

A footfall sounded behind her and she turned her head as Giles came to stand nearby, leaning with one hand on the gunwale.

"I expect you're anxious to reach home—Alhambra, that is," he corrected himself.

Catherine agreed then said conventionally, "I've enjoyed the trip today, however."

"We've had good weather and good luck," he said, nodding.

"And a good pilot?"

A tinge of red appeared under the skin of his face at the compliment. "Don't say that until we get home. There's still a lot of water between here and there."

Catherine smiled without comment. The sun was dying behind the trees in a splendid golden funeral pyre. Indigo blue shadows stretched out over the shimmering water. A freshening breeze blew toward them with the scent of wood's fern and wild honeysuckle overlying the dank river smell. And stretching out from the trees came the spring chant of crickets and peeper frogs, an unending paean.

The man beside her reached out and pressed her arm, a brief contact. "Mosquito," he said showing her the crushed insect. "They will make life miserable when it gets a little darker. Fanny hates them; they are one of the few things she hasn't been able to adjust to here."

"Some people are more susceptible than others. My nurse used to rub mint and sage leaves over her arms and face, and leave a bottle of pennyroyal standing open in her room—" Catherine trailed off, aware of a sudden tension in the big man. Following his gaze, she saw on the river ahead another keelboat bearing down upon them.

Heading downstream, the river provided the power for the other boat. The two or three men standing with poles in their hands had nothing to do but steer. As the distance between the boats closed, these steersmen were joined by others. Catching sight of a fair haired woman, they began to shout and gesticulate, though their words could not be heard.

More men crowded to the front of the oncoming boat, rough men dressed in buckskin, half cured pelts, and other coarse, colorless materials. Their hair grew long and matted and their faces were covered with a heavy growth of beard, giving them a bestial appearance.

Kaintocks, Catherine thought, with a tight feeling in her chest, then saw with dismay that the boat had changed course, veering toward them.

Giles straightened, shouldering in front of her, shielding

her from view with his body in an instinctive gesture of protection. He had time for no more before a hard voice rang out behind them.

"Catherine, go below. Now."

She felt the stinging condemnation of Rafael's tone like a blow, but, staring at his set face and the sword balanced in his hand, Catherine knew it was not the time to argue. She did as she was told.

Strained minutes passed, minutes made horrible by the jeers, the insults and cat-calls that grew more than plain enough to be understood. Then the voices began to fade. Whether the men had not liked the prospect of a more or less even fight, the look of naked steel, or had simply decided the possible sport was not worth the risk, the other boat swept past without touching. The danger receded into the distance downriver, and was gone.

CHAPTER TEN

Long after the sun had dropped below the horizon and the shore on either side was shrouded in darkness, a pale, refracted light on the water allowed them to make headway. When that was gone they fastened a lantern to the bow and continued on. Catherine lay on her bunk, her arm thrown over her eyes, pretending to sleep. That harsh order given to her still echoed in her mind, mingling there with a sense of hurt and affronted pride. She was aware too of Solange's tittering enjoyment of her discomfiture and Fanny's unspoken sympathy. Retreating from both into a pose of quiet dignity, she prayed silently for this endless journey to be over.

The moon was striking a shining silver path across the water when at last they steered toward shore. The boat scraped with a screeching rasp of wood along a mooring pole, and came to a stop. A shouted command, and the boat was secured, bumping rhythmically against the landing with the wash of the current.

"We have arrived, ma petite," Madame Thibeaut said to her charge in over-bright tones. "Come, let me help you. You will feel better once you are upon solid ground. Give me your hands and I will pull you up, so. And now an arm about my waist—there, that isn't so bad, is it?"

"My head is swimming," Solange moaned. "Where is my vinaigrette? I must have my vinaigrette."

From the top bunk, Catherine saw Fanny motion to her. She slid down with alacrity, and together with the other girl's maid they slipped from the cabin, out into the cool night air.

For a moment Catherine thought there might be some mistake. Though they were near the shore and a faint light glimmered through the trees, water surrounded the craft. Then she saw the signal lantern with its sides of red glass hanging from the pole to which the boat was moored, and she realized the landing was submerged by the high water. A skiff tied also to the mooring pole, suggested their means of getting to shore.

Giles stood with Rafe in the bow, a silver timepiece the size of a turnip filling his large hand. Rafe, with his hands on his hips, grinned derisively at his friend.

"I don't need one of those tickers to tell me my time was better than yours."

Giles squinted at the face of his timepiece in the poor light. "I make it an hour and forty minutes better," he agreed with a shake of his head. "I don't know how you did it. No one could make better time then we did today —or have better luck."

"You owe me a drink," Rafael reminded him. "I will collect it as soon as I set a few things in order. In the meantime, if you must have a culprit, blame the pilot."

"What do you mean, you rascal? I'm the pilot."

Both men laughed as they turned towards the arriving women.

It was with great reluctance that Giles and Fanny Barton finally accepted an invitation to stay the night. Plainly they did not like to intrude on Catherine and Rafael's first night together in their home, and yet, as Rafael had pointed out, Giles was a prudent man, with no liking for the unnecessary risk of traveling the five or six additional miles upstream at night. Morning would be soon enough. Still it was only after Catherine added her earnest pleas for their company that Fanny and Giles agreed.

There was a brief argument over who should have the first use of the skiff, but Rafael would not be outdone in politeness. It was Giles who jumped down into the small unwieldy boat and lifted his sister and her maid over the side to join him.

They had not gone more than a half dozen strokes of the paddle before Rafael leaped over the side of the keelboat, plunging above his knees in the water before he found a secure footing on the submerged deck of the landing stage. Laughing, he turned to Catherine, holding out his arms.

"Jump," he invited, a dare in the mocking sparkle of his black eyes.

Catherine took a deep breath. He had practically ignored her all day. Did he now expect to be able to tease her back into humor with him? Of course there were other reasons for her ill-mood that she did not wish him to suspect. Moreover, it would be churlish to refuse such a handsome offer of transportation, wouldn't it?

Putting a hand on the gunwale, she sprang to a seat on top of it, then swung her legs over it. She balanced there an instant, then leaning forward with outstretched hands, let herself fall into his waiting arms.

He had waded half the distance to the shore when a cry rang out behind them.

"Rafe! Wait!" Solange screamed. "Wait for me. Don't leave me, Rafe. Don't leave me alone!"

He turned back, the grip under Catherine's knees and across her back tightening. Solange leaned over the side of the keelboat, waving frantically, with Madame Thibeaut at her side trying to restrain her. At the stern, the Negro slaves were deserting the boat, following Rafael's example. They were jumping one by one to the water-covered landing carrying with them the bundles and trunks.

Catherine could feel the tension in her husband's grasp and the uncharacteristic indecision. "Perhaps you should go back," she said, forcing the reluctant whisper from her throat.

Abruptly he shook his head, swung about, and strode on to the top of the levee. There, he set her on her feet, pressed her hand for one brief second, then returned to the keelboat.

It was Solange he carried down the slope of the levee and up the wooded rise to the lighted house. His sister leaned her head against his shoulder, sobbing like a heartbroken child. Catherine, her skirts held above the dewsoaked grass, trailed after them.

A double, curving staircase led directly to the main rooms on the second floor of the house, by-passing the raised basement. As the procession mounted the stairs, the wide front door opened, spilling light across the darkened recess of the long front gallery. A manservant stepped out into the orange-gold shaft and bowed low with a ceremonial obeisance.

"*Bienvenu,* Maître Rafe, Maîtress. Alhambra welcomes you," he said.

The voice, oddly accented, precise, without the slurred *patois* of most slaves, was a warning. As the manservant straightened to his full height, Catherine drew in a silent breath of surprise. That the blood of some ancient desert tribe ran in his veins was obvious. His face, with a metallic brass sheen on the brown skin, held a mask-like reserve. Deep-set brown eyes looked from under higharched brows. The nose had the shape of an aquiline-ridged hook, while the full mouth beneath it was outlined with a harsh sensitivity. About his head was wrapped a small, neat turban.

Waiting for some acknowledgement of the greeting by her husband, Catherine hesitated. In that instant, Madame Thibeaut pushed forward.

"Go at once, Ali, and inform the maid of Mam'zelle Solange that we have need of her. Mam'zelle is unwell.

145

She must be put to bed with a soothing draught and heat at her feet as soon as possible. Then inform cook that we have arrived and desire a small repast to be served in the dining room in half an hour."

The hard ring of authority in the woman's voice, her determined assumption of the role of hostess, was intolerable. Only disbelief prevented Catherine from countermanding her orders at once. But the moment of reflection convinced her that that course would be unwise; it might even be to step into a carefully planned trap. Was she being overimaginative? Was it possible the older woman had no intention of usurping her place, that her impetuous action had been made solely out of habit and her concern for the welfare of her charge? No, Solange's sudden quietening, her tension in her brother's arms, convinced Catherine of the justness of her first suspicion.

"Wait," she said quietly.

Ali had turned to do the bidding of Madame Thibeaut, accepting her commands with an unsmiling inclination of his head. Now he swung back.

"I think, Madame Thibeaut, that you are forgetting our guests," Catherine said. "I'm sure my husband knows the way to his sister's room. While he is installing her there, perhaps you will ring for her maid—or find someone to carry a message to her. Ali will then be free to conduct Mr. Barton and Fanny to the rooms prepared for them, and then to see to the housing of M'sieur Barton's servants."

As Fanny started to protest that she could find her own way, Catherine turned away. "Can you be ready for a light supper in half an hour, Solange? Good. Then, Ali, you may inform cook that it can be served at that time."

"Madame Ti must come with me," Solange cried, but her voice was too querulously, childishly, demanding to be heeded. A fortunate thing, Catherine thought. It would not have done to appear callous to the needs of Rafael's sister when she had been ill.

As it was, Rafael answered her in a brusque tone as he carried her into the house, "Madame Thibeaut will be along as soon as she can."

146

Solange retreated into a martyred pose as Rafael carried her out of sight.

They passed through a wide entrance hall, furnished as a sitting room, out onto a back gallery. The bedchambers could be reached by moving through the other rooms, but this narrow gallery overlooking the courtyard was the quickest way. When everyone else turned to the wing on the left, Catherine trailed along with them, realizing belatedly that she had no idea where her own room was located.

This inauspicious beginning did not improve. After finally being shown to her room, she found drowned gnats floating in the water in the ewer upon the washstand, and no face towels on the rack. The furniture had been dusted but it had also been oiled with something which, from the smell and the trail of ants devouring it, appeared to be bacon fat. The meal provided for their delectation consisted of a thin gruel which passed for soup, and ham between slices of buttered bread. The butter was rancid, the bread dotted with gray mold on the bottom of the slices.

Fanny and Giles took the deficiencies in good part, seeing them as evidence of the need of the firm hand of the new chatelaine. To Catherine they had a more sinister implication.

If Rafael had joined with them in bemoaning the poor fare and the tendency of a house to decline without a mistress, if he had indicated in any way that he supported her in her stand against his sister and her companion, she might have been able to view what lay ahead with some degree of confidence. He did not. Instead, he sat at the head of the table playing with his wine glass, drinking more than he ate. He scarcely spoke, and then only to Giles. Once Catherine looked up to find him staring down the cloth at her, a measuring expression in his black eyes, as if she had been tried and found lacking.

The gentlemen sat long over their cognac and claret. Fanny and Catherine, too tired, and by now too familiar with each other to stand on ceremony, did not wait, but went to their rooms immediately after coffee had been served in the salon.

Catherine was asleep when Rafael finally entered the room. She heard him stumbling about in the dark with something less than his usual sure-footed ease. His boots hit the floor with sodden thumps. He barked his shin on the footboard of the four-poster and his muttered curse had a thickened sound. The bed ropes sagged as he got into bed. He fell back heavily and was still.

Catherine lay without moving, staring wide-eyed into the blackness of the tester above her. She strained to maintain the even breathing of natural sleep. Her limbs felt stiff with tension, and slowly, carefully, she forced them to relax.

Rafael lay still. She could just sense the quiet rise and fall of his chest. Was he exhausted, in a drunken stupor —or was he listening, as aware of her as she was of him? Was he trying to decide if she was asleep?

A cold depression settled over her. She felt isolated, set at a distance by his attitude during the evening. It was not a feeling she enjoyed, and yet she would not have that distance bridged by anything less than a warm and personal desire. She could not bear the thought of being taken as casually, as coldly, as any kept woman.

Kept woman or unloved wife, where is the difference? she mocked herself. If there was one, it eluded her. Still, she knew instinctively there would be a great deal of difference in being drawn into the arms of Rafael in his most tender mood, and being taken by the surly stranger he had become today.

She need not have worried. Rafael made no move toward her. The leaden minutes crept by. The tiredness of depleted emotions invaded her senses, and she slept.

When she awoke the gray light of dawn filled the room. Rafael was gone. She was alone in the wide bed.

Sitting up, Catherine reached for the bellrope, a strip of tapestry ending in a silk tassel, hanging beside the bed. The Bartons had planned to make an early start this morning. She and Fanny had said their goodbys the night before, but it was her duty as hostess to see that they had refreshment before she speeded them on their way.

Though she waited long, patient moments, her summons was not answered. Surely the servants were not all still abed? Such a thing was unheard of in her mother's house. The cook should be in her kitchen; the houseservants should be up and about, for their morning meal must be out of the way early so they could start their duties. Many of the chores in the tidying of the main rooms should be accomplished before the master and mistress left their bedchamber.

She must remember, however, that this was not a well run household. Judging by last night's fiasco, there could well be nothing more than a cold fireplace waiting in the kitchen. Sliding from the bed, she threw off her gown and began to dress.

Her fears were realized. When she finally found the kitchen, by treading the front gallery completely around the house and descending a set of steep stairs which led along a path to a small, detached building, there was no smoke rising from its chimney. Stale ash lay caked upon the hearth, and black iron pots of congealed food crawling with ants and buzzing with flies, sat upon the trestle tables lining the walls on each side. Roaches, dark brown and an inch long, rustled away at her approach to hide beneath the table edges. There was no kindling, and only a few misshapen chunks of wood in the woodbox. Less than an inch of sediment-clouded water filled the oaken butt beside the door. Was this the usual practice, or was this slackness due entirely to her arrival? The uncertainty of the question was the only thing which tempered Catherine's disgust and indignation.

Something must be done, and quickly. Turning with a swing of her skirts, Catherine started back along the path to the gallery.

But as she strode along that shaded veranda-like porch at the front of the house, her attention was caught by a movement seen dimly through the trees. Finding an opening between the limbs of the live oaks, she stopped, watching the activity at the landing attached to the levee. There was a hollow feeling in her chest as she saw the keelboat moving out into the channel of the river, the polers looking like dream figures as the boat was swallowed

149

up by the morning mist. Fanny and Giles were leaving. She was too late to bid them a final goodby.

Rafael stood on the riverbank. Behind him a saddled horse cropped the fresh green grass just appearing beneath the trees. Perhaps it was just as well he had let her sleep. The departing couple were his friends, his guests. Her presence was not necessary—maybe not even wanted. That she had been unable to offer coffee and a croissant was not a tragedy. Fanny's maid was equipped on the boat to provide that as well, even better, than she. It was irrational of her then, watching her husband mount his horse and ride away in the opposite direction to the house, to admit to a desolation such as she had never known before.

The sun was high before the house began to stir. By that time Catherine had mapped out her campaign in her mind. She must move warily, but she had no intention of letting the conditions she had found at Alhambra continue. Regardless of the reason for them, they were an offense to her fastidious nature and her instincts as a housewife.

She waited patiently for some sign that Madame Thibeaut and Solange had arisen. When she saw coffee being carried to the wing across the court by a shuffling maidservant, she nodded in satisfaction. Grim-faced, she left her room and moved along the back gallery to knock upon the door which the maid had entered.

Madame Thibeaut turned in the act of handing a cup of coffee to Solange, propped in her bed. Her thin brows shot up in elaborate surprise as Catherine entered.

"My dear Madame Navarro!" the older woman exclaimed.

Her voice had an affected ring. She was dressed, her black gown buttoned tightly to her throat, and her hair pulled into a small hard knot on the top of her head. Spots of color, perhaps of irritation, burned upon her sallow cheeks.

Solange took a deliberate sip of her coffee. "What do you want?" she asked without pretense to graciousness.

Steeling herself, Catherine gave the girl a pleasant

smile. "I'm sorry to intrude upon you at this early hour. I do hope you have recovered from the ill effects of yesterday's journey?" At the girl's reluctant nod, she went on. "Rafael has gone, riding over his acres I expect, and it seemed a good time to make myself familiar with the house. I thought I might persuade Madame Thibeaut to be my guide, since I am depending upon her to put me into the way of things here."

"You must wait. Madame Ti has not had a morsel of breakfast," Solange said.

"Neither have I," Catherine reminded her gently. "A pity, is it not, that we must wait upon the convenience of our servants? Do you think, Madame Thibeaut, that this is one thing we might remedy between ourselves? Rafael, you know, is an early riser, in the ordinary way, and I do not like to think of him beginning the day with nothing to sustain him."

The woman could hardly refuse a request couched in such terms of wifely concern for the benefit of the master of the house. The impulse to do so passed as a brief spasm over her countenance and then was gone.

"It shall be attended to at once," she said.

"Thank you. I knew I might depend upon your understanding, Madame Thibeaut. There is also the matter of the—animal life—I have seen in the house. I have it on the best authority, no doubt due to his recent years of living aboard ship, that Rafael cannot abide insects. Do you suppose we could find some means of making them —less noticeable?"

"You seem to have made a study of my brother's likes and dislikes," Solange said suggestively.

Catherine gave her a limpid smile. "It pays a wife to do so, does it not? But there. I will leave you to drink your coffee in peace. Ah, Madame Thibeaut, perhaps when you are done you will have the goodness to ring for a maid for me. No doubt your system of ringing is different from that used in my home, for I have rung several times to no avail. If you receive an answer, would you inform the household that I would like to see them in the sitting room directly after breakfast?"

151

"Certainly, Madame Navarro, I will conduct them there myself."

Before Catherine left the room, she inclined her head, being careful not to smile. She had expected no less from the former housekeeper for Alhambra. She could be depended upon to see that everyone foregathered as requested, if only to be certain that she herself was present during Catherine's address to them.

Ideally, Rafael should have made the introduction to his staff, presenting her to them as their mistress. Since he had not seen fit to do so, she would make her presence known in her own way.

Alhambra was not overly supplied with houseservants. Eight filed into the sitting room at the appointed time, five or six less than her mother had kept for the smooth running of her small house. It was not unusual for there to be a maid or manservant for every person, plus one or two extras for guests and a servant for every public room whose sole duty was to keep it constantly ready for visitors. Meat cook, pastry cook, sculleries, gardeners, all added to the total.

First before her was a woman most likely to be the cook, a large, round woman with the marks of a Congo on her broad forehead. Her expression was benevolent but her slovenly appearance reminded Catherine forcibly of her kitchen. For assistants, she had two sculleries, shy, plump girls who might have been her daughters though with hands too soft and nails too long for them to be efficient at their jobs. The washerwoman was a gangling, thin figure whose stiffly starched apron and kerchief was an indication of her position. Ali, Rafael's valet, was nowhere in evidence and Catherine thought it likely that he had gone with his master, though she had not seen him leave. There were, however, two other menservants. Their duties were to serve at meals and clear up after them, to answer the door, lay fires, see to the needs of men guests, and make themselves generally useful. They were quiet appearing men, one elderly and gray-haired, the other little more than a teenager, but both had sensitive faces and intelligent eyes. The maidservants were not so satisfactory.

One was the shuffling creature Catherine had seen earlier, an older woman, graying, with a vacant expression and a quid of tobacco in her cheek. The other was a young girl with a tendency to giggle and a ready knowledge of her own sensual appearance. The bodice of her dress of printed cotton, a possible cast-off of Solange's, was open in a deep vee and the corners of her kerchief stood stiffly erect like the ears of a cat.

Glancing at the list in her hand, Catherine wondered if those gathered before her would be enough for the task of renovation she had set herself. Were there others suitable for working in the house? If she asked for them, would they be given to her? She did not know, and at this point she thought it best not to make an issure of it.

She got to her feet, unconsciously straightening her shoulders as she stood with her hand resting lightly on the secretary-desk beside her. Her stance was a commanding one, but her smile was warm and friendly as she glanced about the room. Then as she drew in her breath to speak, Madame Thibeaut stepped forward from her post near the door.

A compelling look from her deep-set eyes drew the servants' attention. "You have been called here to be presented to the new wife of M'sieu Rafe. Allow me, Madame Navarro, to make known to you, Cook, her two daughters and helpers, Marie Belle and Marie Ann, Hattie, our laundress, Oliver and Charles, the menservants, and the maids, Nonnie and Pauline."

As their names were called the servants sketched a nervous bow or dropped a quick curtsy.

That Madame Thibeaut had deliberately omitted her given name and her new position, that of their maîtress, did not pass Catherine's notice. She did not trouble to correct it, however, depending on her bearing to make the matter clear.

"Thank you, Madame," she said, allowing her level gaze to slide over the woman as less important than the others before her. "I wanted only to make myself known to you, and to inform you that the residence of your master and myself here at Alhambra will be permanent."

Smiling to herself at the guarded glances they cast each other, Catherine continued. "You must realize this will mean change, and I hope you will consider it for the better. I plan today to inspect the house—the kitchen I have seen already this morning. I will look in upon you again, Cook, just before luncheon. I will not consult with you upon the menu today. I hope you have something sustaining planned, since my husband did not have breakfast this morning. Beginning tomorrow I will discuss the meals with you in advance, and I would like you to hold yourself ready each Monday morning at this time to receive menus for the week ahead.

"For those of you who work inside the house, it cannot have escaped your notice that spring has arrived and summer is fast approaching. It is time to roll up the rugs, put down fresh matting, and clear away the smoke stains and cobwebs of winter. We will begin this chore tomorrow also.

"I am a hard taskmaster," she finished with a lift of her chin, "but I believe you will find, when things are back in order, and your new duties explained, that we will all be more comfortable. That is all."

None of what she had said could be construed as criticism of Madame Thibeaut's housekeeping, and yet, before she finished speaking, the older woman had swept out of the sitting room. Catherine, watching the servants passing through the same door, thought she could sense an uneasiness about them, almost a fear, far in excess of anything her words to them could have caused.

Were they worried that they would have to serve two mistresses? The impression was strong. Surely there could be no comparison between the authority of the mistress of the house and that of a paid companion? With a shake of her head, she dismissed the idea.

The morning passed as Catherine moved slowly from room to room, beginning with the bedchambers. All were well appointed with heavy tester beds, armoires, and dressing tables, some with carving, others inlaid with tulip wood in patterns with a Moorish influence. The drapes and hangings were in the Spanish style of velvet and

154

Egyptian cotton brocade in dark colors. Faded and threadbare, except in the rooms which had been redone for the Navarros, they were an indication of the decline in the fortunes of the Fitzgerald's before the change of ownership. Dirt had been ground into the designs in the jewel colors of the Persian rugs upon the floors, but they were still whole, still beautiful.

However, there gradually grew upon Catherine an impression of starkness in the rooms, traceable to a lack of the small, intimate things that made a room interesting and habitable. Where were the silver candlesticks and dressing table accessories, the china bibelots, the vases and other ornaments that should be sitting upon the mantels over the fireplaces in each room, or the crucifixes that had left their ghostly imprints above the beds? Some might have been taken as the personal belongings of the Fitzgeralds, but surely not all. She had never heard that, previous to the fatal card game with Rafael, Marcus was in such straits he had been forced to liquidate such small items of value.

The main rooms had the same stripped appearance. Large pieces of furniture remained, the chandeliers and girandoles with their filmed and dull crystal lustres, but there were only one or two inferior paintings among the fresh squares outlined in gray smoke upon the caramel-striped silk wall covering. The white-washed walls of the dining room above the wainscoting, which seemed to cry aloud for the glowing color of tapestries, stretched as bare as bleached bone.

Amazingly, the silver still reposed behind the glass of a dining room cupboard, though the lock upon the door may have accounted for its presence. The drawers of the long sideboard which covered one wall, as well as the knife boxes on top of it, were also locked. No doubt the keys to these, and the other doors and cupboards in the house, were in the possession of Madame Thibeaut. Catherine made a mental note to ask her for them.

What to do about the missing items? Was Rafael aware they were gone? If he was, and if there was some simple explanation which she could not see, she would not like to appear jealous of their loss, or too conscious of their value. If he was not, it was without doubt her duty to report the matter to him.

Pondering the problem, she walked through the entrance hall and out onto the back gallery. The courtyard below beckoned, and she leaned on the railing, staring down into that small, enclosed space. The fountain with its four guarding lions was dry, the basin filled with leaves and trash. Weeds sprouted between the paving stones, and in a bed left for planting, purple violets were choked by the bright green of winter grass and the dead stems of last years flowers. A clump of palmetto rustled its leaves in a corner. Yellow jasmine gone wild swarmed up the spiral staircase of wrought iron to drape itself along the upper railing, its flowers releasing their sweetness upon the warm air. Cascading from a pair of giant terracotta ollas were fresh green fronds of native fern.

There should be roses to perfume the court in summer, she thought idly, and lilies to bloom when the roses were gone. She must see about them the next time she was in New Orleans.

"Don't tell me your energy has deserted you already," Solange said sweetly, strolling toward her along the gallery. "We are not all in order yet."

Turning her head, Catherine asked, "Have you come to point out what I have missed?"

Solange's smile faded. "Aren't you clever? Have a care that you don't outsmart yourself."

"Meaning?"

"Meaning you will not find Madame Ti an easy opponent to vanquish."

"I had no idea we were at war," Catherine said lightly.

"Oh, come. You needn't pretend to be dense. Did you really expect to win our servants over with a smile and a pretty speech? They won't work for you, you know. They don't dare."

Catherine stared at the malicious enjoyment on the girl's face. "I have not the least idea what you mean. Are you saying the servants will defy me?"

"Oh, no! That might bring them to my brother's notice.

156

They will accept your orders, they will smile and bow, and as long as you watch them, they will try to do as you ask. But the moment your back is turned they will stop, and, questioned, will find a thousand excuses for not having accomplished the tasks they began. And, if your orders are not given face to face, they will be routed through Madame Ti for her approval."

"Why?" Catherine asked abruptly.

"Because she, not you, is their true mistress. She holds their hearts and their souls in her hands. There is no need for your crusade of cleanliness. Now that Madame Ti has returned the food will improve, and so will the condition of the house. All you need do is step down from your ridiculous pose as beloved and concerned wife and mistress of Alhambra, and allow things to continue as they have done for years."

"And if I do not?"

"You will be forced to do so. You will find there is no other way. You have already made one serious mistake, you will make others."

Had she underestimated Solange's companion—or overestimated her own ability to assume control? She did not like to think so, but it would be best to know it, if it were so.

"Mistake?" Catherine asked.

"You took it for granted that your appeal to the baser side of my brother's nature would last. You moved your person and your baggage into my brother's bedchamber without consulting his wishes in the matter. If you had consulted him, you would have learned that, for the most part, he prefers his own company. The exception is those occasions common to all men when a woman becomes a necessity. I have often heard him say he would hold to the tradition of the Navarro men of sleeping alone. You may imagine the benefits to the men of an arrangement of separate bedchambers? No doubt my brother will make his wishes known eventually, but if I were you, I believe I would spare him the trouble. He can be quite brutal when he finds it necessary."

"Your concern for my welfare overwhelms me,"

Catherine said with irony. "I find it almost as unbelievable as your pretense to a knowledge of men."

"Everyone knows what men are like," Solange looked away from Catherine's candid gaze.

At least the girl still had the grace to blush, Catherine thought. "Do they indeed?"

"Madame Ti explained to me the carnal appetites of males and their vulgar behavior in the marriage bed."

"Did she?"

"Yes," the girl flashed. "And she has also told me of their lack of appreciation of the sacrifices women make for them, and their lack of concern or caring for a woman when they have had what they want from her."

Catherine tilted her head to one side. "And you expect to be treated in this boorish fashion, by your husband when you are wed, even if the man is Marcus Fitzgerald?"

The startled look which entered Solange's eyes was Catherine's answer. Turning to saunter toward her bedchamber, she spoke over her shoulder. "Think of this then. If you should marry, you will have no need for a companion—such as Madame Thibeaut."

CHAPTER ELEVEN

Solange proved an able prophet in the matter of the servants. When Catherine visited the kitchen shortly before midday, there was no sign of the frantic activity she had expected. The cooking pots had been washed, it was true, and a side of beef turning on a spit over the fire sent a savory scent into the close air mingling with the fragrance of yeast bread baking. Either Marie Ann or Marie Belle—she could not tell them apart—was stirring a custard over the fire. Dishes of soup and vegetables lined the trestle tables. But a dog gnawed a bone in a litter of straw and vegetable refuse beneath a table, the cake of ashes spilling out onto the hearth was thicker and more dangerous to the wooden building than before. To enter, she had to pick her way over a puddle of greasy dishwater, shooing aside the scraggly chickens picking at the bits of softened food that had been thrown out with it.

Catherine was nonplussed, especially when she considered the consternation in the kitchen caused by the impending arrival of her mother on a tour of inspection. Was this signal dearth of excitement here a lack of respect, or, as Solange had indicated, a show of fidelity to Madame Thibeaut? That it could be the last was difficult for her to accept. In every household she had ever entered, the position of companion was one without honor, and with precious little authority. For the wishes of a companion to be placed above those of the mistress of the house was unthinkable. They were more likely to be considered last, behind the nursemaid, perhaps, because such a person had no way of enforcing her wishes. Was that the key? The servants did not expect their new mistress to be able to enforce her commands?

It was always possible that the state of the kitchen was due to a difference in standards of cleanliness. So there could be no misunderstanding, Catherine gave careful instructions for the cleaning of it. Clutching at a dingy red flannel bag hanging on a thong around her neck, the cook agreed, but something in that round, tattooed face told Catherine her orders would not be carried out.

If Solange was right on one count, could it be she was right on the other? For all her brave words of the morning, Catherine mused, what, after all, did she know of the likes and dislikes of the man she had married? During their five days together Rafael had never seemed resentful of her presense. However, they had been occupying her room in her home. He had gone to a great deal of trouble to arrange a private bathing room. Had that been for his own sake, rather than for hers?

Last night he had given no sign of being pleased to find her in his bed; indeed, he had given no sign that he knew she was there. Perhaps, lying awake in the middle of the

159

night, he had wished her gone, but had not wanted to awaken her to send her away.

In the bedchamber Catherine had shared the night before with Rafael, she stared about her, trying to decide what to do. Her boxes and trunks still stood about the room. She had no maid to unpack for her, and had had no time to attend to it herself. Her trousseau linens must be shaken out and put away, she thought distractedly. There must be a linen cupboard somewhere.

This bedchamber was slightly larger than the one connecting to it, the middle one of the three in this wing. Both were furnished with similar pieces and colors, almost as if they had been designed as a suite. It would be an easy matter to transfer her belongings to the smaller of the two rooms.

Her own parents had slept in separate rooms, but that was because her father snored; she had often heard her mother speak of it with a laugh and a catch in her voice.

What did she herself want? There could be no question. She must be in favor of anything that would leave her less at the mercy of Rafael Navarro. Still, she would not like for him to think that the reason for her removal was because she wanted to avoid him.

Such agonizing over what was, in truth, a simple thing. If he wished her to stay with him he had only to say so, did he not? So far, he had not been backward in making his wishes known.

Catherine took one last look around the room, at the tester bed with its blue velvet hangings looped back with the blue muslin mosquito baire, at the tall armoire and matching washstand with china accouterments painted with violets, and the chaise lounge covered in pale lavender silk. With sudden decision she nodded her head and bent to catch the handle of a trunk, dragging it into the connecting room.

Rafael and Ali did not return to the house for the noon meal as expected. It was late afternoon before they put in an appearance.

Catherine had finished her own packing, putting her things away in one of the spacious armoires. Wandering into her husband's bedchamber, she had noticed his port-manteau gaping open. Shirt sleeves and breeches legs dangled over the sides, as if he dressed hurriedly, pulling what he wanted from it by touch in the dark. From straightening the contents of the box, she progressed to unpacking it. She smoothed the shirts, folding them and placing them in neat piles, and shook out the frockcoats and pantaloons.

When the door opened with an abrupt swing behind her, she turned, clutching a stack of starched cravats to her chest.

Ali came into the room then stood aside for his master to enter before closing the door behind him.

A frown drew Rafael's brows together as he saw her. "What are you doing?" he asked.

"Unpacking," Catherine answered, feeling, unreasonably, as if she had been caught prying into something that was none of her concern.

"There is no need. Ali will see to it." He threw himself down upon the chaise lounge, lifting one foot so the valet could help him off with the calf-high riding boot.

"It was nothing. There is nothing else—" Catherine began.

"Isn't there? I would have thought, from the state of this house, there is a great deal to be done," he said irri-tably. "Don't stand there, crushing my cravats. Put them down somewhere."

With a lift of her chin, Catherine tossed them onto the bed. "About the housekeeping, there are a few things I need to ask."

"Later, if you please. I am starving, and more than anything else in the world, I would like a hot bath to re-move the smell of horse. At any rate, I expect Ali could tell you more than I. He has been here trying to cope with it six months or more. Considering the results I would say he makes a much better valet than a house-keeper. It is doubtful even he will give you satisfaction."

Though the valet remained silent, Catherine thought a flicker of compassion crossed his face as he glanced at her.

161

"I will be most happy to serve you in any way I can, Madame," he said quietly.

"Thank you, Ali. If you could wait upon me in the morning in the lady's sitting room, I would be grateful." Glancing at Rafael, now unbuttoning his shirt and stripping it from his waistband, she asked, "You ordered the bath?"

Rafael nodded. "And a little something to eat now, before dinner. I forgot to tell them to serve it here, rather than in the dining room. Would you mind?"

"Not at all." Accepting her dismissal, she passed out of the room as Ali reached to hold the door open for her.

It was not necessary to wait until morning to speak to Ali. Rafael had not finished his impromptu meal before a message came from Giles Barton for him.

Catherine, nursing a small glass of sherry at Rafael's command to keep him company over his meal, watched him scan the missive.

"What is it?" she asked.

He tore the note across four or five times and dropped the pieces among the crumbs on his plate. "Nothing to cause you concern. I must go to Cypress Bend."

Catherine was not deceived. He was keeping something from her, something important if he could be induced so readily to forget his fatigue. As she watched Ali dress him at speed in a coat of blue superfine and cream doeskin breeches, she had time to wonder what it could be. Her mind turned to Fanny, but only for a brief moment before she dismissed the idea. Rafael was not the man to come running at any woman's behest, nor was Fanny the type to presume upon their friendship. On the other hand, a discussion of crops or estate management with Giles scarcely called for a hurried evening visit. Perhaps she was refining too upon the matter, showing her vanity in thinking it would take something weighty to draw Rafael from her. The note may have been no more than a reminder of the drink due her husband from Giles.

Still, when he had gone, she could not help moving to the window to watch him ride away down the road that was little more than an overgrown bridal path along the river and through the swamp to Cypress Bend.

"Do not fret, Madame. He will return safely."

At the voice behind her, Catherine turned away. She had almost forgotten the presence of the silent moving valet. "I'm sure he will," she returned.

Ali went on with his work, picking up the towels, the strewn clothing, and finishing the job of putting away Rafael's belongings that Catherine had begun. She was only in his way, she saw. Moving toward the door of the connecting bedroom, she paused only as Ali coughed, a small sound to attract her attention.

"Madame wishes to dress for dinner?"

The evening seemed suddenly flat, stretching long and monotonous ahead of her. To dress without a man to appreciate the effect hardly seemed worthwhile, and Rafael could not be expected back in time for anything more than a late supper. As she hesitated, searching for a polite way of saying no, he went on.

"One of the house maids would be honored to assist Madame. Shall I ring?"

Catherine shook her head. "I think not. I am not particularly hungry. Something light on a tray will suit me well enough—though you may leave the bathtub, if you will?"

"I will see to it, Madame, with pleasure. But—"

"Yes, Ali?"

"Madame should have a personal maid; a maid to run small errands, see to your comfort, and to the care of the clothing. That one, that Hattie, in the wash house is very well for the linens and the clothing of houseservants, but she has no idea of the care of delicate fabrics. In addition, a maid lends consequence, weight, to the position of mistress of the house."

"You are convincing," Catherine said with a wry smile. "However, my husband has promised to find someone for me. Perhaps he will remember in a day or so."

"There is a woman, such a one as I am sure would suit Madame. Her name is India."

Catherine, wise in the ways of servants, sent him a

163

quizzical glance. "This woman, this India, means something special to you?"

A smile came and went in his heavy lidded eyes, and he inclined his head in a faint gesture of respect. "She is my soul," he said, "the moon of my desire. You are surprised, Madame? Surely you guessed. But no, it is my words, *n'est ce pas?* You will know, Madame, that I was born and reared in the desert of North Africa. My father was a Bedouin, my mother an Ethiopian. In my ninth year, my father, the Rif, the chief of our tribe, was killed by my uncle. I was carried into the desert to die, but my cousin, a youth of ten more summers than I, was greedy. He sold me, instead, to a slave caravan. My native tongue, so many eons ago, was Arabic, my religion Moslem, though now I have taken the god of my master. My India, I fear, is a pagan, but I hope still to persuade the priest, when next one comes, to bless our union."

"There is something I don't understand. My husband spoke, just now, as though you had been here at Alhambra for some time. I quite understood that you were with him in his travels, indeed, that you were with him in New Orleans when he first returned from abroad."

"That is so, in part. Six months ago M'sieu Rafe had word from M'sieu Barton of the near ruin of the plantation, and the suspected venality of the man he had left in charge. Before he acted, however, he wanted proof, proof that might not be available if he himself came. Too many were interested in his past activities for him to arrive quietly. He sent me ahead. I came, saw what was happening, and reported. It took some time before M'sieu Rafe could arrange the permission for his return. When he landed at last at New Orleans, I journeyed to the city to serve him, and explain the events here more fully. After three weeks in the city, M'sieu Rafe instructed me to return and prepare for his arrival with you. I regret, Madame, that the task was so poorly done."

"I'm beginning to have some understanding of your difficulty," Catherine said lightly. "And I'm certain you did the best you could under the circumstances."

"Exactly so. The plans had been made for your—

164

welcome before I returned, long before. Please believe that I do not seek merely to justify my failure in your eyes. Such a thing is not possible. My embarrassment is boundless, my shame knows no end." His eyelids came down, veiling the passionate self-abasement. "If it would undo the harm that has come to you, I would cut off my right arm. But it will not. Instead, I have dedicated its puny strength to you, Madame, that you may better defeat your enemies."

The avowal was disconcerting, its sincerity was also touching. "Thank you, Ali," she said simply. "The time may come when I will need a strong right arm. In the meantime, please don't think that I blame you."

"Nor, I think, must you blame the others," he suggested. "They are tools, frightened tools. My India could not be used so, for being a pagan of the clean deep woods, the fields and streams, she worships the sun, the giver of life. She has no need nor fear of the magic of the darkness."

Frowning, Catherine said, "I don't think I understand."

Before he could answer, the door was thrust open unceremoniously and Solange walked into the room.

"Where has my brother gone?" she demanded in sharp tones.

Without answering her, Catherine said to Ali. "About the matter on which we were speaking, if you can persuade my husband, I will abide by his decision."

"Very good, Madame, and I will not forget your dinner tray or bath." With his most formal bow Ali took his leave. The door had closed behind him before Catherine turned to Solange. "You were saying?"

"I was asking for my brother!" Solange spit the words out, her face mottled with indignation at being forced to wait behind a servant for Catherine's notice.

Catherine had not meant to antagonize the girl further, only to remove Ali from her field of fire. Taking a tight rein on her temper, she asked, "Did no one tell you? Rafael received a message from Cypress Bend."

"A message? What kind of message?"

"Something about a wager," she said, having no intention of revealing that she did not know herself. "You know men and their debts of honor."

"At this time of the evening?" Solange said in disbelief.

Managing a smile, Catherine answered. "Yes. I do not expect him back until quite late. Was there something special you wanted to speak to him about?"

"No—no," the girl said, looking away. "Nothing special. But I do think he could have told me."

Conscious of something near sympathy at the forlornness of her tone, Catherine replied, "I expect he would have, if he had known you would be upset. You must remember that he has lived for only himself these last years, and is not in the habit of accounting for his absence."

Solange nodded. Then a sly look entered her narrow eyes. "How understanding you are, to be sure. For myself, I would not care to have my bridegroom ride away and leave me, scarcely a week after the wedding. Are you wise to keep him on such a long chain? I confess I would be tempted to shorten it in your place, especially with a man like Rafe, a man with the instincts of a hunter. The Navarro men have always enjoyed the chase, you know. However, they are prone to become bored with their prey once it is firmly within their talons. Of course, you will be all right, so long as Rafael does not try to bring his new quarry home—as my father did."

"Who told you that?" Catherine asked sharply.

"How can I say? I don't remember. Did you think such a topic too raw to sully my young ears? That is foolish beyond permission, Catherine. I do not doubt that I could tell you a thing or two, for all your married state."

"Indeed? More of Madame Thibeaut's instructions, I suppose?"

"Madame Ti feels that for a girl to be ignorant of these things is folly."

There was truth enough in that, though Catherine, for all her inexperience, knew it was not the complete answer. The desire of a man for a woman, the joining together of their two bodies in that desire, was not the unpleasant thing Solange had been given to understand. Before

166

Catherine could find the words to convey this thought the girl had turned away, placing her hand on the door knob. A mocking smile grew on her face, giving her a fleeting resemblance to her brother.

"Madame Ti says also that a woman who trusts a man is a fool who deserves her betrayal."

Ignoring the malice of that thrust, Catherine allowed a reflective expression to color her voice. "Some man must have hurt your companion when she was younger. It is a great pity, Solange, for your sake."

"Your pity is not needed," Solange cried, her face flushed with sudden rage, "only your absence!"

As the girl slammed from the room, Catherine sighed. Had she reached her at all? It seemed doubtful, considering the strength of Madame Thibeaut's influence. How had she gained such control of Solange and the servants? If it was a control based on fear, of what were they afraid? The magic of the darkness? Did Ali mean, could he mean, black magic?

The door of Catherine's bedchamber swung open to crash against the wall. Rafael stood in the opening, framed in a gilded nakedness by the candlelight in the room behind him. Catherine sat up in her bed, her eyes wide and startled in her pale face. She had known her husband had returned, for she had heard him moving about in the other room, heard the closing of the door as Ali left him. She could not account, however, for the anger evident in the lithe lines and planes of his body, or the menace in his cat-like stride as he moved toward her.

"What is it?" she asked, deeply ashamed of the thread of sound that was her voice.

Rafael made no sign that he had heard.

A *frisson* ran along her nerves. Her composure splintered before the lynx-wild fury that raged in the black caverns of his eyes. She swung away, whipping back the covers. Her arm was caught in a cruel vise and she was hauled against him. A hand raked through the tangled mass of her hair, twisting it, dragging her head back, raising her face to meet the hard pressure of his mouth as it

167

descended upon hers. An instant later the breath was crushed from her lungs as she was hoisted over his shoulder with his arm clamped about her knees. A red haze of pain before her eyes, she felt herself carried from the room.

She was flung through the air with a force that snapped her head back, and as she landed on the softness of a mattress there was the taste of blood in her mouth where her teeth had cut her lip. Her chest heaved and she drew a gasping breath, then Rafael was beside her, his hands firm and demanding on her flesh. With a rending sound, her nightgown gave way, and his warm, hard body covered her. She moved her head from side to side in a feeble negation that went unheeded. Her fingers curled into claws, digging into the corded muscles of his arms. Then a shaft of cool sanity struck her, and with it came comprehension. Her hands fell away to relax upon the sheet. With her eyes closed, she lay passive, her mind drifting away into nothingness, to return only when he rolled away from her.

They lay in silence for long, panting minutes. Abruptly he turned back and drew her against him with a fierce gesture.

"You are my wife, Catherine," he said, his voice low but intense against her ear. "Forget it, or ignore it, at your own peril."

"I am not likely to forget," she answered when the constriction in her throat had eased.

"Why this remove to a separate room then?"

"I—I understood the Navarro men sleep alone." She had very nearly said that Solange had told her, but the memory of Fanny's words concerning Rafael's attitude toward his sister prevented her.

"My father did, at my mother's insistence, which is one reason I have pledged never to have such an arrangement in my own marriage."

"And the other?" she asked daringly.

"A continual need of you, chérie, a need that eats at my entrails, destroying the power of will or containment.

168

It is stupid of me, I'm sure, to tell you so, and yet, perhaps I owe you that much."

"You owe me nothing," Catherine said, flinging one quick look at him before lowering her silken lashes again.

Heaving himself up on one elbow he asked, "Do I not? Deny then, if you can, that you resent me. That you withhold something of yourself from me always."

"I am not aware of it," Catherine said in a voice stifled by acute embarrassment.

"You lie. You know it very well, and I do not refer to what you suffered so gallantly just now," he said with soft sarcasm.

Casting him a look of accusation, Catherine shook her head.

"I can think of a number of reasons, but none of them are totally satisfactory. Shall I enumerate? The first is a basic coldness of disposition, a fault I have been at great pains to disprove—to my complete satisfaction," he added with a faint smile. "The second," he went on, reaching up to take a lock of honey-gold hair and draw it down across the fullness of her breast. "The second is a deep resentment of our first encounter which led to our marriage. This might be overcome, given time and patience. The third possibility is—the memory of another man." He frowned. "You will not be surprised, I trust, if I find this the least acceptable. And then, there is one other—"

"Please," Catherine said with a shade of desperation.

"Do you still deny it?"

The bright mockery in his eyes was like a goad. "You have the free and legal use of my body," she said, her amber eyes flashing. "What more do you want?"

"Everything, my elusive yellow-haired witch. Everything you have to give."

"While you give nothing in return?"

For a moment his expression was grave, then he smiled. "I give only as much as you are able to take." He paused. "Did you really think that I preferred to sleep alone?"

His change of subject—if it was indeed a change—was

disconcerting. Was it meant to be? But she must answer literally. "You gave every sign of it last night," she said after a moment.

"I had drunk deep of cognac and of absinthe, my *bete-noire,* the leaf-green wine of forgetfulness. I thought to spare you the taste of it—and the memory—and to take pity upon your tiredness by not disturbing your slumber. "Truly," he asked, a smile in his voice, "did you feel unwanted? Should such lack of conceit be rewarded, or remedied?"

Catherine bit her lip. She would not be cajoled so easily, she told herself, though she shivered a little at the warm slide of his lips along her collarbone to the vulnerable curve of her neck. "Would you threaten me one moment and make love to me the next?" she asked.

"Lamentable," he murmured, "but that is my inclination."

"It isn't mine," she said stoutly.

"No?" He drew back so he could see her face. "Why? For the sake of your pride? Will you set it between us like a stone? Is that what you want?" He shook his head. "I cannot allow it. I will make amends, an apology of caresses, even if I have to force you to accept it."

"Would that not defeat the purpose?"

"Perhaps," he agreed in the same quietly calm voice, "if I fail."

"Rafael—" She turned her head, staring into the depths of his black eyes, but all she saw was her own reflection. Whatever she had expected to find was obviously not there. The question that had hovered ghost-like at the back of her mind died unspoken.

"Yes, chérie?"

"It will not be necessary," she whispered.

Later, lying in the dark under the mosquito baire, Catherine knew Rafael was right. She did withhold something of herself. Not that she remained cold in his arms, there was little hope of that. Still the reserve remained. It was not a conscious thing; indeed, she had been unaware of that inner core of resistance. Now, made aware of it, she had no idea that she could control it. It was not an active resentment. It was more a withdrawal of some secret part of herself into the fastness of her mind. Why? Some residue of close-held offence for the abduction and the despoiling of her virginity as Rafael suggested? She did not know.

Nor could she come to terms with Solange's deliberate attempt to drive a wedge between Rafael and herself. Why did Solange hate her so? She posed no threat to the girl. It was possible she was merely championing Madame Thibeaut. And yet, there was something unbalanced in the virulence of the younger girl's dislike.

She would like to confront her about her advice, but she would not give Solange the satisfaction of knowing that her stratagem had been effective, of knowing how near she had come to causing a permanent rift between Rafael and herself. No, she would not confront her, but she would remember, and be on her guard.

CHAPTER TWELVE

A week of fine weather gave way to a fortnight of rain. Gray clouds blanketed the sky day after day, making an unnatural twilight within the house, so that candles had to be lit even at noon. Storms with continuous thunder, like the sound of *Le Bon Dieu* rolling his stones, alternated with periods of monotonous drizzle. Outside, even the light seemed to have a green tint as it was refracted from the wet, glistening surfaces of fresh grass and tender new leaves.

Rafael, prevented by the inclement weather from riding out, spent much time in his study, going over the account books. Catherine was balked at this pastime. When she had asked for the account books for the house, containing the amounts and prices of food staples, clothing, and other supplies bought and doled out for the use of the household and the people in the quarters, she was calmly told there were no such books. The reason given was simple. There were no such items parceled out at Alhambra.

Catherine had stared at Madame Thibeaut in amazement. Her own mother, self-centered and careless of others as she undoubtedly was, had given out supplies of beans and pork side meat, meal, flour, lard, eggs, and fruits and fish in season. Once a week. Every servant was given a new suit of clothes in summer and fall, from cloth personally chosen by Madame Mayfield, and made to patterns by two seamstresses brought into the house especially for the occasion. The servants had little time or means of providing these things for themselves. If they had not been available at Alhambra, in what situation must the servants be? Catherine resolved to find out as soon as the weather permitted.

But she did not remain idle. Discovering, as Solange had predicted, that the maidservants would not work without direct supervision, she harried them constantly, standing over them while they scrubbed every piece of furniture in the house with soap and water and rubbed them down with a polish made of linseed oil and vinegar. Gray swaths of spider webs were swept from the high corners of the rooms. The rugs were rolled and stacked on the front gallery, ready for a sunny day when the dirt would be beaten from their fibers. After that they would be sprinkled with tobacco, sewn in muslin covers, and stored in the attic until winter. Exposed by the removal of the rugs was what appeared to be a twenty year accumulation of decaying grass matting. During a lull in the rain, these were carried out and set afire. The sifted dirt left behind was swept away and the floor thoroughly mopped before new matting with the fresh scent of newly cut hay was laid.

The polishes, cleansers and matting were brought up from New Orleans by keelboat. As Fanny had indicated, Rafael owned a boat. It was a commercial venture plying up and down between Natchez and New Orleans, stopping at the scattered plantations along the way. The boat

172

occasionally tied up overnight before the house. The crew was seldom in evidence, either from Rafael's orders or a preference for their own rough company. She gave her list of needs to Rafael who referred them to the boat's pilot and they were miraculously delivered at her doorstep.

Ali proved an able ally in the house, always at her side when there was lifting or carrying to be done. He was especially good at routing the maids out of their rooms below in the raised basement, or the menservants from the blacksmith shop at the edge of the quarters behind the house, where they liked to sit hunkered against the wall, spitting into the fire.

For all his closeness to Rafael however, Ali seemed reluctant to broach the subject of India, Catherine's prospective maid, to him. In gratitude for his helpfulness, Catherine, one night at the dinner table, impulsively did it for him.

"A maid?" Rafael asked, looking up with a frown from the dish of squabs being offered for his selection. "Do you need one?"

"Ali insists that I do. You will understand better when I tell you he has someone in mind whom he thinks will be suitable."

Rafael allowed one of the squabs to be placed upon his plate, then leaned back in his chair. "Yes, I begin to see. Is she attractive?"

"I have no idea, I haven't seen her, but I feel sure I can rely on Ali's taste in the matter," Catherine answered, trying to ignore Solange's snort of derision. Madame Thibeaut's interest in their conversation was better concealed by the droop of her eyelids, but it was there all the same.

"What attracts Ali might not be pleasing to you," Rafael commented dryly. "But I did engage to find you another maid, did I not? Since I will not have to exert myself in the search, I am disposed to be magnanimous. Do you know the name of this paragon?"

"I believe Ali called her India."

Catherine thought he did not intend to comment, then without looking up from his plate, he said: "India, an unusual name."

"Yes," she agreed. "Possibly, like Ali, she has a dash of foreign blood."

"You really haven't seen her?"

"No," she said, her fingers tightening on her fork, asperity creeping into her tone at this abrupt turn to censure.

That drew his attention to her in a narrow-eyed gaze through thick lashes. "Then before accepting the girl I advise you to see her, talk to her. She may be ignorant and unskilled if she has never worked inside the house before. If so, you will have to exercise great patience to turn her into the sort of ladies' maid you require. You realize you cannot send her back to her old place without excellent reason. It would shame her before the others, leave her open to their merciless ridicule."

"I had not considered," Catherine said thoughtfully. "Since these are your people, perhaps you would like to pass judgment?"

Reaching out, Rafael took his wine glass, his eyes on the liquid ruby depths. "No," he said slowly. "It is little to do with me. I will trust you to know what you would like."

"Thank you," Catherine said, surprised at his sudden capitulation which left her a trifle breathless. "I'm sure Ali will be pleased."

A smile relieved the sternness of Rafael's mouth. "If you install a maid, I may be able to reclaim the services of my valet."

"I had not realized I was taking him from you when you needed him."

"No, no," he disclaimed quickly. "He had my instructions to make himself useful."

"Did he? Then I am most grateful," Catherine said, meeting her husband's eyes without evasion.

Solange cleared her throat ostentatiously. "It is my opinion Ali gives himself airs above his station. He is becoming entirely too dictatorial to the other servants, and he interferes with the running of the house. Several times he has had the effrontery to ask Madame Ti for the keys to the silver cupboards in the middle of the day, and he only returns them when he is asked directly to do so."

174

"I am afraid that is my fault," Catherine said gently. "He and I spent a day or two cleaning the silver. I wished to see if my family recipe of whiting and spirits of wine would bring a better shine than the silver soap used in the house. There were also a few discolorations from egg which we rubbed with salt."

At the head of the table Rafael frowned. "Really, Catherine. Was there any need for you to involve yourself directly in the cleaning?"

"Only one or two pieces, I assure you. Ali did most of the work."

"I appreciate your efforts," he said, his eye flicking over the shining gleam of the brass and the new coat of blacking around the fireplace, "but I did not mean you to take my comments on the condition of the house quite so seriously. A degree of relaxation is necessary to all of us. You ride?"

"I—yes."

"Then it would please me to have you with me while I ride out in the morning—or you might enjoy a canter along the river at your leisure, so long as you do not go into the swamp. I would prefer that you not overtire yourself."

Flushing a little, Catherine looked away from the sardonically knowing twist of his lips. Without words she understood that, in a house full of servants, tiredness was unacceptable as an excuse to avoid his advances beneath the mosquito baire of their bed. To change the direction of her thoughts, Catherine gave a curt nod, and turned to Madame Thibeaut.

"Concerning the keys," she said. "I wonder if I might trouble you for the one to the linen cupboard. I have a fancy to see to its contents in the morning, and I would not like to disturb you too early."

"I will assist you, of course," Madame Thibeaut began, her small mouth pursed in a dutiful expression.

"That will not be necessary. I know how you hate being aroused before mid-morning, and Ali can help. Besides, there are my trousseau linens to be put away still, and I would like to do that myself, you understand?"

Madame Thibeaut made a noise that might be taken for reluctant agreement.

Catherine, seizing the glimmer of an opportunity, persevered. "It might relieve you of much inconvenience, Madame, if you were to give all the keys into my keeping for the time being. I have a silver chatelaine, a parting gift from my mother, which will hold them in a sunburst effect. Pinned at the waist, the chatelaine is a most practical example of the jeweler's art. I confess," she said, including Solange and Rafael in her most charming smile, "that I am longing to wear it."

The pock marks on the companion's face were dyed an unbecoming red by her chagrined color, while the reflection of candle flames, in the center of the table, seemed to flare in her wide, gold ear-hoops. She took a deep breath, then a hurt look appeared on her plain features. "Why —why certainly, Madame Navarro. I would have been —most happy to surrender the keys to you, if I had known you wished to have them. You had only to ask. Unfortunately I do not have them with me just now. Perhaps in the morning—"

"I knew I might depend on your co-operation." Catherine smiled, her tone brisk. "There are the linens waiting upon the morning however. If it will not disturb you, I will send Ali for the keys later this evening."

"As you wish." The tone of the woman's voice was submissive, but Catherine had never seen anything less servile than the look in her colorless eyes before she bent her head over her plate. Had Rafael been taken in by her pose? Catherine could not tell. His face was impassive, his gaze on the wall before him, as if his mind was busy with other things. She would have liked to have laid her problem before him, but she had no idea how he would react to being embroiled in her difficulties. He had enough of his own. In any case, she had no assurance he would add his weight to her side of this domestic tug-of-war.

They finished their meal in near silence. When desert had been served and consumed, Catherine made a small, unobtrusive signal.

"We will leave you to your nut bowl and cognac," she

began, rising, but when she looked up, she found Rafael already on his feet.

"I think I would prefer coffee," he said, rounding the table to draw back her chair. "Shall we have it in our bedchamber?"

Catherine stiffened as from the corner of her eye she caught the smirk on Solange's face. Rafael's request had been worded pleasantly enough; it was only the look in his eyes which made of it an intimate interlude. It could only be embarrassing if she allowed it to be. With as much dignity as she could muster, she answered, "That would be—lovely."

Taking her hand, he carried it to his warm lips, and then drew it through his arm. "You will see to it, Madame Thibeaut," he asked pleasantly, without looking at the companion.

"Certainly," the woman replied, managing to make it sound as if she were granting a favor.

She was clever, Catherine had to allow her that much. Then she forgot her as Rafael drew her out through the hall to the back gallery.

He released her, to slide his arm about her waist and draw her against him. "You were enchanting there, tonight, in the candlelight. So earnest, so much the mistress of my house with your talk of linens and keys. I find I do not like this business of having you at the foot of my table, so far out of reach. I could not bear it a second longer."

Folly to believe him, a part of her mind whispered, folly to care if he spoke from the heart. It could be a mortal sickness should she come to care too much. Yet, his lips against hers sent her senses reeling. Caution seemed a cold thing. Lifting her arms, she slid her hands around his neck.

A voice of murderous sweetness came from behind then. "Do excuse us," Solange said.

Rafael controlled Catherine's startled recoil by the simple method of tightening his arms. After a long moment he lifted his head. "Your pardon, Solange," he said to his sister, and without glancing in her direction, turned

177

Catherine in the circle of his arms and walked her to the door of their room.

"I'm sorry, Madame. I should have told you sooner. But—" Ali shrugged, "I could not think how to introduce such a matter into the conversation. I am sorrier still that you had the trouble of speaking to M'sieu Rafe of my India for nothing."

"For nothing, Ali?" Catherine asked. "It is dense of me, I expect, but I do not see that India being with child has anything to do with her ability as a maid."

"Already her slenderness is gone, Madame. Her body is swelling with fruitfulness. Soon all will know."

"That is natural, is it not?"

"Assuredly, and a glorious thing, but most ladies have little use for a woman clumsy with childbearing about them."

Such plain speaking was just a little above the line of what was permissable, but Catherine let it pass. This conversation was becoming awkward enough without adding the strain of a reprimand to it.

"I am not one of those ladies," she answered.

"I might have guessed you would not be, Madame. But childbirth is a time much fraught with nerves, not the best time to be thrust into new duties."

Catherine stared at Ali, noting the sheen of perspiration across his cinnamon-brass face, the stiffness of his stance before her secretary-desk in this corner of the sitting room. Was there a shadow of concern behind his eyes?

"Tell me plainly, Ali," she said. "Does your India not wish to work in the house?"

"It is not that. She feels the disgrace of being a field-hand very much. In Santo Domingo, where she and her parents came from seven years ago, her mother was a ladies maid. She herself was companion to the small daughter of the house."

"I see. Could it be that it is you who have changed then? Now that India is carrying a child, she is no longer the—the 'moon of your delight'?"

178

"Ah, Madame, do not say so. The mother of my child must always find favor in my eyes. But—I fear for her."

"You fear for her? Why?"

"I have learned that India knew Madame Thibeaut in Santo Domingo, and though only half-grown, she had no liking for her or her ways. In the years they have been here, India has kept out of the woman's way, kept her eyes downcast as though she did not remember. Still, in her veins runs the wild blood of the Indian tribe from which she sprang. The lessons of obedience, silence, and self-control learned by her people in slavery are only skin deep. If she was pressed as you have been in the weeks past, she might not be accountable for her actions."

"Indian tribe? American Indian?"

"Yes. She is descended from a noble of the Natchez Indians who, eighty years ago, arose against the French. They were defeated and enslaved. The chief of the tribe and several of his most fierce warriors were sent to the island of Santo Domingo. India has lived under the yoke of slavery all her life, but she is proud, with the kind of dignity and honor that is her heritage. She has also the notions of freedom nurtured these last few years on that sun and blood-soaked isle."

Catherine was quiet a moment, a frown between her brows. "You think then, that Madame Thibeaut would seek to cause trouble for her?"

Ali's smile was touched with an odd sadness. "I am not certain, Madame. I am just—afraid."

"Your India sounds the type of ally of which I have need," Catherine said, "but I would not have you go against your foreboding. There is no great hurry for a maid; I have grown adept at doing up my own buttons." She smiled. "My husband has given me full authority in this matter. I convey it to you as my seneschal."

"You are kindness itself, Madame Catherine," he said, bowing with his hand on his heart. "I am sorry if I have caused you any inconvenience. There is something I must learn, then you will have your final answer."

He did not elaborate, and because of the austere expression in his dark, slanted eyes, Catherine hesitated to question him further. At that moment Madame Thibeaut, looking for a piece of misplaced petit point, entered the room. Ali, pleading other duties, made his escape, and the moment was lost.

His inquires must have been time-consuming however. Days went by without India being mentioned again. In the end, the decision was taken from his hands.

It was the first clear spell after the long days of rain. Rafael had taken the opportunity to ride out to view the level of the river and set a crew of men to work shoring up the levee where it showed signs of weakening. Madame Thibeaut had enticed Solange from the house, like the simplest of schoolroom misses, with the prospect of a morning walk. Catherine had not been sorry to see them go. They had all had more than enough of each other's company.

With Rafael near, demanding her attention, Catherine had not been able to get to the linen cupboard as she had planned. As soon as everyone was out of the way she vowed to tackle the task.

Holding the keys attached to the chatelaine at her waist so they would not rattle, she went along the back gallery and down the winding iron staircase. At the bottom to the left was a small, unobtrusive door into the lower floor of the house, the raised basement, where the storerooms were located. The linen cupboard, though adjacent to the servant's sleeping quarters here below, was still inconveniently located, in her opinion, with definite possibilities for damp and mildew. Another reason for her delay in seeing to it was a plan at the back of her mind to remove the linens to the upstairs. The back bedroom of the wing in which she and Rafael slept was not in use, and had not been in some years. It served, apparently, as a catch-all for boxes, trunks, and odd pieces of furniture.

The hallway dividing the storerooms from the sleeping apartments was a dark tunnel-like affair. It was bad enough in the daytime; what must it be like at night, Catherine thought, and made a mental note to install candle brackets along its length.

"Madame! Madame Catherine!"

The alarm in the call sent Catherine running back along the hall toward the sound of Ali's voice. He had raced up the stairs and was running along the gallery before she reached the courtyard.

"Ali," she cried. "What is it?"

He halted like a puppet whose strings have been jerked. His face was ashen as he leaned over the railing. "It is India. They are beating her."

"They? Who?"

"Madame Thibeaut and Mam'zelle Solange," he said, waving toward the trees that crowded up behind the house. "You must stop them. They will kill her. Please, Madame!"

"Where is M'sieu Rafe?" she asked, following the tense figure of the valet as he started back to reach her, spinning down the spiral stairs.

"I do not know, Madame. There is no time to find him. You must come."

Catherine stared at him then gave a nod of sudden decision. "Very well. Let us go."

The trail to the quarters at the rear of the house was only a path of beaten earth. Dew lingered on the high grass that bordered it, dampening the hem of Catherine's skirts as she brushed passed. Beneath the trees where the sun did not penetrate, it was cool, and spider webs strung from branch to branch glistened like wet silver threads.

From a distance, the quarters appeared to be a small but fairly clean and well organized village. A single straight street ran through it, going on to the barns and stables hidden in the trees just beyond, where they opened to cleared pasture and fields. On the nearer end of the street was the blacksmith shop, the carpenter's shop, the cooperage, a large, tight smokehouse, a boarded-up building that might have been a hospital or nursery, and a shed with one tiny barred window which served, without doubt, as a jail.

The double-room cabins further along were of the same bousillage construction as the main house, with mud-daub chimneys on each end, and long porches across the front. An even dozen of these cabins, each holding two families,

181

faced each other across the street. At the far end was a pair of larger cabins, dormitories for the unattached males and females, set well back from a small square. In the center of the square was a curbed well with a deep wooden trough on each side. The kind of stocks found in any small town stood to one side, while on the other was a snubbed whipping post with rings attached to its sides.

The long street was awash with mud in which pigs wallowed, and chickens made dainty, pronged tracks. Emaciated dogs slunk around the cypress log pilings of the buildings. There were no facilities for sanitation. Slops and night soil had been thrown from the back doors, out into the rank, dark green grass.

An unnatural silence, as thick as the miasma of oders brought out by the strengthening sun, hung over the quarters. Most of the men were out with Rafael, but where were the women who should be coming and going, washing clothes in the troughs, cooking, sweeping, gossiping, calling to their children? Indeed, where were the children? Were they cowering, afraid, behind the tightly closed doors? The quiet emptiness was ominous. Catherine felt a prickle of unease move over her.

And then as they neared the dormitory on the left at the end of the street, Catherine heard Solange's voice rising shrill with excitement.

"Hit her again, Madame Ti. Hit her again."

There was the sharp crack of flesh against flesh, followed by words too low to be understood. Ali began to run. With Catherine behind him, he pounded up the uneven steps and threw open the door.

Inside was a large common room. A table surrounded by several home-made chairs stood in the center. The remains of a sketchy breakfast lay upon it, and the fire on the smoke-blackened hearth at the end of the room had sunk to a bed of gray coals. Crude bunks, the upright posts, formed from the knobby trunks of small trees, were built against the walls.

Tied to one of the posts with her arms crossed above her head was a sullen faced young woman. She reminded Catherine at first glance of the quadroons she had seen;

182

there was the same refinement in her copper-tinted features, and, even in her dishevelment, the same faintly insolent pride. Blood from a split lip trickled down her chin. A livid bruise rode one high cheekbone. Her coarse, straight hair, worn in braided coils over her ears, had come down on one side. The rough sacking of her blouse was torn away at the neck revealing the lacerations made by razor-sharp fingernails. Her body, strained back against the post, showed the rounded fullness of advancing pregnancy.

Solange swung around at their entrance. A guilty fear flickered in her eyes, a fear that sat oddly with the excited color burning in her face. It was the expression on the features of Madame Thibeaut that stopped Catherine where she stood. Never had she seen such feral hate and animosity.

Madame Thibeaut glanced at Solange. The girl stepped forward. "What do you want?" she demanded.

"We have come for India," Catherine said, speaking directly to the older woman, her clear brown eyes unwavering. "I have decided that I have an urgent need for a maid. None other will do."

"I am afraid you are doomed to disappointment," Solange sneered, recovering her composure. "This girl is a savage, unfit to be a houseservant. She is impertinent and wholly immune to taking orders."

"Indeed? I assume that is why she is being punished?"

"Yes—yes, of course."

"May I ask the circumstances?"

Solange flung a questioning appeal to Madame Thibeaut. Receiving no encouragement, she turned back to Catherine. "No, you may not," she said tightly. "The affair is no concern of yours."

"I think you are mistaken," Catherine said, a trace of iron running through her quiet tone. "As mistress of Alhambra, the welfare of all the servants is my concern. This girl is particularly valuable. She carries the child of my husband's valet. Naturally, M'sieu Rafe would be most displeased if anything should happen to her. Ali, you may cut her down."

Catherine felt the eyes of the Indian girl upon her. There was no concern, no gratitude in their obsidian depths; neither was there fear and cringing, only an acceptance of pain. There was a hardness about her, as of a soul tempered in too strong a heat, a heart with the emotions seared in.

"No!" Solange cried, as Ali took up a knife from the table and began to slash the thongs. "By what right do you interfere? You may be mistress here, but you are not a judge of these matters."

Catherine smiled, choosing to take the objection literally. "You are quite right. My husband is judge, is he not? Shall we allow him to decide the issue?"

India, rubbing the feeling back into her wrists, went as still as a doe scenting danger in the forest.

"There is no need—" Madame Thibeaut said with an abrupt gesture.

"And why not?" said Solange. "My brother has meted out enough whip justice himself since he returned. You may just find him in agreement with us, my dear Catherine. That would take the bloom from the rose, would it not, to see how merciless our Rafe can be?"

Catherine hesitated only a moment, then she lifted her chin. "He will have the chance," she said, indicating with movement of her hand that Ali should help India from the cabin.

"I forbid you to take that girl out of here!" Solange cried, her face twisting as she glanced about as if for help.

Swinging around, Catherine said, "Forbid? Forbid, Solange? Who do you think you forbid? Certainly not me. Come, Ali." Picking up her skirts, she marched out like a general with her troops behind her. She did not stop until she had reached the courtyard of the big house.

At the wrought iron staircase she turned.

"Madame," Ali said, one arm about the girl called India. "My heart is full. Gratitude chokes my mouth."

"Then leave it unsaid," Catherine answered gravely. "And let us see to India's hurts."

"Yes, Madame. But—that one is a powerful conjure woman. The forces of evil in her body are strong. She makes the knees of the strongest men on the plantation turn weak. To see you face her as brave as *La Lionne* fills my soul with joy to be your servant. When your tawny eyes, like the desert cat, flash with pride and anger, I see more than ever why M'sieu Rafe chose you for his own. It is most fitting that the black panther mates with the golden lioness."

For one disconcerted moment, color rose to Catherine's cheeks, then as she saw the earnestness in Ali's eyes, she knew he meant only to express his admiration; he had no idea of disrespect.

"Thank you," she said softly. "I have grave doubts that I deserve such extravagant praise, but I will remember your words."

In truth, it might have been the bolstering effect of Ali's compliment which led her to intrude upon Rafael in his study that night after dinner. She could have waited until he came to their bedchamber. She thought, however, there had been enough discord between them on that battleground. Moreover, he was seldom in the mood for discussion at that hour.

"Entre," he called at her knock. When he saw who it was, he threw down his quill and stretched achingly, clasping his hands behind his neck. A smile curved the firm lines of his mouth as he watched her advance to stand before the wide table that served him for a desk.

"Such formality," he drawled. "I suppose I need not hope that you have come to drag me away from my labors?"

"I'm afraid not," she said, summoning a smile. "I would like to speak to you, if I may?"

The tiredness around his eyes seemed to deepen. He answered shortly, "Of course you may. What can I do for you?"

"It is about India—" she began, and proceeded to tell him what had taken place. A frown appeared between his eyes as he listened, though she had no means of telling whether he was displeased with her conduct or that of his sister. Whatever the reason, she refused to be daunted. "Solange feels, because you have ordered whippings your-

185

self, you will condone what she was doing. For some reason she is totally against having the girl in the house."

"Do you know why?" Rafael asked, staring at a point past her shoulder.

"I'm not certain. It may be because India knew Madame Thibeaut in Santo Domingo and dislikes her—and because she isn't afraid of her."

"Afraid?"

"I understand your sister's companion has a reputation as a—conjure woman. I—I cannot help but wonder about the influence she has over Solange."

"Like that of your Dédé over you?" he asked dryly.

Did he suspect her of making something of nothing because his dismissal of her old nurse still rankled? She let the idea pass, refusing to be drawn.

"No, there is no hint of drugs," she replied slowly. "But something is amiss, and I can only suspect the woman's influence. Solange hardly moves without her, and then—there was the affair of the mice this afternoon—"

"Mice? I don't see—"

"Pauline and I finally found time to turn out the linen closet after luncheon. It had come to a dreadful pass. Quite half the sheets are in need of mending. A goodly portion were rotten with mildew, fit only for the rag bag. There were silver fish everywhere, because of the damp, and among a stack of coverlets we found a nest of newborn mice, tiny, blind, pink creatures smaller than my little finger. I sent Pauline to dispose of them. She came back to tell me that Solange had taken them from her. They had to be killed, of course, but Pauline said Solange threw them on the stones of the court and crushed them with the heel of her slipper."

He was quiet a long moment. "You are placing this at Madame Thibeaut's door?"

"I can think of no other explanation."

"No. Do you recommend, then, that we dispense with her services?"

"That is for you to say, but would it not be better?"

"I don't know," he said, leaning forward on his elbows

to press his fingers against his eyes. "You see, Solange has had no one but this woman since she was little more than a child. She is the only person for whom she has developed an affection. When our mother died, she had a succession of nurses, none of whom could suit my father's unreasonable demands for keeping her secluded. I, much to my regret, had little time for her. Then, for these last two years, she has been deserted except for her faithful Madame Ti. Is it surprising that she harbors resentment which comes out in violence, or that she is dependent upon the one stable person in her life?"

"An unhealthy dependence, surely?"

"Granted, and yet, all she has. How can I take it from her?"

"But this woman may be using a worse form of juju than that you condemned Dédé for using," Catherine said, using the argument she most wanted to avoid in a desperate appeal.

He sighed, and getting to his feet, moved around the desk to sit on its edge, swinging one booted foot. "Yes. You do not need to tell me of the dangers. But let's not quarrel over it. I am grateful for your concern for Solange —for I am more aware of what occurs in my absence than you imagine. I will take what you have said under consideration, and keep watch. For the present, I am reluctant to do more. As for India—" he continued, reaching out and taking Catherine's hand, caressing the palm with his thumb. "You are determined to have her and no other?"

"I—would like to have her, yes." Catherine answered as she was drawn nearer to him.

"Then I will attend to it."

"And if Solange applies to you—to continue the punishment?"

"You may rest easy. I will know how to answer her."

"I am grateful," she said in a low voice, though she refused to look up for fear of the laughing demand for a demonstration of it that she might see in his eyes.

But when he replied, his voice was grave, "Don't be. I

do it for Ali also. He, too, would like India, or so I understood while I changed for dinner."

"You are very fond of him, for a slave."

"Ali is like my brother," he answered shortly. "And he is not a slave. I freed him in Paris."

"And he returned here with you?"

"Yes. Does such loyalty surprise you? I'm sure it does, knowing your opinion of me. I cannot take the whole credit however. I was with Ali when he journeyed back to Arabia. I thought for a time I would lose him to the desert, but his place in the line of succession, as chieftain of his people, had been taken from him. He found too that he no longer had anything in common with the people of the blue tents. As he put it so gallantly, I am his tribe. I am certain he now includes you, chérie."

"I am happy to think so," she answered with a slight smile.

A small quiet fell. Catherine could feel the magnetism he exuded, willing her to respond to him, to come freely into his arms in response to the slight pressure on her wrist. Before she capitulated, before her courage could fail her, Catherine asked, "Is it true, what Solange said? Have you ordered whippings here at Alhambra. You, of all people?"

"Yes," he answered.

She looked up, searching his face unconsciously for a sign of the same blood madness she had seen in Solange's eyes. "But why?"

"I think I told you that the hands here have been brutalized for years—and yet they are all I have and there is so much that must be done at once if everything is not to be lost. The levee must be repaired and strengthened to prevent a crevasse which could wipe everything away. The livestock must be rounded up, counted, evaluated, and cared for. Fields need plowing, the fences need work, plus a thousand other minor jobs. There is no time for disobedience or insubordination, no time for mutiny against the change of authority. At present, the only authority these people recognize or respect is one based on fear. The only thing they fear is the whip. Kindness, trust, are looked upon as weaknesses to be exploited. There are times when the situation reminds me of our marriage, my sweet Catherine."

He cupped her chin, tilting her head so that their eyes met. "If I were to tell you I love you, you, who care nothing for me, would be able to use that love as a weapon against me. I dislike feeling you tremble beneath my hands, and yet, so long as you are unsure, so long as you are just that tiny bit afraid of me, you must remain, docile, at my side."

"How do you know I won't take fright completely and run away from you?" she asked, her voice, which she had meant to be so defiant, holding a husky timbre.

"I will never let you go," he said, his grip crushing her hand, all laughter vanishing from his eyes. "Never."

CHAPTER THIRTEEN

"Marcus!"

The cry of joy rang through the quiet woods. Solange set her spur in her horse's side and rode at a headlong gallop toward the man standing in the shade of a gnarled live oak tree. She flung herself from the saddle and into the arms of Catherine's former suitor.

Her face grim, Catherine brought her horse to a halt next to Solange's. She should have known, she upbraided herself. She should have guessed there could be nothing so innocent as a morning ride in Solange's unexpected invitation. What a fool she was for thinking the girl's attitude might change, or that she might welcome her as a friend. Intent on proving to Rafael that she was not always at odds with his sister, she had been an easy dupe. It only remained to find out whose idea it had been that she come.

Marcus was there beside her when she started to

dismount. He lifted her down, and took her hand, pressing her fingers to his lips.

"So, you came," he murmured.

"As you see," she answered, unable to keep the irony from her voice.

"It was gracious of you to bear Solange company," he continued, matching her tone so exactly that Catherine glanced at him in puzzlement.

"I am happy you think so," she returned, "but it might clarify matters if I say I had no idea we were to meet you."

Marcus looked at Solange, whose thin lips took on a mutinous twist as she shrugged. "She would not have come, otherwise."

"No?" Marcus asked, his eyes on Catherine's face though he pretended to speak to the girl. "Considering the rumors of how hard our Rafe has been working, I would have thought that any woman would have been bored to distraction by now."

"I am not—any woman," Catherine countered significantly. "I am his wife."

"Yes, indeed."

Marcus's tone was so cold Solange glanced from him to Catherine before she spoke. "You need not act so pretentiously, Catherine. You are here merely as a chaperone for me. Marcus is most jealous of my good name. He refused to meet me here again unless you agreed to accompany me."

"Did he?" Catherine asked. "It is strange, but I do not remember agreeing."

"Come, Catherine. Don't be difficult. You know it causes the most unsightly lines in your lovely face—and I have no wish to referee while you and Solange pull caps. Do you still hold what happened in New Orleans against me? I would be most sorry to think so. I meant nothing dishonorable. I had been given to understand by your mother that there was every possibility of a match between us. My one desire was to set the wedding forward. Is that so terrible?" He paused. "Well, yes. Perhaps it was —for you. My method was—unfortunate, but I have lived

190

to regret a thousand times over the pass to which my folly has brought us."

"Marcus—" Solange said uneasily.

He stepped away from Catherine at once. "You need not be jealous, my love. Catherine and I have known each other all our lives. It should not be surprising if we have a thing or two to discuss. I must say, I prefer her to your usual companion. I don't think your Madame Ti was any more comfortable with me than she was riding pillion. Which reminds me—" Taking up the reins of Catherine's horse, he handed them to the girl. "Be a dear, and find a patch of grass for your mounts to crop so they will not become restless. Then the three of us will stroll through the woods together for a short way."

The instinct to resist the soft blandishment in his voice struggled in Solange's face, but she did not have the will power. With an abrupt gesture, she snatched the reins from his hand and walked away a small distance to a grassy glade where the sun fell through the trees. There she tied them to a sapling near Marcus's own mount.

As soon as she was out of hearing, Marcus turned to Catherine. "Forgive the subterfuge, chérie, but I had to see you, and your husband was hardly likely to welcome me at Alhambra."

"You mean you have no intentions toward Solange? I think that is a despicable trick, Marcus, if her feelings are engaged."

"They do say all is fair in love and war."

"And which do you consider this?" she said rudely.

He laughed. "You suspect me of planning revenge? That, chérie, is more in line with dear Rafe's conduct. I will tell you plainly that all I want is you. The means I use, fair or foul, matter little."

There was a moment of silence as if Marcus was judging her reaction.

"Are you flattered?" he asked finally.

Directing a level look at him, Catherine said, "Not particularly."

"You should be. It is not every woman who inspires such devotion."

191

"A devotion to my fortune, was it not?"

"I would have you still, if you would come with me," he told her, his hazel eyes suddenly serious. "If you did, you would be penniless, you know. Now that you are married, your husband controls your fortune. Only death can release it—or you—from him."

"I had not thought of that—in which case, I am indeed flattered," Catherine replied slowly. "But I must tell you Rafael will not release me. He has said so. Are you certain, then, that you still have no designs on Solange?"

"Testing my loyalty?" he murmured, his chestnut hair catching a gleam of sunlight as he leaned closer. "You have no need for concern. It has occurred to me—if I could persuade the fair Solange to elope with me, that Rafe might eventually be reconciled to my presence for the sake of her happiness. Then, as your brother-in-law, I could take up residence in the same house."

"That is hardly a reason for making another woman your wife," Catherine protested, unable to believe he was serious.

"I would go through worse ordeals willingly for such a prospect. It certainly bears thinking on," he said, his smile far from reassuring as he rose, and, with outstretched hands, went to meet Solange.

It did indeed. As Solange chatted to Marcus, her face relaxed and glowing under his compliments with something near beauty, Catherine walked quietly beside them, her mind in turmoil. With a sinking feeling in the pit of her stomach, she wondered if, allowing herself to be led by Rafael, she had misjudged Marcus all those weeks ago. It could not matter now, but she did not like to think so. Did he care for her? His manner of expressing his devotion left her uneasy, but it had been an effective one. Surely he would not have gone to so much trouble, cultivating Solange, gaining her co-operation, if he did not care.

He was an attractive man, made in a softer, more pleasant mold than Rafael. He was able to keep up a flow of light conversation that was easy to answer, interspersed with compliments meticulously divided between the two women on his arms. The sadness, the adoration hidden in the depths of his eyes when he turned to her was balm to Catherine's sore vanity. Still, she could not bring herself to trust him.

Her smile, when they parted at last, was pensive, and she did not return the pressure of his handclasp.

Solange was quiet on the ride home. A small frown rested between her thick brows as she stared straight ahead. Catherine felt even less inclined to talk. It had been nearly three weeks since the last real rain, but there had been light tropical showers nearly every evening. The black, alluvial mud of the forest trail was slick in places and she needed her attention for the footing of her mount. Though the ground was drying and the river beginning to drop a little between its banks, thick layers of gray clouds moved with rain-heavy slowness around the horizon, occasionally blocking out the sun. A breathless, humid heat hovered over everything, making activity an effort. Catherine found the dark, hunter's green velvet of her riding habit more than a little heavy. It had been made for a stately promenade along the levee and around the Place d'Armes in the height of the winter season, not for this jaunt through the woods in the heat of the morning.

Reaching up, she removed her plumed hat, and transferring it to her left hand, loosened her stock.

Glancing at the girl riding beside her, Catherine's conscience pricked her. Solange was so young, and despite her outrageous behavior at times, so vulnerable to a man like Marcus. Only a year older in terms of years, Catherine felt eons the senior in experience.

"Solange?" she said hesitantly.

The other girl slanted a glance in her direction but did not answer.

"Do you think it is wise, meeting Marcus like this?"

The girl shrugged. "Maybe not, but what has that to do with anything."

"It depends on what you want. If you love him, if you wish to be married to him, then I think these proceedings are ill advised."

"Why?" Solange asked with a show of indifference.

"A woman is unprotected in this type of clandestine affair. If the man is not liable to the girl's guardian, it is far too easy for him to carry on a light flirtation which means nothing."

"Are you suggesting I invite Marcus to come to Alhambra so that my brother can ask him his intentions? Very amusing. Rafe is much more likely to offer him a challenge, which is your doing."

"Is it?" Catherine asked. "Would it surprise you to know Marcus and Rafael were enemies long before I came upon the scene?"

Solange swung her head sharply to search Catherine's face. "Why should they be enemies?"

"That is something you must ask Rafael—when you speak to him about Marcus."

"You must know I have no intention of doing any such thing."

"Because he might find a way of preventing you from meeting?"

"You know he would," Solange exclaimed in exasperation. "Rafe would never allow him to court me, if only because of his lack of means."

Catherine sighed. "You know Rafael would approve if the man were suitable. Fortune isn't everything."

"I don't care! It is Marcus I want, and Marcus I will have. And I will see him, no matter what Rafe says, no matter what you say!"

"Will you? I understood Marcus will not meet you without my presence as chaperone. What if I refuse to go with you?"

"You will not dare," Solange said, her mouth tight. "If you do, I will go to Rafe and I will tell him it is you who has been meeting Marcus in the swamp every day this past week. Do you think, my dear sister-in-law, that he will believe you when you deny it?"

Staring into Solange's bitter black eyes, Catherine murmured, "We shall have to see, won't we?"

Despite the bravado of her words, Catherine was not confident. Solange's threat carried little weight since it was unlikely she would deliberately jeopardize her meetings with Marcus, but who could say with certainty what she would do? Of course, to erase the threat completely, Catherine had only to go to Rafael and tell him frankly that she had seen Marcus and his sister in the woods and suspected his old enemy of casting out lures to Solange. But would that serve? When she thought of the smouldering enmity between the men, one of her most forceful memories was of Rafael standing over her in that Rampart Street bedchamber, his eyes glittering with anger as he accused her of joining with Fitzgerald in a plot to entrap him. He knew of Marcus's protests of love. Would it sound reasonable that he could transfer his affections so quickly to Solange, or would it have the sound of another plot? She had had more than one taste of her husband's temper. She was not certain she wished to risk another.

As Solange and Catherine rode before the mounting block at the front of the house, two men rose from chairs on the gallery and descended the stairs to meet them. One was Rafael; then as the other stepped into the sun and it caught the silver-gold of his hair, Catherine recognized him.

"Giles," she called, her pleasure ringing in her voice. "How good to see you again. Have you brought Fanny?"

Even as she spoke, the slender shape of his sister moved from the shadowed doorway of the house. "You don't think I'd let him come without me?" Fanny called.

Rafael strolled to help his sister dismount. The young girl, with no more than a muttered greeting, sprinted up the steps. There she was taken under the wing of Madame Thibeaut, waiting like a malevolent spirit in the dimness at the end of the gallery.

Giles held up his arms to Catherine. Kicking free of the stirrup, she allowed herself to be swung down. There was an instant when Giles's fingers met around the slimness of her waist in the tightfitting jacket of the habit, so different from the usual high waisted gowns. Catherine had to smile at the expression of surprise and gratification that passed over his face. Then she was on her feet moving up the steps to greet Fanny with all the fervent happiness and enthusiasm of one reunited with a sister.

195

"What have you been doing with yourself? You are worn to a shade."

"Oh come, Fanny," Catherine laughed. "Next you will be telling me I'm looking positively haggard."

"I would never say anything so infamous—or untrue," Fanny exclaimed.

"And I thought you prided yourself on your outspokenness."

"I try never to hurt my friends," Fanny said, her smile fading before it returned with even greater brightness. "But I have come to invite you all to a party. Lent is over, Easter behind us. It rained through May Day, but soon it will be Midsummer night—"

"A month or more," Giles reminded her as the men joined them on the gallery.

"Not long at all when there is so much to be done, and a perfect time to be merry. Any later, and it will be too hot to dance the night away, too hot to do anything but perspire under the mosquito nets. Besides, Catherine must be introduced to her neighbors. The two of you cannot stay in isolation forever, as pleasant as it may be. You must come out and satisfy everyone's curiosity about how you are dealing together."

"Fanny, mind your tongue," her brother told her in a voice that brooked no nonsense. "You are embarrassing Catherine."

"Am I?" Fanny asked, her gray eyes contrite. "Forgive me."

"There is nothing to forgive," Catherine assured her, much more distressed by Giles's solicitude than by Fanny's frank summation of the general attitude.

"You will come to my party then?"

"Certainly, if Rafael—"

Fanny turned at once to the dark, unsmiling man who seemed to rouse himself to recollect his company. "I'm sure we would be delighted," he said.

Catherine, caught by the sardonic emphasis of his voice, cast him a quick glance, but his face revealed nothing.

Fanny touched her arm. "Rafe has been telling us of

196

the improvements you have been making for the benefit of your people. You must show them to me."

"I would love to," Catherine said with one last glance at her husband, "as long as you don't mind walking to the quarters."

Catherine's particular pride was the nursery which she had caused to be reopened. The boards had been taken from the windows, and new shutters set in place. A fresh coat of whitewash brightened the interior, and grass matting had been put down for a safer crawling surface than the splintery split-puncheon floor. Makeshift cribs had been hammered together by the carpenter, and the left-over pieces of wood and tree rounds sanded for toys. There had not been enough mosquito netting to cover all the cribs, so a single baire had been cut up and the squares used to cover the windows. Now the children of the women workers could be left in safety, watched over by a pair of older women.

The next project Catherine had in mind was a proper hospital. Among so many people, nearly two hundred, counting the children, there were always accidents and illness. Most could be treated in their cabins, it was true, but occasionally there was a case that needed quarantine, or a degree of care which could not be given by the family. She needed a building at least as large as the nursery, but far enough away from the other cabins for isolation. When planting was over Rafael might be able to spare the men to build it. In the meantime she had cleaned out the jail for this purpose, it being the only building not in use.

Fanny missed not a detail of the changes Catherine had brought about, commenting with marvelous frankness on all she saw, including the pens built to restrain the ramblings of the population of pigs, and the new privies which stood behind each cabin.

Her efforts, Catherine realized, were made in a rather obvious attempt to mitigate what she considered to be Rafael's harsh, uncompromising attitude. She often wondered that he did not resent it. Instead, she was left free to do as she wished, so long as she did not hinder the usual work of the plantation, a form of tacit approval. She would often feel the inclination to ask his advice, but she had little encouragement to do so. Each involved in their own work during the day, their nights were times for coming together that seldom had anything to do with words. They were weaponless passages at arms which neither could win, bloodless duels beneath the mosquito netting, with both antagonists armored in pride.

"This party," Catherine asked as they started back toward the house, "will it be a large one?"

"I have not fully decided, but I expect it will end that way. In a community so far from civilization as ours, it seems a crass incivility to leave anyone out who might conceivably wish to come. I am constantly surprised at the distances that people here are willing to travel for the sake of amusement. Giles tells me the river track, both above and below us, is passable. I expect the Trepagnier family, some fifteen miles below us, will get out their new landau and give us the treat of seeing them arrive in it. I hear it has blue upholstery and silver fittings, very fine."

"Did you and Giles drive over today?"

"Yes, indeed. Giles has a phaeton that is his special pride. You will be suitably impressed, I'm sure, when I tell you he allowed me to take the reins for a short distance through the swamp, though that may have been so he could keep a firmer grip on his horse pistol against a sight of our runaways."

"Runaways?"

"Rafe did not tell you? Several more of our hands took to the swamp during our stay in town, along with a number of yours. We discovered it the day of our arrival. Giles sent for Rafe, but it was decided that their trail was too old to make pursuit practical. The men have set a reward for their return and are watching. If they try to form a band something must be done. So far things have been quiet and we can only suppose they have dispersed."

"That must by why Rafael warned us away from riding along the swamp road."

"An order without explanation?" Fanny grimaced. "It sounds like him."

Oddly reluctant to discuss her husband, Catherine merely agreed and went on, "I didn't know you could drive."

Fanny nodded vigorously. "It is one of the few compensations I have found for being a spinster. It quite makes me resigned to—how do you say here—'throwing my corset on top of the armoire?' People no longer expect a woman out of the marriage race to be quite so circumspect. Now if they would only give up expecting us to wear those incredibly dowdy spinster's caps—"

"Nonsense. You can't be old enough for any such thing."

"I assure you I am, and I am quite content with keeping house for my brother," Fanny said brightly. "The only thing that could change it would be Giles's decision to wed, but I see no prospect of that. He and I have not been fortunate in our choice of loves."

As they crossed the courtyard and climbed the winding stair, Catherine was tempted to question the other girl about that last statement, but she desisted. The voluble Fanny might be moved to answer more truthfully than would be comfortable for either of them. It was a wise decision, she found. There was no mistaking the relief that crossed Fanny's features before they entered the house and she broke into effusive praise of the changes Catherine had made inside and her progress toward spring cleaning. She was interrupted only by the approach of Madame Thibeaut.

"Pardon, Madame Navarro. Cook wishes to know if Mademoiselle and M'sieur Barton will be with us for luncheon."

"You will, won't you?" Catherine asked, then without waiting for an answer, turned back. "Tell Cook of course they will, and instruct Oliver to lay two more places at the table."

When Madame Thibeaut had moved away, footsteps silent in the carpet slippers she liked to wear in the house, Fanny turned to Catherine.

"And how do you get on with the enigmatic Madame Thibeaut?"

"She is good with Solange," Catherine said.

"I confess it would give me chills to have her creeping about my house. She looks the kind to listen at doorways to me."

"There is something in what you say." Catherine's smile was rueful. "I have clashed with her a number of times, and I haven't always come out ahead. Tell me—have you ever heard that she—dabbles in voodoo?"

"I have often wondered, to be honest," Fanny replied, a frown between her gray eyes. "I have heard my servants say there is an obediah woman here at Alhambra, a woman who makes love philters and charms—and other less harmless potions. I could conceive of no one else it could be. Surely that is a strange occupation for a woman of her class? I don't like to frighten you, Catherine, but it hints of an unbalanced nature that could be dangerous."

"Dangerous, in what way?"

"Who can say? But I'm told poison figures largely in the miraculous feats of the voodoo cult. If I were you I would make certain I ate only what Solange or Rafael eats."

Her face thoughtful, Catherine said, "She has never threatened me personally."

"No. That would be unwise, would it not? I have made a study of this business of magic and spells in connection with missionary work back East. I think that this woman, if she sees you as a danger, will not try primitive magic with you, but will try to strike at you through someone else, someone you care for."

Catherine stared at her. "There was the incident of Ali and India. I never could quite see why the girl was attacked."

When the circumstances had been retold, Fanny mused, "India. There was something—" After a moment, she shook her head. "I can't remember. Something about her parents."

"She claims the blood of the Natchez Indians, I believe."

"That could be it. But what is more important is

Madame Thibeaut. I strongly advise you to speak to Rafe about her."

"He will not listen."

"Will he not?" Fanny asked. "I can scarcely credit that a man would not prefer to listen to you, Catherine, than to a sister, however well loved."

A smile flickered over Catherine's face. "You do not understand."

"That may well be. Is he still jealous of Marcus Fitzgerald's presence in the vicinity?"

"Still?" Catherine asked faintly.

"He was livid at the prospect of our original trip up-river together. Didn't you know?"

Mutely, Catherine shook her head.

"Giles said he had never seen him in quite such a murderous mood. I noticed it myself after Solange spoke of it—and took it for granted he would give you the opportunity to allay his suspicions. How perverse of him, especially with Fitzgerald visiting up and down the river, making himself quite at home in the neighborhood." Fanny's voice sharpened. "You realize he is the house guest of the Trepagnier's. If they are invited to my party he must come also. Have you considered what that will mean?"

For a moment Catherine was tempted to tell Fanny of her meeting with Marcus and his pursuit of Solange, then the impulse died. "It will mean nothing to me," she said firmly.

"But to Rafe?"

"You are well aware, Fanny, that ours was a marriage of necessity. Let's not pretend. I fail to see why Rafael should be concerned—unless, of course, you consider that jealousy can stem from pride of possession?"

"I can not, somehow, feature Rafe marrying for anything less than an intense, personal desire," Fanny said slowly.

"Not even for honor?" Catherine's smile was almost painfully ironic.

"Forgive me, I did not mean to pry, or to embarrass you. It is only that you and Rafe—you look so perfect together, so suitable. It would be tragic if you were not happy."

The subject was allowed to die, and, as good manners indicated, they went on to speak of other things. At the back of Catherine's mind a relentless fear hammered. She had discovered in her husband an uncanny ability for knowing what was happening around him. It seemed he had known all along of Marcus's presence on this section of the river. And if he knew that much, how much more did he know?

It was late afternoon before Giles and Fanny took their leave. Catherine stood on the gallery, waving until they were out of sight. Then, long after Rafael had returned to his study, she sat on the steps of one arm of the double front staircase. She watched the flittings of blue jays, cardinals, and mockingbirds, and the swooping, quarreling flight of mating sparrows among the trees, but her thoughts wandered without control. A restless feeling crept along her nerves. She was conscious of a sense of strain, of a tight-stretched anticipation of she knew not what.

When a scuffling footstep sounded behind her, she swung around with a start.

"I crave pardon, Madame. I did not mean to come upon you unaware."

That voice of grave politeness was unlike Madame Thibeaut. Catherine stared at the woman, trying to see the expression that was hidden by the shadow of the gallery.

"Yes, was there something you needed?"

The woman caught her bottom lip between her teeth, moving a step closer. "It is Mam'zelle Solange. If I might speak to you about her?"

"Certainly," Catherine said, though she was unable to infuse any warmth into her voice.

"You went riding with her this morning?"

Catherine agreed.

"Did you—did she meet anyone? A man?"

The woman's voice was tentative, as if she doubted the wisdom of what she was doing. Catherine's eyes narrowed, then she gave an abrupt nod of her head.

202

The pock marked face hardened, the bony shoulders were drawn back. "Very well then. So long as you know." Turning on the heel of her slipper, she marched away.

What had prompted such a piece of tattling? Duty? Hardly. Fear? Jealousy? Much more likely. The same kind of jealous self-interest which had made her fill Solange's head with tales calculated to give her a disgust of marriage. What did the woman expect her to do? Run to Rafael with the tale, thereby earning Solange's fury for herself—rather than have it fall on Madame Thibeaut's own head? Solange had already blocked that possibility. What was she to do? Would Rafael believe her, or his sister?

Theirs had been far from a trusting relationship. Her knowledge of the whippings carried out under his orders had placed it under a greater strain. Not that there was any overt sign between them, and yet, her feelings for him had undergone a change. Her feelings? What feelings? She cared nothing for him, nor he for her. They had made that plain in the beginning. Still, it was impossible to live with a man, to share his bed, without coming to some accommodation. She was disappointed in him, he had lost stature, respect, in her eyes, that was it. He had shown himself as less human than she had believed.

Catherine sat on, lost in thought, her chin resting in the palm of her hand. The sun sank behind the trees, leaving a golden tinged purple twilight that moved swiftly to a gray dusk. Frogs croaked in the gathering evening, and from far away came the mournful, desperation-haunted call of a whippoorwill. The smell of woodsmoke hung in the air, mixed with the pervasive scent of yellow honeysuckle from the woods, and the dank odor of mud from the river. The air turned cool and damp on her face. Reluctant to go in, she made no move until the sting of a mosquito broke her mood and forced a retreat into the house.

She found India waiting for her on the back gallery. The girl said nothing, only curtsying with an awkward grace and opening the door of the bedchamber so that Catherine could enter. As she stepped across the threshold, Catherine glanced at her in surprise, wondering why she was hovering outside rather than waiting within the room where she could sit down. Then she had her answer: Rafael lay stretched full length upon the bed with one hand behind his head.

He flung Catherine a look of mocking amusement as she entered with India trailing behind her. He made no move to take his leave, and after a moment's hesitation Catherine signaled to India to begin to dress her for dinner.

The maid obeyed, but her fingers trembled and she made slow work of the row of tiny buttons down the back of the gown.

It was odd to have Rafael there in the room. It was seldom he was in from the fields until she was done. For a second it reminded her of the night he had watched while Dédé dressed her for the theatre. Wincing away from the thought, she asked, "Aren't you going to change?"

"I wanted to speak to you first," he answered.

"Now?"

"If it's convenient," he said dryly.

Stepping out of her gown, Catherine nodded at the maid. India picked up the garment, and went slowly from the room with it over her arm.

"That girl doesn't like me, does she?" Rafael said, his eyes on Catherine's face.

"India? Why shouldn't she?"

"I was asking you."

"I—expect she is just shy of you, and a little nervous."

"Is that how she strikes you?" he asked in obvious disbelief.

Catherine had recognized the hidden hostility behind the girl's demeanor, but her first impulse was to protect her. "I can't think what else it could be," she answered, meeting his gaze squarely.

He looked away up into the canopy above him. "I suppose if you are satisfied, I must be." After a moment he spoke again. "I begin to see why Ali was so anxious to have this girl as your maid."

Busy trying to unknot the tapes of her chemise, Catherine did not look up. "Do you?"

"It appears he is to be congratulated."

"Oh, yes. It is becoming—obvious. I daresay she could use a few larger dresses. The style now is good for concealing a delicate condition, but after a time other measures become necessary."

"Did you know she was quite so far advanced when you accepted her?"

"Ali warned me, yes."

"Did he?"

His tone was so odd that she glanced up from the stubborn knot.

"Forgive me," he said, "but you blush and stammer so delightfully when speaking to me of it. I find it hard to imagine this conversation with Ali. This girl, you took her anyway, knowing her usefulness would be limited to two or three months at best. Why?"

Catherine stared at him, a defiant light flashing in her eyes. "I told you why."

"Oh, yes. You see yourself as her protector against Solange and Madame Thibeaut."

He was in a peculiar mood, Catherine chose to ignore it. "If I am to clothe her decently," she said, enlarging on her previous remarks, "I will need cloth, and while I am about it, the other servants, the field hands and outside workers, appear to be dressed in rags, tatters, and animal hides. They tell me they have not been issued new clothing since before the Fitzgeralds left two years ago."

"Not so. I gave instructions for outfitting them myself last year."

"They do not appear to have received it. Do you think I could have materials sent upriver?"

"On the next trip," he said, his face hard. "Let me know what, and how much, and I will see to it. But are you sure you will have the time to do this sewing? I don't like to see you overtired. Fanny was right, you are thinner."

Was there a rebuke in his voice or had she imagined it? Had he noticed she was deliberately finding tasks to occupy her hands, problems for her mind? Fatigue dulled the senses. It did not spare her, but it helped her to resist the subtle beguilement of his hands upon her, and her own sensual response to him, a response which seemed, under the circumstances, degrading.

Catherine tugged futilely at the tapes, allowing a sharp edge to creep into her voice. "Of course I will have the time. I don't intend to do them myself, you know. There are several women in the quarters who have some skill with a needle."

With a fluid movement, Rafael left the bed and moved toward her. "You needn't show me your claws, *La Lionne*. I have no quarrel with you. At least," he amended, "none that I am aware of."

Catherine looked up, her golden brown eyes wide. "What did you call me?"

"The lioness. It is what our people call you behind your back, for the yellow mane of your hair, and your courage. You have also captured Ali's admiration, a thing not easily done by a woman, considering his Arabic heart. Did you not know?"

Placing his hands on hers, he stilled her frantic efforts at the knot. With a single jerk, he tore the tapes loose, freeing her from the clinging silk of her chemise. There was no mistaking the purposefulness of his touch as his hands slipped beneath the silk, pressing her naked form against him.

"You—you wanted to talk to me," Catherine reminded him as a distraction.

The muscles in his arms tensed, then relaxed once more. "Odd. I no longer feel like—talking."

"India will be waiting," she gasped.

"Let her wait," he murmured, pressing his face into her hair.

CHAPTER FOURTEEN

If Rafael had asked her about Marcus, as she had half expected, she could have told him everything. At it was, she let the days go by without speaking out, unwilling to disturb the uneasy peace between them, or to provoke the kind of acrimonious scene she expected from Solange. No further mention was made to Catherine of a need for her chaperonage. Whether Solange and Marcus were still meeting, she did not know, nor did she wish to. She knew a guilty hope that the girl would tire of her flirtation—or that Marcus would. Failing either of these, she was certain Madame Thibeaut would find a way to put a stop to the meetings. Such optimism might have been unfounded, but it helped her to keep her balance on her life of knife-edged uncertainty.

Within the walls of the house, the silent battle over authority raged on. India, growing daily larger, and more majestic with it, ranged herself solidly with Catherine. Instead of avoiding Solange and Madame Thibeaut, as Catherine had expected, she seemed to go out of her way to flout them. She would not accept orders from either without first referring them to Catherine. She terrorized the other maids with her black, inimical stare, so that between the former housekeeper and the Indian woman, they were in a constant quake, afraid to perform the tasks assigned them, afraid not to, glancing over their shoulders a thousand times a day as they went about their work.

Her presence made a difference to Catherine. She grew to rely on the girl to transmit her commands and lend support. A bond of admiration, of shared respect, developed between them—but no more than that. India, encased in her hard shell of pride, was immune to friendliness. She never smiled. Her eyes had no depth, only the look of flat, polished steel mirrors, reflecting nothing of herself.

It was with genuine thankfulness that Catherine saw the arrival of the materials for the servants' clothing. Surely here was something all could co-operate upon? No. That, too, became a subject of discord as she saw Rafael actively encouraging Madame Thibeaut to take over supervising the cutting and sewing of the garments and their distribution.

Madame Thibeaut accepted the task in an attempt to make a good impression, but Solange resented being pressed into service as a seamstress for the slaves and temporarily deserted her mentor. Solange was not at outs with her companion, precisely, but there was discernible friction. Catherine thought Madame Thibeaut's disapproval of Solange's meetings with Marcus contributed to it, though nothing was said. At any rate, Solange grew slightly more approachable. She would drop into Catherine's room as she was dressing, fingering her gowns in the armoire, turning over the trinkets and her few pieces of jewelry in her jewel case, and watching critically as India put up her hair. When she admired some bauble, a pair of hair ornaments composed of pink silk roses, or a set of paste shoe buckles, more often than not Catherine insisted she have it. She could not acquit herself entirely of trying to bribe the girl, and yet, Solange took such pleasure from the merest nothings that Catherine enjoyed bestowing them upon her.

One day Catherine ventured to suggest a change of hairstyle, replacing the severity of the mode Solange used with one of the new styles copied from ancient Roman busts. To her surprise, Solange agreed, allowing Catherine to snip the hair around her face and use a curling iron to make a frame of soft curls. The effect was so charming, the improvement in Solange's disposition as a result so dramatic, that Catherine dared to suggest the careful application of a little lampblack in oil to her lashes, a whisk of rice powder paper, and a brisk rubbing of the cheeks and lips with crushed petals of wild roses. These attentions, like the hairstyle, were accepted grudgingly at first, but, once begun, soon became a morning ritual. Solange was even, once or twice, seen to smile at the result. Rafael was generous with his praise, but Madame Thibeaut, in a rare error in judgment, called the artistic embellishment painting.

When Solange did not arrive one morning during her toilette, Catherine accepted it philosophically. She could not expect to win the girl over so quickly. She did not trouble about her until the girl failed to come down for luncheon. This was extraordinary enough to attract notice, and Catherine moved along the gallery to knock on her door.

"I am sorry," Madame Thibeaut spoke around the edge of the panel in answer to her inquiry. "Mam'zelle cannot speak to you. She is unwell."

"Unwell? In what way?"

"An affliction of the stomach, you understand, one of those trying bouts which overcome us all at times. She will be well in a day or so."

"None of the rest of us are ill—" Catherine began.

"For which you must thank *Le Bon Dieu*. I, myself, feel a tiny bit queasy. I am not at all sure the fish cook made for Mam'zelle, in her special tomato sauce with oysters, was fresh."

"I remember no such dish."

"As I said, it was made especially for Mam'zelle. I brought it to her myself. You will remember, she did not care for your menu last night."

That was certainly true. Solange had picked at the food on her plate, though she had been amazingly quiet about it, for her.

"Perhaps she was sickening for something earlier. If I could look at her—"

"She prefers to be left alone, to lie quietly in her bed in a darkened room. I have given her a sleeping draught, and she is just drifting off. I feel confident she will be much better when she awakes."

"I will not disturb her. No doubt you are correct in your diagnosis, Madame, but I have some small experience in disorders of this sort. I'm sure you won't mind if I step inside and confirm your belief?"

"Indeed, I do not like to refuse you, Madame," the older woman said with exquisite politeness and a quite convincing show of uneasiness, "but Mam'zelle will be in a rare taking if I allow anyone to enter and disturb the air so as to bring back her headache. I'm sure I don't care to be responsible for the consequences—"

"Then you must leave them to me, mustn't you?" Catherine said, refusing to be balked. By this time India had come to join her. Placing her hand on the door, Catherine pushed into the room, more in defiance of the tight-lipped companion than from concern for Solange.

The instant she saw the girl, her sympathies were aroused. She was pale, lying against her pillow with her hair in a long braid falling over her white, high-necked nightgown. Pale, and incredibly young.

Her eyelids fluttered open as Catherine took her hand. Her lips curved in the beginning of a smile. "I knew you would come," she said.

"How do you feel?"

Solange moved restlessly. "Better now, but weak, so weak."

"Can I get you anything? Broth? A cool drink?"

"I—yes, a drink, but—you go, Madame Ti. Perhaps you could put a little orange flower water in it. You know how I like it."

"There is water here on the stand—" the woman began.

"No, fresh water, fresh from the well. I want no other."

"Really, petite. This is not seemly."

"I want no other," Solange repeated, tears of frustration springing to her eyes as her voice rose. "I want—no—other."

"Very well. Do not distress yourself. I am going."

It was plain the woman left the room with great reluctance. The reason for it became obvious the moment the door closed behind her.

The grip of Solange's fingers tightened. "Catherine. You must do something for me."

"Certainly, if I can."

"Promise?"

Caution made her hesitate.

"Promise!"

"I will do anything within my power."

"Good," she breathed. "Marcus. He is waiting near the edge of the swamp. You must go and tell him why I cannot come."

"Solange, I—"

"You must! Madame Ti will not. She hopes he will give up and go away. She doesn't understand. She doesn't know how I feel, thinking of him, waiting out there."

"I cannot go without a groom or someone else with me. Rafael has said—"

"There is no need. I do not go into the swamp anymore. Marcus will not allow it. I will tell you how you must go. The way is not long, but it is safe."

"Perhaps India could go, with a note from you?" Catherine suggested, and the Indian girl nodded from her post near the door.

A look of indecision crossed Solange's face, then she turned her head back and forth on the pillow. "Marcus said I must send you if I cannot come. He will not trust any other messenger for fear of a trick, some ruse to make him stay away."

Plausible, so plausible. There was even a feeling of inevitability about it. Clever Marcus.

"Madame, the other one returns," India said into the stillness.

"Catherine, please? Please!"

Those black eyes, beseeching, without a trace of hostility. How could she refuse? "I'll go, but India goes with me."

"India? Oh. Yes. She may as well." Listless, slightly petulant, as if she envied Catherine her outing or doubted the wisdom of letting her make it, Solange agreed. She dropped Catherine's hand and turned her face away as Madame Thibeaut entered the room.

"Consider it, Catherine. I ask no more than that."

Catherine sighed. "Don't you, Marcus? It appears to me that you ask a great deal more."

"Only that you give up a husband you can't love and a home which will never be truly yours. I know what you go through, you see. I know, and it tears my heart out. Can you imagine what it does to me, knowing you are persecuted at every turn, knowing you sleep at night in that pirate's arms?"

"And do you realize what you are doing to Solange, inducing her to love you while you care nothing for her?" Catherine asked, drawing away from him. Considering that impassioned speech, she was glad she had asked India to wait at a distance in order to keep watch.

"What does Solange count for, compared to my feelings for you?"

"She is not like other girls. She has had no other admirers to give her perspective. You must not hurt her, Marcus."

"So much concern for Solange, Catherine. Have you none for me? Don't you care how I feel about you?"

"You know I do, but I can do nothing about it."

"You can. You can come away with me. Now. This minute. I know you feel little for me beyond—I hope—a mild affection. I have love enough for both of us. You will come to care for me, given time."

They had come full circle. Catherine had not wanted the meeting to come to this, still, it was difficult to halt a declaration if the man was determined to make it. In addition, she was haunted by the feeling that she was in some way at fault for Marcus's feelings. She had not encouraged him, there was nothing she could do to prevent it, still, she felt obligated to try to alleviate the pain he felt.

"I'm sorry. Rafael is my husband, under the law and before God. I cannot change that."

"You are not happy."

That was undeniable. She only smiled a little without speaking.

"I would give my life to make you happy, to see you laugh and dance as you used to do."

"Please, you are making me feel quite sorry for myself—and there is no need. You must know that few women in the *haut monde* are happily married, yet they manage to exist."

"Yes," Marcus said, taking her hand. "If they are discreet—no, don't turn away. You must know it's the truth—at least for those who are not overtaken by motherhood every year. There, I won't speak of it if it disturbs you. I will only say this. I am here, if you should ever need me. The smallest billet, a message of any kind, will bring me to your side, ready to serve you in any way I can."

"That is a very generous offer."

He bowed slightly, his hazel eyes glinting green with emotion held in check. "Not at all. I pray you will take advantage of it."

Her smile was a nice blend of appreciation and dismissal. "I must go now, it grows late."

Brushing her hand with his lips, he released it. "Remember what I have said."

"Yes."

"And you may tell Solange she is not to disturb herself. I will see her at the Bartons' soirée—and extend my sympathies and commiserations, if you will?"

Marcus would have escorted her back along the path to where India was waiting. This Catherine would not allow. In truth, he was too close to the house as it was. It might have been necessary to accommodate Solange, but there was no need to risk going closer.

What did she feel for Marcus? she asked herself as she walked back along the rabbit trail she had followed. That he was not overly scrupulous, she recognized well enough. That did not necessarily keep him from being sincere in his protestations of love. She was fairly certain her own heart was not involved, and yet, she felt a certain sympathy with him. Such devotion was gratifying; it could not help but put her in charity with him. Perhaps that was what it was meant to do?

A flicker of movement off to her left caught her attention. She turned in time to see a shadowy form slide away

213

among the trees, the form of a barefoot man dressed in hanging rags of gray osnaburg. Fanny's words rang in her mind. Runaways. Runaways in the swamp. The tales she had heard of the atrocities on Santo Domingo, the children decapitated, women dismembered, half-heard whispers of worse deeds, rose up in her mind. The secret horror of every slave owner since time began shuddered along her veins. Surely it could not happen here? There had never been a major insurrection of the slaves in the lands known as Louisiana. Why should there be one now?

"Madame! Here, Madame."

"India," Catherine gasped. Not until she felt relief move through her body did she realize how frightened she had been. "India, did you see someone, a man, out toward the swamp?"

"No, Madame," the girl said, her face impassive, without curiosity. "I saw only the man who came to tell me the Maître turns toward home. We must hurry if we are to reach the house before him."

Could the man have been the same? Even so, Catherine did not like it. How many more were involved in this piece of deceit Solange was practicing? The more who knew of it, the less likely it was to remain—deceiving.

There were no repercussions. Solange did not quite regain her health. She suffered a persistant *mal de tête* and lassitude which caused her to neglect her appearance, withdrawing to her room. When she appeared at the table for meals her moods fluctuated wildly from tears to laughter edged with hysteria. Her imperfections obsessed her. Speaking to her became a chore, for she must have constant reassurance. Care had to be taken that some remark uttered in innocence did not become a two-edged sword which the girl could use against either herself or whomever she was speaking to. How much of her nervous state could be laid at Marcus's door was hard to say; Solange was unsure of herself, and therefore of him. She may also have sensed the basic insincerity behind his pursuit, though Catherine was inclined to suspect Madame Thibeaut of undermining the girl's confidence.

Grim-faced, the companion waited upon the girl,

hovering at her side like some patient bird of prey, whispering to her, petting her, watching everything and everyone with her round, lashless eyes. The days grew steadily warmer, taking on a summer tempo of early rising, to take advantage of the cool mornings, and mid-afternoon rest.

On the day of Fanny's party, Catherine retired immediately after luncheon. Her ball gown of shaded rust and gold silk muslin with its short, sleeveless spencer of rust velvet, the matching slippers, the jewel box containing her topazes, and her other accessories were packed in a bandbox. Since they would be arriving early she would wait until they reached Cypress Bend to dress. Her coiffure must be done in advance, however. India had asked to be spared the trip in the ancient berlin carriage left by the Fitzgeralds. Catherine could not altogether blame her. She herself would have preferred to ride, but Solange did not feel up to the effort and Madame Thibeaut lacked the skill.

Catherine did not wish to keep Rafael waiting, nor did she particularly wish to be present while he had his bath and was dressed. She was just about to ring for India to do her hair when a knock came at the door and the maid entered.

Her face with its high cheekbones carried a look of unusual animation. The basalt eyes flared with rage and the slim fingers were clenched upon her apron.

Before Catherine could speak, she cried in a low grating voice, "Maîtresse, you must do something about that woman!"

"Madame Thibeaut?"

"Yes, that one, that evil she-dog, that devil woman!"

"Calm yourself, India, and tell me what she has done."

"She has robbed the slaves of what miserable little they possess! I have watched for years while she stripped this house bare, and sold the food meant for all. What did I care for the belongings of owners? We had our pigs, our chickens, the little we could scrabble from the good earth and scavenge from the forest. But now this creature gives the clothes made for the people, and then demands the

215

pigs, the chickens, the vegetables in return, as payment. If everything is not given, she threatens the silent death of the voodoo priestess. Already three of the old people who have nothing to give have lain down upon their pallets, waiting for their end."

"It is a lie."

The denial came from the doorway. Madame Thibeaut moved quietly into the room with Solange behind her. Her expression was grave but without undue concern. Her hands were clasped loosely at her waist.

"It is not a lie. These things I know," India said proudly.

"Why? Tell me why I should do such things?"

Catherine did not care for the companion's assumption of the right to interrogate the maid, but the question was a valid one. She did not interfere.

"For the money, money for your lover, that brute of an overseer turned off by M'sieu Rafe. You thought he would take you with him when he went. Instead he left in the night, like the thief he was, with all you had gathered between you."

"Ridiculous," Madame Thibeaut snapped, a flush rising to her face, though Catherine could not have said whether anger or embarrassment caused it.

India went relentlessly on. "And now you feel Mam'zelle Solange slipping away. Soon she will need you no more. With Madame Navarro against you, you have little hope of the settlement you feel is your due. You must have money, money to keep you, to allow you to play the lady."

"Enough! I will not let you defame my good name further. There is only your word—"

"Yes, because the others are too afraid to accuse you."

"Slaves. Only slaves. Who would listen, even if it were true—which I do not admit?"

She was right. No court would accept the testimony of a slave. Not that it had come to that yet. Turning to India, Catherine asked, "Do you have anything to prove what you say, anything at all?"

"How could I, Madame? This one is clever. Would she

216

touch a pig? Not her. The slaves must deliver their small wealth to a rogue on a keelboat tied up at night down the river. It is delivered in the same way as the valuables from the house, to a merchant of bad reputation who disposes of it and holds the money, less his share. There has been one slave, or possibly more, who has been listed as a runaway, who—was not. Slaves bring much money, more than chickens or silver candlesticks. I do not know this merchant's name—or that of the boatman. There are many such who care not what they deal in. They are like rats in the kitchen, disappearing at the first sign of light."

"This is outrageous. I have long realized, Madame Navarro, that you disliked me. However, that you would seriously listen to a slave making these vile accusations against me passes all belief!"

"I am not interested in personalities, Madame Thibeaut, only in justice," Catherine replied.

Solange, quiet until now, stepped forward. "You seem to know a great deal about these dealings, India. How does that come about?"

A cold smile passed over the Indian girl's face. "I know because it was the same in Santo Domingo. This woman likes to pretend she was of the gentry upon that island, and in truth, she was raised in that fashion with a nurse who practiced the ugly magic of the juju and taught it to her charge. Some say Madame's father drank away his health and fortune, others that the voodoo woman took revenge for some slight. When he died there was nothing. Madame was forced to marry a merchant, a man who, like the man in New Orleans, did not care what he sold."

"Madame Thibeaut, is this true?" Solange asked, her eyes wide.

"Of course not. The merest drivel, dragged out to persecute me."

And yet, in New Orleans the companion had not been anxious to mingle with her fellow refugees.

"I think this has gone far enough then," Solange said, drawing herself up. "It is only this person's word against that of Madame Ti."

217

"That, unfortunately, is true," Catherine was forced to agree.

"It is," Madame Thibeaut said, a cruel smile thinning her mouth, "and it comes well from the lips of the daughter of an insurrectionist and a killer, does it not?"

"My father killed no one!" India cried.

"No, and he did not partake in the rebellion in Santo Domingo either, I suppose? Indeed he did, which is why he was sold into Louisiana with his family when he and his followers were captured in the hills. And he helped murder M'sieur Rafael's father—that is why M'sieur Rafael killed him!"

There was a stunned silence. Then India made an abrupt movement forward.

"My father killed no one!" she hissed. "He ran away, yes, when he could stand the treatment he received no longer. But he would never have killed a man in cold blood. He was himself murdered—by your M'sieur Rafe—for the crime of being in company with the killers!"

"Oh, come—" Madame Thibeaut began, but Catherine made an abrupt gesture.

"That will do," she said.

There was a peculiar element of trust in the gaze India turned to her. "You will not let this evil woman get away with her deeds?"

"I must think what is to be done."

"Think? What is to be thought of? She should be placed in the jail and kept there until she can be taken away to New Orleans."

"It isn't that easy. There must be proof."

"What you mean is, you will do nothing," India said, her voice bitter. "It is always this way. Something always makes it impossible for justice to be done for us. No matter the cruelty, no matter the crimes committed against us, it is we who suffer in the end."

"That isn't true," Catherine said, moving toward the girl. India backed away, the smile on her lips chilling in its hate.

"Isn't it?" she asked. "How little you know. I thought,

218

Madame, that you were different. I find instead that you are only—stupid."

Whirling, the Indian woman ran out the door, knocking against the frame in her clumsy haste.

"Well!" Solange said.

"May I commend you, Madame Navarro, on your self-control?" Madame Thibeaut said, her voice laced with irony. "Come, Solange."

Catherine made no move to stop the pair. Mechanically, she took the pins from her hair and brushed it into a smooth knot. Perhaps Fanny's maid would be able to dress it more festively for her. She must go on with the party, naturally. She would need at least that much time to decide what must be done.

Her first inclination was to inform Rafael and leave it in his hands. Where would that leave India? He might believe her, enough to make the investigations that would turn up proof to be used against Madame Thibeaut, but her parentage could hardly be kept out of it. Rafael could not be expected to tolerate her near him when he knew.

Was there any way she could institute inquiries? Marcus had little liking for Solange's companion. She would see him that evening. Might he not be persuaded to look into the affair for her?

It was an uncomfortable ride to Cypress Bend. The cumbersome old carriage lurched from side to side down the rutted lane which passed for a road. Grass, weeds, and small saplings growing between the ruts brushed the bottom of the coach. Tree limbs scratched along its sides. Swarms of gnats invaded the interior, making it necessary to tie the leather curtains down securely, while this, in turn, increased the stuffiness and the heated smell of musty, mildewing cushions. Before they were a mile from the house, Solange became ill and had to be let out to run into the woods a short distance. They carried on with the smell of her vinaigrette sharp in their nostrils and her lamentations ringing in their ears. Catherine could only be glad Rafael had elected to ride along side and delegated Ali to the place beside the coachman to keep guard with a fowling piece upon his knees. They were at least not overcrowded.

They arrived later than first planned, but in good time for Catherine to drink a cup of tea with Fanny and exchange the news before they began to dress for dinner.

Giles was pouring a sherry for Rafael as they entered the salon. "Ah, the ladies—at last," he said, handing the glass to his friend.

"Nonsense," Fanny scoffed. "We aren't late. You are early."

"That's as may be. Our guests will find us still at table if we don't go in quickly."

"You worry far too much," she told him.

"And you not enough."

A shadow passed over Fanny's face. "I wouldn't say that."

"No, maybe not. I will make you a handsome apology by telling you how well you look." Taking his sister's hand he made her a courtly bow. "That gray-green color becomes you, my dear, and the silver lace with your ribbon headdress is just the right touch."

"Quickly, Catherine," Fanny said, turning to give her hand to Rafael, "Giles seems to be in need of distraction."

"You need not instruct her," Giles replied, lifting Catherine's fingers to his lips. "She could drive any man to distraction."

Mere banter, of course, but Catherine glanced from the sudden grave look in Giles's blue eyes to meet the sardonic gaze of Rafael.

"Including her husband," he said to his friend. "You have my permission to escort her in to dinner, however."

At the table, Fanny directed the conversation to safely dull channels, principally politics, with a comment on the census being taken in the territory. The proposed convention to frame a constitution for use the moment statehood was achieved came under fire next, dissolving naturally into the subject of admittance of the territory into the union.

"I had a letter from Claiborne the other day," Giles said.

"Ah yes, your friend," Rafael mocked him gently.

"And yours, if you but knew it. At any rate, the governor is of the opinion that statehood for the lower portion of the purchase is only a formality. There can be no question of a scarcity of people."

Catherine let her mind wander. Cypress Bend, as Fanny had said, was much like Alhambra in construction. There were the same wide galleries, the same whitewashed bousillage outside. There were no wings however. The main rooms were lined across the front with the bedchambers strung in a row directly behind them. Interest was added by the small twin buildings on each side, on the left a garçonniere for the overnight accommodation of young male guests, on the right a pigeonnier to provide a supply of tender squab for the table—and the neighbors.

Inside, there was a subtle difference in the décor. Less ornamentation was in evidence than in a Creole home, less bric-a-brac and gold leaf, fewer patterns in rugs and drapes. The furniture had simpler lines, the colors were more subdued. The grand salon and petit salons had been thrown together to form a ballroom. Rugs and matting had been removed and the gray cypress boards of the floor colored with a decoction of red oak bark, then rubbed with beeswax. When polished it took on a high gloss, reflecting the chairs set at intervals along the walls and the massed flowers; roses, larkspur, and wild gardenia, which formed alcoves around the floor to ceiling windows.

The flowers were a hobby of Fanny's, grown in an English style garden at the rear of the house. Thinking of it, Catherine made a mental note to ask her for the names of her roses, especially the dusky pink with the mossy looking bud. She had still not gotten around to refurbishing the courtyard at Alhambra. How foolish she had been that morning when she had stood looking over that unkempt area. She had expected no problems in her life greater than taking a neglected household in hand and making something of beauty out of ugliness.

221

"Don't you think so, Catherine?"

"What?" she asked with a guilty start. "I'm afraid I wasn't attending."

"I asked if you didn't admire Fanny's necklace," Rafael said with thinly disguised impatience. "Oriental jade, I think."

Catherine glanced at the pendant on a fine gold chain. A small carved elephant was not her idea of beauty, but she had to agree it was unusual.

"It was a gift from my father on my sixteenth birthday, a long time ago," Fanny said. "He was a sea captain, you know. He picked this up in the Spice Islands on the last trip before his death. He claimed it was a good luck piece, a far eastern superstition, because the elephant has his trunk turned down."

"Show them your bracelet," Giles said lazily from where he leaned back in his chair at the head of the table, playing with a cluster of watchfobs hanging from his waistcoat pocket.

"Oh yes," Fanny said, obediently presenting her wrist. "It is a mate to my elephant, fastened to a band of jade and gold. I found it in Natchez, of all places. There is a man there, a Mr. Martin. He is a planter in a small way, I believe, but he makes a hobby of collecting and selling unusual things of this sort."

"I seem to remember a girl I knew at convent school, Helene Dubois, marrying a Martin at Natchez," Catherine said.

"Quite probably," Rafael commented, "since every girl in the territory with any pretension to education has gone to the convent."

That was so true Catherine had to smile. "Yes, but Helene was a good friend—until she went to visit relatives in Natchez nearly three years ago and never came back."

"The way you say that, you would think Natchez was at the edge of the world," Fanny teased.

"No, no," Catherine said with a smile and a shake of her head, "that is at New England."

They were not caught at the table by the guests, but it was a close thing. When the first carriage was heard upon the drive they were just entering the ballroom and had to arrange themselves hurriedly to receive.

Solange had declined to be present at the dinner table, preferring a tray for Madame Thibeaut and herself in the room assigned to them for their dressing. The pair was seated on a camel-backed settee, talking, quietly at ease when Catherine noticed them. She stared in a mingled indignation and pity, but had no time to do more before the first guest was announced. She was aware, however, of Rafael's stiffening beside her and the thinly veiled suspicion in the penetrating glance he sent her.

"What have you done to her?" he grated under his breath. "She looks like a *fille de joie.*"

There was no time to answer. It was, in any case, all too true—and it was possible she was to blame. Rouged cheeks, red mouth, face dead white with powder, hair frizzed into a tortured arrangement by a too hot curling iron, the girl looked like a painted doll—or a "soiled dove" from one of the bagnios on Tchoupitoulas Street in New Orleans. The dress she wore, of pink silk trimmed about the appallingly decollete neckline with a wide band of diamante, had never been approved by Madame Mayfield on their shopping trips together. Catherine could not imagine where the girl had found it. Topping off this toilette, like a badge of approval, was Catherine's cashmere shawl, the shawl Rafael had given her in her marriage basket.

Who was responsible for this travesty? Solange? Or was it Madame Thibeaut? There seemed only two possible explanations for it. Ignorance was one. The other, sheer malice, the kind of ugly malice that would expose a young girl to ridicule for the sake of scoring a point over someone else. For it was Catherine who had encouraged Solange to use paint—and Madame Thibeaut knew it.

The girl could not be allowed to disgrace herself. After greeting the new arrivals Rafael left them talking to Fanny and Catherine and went to order Solange to her room. The argument was quiet, but no less fierce or bitter for that, from what Catherine could judge. Still, at last Solange obeyed her brother.

A little thought convinced Catherine that her husband's sister could have nothing else suitable to wear. She had brought only the one gown with her. Something must be contrived. As soon as she could do so without attracting undue attention, she followed Solange.

Fanny's clothes were hopelessly large, being both too wide across the shoulders and too long. She did have a lace bertha which her maid found to contribute to the cause. The removal of the diamante made a vast improvement. With the lace across her bosom, most of the paint removed, and the application of a bit of pomade to her hair, Solange began to be presentable. Still, when the time came to re-enter the ballroom, the girl balked. In a fit of temper she ordered everyone out of her bedchamber. Privately, Catherine was of the opinion it would be a good thing for her to be alone for a while. She was not so certain when Solange drew her to one side and asked her to send Marcus to her the moment he arrived.

Catherine could not do so, of course. All the rules of common sense and propriety strictly forbade a meeting in a bedchamber. In the state Solange was in, it would have been most unwise. What Rafael would say if he discovered such a ruse was best left to the imagination. There must be an alternative.

Frowning, Catherine made her way back to the ballroom. She danced a quadrille with Giles. It was a fast set which they frolicked through with much laughter. One or two other gentlemen begged dances and she obliged, though she was careful to sit out several also in order to safeguard against being called a fast young matron, and to find time to speak to several of the older women ranged around the walls.

The Trepagniers were late in putting in an appearance. According to M'sieur Trepagnier, a haughty looking man with a permanent stain under his nose from taking snuff, it was due to a slight contretemps over their new carriage. A piece of the silver molding had been missing, and he had refused to leave the house until the culprit who took it was found and soundly whipped. It was discovered to

224

have been a gardener's child who took it because it was shiny.

Marcus was resplendent in a coat of dark blue super-fine, whisper gray pantaloons, and a waistcoat woven of gray and gold striped silk. An added touch was a gold tassel hanging from the hilt of the inevitable dress sword. Catherine watched with approval from across the room as, with consummate tact, he led his hostess out onto the floor. Still, she was not surprised when he sought her out during the first interval.

It was warm for exertion, and she sat trying to cool herself with a fan of painted chicken skin in one of the flower decked window alcoves. The scent of the roses and gardenias was overpowering and she leaned back, breathing the freshness of the outside air with gratitude.

"I lost you once in a window like this."

She turned her head to smile at Marcus. "Through sheer neglect on your part," she answered, refusing to fall in with his nostalgic tone. "Tell me, did you ever collect your wager?"

"You must know there was none," he said, his voice blunt.

"No, I only suspected." His face was drawn. Dark circles of tiredness shadowed his eyes. When he made no answer, she continued, "Solange wants to see you."

"Does she?"

"Don't be like that!" Catherine's voice was sharp. "She has looked forward to this now for weeks. The least you can do is ask her to stand up with you."

"The thought crossed my mind, but I don't see her on the floor—or along the wall, for that matter."

"No. I expect she will leave her seclusion for you, how-ever. There is a sitting room across the entrance hall. If you will wait there, I will send her to you."

"And her crone of a companion too, I make no doubt," he said with a grimace. "Very well." As Catherine made a move to go, he touched her arm. "First there is something I must tell you."

"Yes?"

"I—will be leaving the day after tomorrow."

225

"Returning to the city?"

He nodded assent. "There is a limit to the hospitality of the fondest relative, and a limit to my funds."

"You have given up the idea of marrying Solange?"

"Bravado, chérie, nothing more. You know as well as I our Rafe would rather see me dead first. Besides, she hasn't a picayune."

"A disqualification of the first magnitude," she said gravely.

"It counts," he agreed, "when you can't have what you really want."

Catherine was silenced. "Well, I will send Solange to you."

"Do that," he said, flashing a brief smile, "but I will leave it to you to tell her I am leaving."

"You are too kind," she mocked, and made her escape.

Hardly had she returned when Rafael claimed her for a new dance imported from Austria via France, the waltz. It was thought to be rather vulgar, not the thing for young girls, but acceptable for husbands and wives. Catherine had practiced it at home but this was her first opportunity to execute it in public. It was a novel sensation being so close in a man's arms in full view of everyone. She and her husband did not speak. Attending to her steps, and the strength of the guiding arm about her waist, Catherine had little time for coherent thought. It was only as the music ended that she realized she had forgotten to ask Marcus to check into Madame Thibeaut's clandestine activities. She was given no opportunity to remedy the oversight, however. Her husband did not leave her side for the rest of the evening.

CHAPTER FIFTEEN

Rafael rode close to the door of the carriage, his hand resting on the hilt of his sword, on the return trip home. There was no need for them to make the night journey through the swamp. Fanny had asked them to stay on, and Catherine would have preferred it, but Rafael had insisted.

Staying would not have been the best arrangement, she had to admit. There had been several guests who were sleeping over, and they had left Fanny counting on her fingers as it was. Catherine would have suspected Rafael of objecting to spending what was left of the night in a room made uncomfortable by the snores of other men, if it had not been for Solange. The girl had never recovered her poise after her unfortunate start. The idea of prolonging their stay had sent her into near hysteria.

There was little need for their side lanterns. A full moon shone down, turning the Spanish moss hanging from the trees to silver-gilt plumage. In its glow Rafael took on the look of some mythical horseman cast in metal, condemned to ride on forever into the night. There was no movement in that moonlit silence. No wind stirred the trees; the shadows beneath them lay dark and still. No prowling night creatures with shining eyes crossed their path. Their coachman, oppressed by the quiet, drove without outcry, and the sound of the carriage was a loud, unnatural clatter.

Inside, there was the smell of dust and the grass crushed by their wheels—and something else—the sweetly sour fragrance of honeysuckle, as pervading and nauseous as any found growing on a graveyard fence.

Then came the hooting of an owl, a long drawn hunting cry. Catherine knew a fleeting relief until Solange sat up, her eyes glistening, round, in the dimness.

"An owl. The night cry of an owl means a death before morning."

Madame Thibeaut sat like an image, staring out a slit in the curtain as if she had not heard.

"Don't be silly," Catherine said bracingly. "Owls are night creatures. When else would you hear one?"

"I've heard it said all my life."

"Superstition, nothing more."

"Superstitions start from something. Night creatures know secrets day ones don't. They can sense when death is near."

Catherine made her voice as quiet, as calm, as she could manage. "Don't upset yourself, Solange. We will be home soon."

The girl glanced at her, then slowly subsided. Catherine did not relax until she saw the bulk of Alhambra looming up with the river gleaming before it.

When the coach rolled to a stop, Ali jumped down, let down the step, and opened the door. Madame Thibeaut was first out. She waited to see Solange alight, then started up the steps.

Rafael dismounted and tied his reins to the rear of the carriage. He paused a moment to give the coachman instructions concerning the care of his horse before following Catherine and Ali.

The house was dark, but Catherine had expected no less in their disorganized household. She had left candles and a tinder box on the table in the hallway against such an eventuality. She opened her mouth to call to Madame Thibeaut, at the head of an arm of the stairs, to tell her so, when the front door swung open. There was a great orange blossom of fire, a deafening report, and the companion was hurled backward, crashing into Solange, carrying her with her down the steps.

A gun, Catherine thought, standing stupidly staring for a shocked instant. Then hard hands dragged her down.

"Stay there," Rafael hissed, his words drowned as Ali fired the charge in his fowling piece from beside them.

She was left alone as the two men charged up the stairs, Rafael drawing his dress sword as he ran.

The night erupted with hideous yells as a stream of brown bodies streaked with white paint came from the house. Armed with sticks and axes, hoes and crude rakes, they formed a ring around Rafael, held at bay only by the flickering point of his steel. A lunge, a grunt, and the blade glittered red while a man fell. The hand of a slave wielding a hoe was severed at the wrist and the man skewered when he stopped to clutch the stump. From nowhere Ali brought forth a knife with a wicked half-moon blade, dropping his useless muzzle-loaded gun. The smell of blood, warm and sickeningly fresh, assailed the air. An unearthly scream of horror bubbled and died as a man was disemboweled with a twisting motion of Ali's wrist.

That cry broke the attack. Two men on the outskirts of the fray bolted, leaving the high porch with flying leaps into space. Another fled down the steps, passing Catherine with his eyes wide and staring, as if he did not see her. One by one those who fought on were pressed back, pouring blood from a half dozen cuts, leaving a slippery trail through which Rafael and Ali followed relentlessly, stepping over the bodies of the slain.

Suddenly it was over. There was a wild rush for the other arm of the stairs. Catherine thought for a moment Rafael would follow, then he dropped the point of his sword and turned away.

Rising slowly to her feet, Catherine spared a glance for Madame Thibeaut sprawled halfway down the steps. A great hole, with the blood already turning black, gaped in her chest. Her eyes were wide and staring in death, frozen in an ageless expression of disbelief. Beneath her lay Solange, her chest rising and falling, but with her eyes closed in a merciful unconsciousness.

Catherine looked up to tell Rafael. A flutter of movement in the open door caught her eye. There was the glint of an upraised knife, and a figure launched itself at her husband.

"Rafael! Behind you," she cried.

He had already transferred his sword to his left hand, as he moved toward Catherine and Solange. It was Ali who whirled, catching the blade on his forearm, bringing his own knife up in a continuous swing.

Abruptly he checked. The assailant, thrown off balance, went down in a flurry of skirts, falling heavily in the gore on the gallery.

Catherine mounted the steps without conscious thought, her hand reaching out to clutch Rafael's arm as if to stay his blow. "India," she breathed, her gaze fastened on the enraged, half-crazed black eyes of the woman struggling in Ali's arms on the floor. "Oh, India."

Catherine got to her feet as Rafael entered the door of the study. His face tightened when he saw her, then he closed the door firmly behind him and moved into the room.

"You wanted something, chérie?" he asked pleasantly as he tossed his riding crop on his desk and sat down.

There was a trace of hardness in her voice when she spoke. "I went down to the quarters just now."

"I see."

"I'm sure you do. They were driving stakes, four of them, and digging a hole—"

"Catherine—"

"A hole for India's belly, Rafael. And four stakes to tie her arms and legs to."

"She must be restrained. There is less chance of her coming to harm in that position."

"You will kill her! It is inhuman. Even if she withstands the whipping, she will never survive the indignity! But to tie a woman big with child down and beat her—I can't stand it. I can't stand it!" A shudder of such intense revulsion ran over her that she swung around, her hands moving over the goose flesh on her arms.

"Catherine, listen to me," Rafael said, coming to stand close behind her. "India is a renegade. She sent for these men, men she had been communicating with in the woods. She helped them arm themselves and let them into the house so they could kill us. For such a crime the penalty under any other master would be death by flogging, after which, her head would be struck off and put up on a pole as a warning. And this regardless of the child she carries. Compared to that, isn't fifty lashes, twenty-five today, twenty-five a week from today, more humane?"

"She will lose the child."

"Maybe, maybe not."

"Couldn't you wait?"

"Two months? And encourage the rest of the restless element in the quarters to join the rabble in the swamp? Impossible."

"Why?" she demanded, turning to face him, her amber eyes dark with despair. "Do you hold life so cheap? Does Ali's child mean nothing to you?"

His face was hard, his voice deliberate when he answered. "Do you think I spare your India so much for her own sake, the daughter of the man who killed my father, a woman who has the death of another upon her conscience? Or had you forgotten Madame Thibeaut as soon as she was buried? Convenient, but it does not say much for your humanity, Catherine."

"You—you knew about India, about her father? Then—why did you have her here?"

There was irony in his smile. "You begged so prettily, ma chérie."

So she had, for Ali's sake. He had been so enthusiastic—at first. Then he had changed. Had he discovered India's secret, and seen the danger of having her in the house? In the end nothing might have come of it, if it had not been for the interference of Solange and Madame Thibeaut.

"I did not know—then," she said with a helpless gesture. "I only discovered it yesterday, before we left for Cypress Bend."

"I am to believe that without question, of course?"

Catherine met his black gaze with a startled expression. "It is the truth."

Rafael made no comment, nor did his eyes waver. Catherine would not be the first to look away. The moment stretched taut between them, then he swung on his heel. "Your pardon," he said brusquely. "If you will excuse me?"

"Rafael—Rafe, please—" There was no encouragement in the broad back he kept turned to her, but she continued. "Couldn't you release India, let her go away with Ali, far away, perhaps back to the desert?"

He was quiet so long that Catherine grew hopeful, then he shook his head. "If it was only myself, I would consider it. But it isn't. The life of every man, woman, and child along the river, every one who lives in contact with slaves, may depend on my decision. We live always one breath away from the holocaust of rebellion. Compared to what could happen, the affair last night was no more than a fencing match."

"Killing India will prevent this?"

"I think, Catherine, that you are deliberately refusing to understand. Hasn't it occurred to you that you could have been killed, mutilated—and worse—for all India cared? A few minutes more of waiting, a little less determination to obliterate Solange's companion, and we would have been trapped like rats in the hallway. And from there, what? Cypress Bend, the Trepagnier place, a general uprising? It is all too likely."

"It didn't happen," she said, her face pale, but her mouth set in a stubborn line.

"And it won't, not if I can prevent it."

What could she say against such grim purpose? He was convinced he was right, and, she had to admit, he did have reason. But that did not prevent her sick horror at the thought of what was going to take place later that afternoon.

It was possible her presence would have the effect of moderating the punishment to be meted out. With this in mind, she made her way toward the square at the end of the quarters street at the appointed time.

The sun slanted through the trees, throwing the dark shadows of the cabins across the road. Because of the whipping, the hands had already been called in from the fields, driving the plow mules and oxen before them. The smell of dust and horse dung hung in the air with the reek of honeysuckle. It was warm, though not unbearably so. Gnats hovered in clouds, and yellow butterflies tentatively investigated the purple head of a nettle. That only the night before they had been in danger of a bloody death seemed as impossible as looking back upon a bad dream, until she saw the blank faces of their people like so many brown masks.

They stood in stolid patience, the slaves, arms folded, elaborately at rest, waiting for the start of the rare show they had been ordered out to watch. A sullen fatalism was a part of their attitude, but there was something more, something that remained hidden. Their gaze passed over Catherine. To force some sign of recognition, some change of expression, she would have spoken, then she realized that their attention was focused behind her.

Turning, she saw India with her hands tied before her, walking between a pair of husky field hands. Her bearing spoke of pride, of dignity, her face mirrored nothing but a quiet scorn. Following her were Ali and Rafael, the latter on horseback. Catherine's husband rode with a casual grace, but she was conscious of the alertness beneath his manner and the unaccustomed presence, during the day, of the sword strapped about his waist.

She stared longer, however, at the whip coiled over Ali's shoulder. Surely he did not intend to use it? Rafael could not be so unfeeling as to give such an order, nor Ali so lacking in free will as to accept it. Then as Ali singled her out of the gathering, as she saw the black suffering in his eyes, she knew she was wrong.

India was forced to her knees and the ropes tied about her ankles. A spasm crossed her face, but she made no protest as she was stretched over the hole in the ground and her wrists fastened to the other two poles. A woman stepped forward with a knife to slit the back of her dress and draw it aside. A shiver ran over Catherine at the thought of blows on that bare copper back, though she knew it was better not to have shreds of material forced into the skin.

Staring into the distance, the muscles of his jaws standing out in cords, Ali shook out the long whip of plaited

233

leather. The two field hands stepped back. Rafael raised his hand. When complete silence moved over the crowd, he let it drop.

Slowly, as if he had to force himself, Ali's arm went back. He drew a deep breath, and the whip slashed downward. The muscles of India's back jumped, her hands curled into fists, but she made no sound. Again and again the whip cracked, no two blows landing in the same place. On the fifth blow India closed her eyes, writhing, straining against the ropes, on the seventh a grunt of pain escaped her clenched teeth, on the twelfth she went suddenly limp, unconscious.

Still the blows fell. Sweat beaded on Ali's forehead, running into his eyes, streaming with salt tears down his face. His lips were drawn back over his teeth and his chest heaved.

Blood began to ooze in thin runnels from several of the lacerations. Catherine swallowed against a rising sickness, counting in her mind. Twenty-one. Twenty-two. "God," she whispered. "Please, God."

"Enough," Rafael said quietly.

The word brought a collective sigh of held breath from the crowd. Catherine sent her husband a glance, noting without interest the paleness underneath the bronze of his face.

"No, no!"

The scream came from Solange who had crept unnoticed into the forefront. Rushing at Ali, she grabbed the whip from his hand and began to strike clumsily at India. "Kill her! I want her to die! She killed Madame Ti. She killed my Madame Ti!"

Rafael slid from his horse. In a single stride he reached his sister, spun her around, and twisted the whip from her grasp.

Solange, nursing her fingers, stared at her brother. "She killed my Madame Ti," she whispered, and crumpled into his arms.

The sobs of Solange Navarro racked the air. Rafael stared at Catherine a brief moment over the form of his sister, then he swung around and walked away, carrying the girl toward the big house.

Indecision gripped Catherine as she stared after him. The Indian girl at her feet began to moan.

"Cut her loose," she ordered curtly, turning to the task at hand, "and someone bring a blanket."

They returned India to the jail. There seemed nothing else to do, nowhere else to take her, and it was clean, at least. The latter point was important, for they had not reached the small building before India began to turn her head from side to side and Catherine saw the ominous contracting of her belly into a hard mound.

As they laid her upon the narrow cot that passed for a bed, Catherine felt a presence near her. It was Ali, reaching out to brace India on her side with a rolled blanket in the only position which would not be painful to her.

"Send the others away," Catherine murmured. Rafael's valet obeyed.

When they had gone the two of them stood staring down at the mass of angry red stripes and weals, of cuts and torn flesh that was India's back.

"Why, Ali?" Catherine whispered. "Why?"

He understood her as quickly as always. "Why did I ply the lash? Who better, Madame? I could depend on no one else to treat her as carefully."

"You mean—it was your idea? Oh, Ali."

"A prerequisite of love, Madame," he said with a smile that trembled with sadness, "to give pain—and to spare it."

They cleaned India's back, spreading a soothing salve over it and tying a layer of bandage into place. She lay without moving, allowing them to tend her. When they were done, she turned slightly, opening her eyes to stare at them with dull apathy. Kneeling beside her, Ali took her hand. She made no move to resist, nor did she acknowledge his presence by even the tightening of a nerve. Refined by pain, her face held a strange, stark beauty. It was a beauty of line and plane and texture, like that of a graven image with empty, staring eyes.

Abruptly the mask she wore crumpled and her hand gripped convulsively. India twisted upon the bed, though no sound came from her lips.

"The baby—" Ali whispered. Catherine could only nod her head.

Night crept in, gathering as silently as the people who came to keep vigil as they learned what was happening inside. A whale oil lantern was brought, cloths, steaming water, cold water, food, drink.

With the heat of the lantern in that small, enclosed space, the air soon became stifling. The puffs of cooling night air that came in at the high window were mere irritants in their tantalizing freshness. Perspiration soaked their clothing and dampened their hair as they worked with India, holding her hands so she could pull against them, trying to keep her from tossing on the bed and hurting herself. There was fever rising in her body. Catherine wrung cloths in cool water to place upon her forehead, and sponged her body again and again.

As India's eyes glazed, rolling backward in her head, Catherine found herself wishing she would cry out, curse, scream—anything to break that terrible stoic endurance. She did not. Her lips swelled and bled, the palms of her hands were cut by her nails, but she uttered not a sound. Nor would she help herself. She ignored Catherine's instructions, letting the pain tear through her in its ebb and flow.

The moon had climbed above the tops of the trees when India's child struggled feet first into the world. It was a boy, a tiny, perfect man-child. For a shattering moment while she cleared his throat of mucus Catherine thought he would not breathe, then his cry broke the panting stillness. He was anointed by her tears as she cleaned his face, wrapped him in a piece of sacking, and passed him to Ali. He took him gingerly, awkward as all men are with their firstborn.

"India," he said softly, kneeling beside the bed. "Behold our son."

Her eyelids quivered, then slowly raised. The ghost of a

smile brushed her mouth. "Your son, Ali," she sighed, and turned her head away.

Ali flicked a glance at Catherine near the foot of the bed, working now with the chore of the afterbirth. She shook her head. "She is losing blood, too much of it—and she doesn't care."

"India," he said urgently, placing the black-eyed babe on the flaccid flesh of her arm, pressing her hand to its feebly moving legs. "Feel your child, warm and sweet against you? You must cling to your life for his sake. This time will pass. There will be joy again, and love. All the love I have to give."

Her voice was like the rustle of dry leaves in an autumn wind. "That might have been enough—if my baby was not a slave—and you were less a servant—in your heart."

Ali's face altered as the hurt of her words sank into his soul. She was right, of course. The child, under the Black Code of Bienville, took the condition of the mother. But the man born of the desert would not allow his feelings to obscure his concern for India.

"In this world, my India, there are things more important than freedom or the fire and death of rebellion."

"Are there?" she asked in weary disbelief.

"Yes. Among them are loyalty, love, belonging—"

"Words. Only words."

Ali leaned closer to catch her whisper. "The greatest of these is—love," he answered, his eyes, liquid and burning, on the angular paleness of her shuttered face.

India did not answer.

The bright gladness of the summer morning was in its full when Catherine walked back to the house. The newly risen sun sparkled on the dew. Birds called from tree to tree, and crickets skirled in the grass. But none of it penetrated the miasma of fatigue and depression in which she moved.

She found Rafael standing on the back gallery with a coffee cup in his hand, as if he had just come from the breakfast table. He appeared so rested, his linen fresh, his

237

pantaloons neatly pressed, compared to her rumpled and stained state, that she felt irrationally incensed with him.

"Good morning," she said briefly and started past.

"Would you like coffee. You look as if you could use it."

"Do I indeed?" she said, her voice sharp. "That shouldn't be surprising, seeing that I have been all night attending a birth—and a death."

His mouth tightened and she thought she detected a hint of defensiveness. "I can only suppose, from your attitude, that you are trying to tell me India has had her child."

"Exactly—and died of it."

"That is unfortunate," he said after a moment.

Catherine realized that this was not the time to discuss it, not while she was tired and dispirited, her feelings overwrought with what she had just been through, but she could not suppress the words which rose to her lips.

"Unfortunate? Is that all you have to say? Is that all it means to you?"

Rafael tossed the dregs of his coffee over the railing, his knuckles white around the cup handle as he balanced it upon the narrow ledge of wrought iron for the servants to find. "I am not a hypocrite, Catherine. That woman tried to have us all killed. What would you have me do, go into black for her?"

"I would have you show a little civilized compassion instead of this cold mask of justice. Even in decadent Europe pregnant women are exempt from punishment for the sake of the innocent unborn. I find what you did brutal and unfeeling. I don't think I will ever be able to forget it!"

"Catherine, you are becoming hysterical. I think—"

"If hysteria brings out the truth, then let us have more of it. Are you quite certain there is none of the hypocrite in your makeup? Are you certain you aren't glad that India is dead? She was the daughter of the man who killed your father. Is your need for revenge satisfied finally? If not, how much farther will you have to go before you can

238

live with the fact that you were happy when your father was killed?"

Her words hung on the air while the blood slowly receded from Rafael's face. He made no attempt to defend himself, however. There was a deadly silence before he spoke. "You cannot erase the sins of the world, chérie."

"I quite thought it one of my duties as mistress of Alhambra to play the goddess of mercy to your people."

"Then extend a measure to the master—unless you regret me and what I have done so much that you have none—"

Did she? She could not be objective at this moment. His words were only a challenge to be answered. Her gaze level, she answered, "How can it be otherwise?"

Anger—or was it pain?—flared behind his eyes. As his hands closed into fists, Catherine took an involuntary step backward. His lashes came down to veil his expression. "In that case," he said slowly, "perhaps you will be interested in the missive which came for you last evening. It is on your secretary in the sitting room."

An aching tightness compressed Catherine's chest as she watched him walk away. Tears which had nothing to do with anger burned the backs of her eyes. She felt slightly sick, as if she had hurt herself.

The note lay on her secretary, a white square closed with blue wax impressed with the Fitzgerald seal. There could have been no doubt in Rafael's mind who the message was from. Did his cryptic utterance just now mean, then, that he had an idea of the purpose behind Marcus's visit to the area?

Brushing a hand across her eyes, Catherine broke the seal and bent her mind to deciphering the elegant scrawl of Marcus's handwriting.

My dear Catherine: it ran.

I have just learned with horror of the recent events at Alhambra. That you escaped was a miracle for which I thank God, but it leaves me apprehensive for you. The liveliest fears for your safety haunt my waking hours.

My greatest hope is that you will reconsider my

239

proposal and allow me to take you away from the scene of danger. Failing that, I most earnestly beg you will accept my escort, at least, to the house of your mother in New Orleans.

I place myself and my vehicle at your disposal. The hour from ten until eleven of the clock tomorrow morning will find me at the usual place of appointment. If I may be of service to you, you have only to appear.

I remain,
your most devoted and obedient
servant,
Marcus

Tomorrow from ten till eleven. That was this morning, since Rafael had said the missive was delivered the evening before.

Could her husband have guessed what it contained? It was unlikely. Unless he knew of the meetings between Marcus and herself? They were innocent enough, those meetings, but Rafael could hardly be expected to believe that.

She was so tired. She could not bear the thought of facing Rafael after the things she had said. The thought of her room, her narrow bed, in the house in New Orleans was like balm. There was peace there, and freedom from the fear of interruption. She would be able to collect her thoughts, obtain a dispassionate perspective on the events of the last few days. She needed that desperately. India's child, for all his small size, would live. She had found a suitable wet nurse; her responsibility there was ended. Rafael, by telling her of the note, appeared to have indicated his lack of concern. Why not return to New Orleans for a time? Why not accept Marcus's escort? Come to that, why not accept his proposal?

With a grim smile, she shook her head. She was not quite so lost to propriety as that. And she did not intend to journey alone with him down the river, either. Pauline must come. The silly young maid would be wild with excitement at the prospect. She might not constitute a very formidable chaperone, but she would be better than no one.

Her trunk was half filled, chemises, slippers, and bonnets scattered over the floor and bed, when a knock fell on the bedchamber door.

"Yes?"

"A lady to see you, Madame," Pauline called.

Before Catherine could answer the panel was pushed open and Fanny sailed in. "Forgive the informality, my dear. I couldn't wait about in the sitting room a minute longer. I longed to come as soon as I heard of your trouble here, but I had to stay to speed the departing guests left over from the ball—"

"That will be all, Pauline," Catherine said, signaling to the girl to close the door.

Fanny, after brushing Catherine's cheek with her own, took off her reticule and dropped it on the washstand.

"You must tell me exactly what took place the other night—" Seeing the trunk, she stopped in mid-sentence. "Leaving, Catherine? That doesn't sound like Rafael somehow."

"Rafael isn't going."

"He is sending you alone? Alhambra or the river, one is as risky as another, isn't it? I'm surprised you would consider it."

"Are you?" Catherine said quietly. The other girl's intrusive comments might not have troubled her at any other time, but she was in no frame of mind for them now.

"I wouldn't like to leave Giles alone to face this situation. Nor would he consider letting me go downriver without his protection."

Catherine's voice was gentle. "Your case is different, isn't it? At any rate, I do not go alone."

"You can hardly count the boatman. They are not to be trusted—"

"I would trust them as quickly as some gentlemen of my acquaintance," Catherine said dryly. "However, Marcus Fitzgerald had offered me his—protection."

The double-edged word was not lost upon Fanny. She

241

sat down suddenly upon the chaise lounge behind her. "Catherine," she whispered. "You can't."

"Can't I?" she asked without looking at Fanny.

"It's unthinkable. Never try to tell me you prefer him to Rafael."

"All right," Catherine agreed, unrepentant, "I won't."

A frown came between Fanny's earnest gray eyes. "Was it so bad, the night before last?"

"It was not pleasant." Catherine allowed herself a tight smile for this slur upon her courage.

"Giles tells me the ranks of the runaways were so decimated that it will be some time before they think of attacking again. Now the men know they are in the swamp, efforts will be made to find them and bring them in."

"Most reassuring, but I'm still going back to New Orleans."

"You are making a mistake, Catherine."

At that superior, accusing tone, all desire to relent and admit Fanny into her confidence left Catherine. She ignored the sound of a bedchamber door slamming across the court. "That may be," she replied, "but it's mine to make."

Time was growing short. She bent over her packing. Cocking her head trying to see Catherine's face, Fanny asked, "Does Rafael know you are going?"

Uneasiness moved over Catherine, but she made no attempt to prevaricate. "Is it likely I would tell him?"

"No," Fanny answered in an odd tone. "I'm sure it would be unwise."

Fanny did not stay long after that. Catherine saw her to the door and watched as she climbed into her brother's phaeton with her groom perched up behind her. The other girl sat a moment, as if collecting herself, then abruptly she gave her horses the signal to start. Catherine looked after her until the dust of her progress began to settle upon the leaves of the trees.

The trunk was heavier than Catherine had imagined. It was all she and the maid, Pauline, could do to carry it along the wood trail. They had to set it down often. The leather strap cut into their hands, and with their long skirts they could not see where they were stepping, so that tree roots and vines tripped them. Each time she stumbled Pauline giggled, an inane sound which made Catherine long to slap her.

Somewhere in the back of her fatigue-numbed brain there was a nagging question of the wisdom of her action. It served only to make her temper short without deterring her in the least. She could not, would not, bear her situation a moment longer.

Her eyes burned with the sting beneath the lids of salty, unshed tears. How long had it been since she had slept? Not the night before, nor the night before that. In the past forty-eight hours she had kept vigil over two deaths and a birth. And how long before that had it been since she had enjoyed a night of undisturbed repose? It seemed months, years, a lifetime.

The carriage which waited for her was a gleaming black picked out with silver and blue, the new Trepagnier landau, Catherine thought. How kind of them to offer it. Marcus leaned against its side idly whacking his booted leg with a bushy switch when he was not waving it at the flies that buzzed around him. He tossed it to the ground at once when he saw the pair struggling toward him, and moved to relieve them of their burden.

"Thank you," Catherine said breathlessly, trying to smile.

With a show of ease, Marcus carried the trunk to the back of the carriage and hoisted it up onto the baggage rack where the coachman, descending leisurely, began to tie it into place.

"Catherine," Marcus said, taking her hands, and carrying them to his lips. I can't tell you—"

"Nor can I, how much I appreciate your offer to see me to my mother's house," she said quickly, letting the clarity of her voice override his low tones. "I will be eternally grateful."

A shadow passed over his face and a mulish look appeared at the corners of his mouth. He flicked a glance of comprehension at the maidservant, but as he started to speak, the clearing ran with an aching outcry.

"Marcus!"

Solange, her hair straggling around her face, her wild eyes puffed and red from weeping, ran with jerky steps from the shadow of the trees. Catherine could only stare, too shocked by the ravaged look of the younger girl to move.

It was Marcus who filled Solange's vision as she moved closer. "You can't go away like this, you can't. I've lost Madame Ti, I can't lose you too. Not like this, to her. It was bad enough when I knew you were going away, but when I heard her say she was going with you, I thought I would die. Please Marcus—take me. Take me, I beg of you."

"Solange, my dear girl," he began awkwardly.

"I love you, Marcus," she cried beseechingly as she read the refusal stamped upon his face. "Don't do this to me."

For an answer, Marcus opened the carriage door and urged Catherine inside. "Hurry up, man," he shouted in a harrassed voice to the driver.

Solange, with tears starting in her eyes, staggered forward to clutch at his sleeve. "Marcus, listen to me—Please—"

But Marcus shook her off as he waited impatiently for Catherine to step over the tumbled boxes and portmanteaux of his baggage lying in the floor of the carriage.

"I love you, I love you! I will kill myself if you leave me behind for her. I will. I will kill myself!"

"Stupid, deranged, little idiot. Get away from me," Marcus grated. As Solange clung to his arm, Marcus thrust her away with a vicious shove that sent her sprawling to her knees among the decaying leaves.

Bending over as if in mortal agony, the girl gave a piercing scream that tore across the stillness around them before it ended in a hiccuping sob. Unnerved, Marcus swung on her as if he would silence her.

There was no need. She raised eyes swimming with anguished disbelief. "I want to die," she whispered through quivering lips. "I want to die."

With a sound of disgust Marcus turned away. As he set

his foot to the carriage door, his gaze fell upon his shaving box. It was the work of a moment to loosen the leather strap and draw out the honed razor. A flip of the wrist, and the straight-edge in its ivory holder landed in Solange's lap.

"There," he said in a tight voice. "By all means, relieve your misery."

A shout to the driver, and the carriage began to move. The maidservant, standing quietly to one side until now, started forward. A glare from Marcus halted her in her slipper tracks. He swung inside the carriage, landing heavily beside Catherine as he slammed the door behind him.

"No, wait," Catherine said, leaning to see around him out the window.

"Don't upset yourself," Marcus told her. "Solange is too much of a coward to harm anyone, least of all herself."

Catherine hardly heard him. Through the dust thrown up by the wheels she saw Pauline running after the carriage. Beyond her sat Solange with the razor flashing silver in her hand. Even as Catherine watched, the girl took a deep breath and began to slash at her left wrist.

"Stop!" Catherine shouted as she saw the blood running in a dark red stream down the girl's forearm. "Stop the coach!"

Marcus made no attempt to comply. He did not look back.

"She is killing herself, you fool," Catherine exclaimed, holding the hazel gaze of the man beside her. A moment passed, and still he did not move. In that small piece of time Catherine saw that he had no intention of trying to help Solange. He did not care what she did.

Whirling, she pounded with her fist on the roof of the landau. "Stop! At once!" she screamed, reaching for the door.

Suddenly her hand was wrenched away and she was thrown back against the seat. Marcus loomed above her, his lips flattened against his teeth. His arm swung back. A blow crashed against the side of her head. The scene before her eyes shattered into a thousand gray fragments, and she saw no more.

A fiery orange light striking on Catherine's eyelids brought her back to awareness. It was the last rays of the setting sun slanting through the carriage windows to probe the dusty interior. She turned her head to escape the glare, then gasped as agony thundered inside her brain. After a moment the throbbing died away again. She could be a little easier, though the bone rattling pace set by the coachmen precluded true relief.

Sunset. It had been only mid-morning when she had left the house with Pauline. Where had the hours gone? Where was Pauline? Left behind, that was it. Left behind—with Solange.

The bitter taste of horror filled her mouth. Slowly she closed her eyes. Solange. Poor Solange. Too late. The blood she had spilled upon the damp earth of the forest floor would be congealed and blackened by now. Too late. Whatever pale emotion of possessive desire Rafael had felt for her would have been burned away in the fire of his hate. Such terrible treachery could be neither forgotten nor forgiven. She had no right to expect it—none even to wish for it. Too late. She was committed, committed to an uncertain future. With or without her consent, she was bound to the man who watched her so avidly from the dimness of the forward seat.

She could never go back to Alhambra. She could never go back. Ever.

Part II

CHAPTER SIXTEEN

"I'm the slick-sided seventh son of a seventh son! I'm brother to the grizzly bear, cousin to the catamount and my pappy was a pole cat! I can out throw, out gouge, 'n out row any man on the mighty Missasip. I can cordelle further, drink deeper, climb higher, and fall lighter than any man Jack of ye here. I can swaller the Black River and spit out the Red. Daytime, I'm meaner 'n a rattlesnake with a sore tail; come night I use the moon for my crowin' perch! Cock-a-doodle-do! Can you hear me world? Cock-a-doodle-do!"

Catherine stopped in amaze in the doorway of the rough river tavern. A wavering yellow light spilled out into the night from lamps hanging in the gloom beneath the low, smoke-blackened log beams. At one end was a large fireplace with a frying pan and a baking pot hanging over the bed of coals, and a small feisty spit-dog wearily making his round, turning a side of beef suspended in the opening. The room reeked of sour ale and whiskey, of smoke and the liberal be-spattering of tobacco juice soaked into the sawdust on the floor. A collection of unkempt ruffians, river boatmen, from the width of the shoulders under their homespun shirts, sat hunched over their food and drink at the puncheon tables. With open mouths they gazed at the bearded giant standing astride the center table, yodeling at the top of his lungs.

Recoil was Catherine's first impulse, but Marcus was behind her urging her into the noisome room. She barely missed colliding with a scowling, black-browed young man with dark hair to his shoulders. He twisted to avoid her, wincing as his weight was thrown onto a lame foot. Ignoring her apology, he slipped past her out the door. She caught the impression of an intense backward look before she dismissed him from her mind.

"A fancy piece, if ever I saw one!" The coarse greeting came from a darkened corner.

"High in the in-step. Might be right interesting to take her down a peg."

"Take what down a peg?"

"Would ye say her 'ud strip to advantage?"

What was there about her to provoke such comment? There was nothing to which they could take exception in her round gown of gray cambric and bonnet of rose satin trimmed beneath the brim with gray ostrich tips. She and Marcus might indeed have been husband and wife; there was nothing to indicate otherwise. Was it her elaborate toilette? Such a dreary place was doubtless patronized by only the most empty-handed of travelers. Certainly no one of any pretense to family or social standing need stay in a hostelry of this sort. Accommodation and a sincere welcome was most always to be had at a private house. But she and Marcus had not dared to bespeak such hospitality, a fact which, just possibly, put her in the category those men had assigned her. A fancy piece. It was a galling idea; still, after this escapade she might do well to savor the ring of it.

With her head high, Catherine stalked through the wave of ribald laughter. She was conscious all the while of the bruising grip on her elbow, and the silent, unwavering stare of the boatman on the table as he followed her progress across the room.

A short, balding man wearing a greasy apron over his paunch turned from basting the beef.

"Yeh?" There was a fleeting familiarity in the innkeeper's manner which gave Catherine the impression that he knew Marcus and was none too impressed. The marked lack of respect shown to the dress sword hanging at Marcus's side was also revealing. It would, of course, be the height of folly to draw it against such odds, but in like circumstances she could not feature Rafael letting such a consideration weigh with him.

Clenching her teeth, Catherine banished such useless musings, directing her attention to their reluctant host.

"A room, you say?" he queried.

"Yes, and private, if you please. None of your four or five to the bed."

The innkeeper winked with exaggerated slyness. "I know just what you have in mind, Sir."

"Do you?" Marcus asked with an attempt at chill irony while extending a coin between two fingers.

The man spat on the silver and rubbed it upon his apron. "To be sure. To be sure," he said, a shade of doubt coloring his tone as he took in the quality of the stuff in Catherine's gown. His gaze brushed her face, then scurried to the dark corner of the room. "Yeh."

Marcus leaned forward, lowering his voice. "Also, you will forget—if you please—that you have seen us this night."

"Certain sure," the innkeeper replied with a dig of his elbow. "Nothing surer."

Marcus was not satisfied, it was plain, but he had said as much as he dared, too much, in Catherine's opinion. He stepped back, allowing the other man to light the way up a set of rickety stairs.

The upper floor of the tavern was scarcely more prepossessing than the lower. The puncheon rattled with every step, a brisk breeze blew down the dark and narrow hall, coming in at the chinks between the logs, and the portions dividing the space into cubicles were so ill-made that the candles of the occupants were clearly visible through the cracks.

Tittering female laughter alerted Catherine to some inkling of the true nature and use of these small private rooms. The rhythmic creaking of bed ropes, coupled with equally monotonous groaning made her sure of it.

"Marcus—" she began, coming to a halt as a shriek from a darkened room shook the cool night air.

"Not now, Catherine," he grated, thrusting her over the threshold of the chamber the innkeeper indicated. Turning, he ordered: "Supper, the best you have, and a bottle of claret."

"A feed I can give you," the man replied, "but I've not much call in my house for rich man's swill. You'll have to take your choice of corn whiskey, Monongahela rye, or ale."

Marcus's lip curled. "Bring water then, and the rye—and if you would care to do me one more service, you can tell me which of the cut-throats downstairs can be trusted to take us safely downriver."

"Why, that's hard to say. Anyone of them would, I expect, if the money passed merrily enough, and was available only in the City of Sin."

"There's none you would like to recommend?"

"As to that—the man exercising his lungs as you came in is as good as any, and better than most."

"His name?"

"That old moss-face? Why, that's Bull March, the best damn rough and tumble fighter on the river—why, he's done took three red turkey feathers off other bullies this week."

"I require his skill as a boatman, not a fighter."

"He's the best keelboat captain too. They do say he can take on three men, bite off their noses and ears and gouge out their eyes, and never take his hand off the rudder." He winked at Catherine. "And he's got quite an eye for the ladies, too."

Peering into the chamber, Catherine pretended not to notice.

A frostiness crept into Marcus's manner. "I believe I would prefer someone less—colorful—and less likely to delay us while he indulges in a brawl."

"There's always Parson Vail," the innkeeper said, pursing his lips, "a nip-cheese who never bought a round of drinks in his life, but they do say he's as careful with his boat as he is with his money."

"He sounds the very man I need. Another thing, you wouldn't know of anybody who might take a carriage off my hands?"

"Reasonable, is it?"

"Very—for a man with ready money," Marcus said, lowering his voice.

"Maybe, just maybe."

Catherine, moving away a discreet distance, was eyeing the fastening on the chamber door, a simple leather thong and peg latch, when Marcus took the candle from the portly innkeeper and pushed it into her hand.

"Business, chérie," he said, an audacious glint in his eyes. "Amuse yourself until I return."

Latching the door behind him was more of a gesture than a real precaution. She could not but be grateful for the tact of his withdrawal however.

A bare and battered Queen Anne table with a Sweet Gum stump taking the place of one of its curved legs stood in the corner. With a tired gesture, she placed the candle upon it and sank down upon the sagging bed. A rustling confirmed her guess at a corn-shuck mattress. The bed ropes stretched so far that she stood again at once, afraid she would have to pick herself up off the floor. Covering the mattress ticking was a sheet of such a grubby gray that she was afraid it would not bear too close an inspection. Bedbugs, she thought with a creeping sensation over her skin, were a definite possibility. The only other amenity, if it could be classed as such, was a cracked, brown stoneware chamber pot beneath the foot of the bed.

Slowly the position in which she found herself sank home. Mirthless laughter gathered in a hard knot inside her chest and she sank back upon the bed, clamping her hand over her mouth, rocking back and forth. The pressure made her eyes ache, streaming water. Her head pulsed with pain.

With a gulping gasp, she calmed herself, gently probing the soreness of a bruise on her cheekbone. She must not give way to her emotions; her position was her own fault. But, oh, how ironic it was that in escaping from one brutal man she had placed herself in the power of another.

At the thought of Marcus's precautions against Rafael's following them, laughter threatened to overcome her again. He could be easy. Nothing was less likely than that Rafael would come tearing after her, even without the death of his sister to occupy his thoughts. No, she had little fear of Rafael this night; it was Marcus who caused the crease between her eyes and set her mouth in a grim line.

With fingers that trembled visibly, she untied the ribbons of her bonnet and took it from her head. The crown was quite crushed on one side where she had hit her head on the door frame of the carriage when Marcus struck her. Had the blow been the action, perhaps, of a determined but exasperated man?

She must not make excuses for him. His conduct in leaving Solange had been callous in the extreme, if not totally criminal. Still, what did that presage for her own future? What, in short, were his intentions? She had no idea. An uneasy truce had reigned between Marcus and herself for the latter part of their journey. It had been dictated in part by her sick inability to hold a coherent idea in her aching head, but there had also been a most ignominious fear of forcing the issue. Her suspicions might be confirmed.

A wry smile flitted across her mouth as she tossed the bonnet aside. What could be plainer than installing her in this single room in what could best be described as an inn of questionable repute? Still, she could always hope that he intended to make his couch on a bench in the common room below. After all, he had left her alone. Tact, or expediency? Being a civilized man, it might be both, an explanation which she wished had not occurred to her.

To give way to useless speculation served no purpose. Her best course of action might be the cool assumption that Marcus intended to conduct himself as a gentleman. This decision taken, the next step was to tidy herself and await events.

All very commendable, of course, but when, a few minutes later, there came the shuffle of heavy footsteps in the corridor outside and an experimental shove on the door, she stood in the center of the room in quiet, frozen horror.

"Hey," a drunken voice said. "Hey, girlie, let me in."

Catherine was mute.

"I can see you, girlie. You ain't got nobody. Let me in."

It was true. Scanning the crude panel of the door, she could see the gleam of an eyeball through one of the wide cracks. Swinging around, Catherine swooped upon the candle and snuffed it out, then immediately wished she had not. To be a trapped quarry in the dark was infinitely worse than being spied upon.

"I like the dark, too, girlie. Com'n, open the door, lemme in."

"Go away," Catherine said in her coldest tone. "Go—away."

Her answer was a thud and the protesting squeak of leather hinges thrown against their nails scraping along her nerves.

"I'm a-comin' in," the man yelled in a voice of ludicrous drunken merriment, as if he suspected her of teasing him. The heavy thump of his shoulder on the door came again.

Catherine flinched, backing away to the far wall. There was no place else to go, no window, no other door. She would not stoop to crawling beneath the bed. The door could not hold long.

Another assault, and abruptly the latch gave, catapulting the man into the room in a stumbling lunge. He waved his arms wildly, trying to save himself, then crashed to the floor!

With a nimbleness she had not known she possessed, Catherine sidestepped his flailing arms and legs and whisked around the bed to the door. Halfway through it, she was halted by a shout.

"Here! What's going on?" It was the innkeeper, puffing

down the hall toward her with Marcus close behind, trying to get around his bulk in the narrow passage.

For a suspended second Catherine was undecided whether to be glad or sorry to see them. She felt an almost overwhelming impulse to run and keep on running. Then with a sharp, controlled gesture, she indicated her room and the bellowing issuing from it.

The innkeeper bustled inside. Setting down the lamp with which he had lighted his way, he collared the river boatman, hauled him to his feet and shoved him protesting outside the room.

"Chérie, are you all right?" Marcus asked, encircling her waist with his arm.

Her voice was brittle as she answered, "Of course."

"I am to blame for leaving you," he murmured disarmingly. "I would not have done so if it hadn't been imperative that I sell the carriage and try to arrange for a boat to take us downstream. I could never live with myself if harm had come to you."

Ignoring the last, Catherine asked faintly, "You sold the carriage? The Trepagnier's carriage?"

"Shhh," he cautioned. "It was necessary. How else was I to find the money for our passage? Don't worry. My dear cousin will have little trouble tracing it, and he is warm enough in the pocket so that redeeming it will do him no harm."

As Marcus spoke he nodded dismissingly at the landlord, busy contending with his belligerent customer, all the while gently urging her back into the room.

"But that—that is stealing," Catherine said when he closed the door behind them.

A pained expression crossed his face. "Not at all. Merely borrowing against its value. I will repay my cousin at the first opportunity."

"And when will that be?" she asked dryly.

Tilting his head on one side, he stared at her with a thoughtful expression on his handsome countenance for the length of time it took a party of noisy river boatmen to clomp down the hall and install themselves, with clinking bottles and glasses, and demands for the cards to be shuffled, in the room next door.

"Why," he said slowly, "I'm not sure when. It may be as soon as your Rafael makes us his first payment of the generous allowance we will ask of him."

Catherine stared at him, only preventing her mouth from falling open with great effort. Madness, she thought. Rafael would never agree. She was prevented from voicing this conviction only by the arrival of their supper, brought by a slattern of undetermined age with greasy, tangled hair and a complete lack of modesty about the flabby breasts escaping from her bodice.

They balanced their plates on the maimed Queen Anne table, eating standing up. Forcing herself to eat the tough meat and the potatoes shining with grease without showing her disgust was an exercise in self-control which stood her in good stead, for while they ate Marcus expounded further on his plan to extract money from Rafael.

"Your erstwhile husband, chérie, is hardly in need of your dowry, but it would be too much to expect him to turn it over to you intact—especially if he suspected that I might benefit from such a gesture. Still, we need not despair. Our Rafael is a fair man. Moreover, I suspect— on account of his quixotic marriage to you, chérie,—that he possesses one of those major inconveniences, a conscience. A charming note, full of contrition and pathos, should elict from him a stipend of a size to allow us to proceed to Paris. There, in comparative anonymity, we can set up housekeeping and enjoy ourselves without stint. We may not be able to move in the best of society, but I am assured that the *demi-monde* lead amusing lives. In fact, more amusing, filled with more pleasure and gaiety than the staid *haut-monde*."

Catherine put down her fork and pushed the tin plate away with distaste. "There is only one thing," she said slowly. "I have not said I will go with you."

"You are referring to your stupid insistence that I escort you to your mother? Don't be naive, Catherine. I never had the least intention of doing so, as you must have guessed by now. I made the suggestion merely as a sop to your ridiculous notions of the conventions. Haven't you realized how leaving your husband with me will be construed by the circle in which your mother moves—be you and I ever so innocent? They will crucify you, chérie. Your mother will have trouble enough putting a good face on the matter without you showing up on her doorstep."

"Women have left their husbands before," she pointed out in a subdued voice.

"But when they do so with another man they are hardly welcomed back into the bosom of the family, or society, with open arms."

"As you well know, I did not leave Rafael for you. There is a vast difference in leaving one's husband with another man and accepting a friend's escort home."

"Is there? The results will be the same when word reaches New Orleans that we were at least one night, unchaperoned, upon the road."

"We would not have been unchaperoned if you had not left my maid behind!"

"Remiss of me, but she did not, I think you will agree, represent a very formidable bulwark against gossiping tongues."

"She would have been adequate if we had arrived in New Orleans this evening," Catherine insisted.

"But then I would have had to think up some other way of compromising you."

Robbed momentarily of speech, Catherine could only stare at Marcus. He reached across and patted her hand. "Come, chérie. Be sensible. It is extremely uncomfortable for a woman without a man in this world—"

"And even more so for a man without money," she flashed.

An unpleasant look appeared in his eyes. Slowly his grip on her fingers grew tighter. "As you say," he agreed. "There is no need to cut up about it, however. We each can solve the problem of the other. You are an attractive woman, Catherine. I freely admit that you have a heady appeal to my senses. It will be far from a hardship to live with you."

256

"And all your protests of undying love?" she asked levelly.

"Were based on fact."

"You will not, I hope, be surprised if I fail to believe you." The ends of her fingers were beginning to tingle and burn but she refused to be cowed.

He sighed. "Must you make things difficult for yourself?"

She laughed, a cold mocking laugh. She felt resolve grow inside her. "Your scheme has a fatal flaw. I want nothing from Rafael. I refuse to write any such whining letter to him."

Following her ultimatum there was a silence so strained that she grew aware of the muttered comments and the perfectly audible slap of cards from the game in the next room. The hazel eyes of the man across from her narrowed. His features grew livid with a swift rising color. Deliberately he released his grip on her fingers, drew back his hand, and slapped her across the face.

The blow wrenched her head back and sent tears starting into her eyes. Before she could recover, he was around the table, his fingers clawing at the neck of her gown. The back of his hand smashed into the other side of her face. When she staggered he twisted the material in his hand, wrenching her back toward him.

Rage and pain exploding in her mind, Catherine brought her hands up, slashing with her nails at the arm that held her.

With an oath Marcus slammed her against the wall, losing his hold as the lace of her collar and jabot came away in his hand along with a strip of her bodice. A vicious jerk, and the material was ripped to her waist. Free for an instant, Catherine twisted away with a cry of desperation, evading the clutching fingers at the low neck of her chemise. The resistance seemed to madden him for he dug his fingers into her loosened hair to drag her back. Doubling his hand into a fist, he hit her in the chest again and again, striking for the tender globes of her breasts.

When her knees buckled under her, he stood over her, holding her head up by her hair. His breath rasping, he said. "I think you will write that letter now—chérie—unless you—want more of the same."

As a final humiliation he dropped to one knee and covered her mouth with his kisses, forcing her to accept his hot probing tongue while his hand roved over her bruised flesh.

A thumping on the door roused him. He raised his head slowly, and when he spoke his voice had thickened. "What is it?"

"It's about the boat you wanted!"

Reluctantly Marcus got to his feet, tugged his coat and cravat into place, and started toward the door.

A long shudder of purest revulsion shook Catherine. She found she could not stop trembling. Moving carefully against the sick throbbing of her head, she raised herself enough to reach the bed. She dropped down upon it and pulled the sheet up to cover her dishevelment.

It was dark in the hall but even so Catherine got a brief glance of the person at the door. Catherine thought she recognized the young man with the limp who had been leaving the inn as they entered.

If he saw her he gave no sign. He thrust a twist of paper into Marcus's hand and immediately moved away.

Turning the message toward the light of the innkeeper's lamp, Marcus opened it and skimmed its contents.

"It's from that fool of a captain, something wrong about the boat," he said without looking in Catherine's direction. "I will be back."

The last had sounded remarkably like a threat to Catherine's sensitive ears. She wasted no time in either relief or listening to the sound of his receding footsteps. She surveyed the ruin of her gown. Momentarily she was carried back to the night she had met Rafael. She shook the memory from her head. She had managed then, she would manage now.

Gathering up the tattered strips of material with shaking fingers, she tucked them into the low neck of her chemise. Her collar and jabot were located under the table. These were separate, hand-made lace pieces which were not attached directly to the gown with which they were worn. Their button loops were torn, but enough remained to fix them in place over the bare expanse of her bosom. Perhaps in the poor lighting downstairs the repairs might pass unnoticed.

She had not thought beyond leaving the inn—and Marcus—behind. The fear of the future could not be allowed to interfere with the necessity of the present.

Her hair was hopeless, but her bonnet would cover it. Where—

She was brought up short by a tap on the door. For a moment her heart beat high in her throat. She clasped her hands together to still them before moving forward with a rush. It was doubtful that Marcus would knock and wait for an answer on his return.

The young man who had delivered the note stood in the opening. "Compliments of the captain, Ma'am. He—he is of the opinion that you might be glad of an offer of transportation." He ducked his head in the direction of the next room. "We couldn't help overhearing—if you don't mind me saying so, Ma'am."

His voice was rough, his words hurried. There might even have been a tinge of embarrassment in his manner. His gaze flicked over her, then away. Still, there was something intrinsically trustworthy in the set of his shoulders and the way his hands hung still and straight while he waited.

"Your—your captain has a boat?"

He gave a stiff nod. "A keelboat. But you must come now—if you wish to come—"

"Yes—yes, but—you are certain this is not the boat the—the gentleman who is with me has hired?"

"Quite certain, Ma'am."

She knew an impulse to ask where the boat was going, but, after all, what did that matter, so long as it was away from this place. Moreover, all boats going downstream eventually arrived at New Orleans, did they not?

Turning back into the room, Catherine snatched up her bonnet. "Let us go—and quickly!"

Her guide led her in the opposite direction from the narrow stair to the common room. He stopped before a window shuttered with rough boards at the end of the hallway. With a glance around, he lifted the bar that held the shutters closed and pushed them outward.

Below was a dark emptiness, or so Catherine thought until the man swung a leg over the sill and stepped out of the window. He appeared to search for and find a foothold, then Catherine saw the top rungs of a crude ladder fastened against the wall of the house.

"When I'm halfway down, you follow. Don't forget to push the shutters closed behind you—and don't worry. If you fall, I'll catch you."

Before he had finished speaking his head had disappeared from sight. Gingerly, Catherine perched on the windowsill and swung her slippered feet over. Her skirts caught on the corner of one shutter and for a precarious moment she clung to the sill, her breath coming fast through her clenched teeth as she fought for balance. It had been many long years since she had climbed trees or slid down bannisters. Her skirts had been shorter then. How was she to turn— Yes, that was it. Mustn't forget the shutters. Splinters. The devil! *Sacré mille diables!*

Her head swam so that she had to lean against the ladder a long moment when her feet touched the ground. It was not the height, it was the merciless headache, the quivering weakness of her limbs, and the taste of illness at the back of her throat. But she could not stop now. With an effort that brought beads of perspiration to her upper lip, she released her hold on the ladder.

"This way," her guide said in his expressionless voice, and moved away through the night, leaving her to follow as best she might.

Their route to the boat was a circuitous one. Due to the darkness of an overcast night sky, progress was slow, and they halted often in the deep shadow of overhanging branches while the boatman searched the trail behind them and the path ahead. Preoccupied, he made no effort to help her, to give her support over fallen logs or disentangle her skirts from clinging sawbriars. She began to doubt that all his caution, and the long halts that went with it, was for the sake of safety alone. A tremor of doubt shook her, then she dismissed it. She was in no position to question.

She was extremely grateful to see the keelboat riding gently on the water. She did not even mind when her guide scooped her up and lurched through the shallow water covering a small sand-spit to hand her to other willing arms on board.

Such unconcern could not last indefinitely, of course. When she was set on her feet at the center of a group of river roughnecks every bit as sinister as those she had seen in the tavern, Catherine was assailed by a wave of panic. They crowded about her pushing, shoving, peering over each other's shoulders, mumbling among themselves. Then, as the man who had led her there appeared over the side of the gunwale, he was greeted by a hearty slap on the shoulder, and a "So you got her, did ye?"

"As ordered," he grunted, and pushed his way to her side. "You'll want to go below, Ma'am," he said. "It will be better that way."

Catherine could trust herself to do no more than nod.

"Bar the door," he instructed as he turned her toward the door of a cargo box much like the one on the keelboat she had traveled in upriver.

"When—when do we leave?" she asked.

"As soon as the captain has finished his business."

He waited while she entered the make-shift cabin then began to shut the door.

"Wait," Catherine said, placing her fingertips on the panel. "You have been most kind. I appreciate it more than I can say."

"It was the captain's idea, Ma'am. Save your gratitude for him. He will—enjoy it." With a stiff inclination of his head, he limped away.

CHAPTER SEVENTEEN

"What a strange man," Catherine thought as she tried to fit the bar in place across the door. It was a heavy length of wood with a diabolically human stubbornness. Whether it had warped in the river damp, or because she lacked the strength, it would not go into its brackets.

After weary minutes, she ceased struggling with it. The best she could manage was to prop it against the door at a sharp angle, with the foot of it against the head of a peg in the floor.

Straightening, she surveyed the cabin. An oil lamp swayed from the ceiling with the surge of the waves driven by a rising wind. Unlike the other cabin she had shared, this one had only one bed, a low, tightly made-up bunk fitted against one wall. There was a table with a ledge around it bolted to the opposite wall, and a heavy chair beside it. At the far end, built on either side of what appeared to be the base of a mast, were a pair of clothes cupboards. It was Spartan accommodation, but surprisingly clean and—shipshape. A shame to disturb the smoothness of the tucked sheet and blanket, the neatly aligned pillow, but she had to lie down. She had to.

When she opened her eyes once more she was being thrown violently from side to side. The lamp above her danced a dangerous jig, with a fuzzy nimbus about its wildly leaping flame. The wooden bar had slipped down. The cabin door swung back and forth on its hinges, while through the opening came the vivid flash of lightning. Watching the motion with a bemused stare, Catherine gradually became aware of voices shouting over the wind.

"Sure, and the captain won't think of putting out in this storm!"

"You don't know the captain! 'Sides, he'll be takin' no chances of losing his 'cargo'!"

"I disremember seeing him so het up about anything—or anybody!"

"Yeh, that blonde headed yahoo will be lucky to stay alive. The captain sure weren't too happy to hear him laying his fives to 'er!"

"Could think of better things to lay, hisself, I'll bet!"

The men, Catherine thought dazedly, were sheltering from the wind on the lea side of the cargo box. Their voices carried plainly. Too plainly. But she must not be upset. Men talked like that. It meant nothing. If she could just get up and shut the door again—

"Five to one we tie up downriver while the captain pays our ladyfriend a visit!"

"I don't know, this one has got guts. My money says he gets a flea in his ear and no scratch!"

"I'll take it. From what I seen, the captain ain't in no mood to take a no answer!"

Slowly Catherine raised a hand to her head. Dear God, what kind of a mess had she landed herself in? The captain. Could they be speaking of that huge braggart with the cast in his eye she had seen in the tavern's common room? That crowing animal of a man? What had the innkeeper said? He had "quite an eye for the ladies." Was his offer of sanctuary no more than a ruse to have her for himself then? She should have known, and yet she had been brought up to believe in the chivalrous gesture, the generous impulse of men toward a helpless female. A silent laugh shook her. How wrong, how pathetically wrong, such teachings were. In her experience the weakness of a woman, her lack of protection, was more likely to excite the instinct of the hunter.

But was she weak, was she helpless? She had been, in the past. Defenseless against superior strength, she had been tricked, dishonored, coerced, bullied, and beaten. No more. Deep in her breast there was a grim, slow rising revolt. She would commit murder before she submitted to another man's will.

It was difficult getting to her feet in the pitching boat,

but she managed it. Holding to the swaying door, she negotiated the small set of steps back up to deck level.

At the sight of her the boatmen stared, their bearded faces washed a pale gray in the lightning flashes. She herself must look like a bedraggled wraith, Catherine reflected as she gave them a short nod. She turned her back on them as quickly as possible, by no means sure that the tattered condition of her bodice was still a sufficient covering.

As she moved toward the dark stern of the boat she could just see the flicker of lamplight from the tavern, like the gleam of a firefly seen through the thrashing branches of the trees. It seemed a greater distance away than it had been before, then she saw that their mooring line had been played out, perhaps to keep them from being blown aground on the sand bar. The wind was surely strong enough for that. It tore at her gown, molding it to her body and snapping the hem like a flag. Loose tendrils of hair streamed across her face so that she kept pushing them back, trying unavailingly to secure them.

What could she do? Where could she go? She could not stay here and await the coming of the captain. Ashore was Marcus. Inland if she could make it that far, was Rafael. *Better the devil you know*—the old saying went; but no, she would not go back. She could not. Who might help her? Fanny? She had not been at all sympathetic. Giles. Yes, possibly Giles. Without vanity, she realized that he had a fondness for her.

First she had to reach him. How that was to be accomplished, she did not know, but an obvious first step was to get off the keelboat. And it must be done quickly, before the captain decided to come aboard, cutting off her escape.

"Ma'am! Hey, Ma'am!"

The hail came from among the boatmen. Turning, Catherine saw the lame man coming toward her, and at that moment she heard the first drops of rain begin to fall on the roof of the cargo box, felt them upon her face. Her hands tightened on the gunwale. He was coming to lead her back below. Whatever she was going to do must be done now.

She had swum the distance from the boat to the river-bank before, but never in a storm, never fully dressed, and not in many years. Still, what did it matter? If she did not make it—then one death would do as well as another.

She hesitated for only a moment before stepping up onto the gunwale and diving in.

The shock of the cold water took her breath. The river dragged her down, clutching her in its dank embrace. She struggled frantically against it, until, with a final kick, her head broke water. Dimly she could hear an outcry but it faded away before she could pinpoint its direction. All around her was darkness. She had lost the beacon light of the tavern. She could feel herself being carried swiftly along on the river's current. Odd, she did not remember it being so strong, but then her swimming lessons had been given in a different stretch of the river in the doldrums of late summer.

A wave slapped her in the face. She breathed water, choked, and coughed, blinking desperately to clear her vision. Was that the bank, that black, uneven line?

She struck out, arm over arm, straining, throwing muscle and courage into each stroke. Her goal came no nearer. For a moment's rest, she tread water then tried again.

She was alone in an immensity of water, a bit of human flotsam rolling sluggishly in the flow of water. The muscles of her arms and back ached, and her eyes burned. Her legs seemed like heavy weights, her brain a useless thing pulsating with pain.

She would not give up. Another effort must be made, and another.

At some time in that nightmare of chill and wet and the thunder in her ears of water and weather and her own blood, she saw a sawyer coming toward her. In the ghostly flicker of lightning its roots had the look of hands upheld in horror. It scraped along her side, igniting a streak of fire down her cold flesh. She felt herself entangled, caught fast by her hair and dragging skirts among the

265

He paused with one foot on the plank which bridged the space between the flatboat and the sandy river bank. "Nobody is ever terribly busy on the river," he said, a slow smile lighting his gray-brown eyes.

"Someone has to catch all those catfish I've been eating."

He moved his shoulders in a shrug. "I'm sure it's not what you are used to. I'd get you something else, if I could."

"I wasn't complaining," Catherine said hastily, "only pointing out the fact that you have been put to a deal of trouble and work on my behalf."

"It was no trouble."

The words were said so simply that Catherine could not doubt them. In an effort to bring back his smile, she said, "Besides, I have had ample variety in my meals. Haven't I dined on white perch and blue gills, crawfish and frog legs, as well as catfish? And, I am quite willing to credit my return to health to the curative properties of cornbread, dandelion greens, and pot-likker."

"Don't let Grannie hear you say that, or we'll have them for supper again tonight."

"You mean we're having something different?"

"Roast corn, the first of the season," he informed her as he removed a fern planted in an old wooden bucket from a crude, handmade stool, and took its place beside her.

"Sounds lovely. I must be getting well, all I think about is food."

"You need it," he said with unselfconscious candor. "But, tell the truth, don't you miss the good things to eat you could be having if you were—where you belong?"

"I don't belong anywhere," Catherine protested, avoiding the question.

It was a moment before Jonathan spoke, then his voice was quiet, and there was a subdued expression on his strong, square-jawed face. "That can't be so."

"Can't it?"

"Not for someone like you," he said, and waited.

It might have been unfair but Catherine had told Aunt Em and her grandson little of herself other than her

270

name. Sometimes she wondered how much Aunt Em knew, how much she might have given away in her delirium. She did not ask. She did not want to know. She only wanted to forget—or perhaps more accurately—wanted not to remember. While she had been ill the events through which she had passed had seemed far away, the happenings of a dream, though she knew the pain and degredation of them hovered near, like the patient buzzards about that buzzard tree. To think of them was hurtful, to speak of them was more than she could bear. Her throat closed upon a hard knot at the idea.

Reaching out, Jonathan placed his hand over hers.

"Never mind," he said softly. "There's time enough and more for that. Time enough for everything."

It seemed that he was right. The days came and went with a majestic slowness. They were empty days, and yet full ones, containing a myriad of small tasks, fishing from a comfortable chair on the deck of the flatboat, mending with her tiny convent-taught stitches, stirring a pudding sweetened with molasses over the fire in the cabin fireplace.

As her health improved, she went farther afield, searching for poke salad and blackberries with Aunt Em while Jonathan scouted for deer or squirrels to vary their menu. Gradually she fell into the way of moving quietly through the woods, and under Aunt Em's patient tutelage, identifying herbs and other edible roots and berries. The old woman taught her, too, the best method of skinning and cleaning game, and while she was about it, a few other tricks with a knife. Catherine learned to love the smell of tasselling corn and to watch closely the color of the silks as a way of telling where the ears were ready to pull—and which were to be left to dry for Jonathan's special corn whiskey.

The process which turned corn into hard liquor was as fascinating as any recipe, Catherine found, hearing it while she helped wash and scald the demi-johns and small barrels used to hold the results. Privately she thought Aunt Em's blackberry and muscadine wine sounded more potable, though she had to admit they were hardly likely to appeal to river boatmen, the major market for the liquor.

Much of what was distilled could be disposed of to passing boats, but Jonathan did not like to encourage all and sundry to stop at the flatboat. Moreover, a better price could be had at Natchez. Suppose greedy barkeepers added the juice of crushed juniper berries or burnt sugar and sold it for gin and brandy; was that his fault, Jonathan asked?

If both the corn crop and whiskey run were good, and if a tow from a passing keelboat could be arranged, it was usual for Aunt Em and Jonathan to make the trip upriver in the fall of the year. The money made went toward winter provisions, often spelling the difference between a comfortable season in front of the fire or an uncomfortable one beating the cold, wet woods for game.

Clothes for Catherine proved no problem. Away from all who knew her, she cared little how she looked. One of Aunt Em's butternut gowns with the sleeves rolled above the elbow did well enough. With her hair in plaits and her feet in mocassins she had the look of an elusive, golden-haired Indian. Her skin, without a bonnet or veil, took on an apricot tint, a sun-kissed dewiness. The hollows left her cheeks, the color bloomed across them. And if the shadow of remembered anguish never quite left her eyes, it was overlaid by a quiet peace. Life on the river was not unlike the unconsciousness of her illness. It asked nothing of her, expected nothing. With such a bargain, she was, for the moment, content.

CHAPTER EIGHTEEN

"Catherine, you're a darling. I do love you."

The quick pressure of Jonathan's lips upon her forehead that accompanied the words was nothing; it was the caressing note in his voice that disturbed her so that she stared after him over the load of dried corn in her arms. They had been stripping the bleached and rustling stalks in the field and she had volunteered to carry the last armful while he brought the final high-piled bushel basket.

It was hot and dusty. They had started before the sun was up, but now it rode high in the blue-hot metal sky. Perspiration covered them with an itchy film, making the old, faded gown Catherine wore cling to her and darkening Jonathan's hair to auburn.

Going first along the trail, he glanced back to see how she was faring. Catherine smiled without quite meeting his eyes. She had not noticed before quite how attractive he was. She had looked on him as something in the nature of a cousin, and she had thought he saw her in much the same light, with the addition of a protective instinct because of her illness. His preference for her company had not gone unnoticed, but she had put it down to his need for companionship nearer his own age. Now she was not so sure.

It would not do for Jonathan to become too fond of her. An uncomplicated friendship was one thing; she well knew she had no more than that to offer any man.

Is that precisely true?

The question whispered through her mind. Frowning, she looked up from the trail and saw Aunt Em at the rail of the flatboat watching them, her eyes shaded by her hand against the glare of the sun.

"The land and the river are great healers," the old woman said later that evening. She finished rubbing the hard kernels from an ear of corn with her gnarled old hands, and tossed the cob in a bushel basket sitting beside her. Before she took up another, she reached for her snuff and took a liberal dip.

Catherine waited. She had learned that Aunt Em seldom said anything for effect; there was usually a sound reason. Carefully, she raked the kernels in her lap into a pile, noting with a rueful grin the cornstarch clinging to the roughness of her hands with their practical, if childish, short nails. She did not mind particularly, but she wondered what her mother would say.

In fact, she wondered what her mother had to say about the entire situation, if she knew of it. Would Rafael have communicated with her by now? He must have. No doubt her mother thought she had run away with Marcus, just as Rafael—

No, she would not think of it. Not yet.

"You are looking well again," Aunt Em went on at last. "Better, I think, than you have looked in quite a spell."

Catherine smiled her acknowledgment. "With due respect to the land and the river, I believe I owe it to you and Jonathan. I can't begin to thank you enough."

"Now, no more of that, if you please. It's been a pleasure. But, I hope you won't mind if I speak my piece?"

"You know I won't—and I promise not to interrupt again."

A smile flitted over the wrinkled, brown face, but the softening was momentary. "You've helped out, you've pitched in and done your part, I have to give you that. Still it's as plain as the nose on your face you just ain't used to working like this. I don't know where you came from, Cathie, but you don't belong, not to our kind of people, not to the river. From the things that surprise you, the things you take for granted, I'd say you was used to servants and a big house. From the ring on your finger and the look in your eyes, I guess there was a man involved. For a woman with looks like yours that's safe enough. There's always a man, ain't there? You needn't answer. I know. But—there's this. I don't have any idea why you left the life you was used to—and I'm not asking—but if you figure on going back, I think now's the time."

Catherine had nothing to gain by pretending to misunderstand her. "For Jonathan's sake?"

"For Jonathan. I'd hate to see him hurt any worse than need be."

"So would I," Catherine agreed, staring out over the river. "But suppose I have nowhere else to go."

"Not likely—even so, it's no reason to stay on when your heart's not in it."

Stung by the truth of that statement, Catherine said, "You seem very certain that my heart is not—involved."

The old woman sighed. "I wish I wasn't, I truly wish I wasn't."

They shelled corn in a silence broken only by the thud of corncobs filling the basket. They would be used in the fireplace in place of kindling. Aunt Em wasted nothing. Not corncobs. Not words. Not sympathy.

"You and Jonathan should be ready to make the trip to Natchez before long," Catherine said at last.

"That's right." Aunt Em leaned forward to spit with considerable expertise over the rail.

"I have a friend who lives there. She might be persuaded to give me bed and board until I have contacted my mother."

"You're the best judge, I expect," Aunt Em said, frowning at her hands with an air of faint regret, "though I can't believe a mother would not welcome her child back, regardless—"

"Regardless covers a great deal," Catherine said quietly. Aunt Em looked at her silently, then turned her attention back to the corn. Catherine closed her eyes. She knew Aunt Em was right. The uncomplicated, undemanding days had been balm while she was contending with the weakness and lassitude following on her illness. How soon before they palled, now that she was fit again? The simple life required an uncomplicated mind. Considering some of the longings she had felt surfacing within herself of late, Catherine was far from certain that hers was suited.

Jonathan, however, could not be expected to understand. The sun was setting, touching the ripples of the river current with pink fire, when he found her leaning against one of the posts of the rear porch of the cabin.

"Grannie tells me you are to leave us at Natchez," he said, resting his hand above her head.

Catherine turned to smile, the soft light shining on her face with a pearl-like gleam.

"Yes," she answered. "Will you wish me well?"

"If that is what you want."

There was such a baffled look on his face that Catherine swung away quickly, the breath catching in her throat. "That is what I want."

"Why?" he asked in a low voice. "Tell me why."

"Because I must."

"That's not an answer."

"Isn't it?"

"You know it's not. You—you were like something out of a dream. I thought it was meant for me to find you, to save you."

"I am grateful for that. I haven't thanked you enough—"

"It's not thanks I want!"

It was a moment before Catherine could trust herself to answer. "I—I'm sorry."

"Sorry?" he asked, disconcerted. "For what?"

"I'm sorry I can't give you what you want, sorry I don't have it to give."

It was such a long time before he spoke that she thought he had accepted defeat. Instead he had only shifted ground in his search for a reason. "If it's because of the way we live, Grannie and I, we can change. I know you're used to something different."

"No, no. That isn't it, Jonathan, believe me, it isn't. But—you must have known I was married."

"I—saw the ring." He paused. "But only a dead man would let you get away from him."

Catherine felt the pressure of tears at that simple declaration. It reminded her fleetingly of another time, another man. *"I'll never let you go,"* Rafael had whispered then. Words, empty words.

"My husband is very much alive," she said stiffly. "We—we had a misunderstanding."

"You're sure that's all."

Catherine nodded. Why trouble him with her story. It would be kinder in the end if she did not give him any reason for hope.

"You can't care all that much for him then."

"Why do you say that?" she asked, swinging sharply around.

"If you did you would be more anxious to get back to him."

That was so indisputably true that she could not argue with it. She took refuge in a return to her silent contemplation of the river.

"Well?"

"Forgive me, Jonathan," she said in gentle but distant tones, "but I don't have to explain myself to you."

"You don't think you owe me that much?"

"Has it come to that, then? A debt?"

Abruptly he pushed away from the wall. "No. Forget I said it. Forget everything."

"Jonathan—don't be angry," she said as he flung away from her. "I don't belong here, I promise you I don't."

"Don't you think I know," he muttered, his voice a harsh rasp in his throat. "Don't you think I've always known."

His step on the bridging plank was so violent it was jarred loose, falling into the water. He strode along the track, his shoulders hunched and his hands thrust deep in his pockets. Catherine watched until he was lost to sight among the deepening shadows of the woods.

Natchez-Under-The-Hill was a dirty sprawl of canvas shelters, lean-to shacks, and unpainted buildings cut through by muddy, rutted streets. A stench rose above it, mingling with the sounds of fiddle, mouth harp, and squeezebox, laughter and screams, blows and brawling. Above the squalor, on the pure, wind-swept heights of Natchez-On-The-Bluff, the homes of the gentry, built of bricks and mortar and columns and arches, sat upon their elevations like the villas of the patricians around ancient Rome. Citizens of the town often promenaded of an evening past the ruins of old Fort Panmure, along the bluff edge and through the Village Green. From that vantage point they could catch glimpses of the plebians disporting themselves below in the manner for which they were fa-

277

mous up and down the river—with murder, maiming, theft, and rapine.

Jonathan, having a healthy respect for the nature of the town, asked to be put ashore on a low stretch of land downriver from Natchez. Once he found his buyer, he would bring his merchandise into town, but until then he was reluctant to expose the inhabitants of Natchez-Under-The-Hill to the temptation of a skiff weighted down with corn whiskey.

The trip up had been uneventful. Aunt Em had been selective in the keelboat she would allow to tow their skiff. She knew many of the crafts that plied up and down regularly by sight, and refused to trust more than a handful. The boat she chose was run by a man and his wife, a huge woman named Annie who not only dressed like a man but had muscles like one. Several of the crew members were sons of the couple, and a daughter served as cook. They were big, boisterous people with a hearty sense of humor as well as hearty appetites. Company on their journey seemed as important to them as the victuals Grannie had packed and brought along as partial payment of their fare. For the rest, Jonathan worked their way with his shoulder to a push pole. By the time they reached their disembarking point, Catherine was of the opinion that the daughter of the keelboat family, at least, would have been glad to let them ride up and down forever without fare for the sake of Jonathan's presence. And Aunt Em's grandson, though not strongly attracted, did not appear immune to the soothing, if unsubtle, flattery of having his plate piled high with choice food.

As she helped Aunt Em pile brush over the lean-to shelter of their encampment, Catherine had to smile. What would her mother say if she could see her? Or Rafael, for that matter? Rafael, who had not wanted her to tire herself supervising the stitching of servant's clothes. He had had his reasons for wanting her fresh and rested—

Shivering a little, she dragged her thoughts back from completing that mental sojourn. She must be depraved to find such memories increasingly pleasurable. How her husband would laugh to know her most potent image of him contained not the cruelty for which she had condemned him, but tenderness.

Jonathan, leaving his musket with them, went off on foot to arrange the sale of the liquor. Catherine could have gone with him, but she preferred to stay behind with Aunt Em. She was under no illusions that she would be any added protection. In fact, the old woman would probably have to defend her as well as the liquor if they were discovered, but she did not care to see her left alone.

They stopped work at noon for a cup of coffee and a piece of venison wrapped in a cold biscuit. Afterward Aunt Em brought out her snuff box and took a soothing dip.

"Nasty habit," she commented. "I don't know why I do it."

"It doesn't hurt anybody," Catherine observed mildly, staring at the grounds in the bottom of her coffee cup.

"Doesn't help anybody, either," the old woman snapped, then sighed. "There, I didn't mean to be so tetchy. My conscience paining me, I don't doubt. You've been on my mind, child. I'm worried about you."

Catherine glanced up. "There's no need."

"Yes, there is. I'm a selfish old woman, looking after my own, forgetting everything else. I was hard on you, and I know it."

"Nonsense."

"No. It's Jonathan, you see. He's young, easy hurt. Right now I don't think his heart was too set on you, but in time it would be. And I could see you was like the sweet pears at the top of the tree—out of his reach."

"Oh no—that is—"

"You see? You can't deny it. Even if it wasn't so I wouldn't like it. You're too different, you and him. I've already seen with my son how that ends. I couldn't bear it to happen again. Two people always pretending nothing matters but love. I could see tragedy waiting down that road. Again. I couldn't let that happen. But I wish I knew what was going to happen to you. I wish I could be easy in my mind."

"Don't fret," Catherine tried to console her. "I'll be fine. My mother is too much the Creole, too steeped in the importance of family, to turn me away."

"A woman like you should have a home of her own, children."

A curious hurting made itself felt in the region of Catherine's heart. "That's in God's hands, isn't it?"

"Then I'll pray he knows what he's about—" Aunt Em said with a flash of dry humor. "I mean it. I'll remember you in my prayers."

More touched than she liked to admit, Catherine could only whisper, "Thank you."

A short while later Jonathan returned with his buyer, a rotund man wearing the apron of a tavern keeper. They rode at the head of a mule caravan. So it came about that Catherine entered Natchez perched upon the back of a mule with her legs hanging sidesaddle over a cask of corn whiskey.

Catherine wore the gown she had been wearing when she was rescued from the river. Much the worse for its dunking despite careful washing and pressing, with the bodice held together by a thousand tiny stitches, it still had more style than anything Aunt Em possessed. Her slippers had been lost, probably far out to sea. She had no choice but to wear moccasins, and she had no bonnet, no gloves, no calling cards. It would not be surprising if her friend from convent days failed to recognize her, much less admit her.

One of Catherine's fears had not materialized. There had been no trouble in finding Helene. Jonathan had insisted on making inquiries for her, but it seemed everyone knew the planter and jewel merchant, Mr. Wesley Martin, and most could point out his house.

It had to be conceded that Helene had done well for herself. The house, set down at the end of a curving drive which led through grounds and gardens covering several acres, was a Georgian mansion of red brick with a double gallery supported by four massive white columns. A white railing connected the columns and provided bannisters on either side of the steps leading up to the fan-lighted door.

There was a distinction about the place, and, if it seemed austere to Catherine's eyes, that could be put down to her unfamiliarity with that style of architecture.

Catherine had expected it to be hard to say good-by to Jonathan. He made it easy for her. Lifting her down, he took her hand.

"I'll wait until I see you go inside," he said. "Aunt Em and I will be camped for a few days while we round up winter supplies. If there's anything you don't like you can always come back to us." He gave her a quick smile, leaned to press a kiss to her brow, his lips lingering a moment longer than necessary, then he dropped her hand and moved away leading the mules. He did not look back.

Clenching her teeth together to subdue an absurd desire to cry, Catherine climbed the steps. The doorknocker was, in her opinion, a trifle ostentatious, a large snarling lion's head in bronze but it was possible to take a firm grip upon it. To relieve her feelings she beat a vicious tattoo upon the panel, then stepped back in confusion as it immediately opened beneath her hand.

Like most of his breed, the butler before her was capable of taking in her attire from head to toe in the flicker of an eyelid. What he saw left him unmoved. His voice was distinctly cool as he asked, "Yes?"

Catherine drew herself up. In a soft, yet distant tone she replied, "Inform your mistress, if you please, that Madame Rafael Navarro née Mayfield is calling."

It was easy to see that the man's first inclination was to shut the door in her face. Failing that, he was certain she should be left standing on the doorstep while he inquired Madame Martin's pleasure. Doubt stayed his hand. The voice, the manner were correct, but the appearance— It was, perhaps, the inflection of the French tongue so like that of his mistress which swayed him. He made Catherine a stiff bow and indicated that she should enter. As a compromise, however, he left her to sit or stand as she pleased in the entrance hall while he mounted the stairs to the floor above.

Frowning, Catherine stared about her, up and down the hall and through the open door of a salon. The house was

281

beautifully clean, delightfully new, but nothing she saw reminded her of the sweet, rather quiet, girl she had known at convent. The furnishings, English in design, stood about in stiff self-consciousness, paired with angular tables upon which were laid passable, but totally lifeless, ornaments. The colors at the windows, dark greens and reds, were garish to her eyes, used as she was to the pastels beloved of the French cabinetmakers. The paintings on the walls were correctly dull children, animals, and landscapes, no shepherds and nymphs, Venuses, bathers, or classic angels *au naturel*. It was as if every piece of furniture, every ornament and painting, had been bought at the same time and place with no concession to personal likes or dislikes. Such a tasteless display of wealth left her with an odd feeling in the pit of her stomach. It did not speak well for her friend's intelligence or perception.

A high scream jerked her attention toward the stairs. At the top a woman stood poised with her plump hands clapped to her mouth, her small brown eyes wide and staring. As Catherine turned she let out another little cry and started down the stairs in a flutter of lace and pink muslin.

"Catherine! It is you. It is! And they said you were dead!"

CHAPTER NINETEEN

She might have guessed. She might have, that is, if she had allowed herself to recall the events of those few terrible days. She had not. The violent events had been a raw, unfading bruise at the back of her mind. She had not been able to bear touching upon it.

Helene Martin had no such inhibitions.

"My poor, dear Catherine, I can't tell you how relieved—how thrilled I am to see you. Come and sit down.

I must hear at once what has occurred to bring you to me."

Pausing only to issue orders for refreshment to be served to them, she ushered Catherine into the stiff newness of the salon and shut the door.

"You will think it odd for me to appear on your doorstep," Catherine began with a wry smile as she seated herself upon the unwelcoming surface of a horsehair sofa.

"Perhaps," her friend agreed on a trill of laughter, "but I can't begin to tell you how gratified I am that you have. I am right, aren't I, in thinking that you have not contacted your mother—or—or anyone else?"

The vapid look in the eyes of the woman before her was something Catherine had not remembered. Always round of face and figure Helene had also grown rounder, with the beginnings of a double chin and an overabundance of bosom. The glittering rings she wore drew attention to the stubbiness of her fingers and the dimpled backs of her hands.

"That is right," Catherine said gravely.

"Then I am among the first to know you are still alive. How marvelous! I will astonish all those in New Orleans—my mother and my sisters—who think I am out of everything here in Natchez. But tell me how this comes about. Marcus Fitzgerald arrived in New Orleans some weeks ago with a most affecting tale of tragic romance, according to my correspondents. He said that you and he—were in flight from your husband when you were set upon by a gang of cut-throat river boatmen. He was beaten and left for dead while you—you threw yourself into the river to escape that most dire fate which can overtake a woman. I think it the most romantic thing imaginable, if there is any truth in it. Is there?"

Unconsciously Catherine stiffened. Her voice was cool as she answered, "Very little, I'm afraid."

"Oh—" Helen's face fell in a ludicrous disappointment. The avid look faded from her rather small eyes to be replaced by a furtive skepticism as she flicked a glance over Catherine's odd ensemble.

Bitter humor curved Catherine's mouth and she had to

force her words through the constriction in her throat. "Oh, it's true enough, in part. I was leaving my husband. Marcus, however, was merely escorting me to New Orleans. Whether he was injured by the river boatmen, I don't know, but I did choose the river to escape them when his—protection proved—inadequate."

"I don't understand. Marcus hinted it was your husband who caused the attack on you. Are you denying it?"

"Certainly. Rafael would not descend to such a petty revenge—even if he had felt strongly enough to instigate such a thing, or had had the time to arrange it."

"You are defending your husband against your—against Marcus."

"Yes," Catherine said with emphasis, "since there was never any special relationship between us to incline me to favor him."

"Then—why would he hint at it?" the other woman asked, leaning forward, her hands clasped in her lap and her fat, glossy sausage curls bobbing above each ear.

"I can only suppose," Catherine said slowly, "that he wished to wound Rafael. He might have saved himself the trouble."

Helene Martin opened her rosebud shaped mouth, then something in Catherine's face caused her to close it again. A look of crafty patience in her eyes, she said, "Maybe later, between us, we can thrash out his reasons. For now I will expire if you do not tell me how you cheated the river, and where you have been and what you have been doing."

Catherine complied. It was easier than speaking of Rafael. Helene's interest was natural, and she could hardly expect to enlist her aid without explanation. Yet resentment coursed along her nerves all the same. That Marcus had tried to exonerate himself came as no surprise. Still, why had he attempted to implicate Rafael? And why must everyone be so quick to believe him?

"So you see," Catherine finished, choking out the final words, "I have come to you for the simple reason that I know no one else in Natchez and I am uncertain of my welcome in my mother's house."

Those halting words should have been enough to bring forth instant words of welcome, but Helene did not speak. She sat frowning with her bottom lip caught between her teeth.

Something like determination hardened within Catherine's breast, and she continued. "I thought, Helene, since we had been such dear friends not so long ago, and you have often enjoyed the hospitality of my home, you might allow me to trespass upon yours. It will only be for a few days, until I can send a message to my mother and receive her answer."

Helene moved uncomfortably, avoiding Catherine's eyes. "Oh, Catherine, I wish I could tell you at once that I would be in transports to have you stay—you must know it is so. But you realize that a married woman must consult her husband. Wesley is a wonderful man, but—strait-laced, if you take my meaning. I am not certain he would wish me to—to—"

"To extend the hospitality of his house to a woman of such notoriety? I do take your meaning, you see, Helene. And I will bid you good-day."

"No, no, don't go," Helene cried, rising hastily to put her hands on Catherine's wrist as she got to her feet. "You must give me time to approach Wesley. He—he is unpredictable—that is, I may be able to persuade him."

"Don't disturb yourself, it's no great matter," Catherine replied with more pride than truth. "I shall manage."

"I didn't mean to offend you—"

"Certainly not," Catherine said. Her smile was brilliant as she turned away.

At that moment the salon door swung open and a short, stout man strode into the room.

"W-Wesley," Helene said with a definite start, her grip tightening on Catherine's arm.

"Helene, my dear, they told me you had company."

"Yes. Yes, this is Catherine Mayfield Navarro, a friend, an old friend, from New Orleans."

"I've heard my wife speak of you, Madame Navarro," Helene's husband acknowledged the introduction, moving

285

forward to take Catherine's hand in a tight, damp-fingered grip and bend his head over it.

Wesley Martin was considerably older than Helene, perhaps in his early forties, a husky man with thick shoulders and a slight tendency to overweight. His fine yellow hair was receding in front, exposing a bulging forehead covered with brown sun splotches. He was dressed in dark clothes of a somber exactitude that told Catherine at once who had chosen the furnishings for the house. The expression in his pale blue eyes, seen from between a fringe of yellow lashes, left her in no doubt that he had recognized her name and neatly categorized her in his mind.

"Catherine and I were just having tea. If you will join us in our second cup, I will ring for a fresh pot," Helene offered.

"None for me," Catherine said firmly. "I really must be going."

"Nonsense. We haven't visited at all. Stay only a little longer, and I'm sure Wesley will drive you back in to town."

When Catherine glanced involuntarily at Helene's husband she found his gaze upon her, resting in speculation in the region of her breasts. Becoming aware of her attention, he glanced up then away. "Most happy to be of service," he muttered.

Helene, reaching for the bell, cried, "That's settled then. Do sit back down, Catherine. Wesley, you wouldn't believe the adventure Catherine has had. I vow I am pea-green with envy. Let me tell you—"

"Forgive me, my dear, but I would prefer to hear it from Catherine, if you don't mind."

A frown creased the skin between Helene's brows for a fluttering second. She said only, "Yes, perhaps that would be best."

Catherine did not agree, still her version would, no doubt, be shorter and less embarrassing than Helene's.

When she had finished he sat frowning, a hand on each knee. "Then, as I understand it, you are without friends, other than my wife, in Natchez."

"That's right, Wesley," Helene answered before

Catherine could form a non-committal reply, "but she is so proud she prefers the discomforts of a tavern to our poor house."

Wesley Martin frowned, his eyes narrowed. "A tavern is no place for an unattended female, especially a female of quality, as I'm sure you must have guessed after your experience, Catherine—I may call you Catherine?"

With an inclination of her head, Catherine gave her permission. "I am sure I can depend on the company of my rescuers."

"That old woman and her grandson?"

"They protected me for quite a few weeks," Catherine said, her voice stiff with distaste for this argument in support of the false position in which Helene had placed her.

"You were not in Natchez," Helene's husband said unanswerably. "You expect a prompt reply to this letter to your mother?"

"I'm not certain. Naturally I hope for one."

"I suspected as much. It stands to reason that if you were positive you would be welcome at home there would be no necessity for writing in advance of your coming."

"Very true," Catherine said, the only possible answer to such devastating logic.

"Yes. I suspect also that your funds are limited. It only stands to reason. Therefore a protracted stay in a tavern would not only be unwise, but needlessly expensive."

A small break in the conversation was provided by the arrival at last of fresh tea. Immediately after it had been poured, Wesley Martin resumed. "I believe under the circumstances that both Helene and I would feel that we had failed you if we did not insist that you stay with us. Your presence would be a joy to Helene, and I assure you no man ever regrets the addition of an attractive face at his table."

Helene sent her husband a look of brimming gratitude before turning to Catherine. "There," she said in suppressed triumph. "Now will you consent to stay?"

Agreeing was a formality. Catherine found herself caught in the vortex of a storm of furious energy. She was whisked above stairs and installed in a guest chamber of formidable proportions and excruciating formality. When asked if there was anything she would like, Catherine had asked unhesitatingly for a bath. This was brought to her, along with a supply of soap, scented with attar of roses, and soft linen towels.

Helene's maid, when she first entered the room at her mistress's command, was sullen of face. She was hardly reassured by the sight of the small but wickedly sharp knife in its porcupine quill decorated leather sheath which Catherine removed from her thigh before stepping into the tub. After a moment, however, she was absorbed by the challenge Catherine presented. Before long the maid was up to her elbows in the task of shampooing Catherine's long honey-gold hair, and applying goose grease and buttermilk, witch hazel and vinegar, to restore her complexion to its customary paleness.

In the midst of the operation Helene arrived with a half dozen gowns over her arm. She thrust them upon Catherine with a lavish gesture. "There should be something among these which you can wear, chérie, with only the tiniest bit of taking in here and there. They are like new, I promise. I've done no more than try them on. Wesley buys all my clothes in New Orleans. These he refuses to let me wear. He says they make me look too old, a thing he abhors. I don't see it myself, but I try to please him. It was his suggestion that I bring them along. He thought you would shrink, just now, from going out to the local modiste."

Catherine accepted the gowns with a real and proper gratitude since they were beautifully simple, with a becoming sophistication. They were in dark colors, gray, plum, and mulberry, but that suited her mood. A pair of slippers were included in the bounty. They were a bit large but Helene quickly offered the services of one of their servants who had a cobbler's skill. And if Catherine, as a result of all this thoughtfulness, began to suspect that it did not suit Wesley Martin to have his wife seen in public with their house guest, she kept the idea to herself.

Dinner was a quiet meal. Immediately afterward Catherine retired to her room to write her note to her mother. Its composition was time consuming since she had to keep in mind the misapprehensions her mother was under concerning her disappearance. She might have waited a day or two in the hope of improving on the wording, but there was a boat going downstream the next day and Helene's husband had promised to have her missive on it. It was always possible that her mother might prefer to continue wearing mourning rather than face the resurrection of a daughter involved in scandal. However, Catherine could not let her learn of it from any one else.

The days which followed stretched long and empty. Helene's company soon ceased to be a novelty. Her conversation consisted of gossip—all prefaced by her husband's views—and the discussion of patterns for needlework, her sole diversion. In between these two subjects she made constant probing reference to Catherine's ordeal in an effort to prise further details out of her. Her frustration at Catherine's refusal to be drawn left her pettish.

Catherine also discovered in her friend a tendency to jealousy. Wesley Martin could not address a half dozen words to Catherine without Helene joining the conversation, her eyes sparkling with determined cheerfulness. In order to placate her hostess Catherine found herself withdrawing into herself, spending much time alone in her room on the plea of weakness and infirmity she did not feel. She also encouraged Helene to keep up her usual activities, her morning calls and sewing circle, as if she herself were not there. At first Helene refused, but as Catherine persisted in withholding her confidence, she grew miffed enough to ignore the obligations of hospitality. On an afternoon when Catherine had been particularly adept at evading her questions, Helene placed a bonnet trimmed under the brim with coquettish tufts of tulle upon her head and sailed out of the house in a huff.

Watching her go from her bedroom window, Catherine wondered if Helene would regale the ladies of her circle with the tale of her visitor. It was more than likely, and it would be in keeping if she also embellished the tale. Nothing too slanderous, of course; a questioning inflection of the voice, the lift of an eyebrow, would be enough to rip what little character she still possessed to shreds.

It was with surprise then that she heard a carriage returning a short time later. It was unlikely that the early homecoming had anything to do with her; it almost certainly was too early for a message to have been dispatched from New Orleans, but Catherine could not prevent herself from going out onto the stair landing.

Wesley Martin stood in the lower hall. As he caught sight of Catherine at the head of the stairs his colorless lips moved in a smile. He stuffed a letter he had been reading into his pocket, and handed the waiting butler his hat and cane.

"They tell me Helene has gone out and left you alone," he called.

Descending the stairs, Catherine replied, "Yes, I insisted."

"It's such a pretty day, our first cool spell this fall. I thought you two might enjoy a drive in the phaeton. I have a couple of calls to make in the city and then we could have a turn in the country."

"How thoughtful." Catherine meant what she said. She had been inside longer than she liked. An outing would have been an antidote to the anxiety of waiting.

"If I know my wife, it will be hours before she can drag herself away from her friends. By then it will be too late. Could I, by any chance, prevail upon your good nature, Catherine, and persuade you to bear me company?"

Such a drive would be unexceptional in normal circumstances. Catherine knew a moment's doubt concerning the present ones, but if staid Wesley Martin was inclined to brave propriety, why should she worry? She had little to lose.

"I would enjoy it immensely, if you think I might borrow a bonnet from Helene."

A pair of matched bays drew the phaeton at a smart clip along the road into town. In that bustling center they stopped before a squat brick building that carried a sign advertising a jeweler over the door. Catherine was not surprised when Wesley Martin got down and went inside, remembering that one of his many interests was in gem stones. Their next halt was outside the ornamental fence surrounding a small planter's style house with overhanging galleries and neat green jalousies. Explaining that he was thinking of purchasing it as an investment, Wesley asked Catherine for her opinion on a number of improvements. Then at last they headed south, out along the bluff road, winding up through forests of huge oaks hung with grape and muscadine vines. Wesley took the whip from the socket and touched up the team, laughing deep in his throat as he saw the exhilaration shining in Catherine's amber-gold eyes.

It was such a pleasure to be free of the confining walls of the house and of Helene's prying, to feel the vigor of the wind in her face and the joy of life pulsing in her veins. She wanted to drive on forever—or she would if the man beside her was—

The sudden swinging of the vehicle made her glance sharply at Wesley. The reins were still firmly in his hands, but he was taking a turn. The rutted and rocky track lead finally to the edge of the bluff overlooking the river.

"The view from here is said to be outstanding," Helene's husband said, setting the brakes and wrapping the reins around the whip handle before he climbed down.

Catherine, following his example, was forced to agree. Beneath the bluff ran the wide Mississippi, a muddy brown nearer in, but blue as midnight where it spread to the distance-hazed Louisiana shore. The height brought a majestic sweep of gray-blue sky and green tree-line into view, more than Catherine, hedged in all her life by a tree crowded, flat land, had seen in her life. Unconsciously she moved closer to the overlook.

A quick step brought Wesley close to her side. He placed a hand under her elbow. "Take care, the edge may crumble," he cautioned, then pointed across the river. "Look over there, straight across. That's my land, my plantation."

"Really?"

"Ten thousand acres."

Catherine had to smile at the swelling pride in his voice. "Do you plan to build there?"

"No, no. It's too low, swampy, fine for crops, but its unhealthy. Most planters with Louisiana delta land live on this side of the river, in Natchez. But I don't want to get started on that. You see, Catherine, I brought you up here for a special reason. I—have something to tell you."

The grave, faintly portentous tone of his voice was no longer amusing. It sent a shiver of apprehension along Catherine's nerves. "Yes? What is it?"

"When I sent your message to New Orleans I gave strict instructions that a man was to wait for an answer and return here with all speed. He—he returned this morning."

When Wesley did not go on Catherine forced a smile. "He was certainly swift."

"Yes, but—I don't know how to tell you." Wesley looked down. "There was no answer."

"No answer?" Catherine repeated.

Wesley Martin looked back at her. "Your note-of-hand was taken in to your mother. He waited outside for hours, then when he asked at the door, he was told there would be no reply."

Catherine turned her face away, grateful for the concealing frame of Helene's bonnet. She had thought she was ready for whatever her mother decided, but she had been wrong. She knew at that moment that she had never expected her mother to reject her plea for help.

Helene's husband moved nearer, his hand moving up her arm to cup her shoulder.

"I know what a blow this must be," he said. "You will be wondering what you will do now. I think—I believe—I have a solution."

Catherine wanted nothing so much as to be alone. Still, she raised her head, bringing herself to some semblance of attention.

"I am a wealthy man. I can give you almost anything you want, clothes, the house we looked at in town, jewels—I have a bracelet I chose for you just now—"

"And in return?" Catherine interrupted, her revulsion masked by sheer disbelief.

"In return you will give me what I have wanted since I walked into my house and saw you standing in my parlor in your rags—yourself!"

The grip on her shoulder tightened abruptly. Wesley swung her around, dragging her up against the roundness of his paunch. She was engulfed in the smell of stale sweat, made too aware of the hard urgency of his desire for her. With a sharp effort she pushed him away to arm's length.

"No!" she cried. "I will not be your kept woman!"

"What else can you do?" he asked, his smile unpleasant.

"I'll walk the streets first," Catherine declared, throwing her head back.

Anger suffused his face. He jerked her back, his fingers digging into the flesh of her upper arms. "Will you?" he muttered. "Will you? Then you can start with me."

His hot, thick lips slid wetly across Catherine's face searching for her mouth. She felt herself drawn nearer, his arms closing tightly around her, subduing her struggles. That too familiar feeling of helpless outrage screamed within her head. And then she remembered Aunt Em in a wood clearing, her voice quiet, dispassionate, pointing out a woman's strengths, a man's weaknesses.

Shifting her weight, Catherine brought her knee up in Wesley's groin. The instant his hold loosened, she twisted away, trying to get out of reach.

But he was not done. With a bull's roar he lunged, his closing fingers clutching at Catherine's limbs. Together they fell, rolling in the grass. His weight was heavy upon her. She felt his hand pushing up beneath her skirts. Curling her hand into a fist, she beat at his unprotected face, but he did not seem to feel it. He heaved himself higher and his forearm came down across her throat.

She could not breathe. The air was cool on her flesh as her skirts rode higher. His knee was between her legs, forcing them apart.

And then her groping fingers touched the handle of the

knife fastened to her thigh. She gripped it convulsively, tugging it free. Her back arched, and in that unsettled instant she slashed upward, driving the blade through cloth and skin and muscle to the bone. She ended the thrust as she had been taught, with a quick, tearing twist of the wrist.

Wesley gave a hoarse howl and rolled off her, thrashing on the ground like a wounded animal. Catherine scrambled to her feet and backed away with the knife in her hand. Her eyes were narrowed, wary.

After a moment the man was still, then slowly he rolled to his side and, grunting, pushed himself to one knee. His left hand he held pressed to his hip with the leg at a stiff, awkward angle behind him.

"You bitch," he said unsteadily. "You God-damned, whoring bitch. You've crippled me."

There was a long rip in his breeches leg ending at the fleshy part of his hip. Blood had already darkened the material and soaked through to drip upon the green grass with a red gleam.

"I could have killed you," Catherine told him in a voice so hard she scarcely recognized it for her own.

He crawled bit by painful bit to the wheel of the phaeton where he pulled himself up. While Catherine watched unmoving, he clambered into the vehicle and fell across the seat.

Perspiration beaded his upper lip. His panting breath was loud as he settled himself and reached for the reins. Slowly he swung his head toward her while he moistened his lips with his tongue.

"If I—ever see you—again—" he said with difficulty, "you will wish you had—killed me."

Jerking brutally on the reins, Wesley Martin backed the phaeton, then swung it in a wide circle, heading back the way he had come.

For a moment Catherine had been afraid he intended to run her down and had moved prudently near a tall tree. When the sound of the carriage wheels had faded she leaned against the trunk, feeling the rough bark under her forehead as she fought to control the trembling weakness of her knees. Her hold on her knife loosened so that it slipped in her hand. Hearing it fall, she dropped to the ground, wiping the blade clean on the grass with a gesture of repugnance.

Quiet, broken only by the distant calls of birds and the sibilant whisper of the great river, descended around her. Staring at the knife in her hand, Catherine got slowly to her feet. Aunt Em. Jonathan. She could always go back to them. In truth, she was already halfway there. Further along the bluff trail, another two or three miles, was the low shelf where they were camped. If she hurried she could be with them before sundown.

Her sense of time was correct. The last red rays of the setting sun were tipping the waves with rust when she reached the riverside encampment. The brush shelter was there, and the circle of the campfire. But the embers within the circle were cold and black, the shelter empty. No light shone. No skiff bobbed against the bank. They were gone.

Out in the fast current of the Mississippi nothing moved except the endlessly flowing water. She was alone.

CHAPTER TWENTY

The bright light of morning was the time for courage and for hope, the time for a sure and easy step. But in the dark cover of the night lay safety. That it also covered the scream of a panther and the panic-stricken scurryings of smaller animals had to be endured. Somehow. Man was the greater danger.

It was not hard to keep moving. The difficulty was to keep from running, from descending to headlong, ignominious flight from the noises of the night and the fears that stalked her as surely as did the hunting cat of her imagination. Soft, deadly tread. Sinister shadow in the light of a rising moon. Low, vibrating growl, felt rather than heard.

Rafael. Rafe. They had called him the Black Panther, the most dangerous of men, and yet she had known security in his arms. Security and something more, a perilous joy, a trembling ecstasy.

She had tried to deny it. Out of pride and mistrust and a cankering resentment for the manner in which she had been forced to marry him, she had built a barrier against him in her own mind. How wrong she had been. The fault for what happened between them on the night of the quadroon's masquerade was not his alone. Moreover, her experiences with Marcus and Wesley Martin had shown her how different, how terribly different, that night could have been. In her struggles with Rafe she had known instinctively that he would not cause her injury or inflict intolerable pain, that he felt no pleasure in the hurt he reluctantly gave her. Then, and later, after they were married, the strength of his desire had always been tempered by tenderness and a sensitivity to her pleasure.

These gentle emotions had been absent in his judgment of India, but could she blame him for that? Men and women were whipped, branded, pilloried, and hanged every day for lesser crimes. His decision had been as humane as he dared make it. India's death had not been intended. Her condition as a slave and the daughter of a slave had caused her crime. The responsibility for that belonged not to Rafael alone, but to all men.

Time and distance had cooled Catherine's impotent anger. The same forces had softened the memories of agony and stifling, bloody death. In addition she had grappled with her own degree of blame in the death of Solange. It was inevitable that there must be some readjustment in her attitude, some acceptance.

What, she wondered, would have happened if she and Rafael had met in the ordinary way? Would he have felt an attraction to her? Would he have acted upon it? Or would he, perhaps, have dismissed her as a boring ingénue?

A gust of soft laughter caught her unaware so that her

shadow weaved a little over the ruts of the sandy wagon road she followed. If they ever met again her husband would have no cause for complaint on that score. If they ever met again—

The distant whine of a squeeze-box told her she was nearing Natchez. Alerted by the sound, she was able to step off the road, wading through dew-wet heads of pungent black-eyed susans, into the trees in time to avoid a trio of horsemen. They rode past at a tired clop-clop, their carrying voices raised at intervals in desultory conversation.

A few steps further on she came out on a clearing where the road divided. To her right lay the dark and huddled buildings of Natchez with here and there the moon catching a ghostly gleam from a whitewashed wall, a turned post, or a pane of glass. Directly below was the raucous noise and life of Natchez-Under-The-Hill where open doors dumped yellow lamplight upon the refuse strewn streets and the moon shone on warm bisque and alabaster nakedness posed at the red-curtained windows.

What was she to do? Where could she go?

It was unlikely that Helene would help, even if Catherine could bring herself to ask. Doubtless Wesley had concocted some plausible story to account for her absence, one that would reflect little to her credit. A jealous wife could not be blamed for believing nearly anything of a woman already involved in scandal.

A cynical smile twisted the pure curves of her mouth. Slowly she turned from the righteously sleeping houses toward the brutal uproar of Natchez-Under-The-Hill. Were the harridan Fates that tenacious? Was it to be the demi-monde after all? For long moments she faced the prospect unflinching, the darkness in her eyes reflecting the lights below, and then the echoing trill of her silvery laughter rose to salute the face of the benign and careless moon.

"Madame, you have a visitor."

Catherine looked up at the innkeeper's wife in her apron where the woman stood in the doorway. There was a thinly veiled insolence in the clipped, northern voice, but she felt she could hardly object to it. It was because of the vanity of this woman with her thin-lipped face that she had been given a bed, board, and the use of a private parlor. Helene's bonnet had been the sacrifice. Catherine had passed it over without a qualm.

Studying the toes of Helene's slippers, Catherine had been wondering if they were worth another day, or if she might be better advised to offer her services as a chambermaid for her keep. Shelter was the first necessity. That secured, she could turn her faculties to securing a more permanent position. Perhaps as a governess? How this was to be achieved without connections, or without revealing her circumstances, she did not know.

Now she turned her head to stare at the woman. "A visitor?"

In answer the innkeeper's pasty-faced wife stepped aside, revealing a well-dressed woman who advanced with a cordial smile. It was not Helene, Catherine's first thought, and she was not a lady, though Catherine was uncertain how she arrived at that conclusion. The snug cut of the green spencer over her apply green muslin, the vibrant color of her shawl of tartan plaid? Or was the hair curling about her face beneath her bonnet brim a trifle coarse, a bit too golden-red?

"Good afternoon. Permit me to introduce myself. I am Mrs. Harrelson." The woman removed her gloves as with a nod she dismissed the innkeeper's wife.

Rising, Catherine responded automatically, "How do you do?"

"I can see you have no idea who I am or why I have come," Mrs. Harrelson continued. "Perhaps if I could sit down we could discuss both?"

"Certainly."

Catherine could not bring herself to anything warmer. Mrs. Harrelson seemed pleasant enough, with shrewd brown eyes and classic features only a little blurred by aging, but something inside Catherine resisted being managed. With a brief gesture, she indicated one of the parlor's two smoke-blackened settles and perched herself upon the other.

Mrs. Harrelson dropped her gloves and beaded reticule into her lap, placed the silk fringes of her shawl, and looked up. "You are a most attractive young woman."

After a moment Catherine answered, "Thank you."

"It would not be an exaggeration to say your face could be your fortune."

Catherine's eyes narrowed slightly. "You are too kind," she parried.

"Ah, I think you begin to understand me, do you not? In my profession intelligence is not always a virtue, but we will overlook that. Let me be frank. I have it from your genial host here at the Byrd In Bush that you are— shall we say—without resources."

"Not quite," Catherine objected.

"Not?"

"I have been well educated. The position as a governess to young girls would not, I believe, be beyond me."

Mrs. Harrelson smiled. "Forgive me," she said in her calm, melodious voice. "I think you have not considered this very well. If I may say so, a wife would be a fool to take you into her house. As a female in a vulnerable position, unprotected by rank or family, you would be an irresistable temptation to most males, whether they be grandfathers, fathers, husbands, or sons. In addition, I fear, Catherine Navarro, that your past has been too well discussed in Natchez to make you acceptable. It is a small town, you see, and it isn't every day we have a woman return from the dead, especially after flying from her husband. It was amusing also to see one of our most staid but grasping business men accept you under his roof. More than one wager was laid on the outcome. I, having some experience of the gentleman, made a pretty profit."

"And what was the outcome?" Catherine asked stiffly.

"Oh, his wife is saying that you took flight on learning that your husband was coming to Natchez. Our Mr. Martin is telling his cronies that you left in a huff after offering yourself to him at such a high price he refused to pay, while the servants say you and their master went for a drive and only he returned. A most curious case."

"But amusing," Catherine said.

"Did that sound cruel? I am sorry, but that is the way of the world. You do see that what you suggest is impossible?"

The words were unpalatable but Catherine found she did not doubt what the woman said. She nodded slowly.

"Good. Now I, on the other hand, am in need of a housekeeper. Oh, you needn't frown so, you have not misjudged me. I do indeed keep a house of assignation, to put it as delicately as possible. And I will not lie to you. I hope you will decide to forgo the menial task of housekeeping for something less—strenuous. I do not force young women into my house or my way of life, however. Your body is your own. My contribution is only to provide the means to exploit it, and your great advantage, if you wish."

"My—great advantage?"

"Haven't you realized? You are the keeper of the remedy for man's most intense and persistent pain. The fear that women will withhold it is the reason why men have kept us subjugated for hundreds of years. They make the mistake, you see, of believing women as ruthless as they are. In retaliation women have kept from them the knowledge that their need is as great as any man's— explaining why all women have the impulse to lie back and let themselves be taken."

"The reasoning, surely, of a woman who sells herself?"

"You have claws—if a limited vocabulary—do you not, Catherine Navarro? That is good. Spineless women left to their own devices seldom prosper. But tell me, does my proposition interest you? I will tell you freely that you are unlikely to get a better one."

"I had thought of asking if they are in need of a chambermaid here—"

"And find yourself pinned to a mattress by the first amorous traveler who catches you changing his bedclothes? There is no profit in that. Before long innkeeper Byrd himself would be sending you to the unused rooms with an offer of wine and—accommodation. That is, when he tired of following you into the pantry and cellar himself. And I have it from Mrs. Byrd that she will not have you on the premises another night if she can be rid of you without Mr. Byrd's knowledge."

"You seem to have disposed of the alternatives," Catherine said hardily. There were still her betrothal and alliance rings. They would allow her to live for a time, but she was loath to part with them. She had grown used to their weight upon her fingers.

Mrs. Harrelson smiled. "I have tried."

"Let me be as honest as you then. If something should happen to change my circumstances, if I should see a way to make my way without you, I will leave you at once."

"That is fair enough," Mrs. Harrelson agreed, getting to her feet. Reticule in hand, she walked to the door and pulled it open. The innkeeper's wife stepped back, smiled, let it fade, then smiled again.

Mrs. Harrelson surveyed her with grim amusement while she dug in her beaded purse. "I take it you are concerned for your money? There it is, as agreed, and I do trust you will think of me again the next time."

The other woman swallowed, dropped her head, and scuttled off, fingers busily tucking her money into her bodice.

"Do you mean," Catherine asked wrathfully, "you paid that woman for bringing me to your notice?"

"I thought it best for you to know; call it, if you like, the beginning of your re-education. I have little use for anyone with illusions." Mrs. Harrelson gave her a look of wry speculation. "Don't make the mistake of thinking you have seen the depths, however. I fear you have much to learn."

Walking out of the inn with nothing but the clothes she stood up in, journeying a hundred feet further down the street, and down the hill, to the house of Mrs. Harrelson, Catherine was tempted to tell the woman how wrong she was. It was just as well she decided against it. As the heat of late August gave way gracefully to the long golden glide of Indian Summer, she discovered a chastening amount of truth in the statement.

The difference between a bordello, where women waited patiently to be visited by men, and a house of assignation where men of means could rent a place of privacy to bring more respectable women, the wives of their friends, was made plain to her. She learned also that despite Mrs. Harrelson's pretensions, the lady kept both in the same narrow-fronted, two-storied frame structure, with a separate entrance for each. She discovered at first hand the amount of laundry necessary to keep such an establishment in operation, and the part the laundry played in the bordello's social order. For the bordello contained a caste system based on the number of sheets strung on the clothesline in back. By that criterion the inhabitants of Mrs. Harrelson's house were the aristrocracy of Natchez-Under-The-Hill, and behaved accordingly.

Very few of the women were truly beautiful, though all were attractive in their various ways. The majority were vain, lazy, self-centered, and grasping. A few were intelligent, though that type, according to Betsy Harrelson, usually hated men. A few were romantic, mindlessly thrilled by the idea of men, given to toting up the number they had entertained. A still smaller proportion actually enjoyed their work. Most could spin a pathetic tale to account for being where they were; one or two such tales were even true.

Catherine, moving about the house in her black dress, voluminous apron and dainty batiste mobcap, cleaning, dusting, directing the bevy of black maids, was looked on with suspicion by the girls. They resented her failure to become one of them. They resented her implied censure, her preferred status, her dignity, and her fresh looks as yet untarnished by spite, cynicism, or the aching tiredness of being pawed. In the manner peculiar to women they divined her basic inexperience and delighted in recounting for her all the more bizarre and demeaning things that had been required of them. Several tried to make a personal servant of her, demanding that she iron their ribbons, mend their gowns, dress their hair and a dozen other small but wearying tasks. They were incensed by the ease with which she avoided giving them a direct negative but always managed to slip away and send one of the maids to do their bidding.

Catherine never went near the front parlor where the girls waited in silk and boredom for men. In the early days she shunned the halls also, retreating at night to the attic room allotted to her, far beyond the noise of music and the shrieks of gaiety and pain. But after a time, Betsy Harrelson, when she was otherwise engaged, appointed her the task of patrolling the hallways to make certain no girl was permanently injured by a client, and to summon one of the husky men hired to deal with such situations if she discovered it. It was a tactical error. The bestial sounds of loveless love coming muffled through the doors brought the taste of revulsion to Catherine's mouth. Only the realization that she was unlikely to find a different sort of life elsewhere kept her from leaving, running out into the darkness.

And then came the busy night when Catherine heard a tortured squealing. She had hammered on the door from which it came without response. Her actions brought a bouncer. Standing aside, she watched the door broken down. She was the first inside, first to see the girl, young and nubile, with her pretty mouth gagged wide open and her arms bound with her own silk stockings. The girl's eyes had been glazed with pain and the inability to understand, and the sheets of her bed soaked with the blood oozing from the stripes that criss-crossed her body. A man stood naked over her, his face twisted with frustration, a stock whip in his hand.

The incident had set the seal on Catherine's resolve to be gone, one way or another.

The first consideration of leaving, however, was money, something she saw little of. There had been no mention of payment for the duties she performed. Mrs. Harrelson seemed to feel that bed and board should be sufficient recompense for the time being, with the vague intimation of reward when Catherine had had enough of drudgery and prudery. Confronted with the problem, her benefactress was sympathetic, but Mrs. Harrelson's only answer was a mild suggestion that Catherine might take an occasional paying customer.

Catherine recognized both the guile and the miserliness in the proposal. Neither came as a surprise. The guile had been present from the beginning; the penny-pinching had made itself apparent gradually. Nothing upset Betsy Harrelson like the loss of money, nothing brought quicker reprisal followed by dismissal than someone withholding from her what she considered her due. Her greed was obsessive. It was the one thing about which, for all her pretense to good breeding, she failed to be either tolerant or objective.

Now she cocked her brass-gold head on one side, her sherry brown gaze on the stiff lines of Catherine's face. "The idea is still distasteful to you, isn't it, after all this time. If I didn't know better I would say you had never known a man—or no more than one. After the second what does it matter—two men or twenty?"

The color mounted to Catherine's face then drained away again. She said nothing.

"Oh, I see—I am a fool. But you know, I feel I have been more than a little misled."

"Not intentionally," Catherine said at last.

"Perhaps not, but you must have realized that when a woman runs away with a man one assumes there is an urgent physical need which is satisfied at the first opportunity. If not, one might as well stay with the husband."

"There is more than one reason for leaving."

"I was speaking of the usual case," Mrs. Harrelson said with an irritable wave of her hand.

"Mine was not usual then."

A frown flitted across the woman's face, then she allowed a low chuckle to escape her smooth, rounded throat. "Next you will be saying you were in love with your husband. Come, now, Catherine. Let's be sensible. I have had several inquiries for you already. There is something about you—even seen from a distance—which stirs men's minds—and thus their—emotions. You could so easily be rich, if you would but try."

304

Catherine, clasping her hands together, stared unseeing toward the window where dry brown leaves drifted past from the trees that hid the back entrance to the house. There had been frost that morning but there was no fire in Mrs. Harrelson's opulent bedchamber. Wood, bought from the woodhauler, was not cheap. Men lingered longer in warm rooms, therefore fires were not lit in the bedchambers until dark.

At last Catherine said, "I have no need for riches."

"Don't you," she answered, acid lacing the words. "You will think differently as you grow older, I assure you. But the choice is yours. In your place I would waste no time in making it."

The woman picked up a mirror and a pot of pomade, a sign that Catherine was dismissed. She hesitated momentarily, curious to know the names of the men who had asked after her. That might be to show too great an interest, however. It was unlikely they wanted her for any other than the obvious purpose. Quietly, she let herself out into the hall.

Had there been a threat in that controlled voice, a hint that Mrs. Harrelson's careful patience was growing short? It was not often that her will was flouted. What would her reaction be if Catherine continued to resist her persuasion?

These matters troubled the surface of Catherine's mind, but they were trivialities, scattered thoughts which did not distract her from a deeper agitation. It was impossible. She could not be such a fool. Love? Pride refused to countenance the idea. Love was an adolescent fancy, the affliction of poets and madmen. Love was reserved for God, the church, and one's children; it was not an embarrassment to be inflicted upon a husband, never upon a husband.

Why, then, would she stand with a pillow in her arms, inhaling the scent of fresh linens, caught by a memory of Rafael drawing her gently across warm sheets to lie within the curve of his body? Why would she lie at night staring into the dark with slow curling fingers in a trance of sleepless yearning? Give it a name, call it passion, awakened desire. But explain, then, this deep welling desola-

305

tion of salt-savored pain, like a fount of unshed tears?

It was a peculiar brand of honor that had held her inviolate for love of a man who would never touch her again. Perhaps the cure would be to—embrace the vocation Mrs. Harrelson was pressing upon her, to seek in other men's arms some assuagement for this anguish.

A week of indecision passed unnoticed. On the evening of the seventh day Catherine was moving down the hall leading from the rented rooms to the section given over to meaner and more shameless pleasure when she heard a hail behind her. She turned, then her head came up and her nostrils flared. She would have swung around again but that might have looked as if she were running.

"Catherine, it *is* you," Wesley Martin said, a look of sadistic glee lighting his pale eyes. "I thought there could not be two women in Natchez to fit your description."

"I am flattered," Catherine said with obvious untruth. "Since you have satisfied your curiosity, you must excuse me."

"Not so fast, my girl," he said, touching her arm with damp fingers. "There is still a matter to be thrashed out between us."

Catherine shook him off. "I know of none."

"Don't you? I could prompt your memory, with the utmost enjoyment, here in the middle of the floor, but the dirt would be hard on my knees—and I prefer to prolong the reminder. You have much to answer for."

"Indeed. I believe, however, that I must disappoint you," Catherine replied, moving off again.

"I think not," he disagreed, following leisurely. "I am not without influence here, you know. For a price I could have you drugged and laid naked in my bed."

Catherine whirled to give him the lie but the gloating assurance in his tight grin stopped the words in her mouth. She stared at him, unblinking, while the noise of a squeeze box and jew's harp from the parlor beside them dinned in her head.

"That frightens you, doesn't it, the idea of lying helpless, exposed to me, mine to use as I please, how I

306

please? On second thought, Catherine, I think I would rather you were obstinate."

"You may rest assured on that score," she told him, forcing a hard scorn into her voice. "But perhaps you should give a thought to what Helene will say when I tell her of your activities and your threats."

"My wife will say nothing. She is as helpless as you, my dear. She may believe you, having some experience of my methods, or she may not, since you lack credence, if I may say so, coming from the house of the fair Cyprian, Betsy Harrelson." He shrugged. "Tattle if you must. It will avail you not at all."

He probably spoke the truth. If Helene had a large family, a father, brothers, to support her and exact the respect due to her, it might have been different. There was only her mother, her sisters, and an assortment of cousins, and they were many miles away.

Catherine's head came up. "It seems I have no one to depend on except myself. You will remember then that I am not without strength. If ever you have me in your grasp you had best kill me, for I promise you a reckoning in steel!"

"Magnificent," he applauded in heavy irony. "I have grown tired of suet pudding in my bed. A ration of pepper will not come amiss. And have no fear that I have forgotten your whore's weapon. I intend to make you regret leaving your mark on my backside. My initials carved into yours should suffice—"

A rage of revulsion trembled along Catherine's nerves. She wanted to fling his words back in his teeth but her chaotic thoughts could form no phrase scathing enough, vicious enough, to satisfy her. Her breasts rose and fell in her agitation, and his enjoyment of the spectacle, and his obvious reaction beneath skintight pantaloons, gave her a near paroxysm of disgust.

Without conscious intent, her hand reached for the knob of the door to the front parlor of the house. It turned and she stepped across the threshold with Wesley Martin moving in behind her.

The girls, ranged about the room in their thin,

decolette gowns, turned toward her with surprise and alarm, forgetting the men beside them, so unusual was it for her to appear. Surveying them one by one, Catherine's gaze settled on a sullen-faced girl with soft brown hair whose *maquillage*, skillfully applied by Catherine, concealed dark circles under her eyes caused by the fear that she had contracted the trench pox.

"Sophia," Catherine said clearly. "Mr. Martin has need of your services."

Wesley Martin wanted to deny it, but under that battery of eyes alight with ribald amusement at the public exposure of his problem, his assurance deserted him. He only stood, face flushed, while Sophia came toward him.

Catherine waited until Sophia had taken his arm and drawn him free of the door, then she shut it firmly upon their audience. A smile of encouragement for Sophia, and she stepped around them, walking swiftly away down the hall.

But even as she went a familiar face in that room of preoccupied men and women tugged at her memory. It was an intense face under a shock of lank, black hair. The man had been leaning against the wall, one foot thrust out before him, as if the leg was stiff. He had straightened as Catherine appeared, and taken a halting step toward her, ignoring the restraining hand of the girl beside him. Shock had smoothed his features so that Catherine could not bring them fully to mind, but in his eyes had blazed an expression she had dreaded for many a long day.

It was recognition.

CHAPTER TWENTY-ONE

Sunday was a quiet day. It was kept that way by Mrs. Harrelson more as a practical measure than as a form of respect. Rest was necessary to all who labored, except, of course, for those who brought in no return.

Catherine was counting the bottles in the liquor cabinet, listing those which needed replenishing, when Betsy Harrelson approached her. Catherine raised her brows. It was seldom the woman penetrated to her own kitchen, much less to this dark and dingy corner.

"You needn't look so stunned, I haven't come to help. I have an addition for you." With an expansive gesture, Mrs. Harrelson indicated the bottles she carried by their necks in one hand. "One of our noble fellows has seen fit to reward us with champagne. We must see if among us we can remember what we did to deserve it."

Was there a faint slur to her words, an unfocused look to her eyes? The level in one of the bottles she held hovered near half empty. It was not a lot for someone of Mrs. Harrelson's capacity, but she had slept through luncheon as well as breakfast. It was possible she was a trifle mellow.

Catherine took the full bottles from her and began pushing them into the rack. "Was it anyone I know?" she asked carefully.

"I don't think. T'was a wee little man with an Irish accent who fancies himself a connoisseur of wine and women. Randy little goat. Likes girls taller than he is, which aren't too hard to supply. He saw you last night in the parlor. Since you have ventured that far, maybe next time you can earn our champagne for us?"

Without looking at her, Catherine replied, "I don't think so. In fact, Mrs. Harrelson, I am afraid I will have to leave you."

She expected the woman to ask why, and she had ready the tale of the young man with the limp. She had placed him at last. He was the deckhand of the keelboat captain called Bull March who had tried to trick her into his berth. The captain could cause a lot of trouble for her, and for Betsy Harrelson, if he decided to turn his river boatmen loose on the house.

But Mrs. Harrelson did not speak. Glancing at her, Catherine saw a high color mantling her cheeks that might or might not have been from the champagne.

"I am grateful for the charity you have shown me—"

"Are you?" Mrs. Harrelson interrupted. "I'd have thought you would have been glad to repay me with the kind of service I ask of you instead of words—but no matter. One can't always win. Let me wish you good fortune. I'm sure we will all miss you and the many kindnesses you are always doing for us. You were our ray of sunshine, our prop and mainstay. How we shall go on without you, I don't know."

Maudlin sentiment was not at all like Betsy Harrelson, then neither was drinking without a customer to pay double for the tipple.

Catching Catherine's veiled look at the half-empty bottle remaining in her hand, Mrs. Harrelson called over her shoulder to a scullery maid, "Bring two glasses. I want to drink a toast with Catherine, the only woman I ever knew who might have taken my place."

There was no graceful way to refuse, Catherine saw. She could count herself lucky to get off so lightly. And so she smiled and accepted the dubious compliment along with the brimming glass of tiny golden bubbles.

It was a potent elixir, true enough. Catherine felt her head begin to float while Betsy Harrelson stood smiling and asking what she would do and where she would go. When the glass fell from her numb fingers with a tinkling crash Catherine was only dimly aware of the sound. Through blurring vision, she saw Mrs. Harrelson start toward her, smiling, smiling, her rounded arms outstretched. Their scented, silken strength caught at her and dragged her resisting into the dark.

A fool. A fool of extravagant pride, a paragon of trusting stupidity, unfit to fend for a child, much less herself. Self-castigation did not relieve the ache spearing into her head, nor bring the comforting light to the dark space around her. It did prove she was not to be always a dullard with a brain trussed up, like her body, by a bawd's potion.

An error, allowing herself to trust the beneficence of a procuress. Such a one's loyalty was, of necessity, singular. Money was undoubtedly the touchstone. Put to the test of jasper, Betsy Harrelson had shown dross, impure metal. To put it succinctly, she was a slut.

How much had she been paid to persuade her to drink tainted champagne? Except for conceit, what good did it do to ask?

Lying still, she discovered a circumstance which would have been obvious to her earlier but for the sensation of moving seas inside her head. She was on a boat, a craft rocking gently on the current's drift, swinging at its mooring. She could hear the hollow lapping of wavelets against the hull. Beneath her was the hard, rough bedding and narrow width of a berth.

Why would Wesley Martin have her put on a boat? Even if Mrs. Harrelson had wanted her removed from her house—an unlikely event—it was not reasonable that the Sybarite in the man would have allowed him to choose such unstable and cramped surroundings.

Where was he? It was not like him to postpone his pleasure.

Perhaps he had not postponed—

No. Her careful movements brought no discomfort. They brought instead the realization that she was not bound. A coarse sheet, tightly wrapped, confined her. Her apron and her gown of dark gray linen were gone, also her knife whose hilt curved so sweetly to the palm of her hand. She had been left the redeeming modesty of her chemise.

The last was not according to Wesley's plan. It had more the look of Betsy Harrelson's nip-cheese ways, a repossessing of the garments she had provided.

Like a chance intruder, the thin face of the limping man flitted across her groping mind. Was it accident or intent which had brought her to a riverboat so soon after seeing him? Was he the bellwether leading her once more to his master, the captain of the three red turkey feathers, Bull March?

In sudden revolt against restraint, Catherine threw off the sheet and swung her feet to the floor. She encountered slippers under the edge of the berth, neatly paired. Silence was more important than comfort. She left them there,

311

raising herself with caution, afraid of a noisy collision in the lightless cabin.

A table impeded her progress to the far wall. She managed to skirt the edge without upsetting either of the two chairs pulled up to it. The contours of a leather bound chest exercised her imagination farther along, and then the rough lumber of the door with its crossbar was beneath her fingers.

With a slow and steady pressure, she pushed up on the bar. It did not move. Again.

She made the third effort before her questing fingers discerned that the crossbar was nailed into place. Above it was a metal latch of simple yet effective design which gave her no trouble. To be thorough she reached higher, running the palm of her hand along the frame edge.

Her movements slowed. The door was warped, the reason for the bracing crossbar.

A swinging door that could not be barred. The splutter of thunder and stab of lightning. Voices raised in Rabelaisian disrespect. The captain.

The captain. It was satisfactory as an explanation, if not reassuring. It went well with the positive fact that, despite the released latch, the door would not open.

Muffled sound heralded change. The pound of feet sent tremors through the boat's hewn timbers. The swing and bump of mooring ceased. There was a quickening, then a mill-race roll as the rushing river took them. Downstream. Down past Cypress Bend and Alhambra and the shantyboat of Aunt Em and Jonathan in its sluggish backwater. Past the crescent shaped port of New Orleans—past hope and fear and the spectre of ancient forbiddance of the taking of one's own life, past all this and out to sea, as quickly, as cleanly, as possible.

The rattle of a bolt being drawn outside was a warning. Catherine pressed herself against the wall beside the door. The panel swung inward, silhouetting the broad shouldered form of a man before the dim sheen of half-hidden stars.

Catherine did not stop to admire. She slid like released satin around the door jamb, her eyes straining for the

312

glitter of night-black waves, her breath caught already in defense against the chill of the water.

Muscular, burning, an arm lashed out to curl about her waist. She was snatched off balance against a hard body and lifted, kicking viciously, into the air. Fury was trapped like her breath in her lungs. She twisted, clawing at the steely forearm that held her.

The sharp edge of the berth caught her hip and she gasped in pain, flinging herself away from the weight that sought to pin her to the mattress. Caught between unyielding wood and resistless force, she had no hope of escaping. The bulkhead confined movement. Her flailing arms were captured in a steel manacle grip and wrenched above her head. The man's body bore relentlessly down, crushing movement.

Catherine clenched her teeth in grim resistance, setting subterfuge against strength, feigning surrender. He was still, his mouth hovering, mistrustful, above her. Their breathing was harsh in the close cabin. Catherine was aware, with a sharp amaze, of the clean male and fresh air smell of the body grinding into her and the lack of bristling beard.

What difference—a part of her mind screamed. In frustrated virulence she heaved upward and sank her teeth into his lip.

She expected recoil, a fraction of release she might use to advantage. Instead his mouth came down on hers, wet and acid with blood, savagely bruising. He shifted his weight across her thighs, forcing her knees to lock straight. The edge of his forearm pressed hurtfully into her breast, the weight behind it denying her air.

Bitter tears rose scalding to her eyes. For a woman, submission, whether to fate, to nature, or to a man, seemed constant. What did it matter that some men refrained from imposing their will with brutal blows? The results were the same.

Parting her lips in the desperate effort to breathe set her captor free. Minutely, he eased his constricting embrace.

Grief, shattering, final, welled blackly in her mind. The

313

wet tracks of tears coursed into her loosened hair. The despair in her mind clung to the memory of the one man who had ever saved her from anything. "Rafe," she cried out softly, shaking her head in hopeless negation. "Oh, Rafe—"

A soft curse rustled in the darkness. Abruptly, she was free.

Catherine made a small, convulsive movement. She wanted to run, to surge up and out through the half-open door, yet some quality in the strained silence held her rigid.

The moment for going, if it ever existed, was lost. Looming large in the small cabin, the man pushed the panel shut and shot the bolt, locking them in together in the dark.

The rasp of flint informed her of his actions. Blue-white sparks arched onto the tinder, flared, caught. His hands enameled by the small blue and yellow flame, the man dipped a candle into the box to catch the wick, then held it straight, a steady burning star of light. The tinder-box was closed with care, the candle, in its holder, placed upon the table. He turned.

Catherine, despairing, stared into the black and joyless eyes of her husband.

Rafael Sebastian Navarro, the Black Panther, the pirate sailing as El Capitan—The Captain. A plantation owner who had his own keelboat with a stepped-in mast. The cabin was undoubtedly the same. There could not be two with a mast thrusting upward at one end and cupboards athwart. Could there?

"So you knew," he said, his voice like hammered silver.

"No." Let him make of that what he would; accept it or not, as he pleased.

"Then why?"

"Why—speak your name?" Catherine lowered her eyes, letting her lashes filter her distress.

His nod was stiff.

"Why did you go to the trouble of bringing me here?" she asked, perversely.

314

A grim smile lit his face. "I doubt our reasons were the same."

"Do you? I expect you are right," she agreed with a fine show of carelessness. "But then do reasons matter?"

"They matter." He moved nearer, a curious opaqueness rising in his eyes.

Leaner than she remembered, his features were also harder, more refined, as though they had been sheeted with bronze.

"They matter," he repeated, dropping to one knee beside her, "but not so much as this."

His fingers slipped beneath her neck, forcing their way through her hair, scattering the pins, lifting the soft curling strands to let them fall shining over the edge of the berth to the floor. Once more beneath her head, his fingers gripped, drawing her upward to meet the sudden, searing demand of his lips.

Deep inside her was an empty stillness. She tensed for a fresh assault, her flesh prickling with nerves and the apprehension of pain. And then his kiss changed, deepening to a searching wonder of remembered delight. Her lips parted, accepting the sweetness, curving with a gentle passion of giving to meet his need.

His hand, questing, burned upon her swelling breast. She lifted her arm to his muscled shoulder, granting him the freedom of her body. Before the gesture was complete, he took it. Thrusting his fingers through a rent in the much-washed softness of her chemise, he ripped it open from neckline to hem. His touch grew rougher, feeling the curves and hollows that shaped her femininity with the sureness of a blind man in the dark. His lips pressed liquid fire along the curve of her jaw and into the tenderness of her neck, moving in agonizing progression toward the deep rose nipples of her breasts.

Her need grew, a demanding thing, so that she moved under his hands, a near inaudible sound catching in her throat. A moment of chill desertion, and Rafe was with her, drawing her under him, fitting himself to her in perfect and urgent unity. A bursting flood of savage joy caught them, rushing them together toward a cataract of

315

pleasure holding within it the keen edge of pain. Catherine wanted to take him completely within herself, to dissolve her being with his and be lost, safe, in him. But she could not and the realization brought silent, quick-silver tears to her eyes.

Catherine woke to daylight slanting through the hairline cracks in the shutter at the small window. She felt confined, with muscles aching from cramp, but there was a wonderful warmth at her back. With a tremor of shock she remembered, acknowledging also the faint soreness between her thighs. She might well be tender. She and the man whose arm fell so heavily across her waist had awakened in the night with a sudden and ravenous hunger for each other. Coming from the depth of sleep, their consciousness had remained at some primordial level so they grappled, straining together as shamelessly, endlessly, as any creature of the swamp with his mate. Underneath the sheet and rough blanket that covered them, she grew hot with embarrassment thinking of it.

She would have liked to move, but Rafe was a light sleeper. The last thing she wished was to wake him. Her humiliation was complete enough without having to face him as yet.

After her passionate response to him the night before, how was she to comport herself? She had no wish to be one of those pitiful objects, a woman in love with a husband who cares nothing for her. Or, she amended, nothing beyond her function in his bed. He had shown plainly what was most important. That he had missed her, missed having the use of her body, she could not doubt, but he had spoken no word of love.

Was that so important compared to his obvious need? It was. Without love his use of her was degrading. She had no more value than a chance met whore or a *vase du nécessité*.

I am a curious phenomenon, she thought, a puritanical idealist emerging from a whorehouse.

And then she realized he had awakened. His hand began a stealthy climb to the flat surface of her abdomen, brushing higher with persistent sensitivity.

Catherine wrenched over with a suddenness that caught him unprepared. He rallied, blinking sleep from his eyes, raising to his elbow. Quirking an eyebrow, he leaned to kiss her, his hand seeking once more the full warmth it had lost.

Catherine laid the palm of her hand against the flat planes of his chest. The grim turn of her mind led her to a grimmer subject with which to protect herself from his ardor. "Solange?" she said, her amber eyes wide. "Tell me what passed with her."

Color receding, he released her. "Madness," he answered bitingly.

"She did not die?"

"If you mean did life escape her body, then no, but her mind and soul have flown. She sits doddering, prinking, and primping, forever planning to elope with her lover. The nuns are very patient with her."

"She—has entered a convent?"

"She was pushed in, and the door slammed shut behind her."

"I—I'm sorry," Catherine said, staring at the ceiling.

"That helps, of course."

She ignored the sardonic inflection. "Pauline, I suppose."

"Pauline." He paused. "She saved her. And you need not worry. She told us of your heroic behavior in trying to come to Solange's aid, and of the dastardly way your gentleman friend turned on you. I absolve you of guilt— except that, but for you, Marcus Fitzgerald would never have been near Alhambra."

"And but for you neither would I," Catherine reminded him.

"There is that. I do not absolve myself."

She looked at him sharply but could find no hint of his feelings in his cold and withdrawn expression. "You came after me," she said, almost a question.

"Oh yes. I might have been with Solange sooner, but for that abortive chase."

317

"I am right, aren't I? This is the boat I was brought to then?"

"It is. I had in mind to teach you a sharp lesson and return you to my bosom. Instead, I came near to killing you. I thought I had. Do you know," he asked, his voice soft, "that at Alhambra I caused to be raised a tomb in memory of my beloved wife?"

A cold band closed around Catherine's heart. She levered herself up, and dragging the blanket around her, got to her feet, putting distance between her and the expressionless man in the berth. At the small, bolted down table she swung around, her face set.

"How? It doesn't seem possible that you could have arrived so close behind us."

"You have Fanny to thank for that mercy. As soon as she left you that day, she came to find me. You were gone by the time I returned to Alhambra, but the boat with my men on board was enroute there from Cypress Bend above. I rode along the river, joined it and began the trip downriver. Fanny believed you were running away with Marcus. My mood was not benevolent. The slowest boat makes better time along that stretch than a carriage. Mine was not slow."

"And was it luck that led you to our stopping place?"

"Hardly. My men knew about how far the river road was passable. From that point you would have to change to a boat. A sharp watch was kept. No one could have missed the Trepagnier landau."

"No," she agreed.

"I could have stopped it there, at once. But you had struck at my pride and Marcus at my honor. I was of a mind to slash someone to ribbons. I took the room next door to the one you were in and began to lay my trap. What I overheard through the thin walls convinced me that you, at least, had no idea other than escaping from me. By the time I assimilated this fact, you were in dire trouble. I was alarmed—but, I regret to say, unforgiving. I did not go to you, I sent a messenger to decoy Marcus into my vengeful presence, a measure that should have served the same purpose. I then dispatched Dan to see

318

you safe to the boat while my quarry and I repaired to the innyard to try our steel once again."

"I wish you had horsewhipped him."

"Odd, but I had the idea you did not approve of that. In any case, my method was more deadly."

Drawing out a chair with much show of attention, Catherine sat down. "You did not kill him. They told me he was seen in New Orleans, harmed but healthy."

"He owes his life to the fact that you chose the moment of the *coup de grace* to heave yourself into the river."

There was a moment of silence.

"If you are wondering why, I objected to becoming the berthmate of a man who was referred to in my hearing only as 'The Captain.'"

"If you had heard my name would you have gone to my boat?"

Catherine hesitated, then said honestly, "At that point, yes, if you had asked it."

"You regretted leaving then?"

Despite the softness of his voice, that question came too close. She smiled in bitter ridicule. "I won't deny it. I have discovered a woman without a husband is in no enviable position."

A silence followed. The voices of the men keeping the boat on its course penetrated faintly. There was the smell of a hot coal brazier and brewing coffee.

"Is that all you learned from your experiences?"

"I have also been taught something of the tenaciousness of husbands," she admitted, lifting her eyes to his. "How did you find me?"

"Your mother, of course."

"My mother?" Not until this moment had she realized how deeply her mother's rejection of her plea had gone. Her relief was a gauge.

"She sent your letter to me immediately, urging me to go after you. By return messenger she told you I was coming. Tell me, if what you say is true, and you have been reconciled to being my wife, what happened between your river bath and your arrival in Natchez to make you decide you could not bear with me after all?"

It was a moment before she understood. "Do you think I left the Martin house to avoid you?"

"You were not there."

"No, but I never received an answer to my letter. I was led to believe there would be none."

"And so you left. Aren't you going to tell me why, my innocent seductress?"

Catherine stared at his mocking smile with mistrust. "No," she said baldly.

"Let me tell you then."

Tight-lipped, she threw her hair back behind her shoulders. "Do," she invited.

"Wesley Martin, your host, demanded your favors and you pruned him with a sharp knife," he said. His eyes glittering, a smile hovering about his mouth, he watched as shock rippled over her features.

"How did you know?"

"I persuaded him to tell me—no, do not interrupt. At first I accepted Helene Martin's word that you had left, suddenly, after hearing from your mother. Then you did not, after a sufficient length of time, appear in New Orleans—wasted time, but I did think you had a dislike for my company. In my talk with Helene she had mentioned the old woman and her grandson who had pulled you from the river. It seemed possible that you had returned to them. River boatmen, by and large, are co-operative with their own kind. Inquiries at the dock in New Orleans produced the name and location of the pair. Unfortunately, they had not seen you. The young man, however, reinforced a general feeling of mine that Wesley Martin was not a particularly trustworthy individual. I returned to Natchez two nights ago and secured an interview with him without the presence of his charming wife." Staring at his fingers, flexing them contemplatively, Rafe went on. "At first he was reluctant to discuss you, but I was able to help him remember the circumstances surrounding your departure from his house, and also your current address. He even grew loquacious enough to confide to me his arrangement with Mistress Betsy Harrelson to deliver you, drugged, into his hands. I decided to—redirect—the program."

Catherine gave him a tremulous smile. "I am grateful," she told him. "I will even admit, if you like, that I prefer your arrangement. But—why?"

Swinging out of the berth, he was beside her in a stride, drawing her to her feet, pushing the blanket to the floor without nonsense.

"Have you forgotten what I told you?" he asked, his voice rough at her ear. "I will never let you go—never."

CHAPTER TWENTY-TWO

The wind blew fair, the river ran strong, and their passage began to take the aspect of a race. What they were racing toward, Catherine did not know, but, watching her husband scan the great triangular sail above them while he took his turn at the rudder, she could sense the tension that drove him. With his hair whipping in the chill wind and his eyes narrowed in concentration, he seemed remote, self-sufficient. Attuned to his craft, the water and sky, buttressed by the camaraderie of his men, what need had he of her?

The comradeship was not imagined. Early that first morning, while she was still below donning a gown and shawl which, from the smell, must have hung in the cupboard many a damp and mildewed month, she had heard a boatman call: "Easier to steer this morning, ain't it, Cap'n?"

"You had trouble last night?" came the query.

"Oh, aye, turrible trouble, sirrah."

Something must have warned Rafe, for he said only, "All right, out with it, you old sea dog."

"Seems there was a bit of a list to port, and a mighty

321

rocking up and down and up and down. Could hardly keep a true course. I had a mind to go have a look-see in the cargo box, but long about daybreak it finally quit!"

There were shouts of laughter, followed by a splash. Emerging on deck, Catherine found the boatmen lining the gunwale, jeering at their bearded fellow trailing behind the boat on the end of a knotted rope. Choking with swallowed water and glee, it was all he could do to hold on. Rafe steered on, unperturbed.

In Catherine's presence, however, the men showed her an almost comical deference. Their voices disappeared to no more than a mutter behind their ferocious beards. The majority never addressed her directly, and, when speaking to Rafe while she was at his side, looked at the deck, the sky, the sail, but never at her. Of them all she found she liked best the young man with the limp whom Rafe had called Dan. He was cook for the crew, though he held the offices also of purchasing agent and records keeper. On this trip it was he who served Rafe and Catherine their meals. If Rafe had let him, he would have acted as valet in Ali's absence. His loyalty to her husband was fanatic. Rafe had saved him from the pirate crew, of which he was a member, when they had wanted to throw him overboard as useless baggage after he caught part of a load of grapeshot in his leg. According to Dan, the correct name for their activities at that time was not piracy but smuggling, an old and honorable calling along the waterways of the gulf coast.

From what she could discover, Ali had been left behind to keep watch over Alhambra. The situation there had not changed either for better or worse, apparently. Rafe had little to say on the subject. Her nursery was still in order with Ali's son, a hefty, kicking, cooing babe of five and a half months, the most important boarder. Ali had a great attachment for the child. He had named the youngster Rif so that he might not forget his people, the Berber tribe from which his father sprang. Ali slept with him at his side at night, a fact which had, perhaps, influenced Rafe's decision to leave Ali behind, though he did not say so.

Questions about Giles and Fanny Barton brought little more response. They were not at Cypress Bend. They had left their plantation on the river for the amusements of the city. The winter season would just be starting in New Orleans.

Her husband's attitude was bewildering. It was no compliment that his single need of her was to slake his passion. If his understanding was so superior, he must know she required more than that. And yet, though he kept her at his side, though he required her company below in the cargo box not only at night, but often in the afternoon, he did not say the words she most wished to hear.

Catherine came to hate the inscrutable gaze he turned upon her. She resented his impatient answers only a little less than his alienating silence. Imperceptibly, she began to repossess herself, withdrawing by degrees the portion of her heart and mind she had so willingly yielded. She could no longer give herself to him with abandon. It was hurtful, therefore, to give herself at all.

Such shrinking did not, of course, go unnoticed.

"Your eyes, sweet Catherine, reproach me, though your lips smile. How have I offended you?"

They were in the berth. They had been sitting there at first, since it was the most comfortable seat in the cabin, but the sitting had quickly led to other things.

What could she say? *You hold yourself aloof from me. You treat me like a woman you have bought, a pleasing whore. I hate you because you can make love to me, and forget. I hate you because I am afraid you came after me out of no more than vengeful desire.*

"I don't know what you mean," she said.

"I am to guess, then?"

She shrugged, a pettish motion she regretted but could not help.

He caught her chin and turned her to face him. "Look at me and tell me what is wrong."

"I am tired," she said, withstanding his gaze because it mattered so much, "and I long to see Alhambra."

"No more than that?" he asked, but she was not deceived. His sudden stillness had not been natural.

Catherine lowered her eyes. "I have wondered," she said carefully, "what you thought, finding me in such a place there in Natchez."

"What I thought doesn't matter," he replied, his voice carefully expressionless. "I forfeited the right to condemn long ago."

Irony twisted her smile. "And did it never occur to you there might be nothing to condemn?"

"What do you mean?" he grated.

"I was only asking a question." She turned the limpid gaze on him that had confounded the nuns at the convent school.

"Now, having uselessly tested the depths of my affections and loyalty, will you be content with what is between us?"

She answered, "I doubt it."

Forgiveness was to be hers then. She had thought to present to him the gift of her faithfulness, and found it tossed magnanimously back into her lap. That under different circumstances she might have been glad of the gesture made no difference. Instead of trust, he gave her pardon. It rankled.

In the gray and blue transparency of the morrow's dawn, the keelboat under full sail swept past the bearded oaks and shuttered silence of the mansion called Alhambra and continued on through timeless wraiths of river mist toward New Orleans.

The silk clad bosom of Yvonne Mayfield was as plump, as scented as ever, but comforting. She received her daughter in her boudoir. Her dressing gown was a ravishing shade of plum trimmed with rose-point lace. Her hair was charmingly coifed with shining curls of doubtful origin over each ear; her tears, however, were real. They ran convincingly into the deeper creases beneath her eyes, and rolled wet and heavy with salt down her cheeks. Tears stained silk, but Madame Mayfield never noticed.

"So Rafael has left you with me for awhile. That was kind of him," Catherine's mother said.

"Yes." Gently Catherine disengaged herself and looked about for a seat for the older woman.

"A good man in a crisis, but he can be extremely unpleasant also, quite menacing, in fact. Do you know, when he could not find you at Natchez on his first trip he returned here and accused me of hiding you from him? *C'est infâme!* Not that I wouldn't have, chérie. If you had asked it, I would. I have been well served, Catherine, for pushing you into marriage with him, well served, indeed."

"Never mind," Catherine said, helping her onto a new chaise lounge of moire silk and pressing a perfumed handkerchief into her hand. "I am back, Rafael Navarro has gone, and you need not wear black. With so much cause for rejoicing, how can you cry?"

Her mother wiped her eyes and blew her nose. Tear wet, her gaze was still astute. "You have been gone a long time, chérie. You must tell me everything that has happened, but most of all, what has come to you to cause that terrible tone in your voice."

United against a common enemy, the two women moved closer together. Their campaign of action was carefully laid. In the way of women everywhere they struck back at the man through a flank attack at his most vulnerable point; his purse.

It was not a particularly satisfying operation due to Rafael's generosity—he had placed a magnificent sum at Catherine's disposal—but it was time consuming, and it forbade repining.

The first consideration, of course, was clothes. Her wardrobe hung in the armoire at Alhambra. It might have been sent for, but the gowns of appealing innocence contained in her trousseau were no longer suitable. Catherine was in a mood for defiance. She wanted something of surpassing elegance and style, and if it was a trifle *outré*, so much the better.

Transparent taffeta, brocade so stiff it could stand alone, lawn patterned in apricot and black, in a peacock clash of blue and green and lavender; a soft drape of nun's gray linen worked up with cowl and crossed belt of tasselled cord, velvet with jewel-toned nap, the glitter of a jeweled corselet to wear under the bust, a muff of gleaming beaver with a crockery handwarmer included, a gold-fringed Persian shawl, a pleasing flutter of striped, scalloped, and figured ribbons; these and more were commissioned for delivery as soon as possible.

One of the taffetas, the peach, its billowing fullness depressed by a banding of matching velvet ribbon, was completed in time for her mother's weekly "at home." Topped by the lovely jewel colors of the Persian shawl, it gave Catherine much needed confidence. Would all of New Orleans come to gawk, or, worse still, would they stay away? Head as high as any aristocrat, tumbriling to the guillotine, she descended to the salon to see.

She need not have worried. New Orleans was much too maliciously intrigued by the heady scent of *la scandale* to deny itself a glimpse of the notorious Madame Navarro. The women were distant, the men charming, though the least bit encroaching. It was possible to trace the passage of rumor and counter-rumor about the crowded room by the dipping of painted and lacy fans. She had fled her home for fear of the slaves, been captured and held for ransom— She had been abused by river boatmen—no, she had tried to commit suicide rather than live with the Black Panther! *Mais non*, her husband was blameless, such a handsome fellow. She had been left for dead by his slaves, saved by Navarro and brought back to New Orleans to regain her health. Look you, there was another man in the affair. Hadn't her husband found them together in Natchez? A pretty fool Fitzgerald looks, hinting Navarro killed her. She was seen parting most amicably from her husband at the levee.

Indignation sparkled in Fanny's gray eyes as she embraced Catherine. "How lovely to see you looking so well, but isn't it ridiculous, the things they are saying. If they had seen how demented Rafael was when he thought you had drowned they would be ashamed to speak such terrible lies about him. If I have one more impertinent question asked of me I shall scream."

"Which will help not at all," Giles said, bowing over

326

Catherine's hand, the clasp of his fingers firm and reassuring.

"People will always talk," Catherine said, smiling. "As long as they occupy themselves with something less than the truth I am satisfied."

"I confess I am amazed at the number of different rumors currently abroad," Giles replied in his quiet, controlled voice. "One would almost imagine there was some plan afoot to amuse and confuse the populace."

Catherine glanced at him sharply. "You can't be serious?"

He moved his shoulders uncomfortably. "I saw a couple of Rafael's river boatmen entertaining a tavern last evening with a tale of sacrifice—you, my dear, saving a flatboat family's child from drowning before being swept downstream yourself, then you were supposed to have suffered loss of memory after you were rescued. A most affecting tale, in all honesty. If you find yourself a heroine tomorrow we can begin to guess at the truth. It's a clever rogue, our Rafe."

"Yes," Fanny agreed in brittle tones. "If you will excuse me, Catherine, I will go and see what I can do to further his scheme."

"She hasn't forgiven me, has she?" Catherine asked, watching the tall, straight figure of the girl moving through the press.

"It's herself she can't forgive," her brother answered. "She did a noble thing, against her own best interests, and it benefited no one."

"She is in love with Rafe." Catherine could not have said how she was so certain. She simply was.

"And if she had let you go without a word, you would be—who knows where, in what condition of life, now? And he might have turned to her. As it was, you became, for a short time, a martyr to Rafe's ill temper. She had her hopes, but found you as great a rival dead as alive. A discovery such as that does nothing for a woman's vanity, much less her disposition."

"You have seen Rafe, you know what happened? All of it?"

Giles inclined his head. "Rafe visited me before he returned to Alhambra. He entrusted me with the agreeable task of keeping you amused. I am to be your escort wherever you wish to go. Command me!"

"Was my husband afraid I could not find my own escort?"

"No, rather afraid you could find one more attractive than he would care to choose for you."

"Nonsense," she said, her lips curving as they were meant to. "But it is a great deal to ask of friendship."

His blue eyes darkened to cobalt. His reply was abrupt. "Not at all. I would that circumstances were such I could do more."

Following the "at home," invitations began to pour in. Soirees, routs, masquerades, balls. She began to feel she was asked as a curiosity. True to Giles's prediction, in a matter of days so many contradictory tales had been circulated that she became a figure of mystery. Her name was even whispered in connection with that of former Governor James Wilkinson who had been defending himself before various courts martial against charges of treasonous activities and being a Spanish agent for some time.

Catherine put a good face on the public appearances; that much, at least, she had learned from Rafe. With Giles's solid form at her side, she danced, smiled, parried questions, and chilled the insolent in high form.

To a performance of mediocre opera at the small theatre on Orleans Street, she wore gold velvet. The wide, medieval sleeves, edged with fur tinted to match, lay folded on the floor as she sat watching the singers struggle through their parts. Her hair, fashionably cropped on top and at the sides was brushed into a profusion of tawny gold curls. A murmur, starting in the parquet, moved gradually about the single tier of boxes. *La Lionne—La Lionne.*

Catching the muted syllables without knowing for whom they were meant, Catherine was cast back to a dew-bedraggled morning and Ali, standing earnestly before her. *La Lionne,* the lioness, he had called her. Such a pity she had done nothing to deserve the name.

But once given, the appellation was impossible to repudiate. With sardonic humor, Catherine even began to play up to the crowd's inclination for drama which had occasioned it. Golden fur in tippet and muff and cloak's hood became her *griffe,* her signature.

At first Fanny and Madame Mayfield accompanied Catherine and Giles in their gay and frenetic round. Fanny was the first defector. She could never regain her old ease in Catherine's company, could not begin to understand her seemingly frivolous attitude when she hersel would have been either forcing herself on Rafe's notice or waiting repentantly for his return.

But then Fanny had not, like Catherine, parted from Rafe with an aching smile and the brittle agreement—once Alhambra was well behind them—that yes, she would be pleased indeed to spend an indefinite amount of time with her mother. She had not had to face that most bitter of all rejections; that of a woman who has been tried, and found wanting. It was possible, however, that Fanny had suffered a rejection of some fashion. She could not otherwise account for the girl's aversion. Giles's sister turned to former friends in the American sector of the city forming above the canal, and Catherine was not surprised when she learned that the girl was packing to travel back east with a family group leaving after the first of the year.

"There is no enemy so implacable as one who was once your friend," Catherine's mother said with philosophical candor. "You must forget her, forget everything. Look about yourself for a new life, new friends, a new man. One does not mourn the passing of the full moon, however splendid its light; one enjoys the next phase, and the next."

"That's very well for you, Maman," Catherine agreed, "but you are a widow."

"There are ways—" Madame Mayfield had begun, but stopped then, her gaze clashing with the look of arrested warning in Giles Barton's eyes.

That Yvonne Mayfield's philosophy worked for herself could not be doubted. The stairs to her bedchamber rang still with the footsteps of a number of men, all engagingly young and unsure of themselves, all enjoying varying degrees of favor, from the mere lending of a matronly ear, to the most intimate. Catherine, tinglingly alive to the demands of her own physical appetites, discovered tolerance within herself for her mother. She was not particularly comfortable in the presence of the young men, but with her own large and handsome *cavaliere servente* in tow, she could scarcely object.

Gradually, as she saw Catherine accepted once more into the woof and warp of the New Orleans season, Madame Mayfield also withdrew. She had her own circle of familiars, her own amusements. She had caught the fever for gaming, perhaps from some of her young men, and spent hours at the tables in the elegantly appointed gaming houses. Without being able to appreciate her fascination, Catherine still had few fears for her mother. She was an innately cautious woman, as frugal with the sum she allowed herself for testing *la bonne chance* at faro as she was with her housekeeping money.

Giles, alone with her in their journeys about town from one place of amusement to another, behaved with exactly the same propriety as when they had been so well chaperoned. He did not probe or invite confidences. He did not make pretty speeches or pay her court. His was a soothing personality, one that made no demands, still she was constantly aware of his admiration, his gallant sympathy, and something approaching ardor. It was present in his eyes, in the arm he held to protect her in the crush of a crowd, in his adroit turn of the conversation when it approached too close to her, in the delicate use he made of his size to shield her from the overt attention of other men. Her debt to him grew each day, as did her gratitude.

At no time was she quite so thankful for his presence as when she came face to face with Marcus Fitzgerald.

The occasion was a rout party given by one of the rather fast young hostesses who had taken up *La Lionne* in much the same spirit as they had begun to invite opera singers and artists to their homes. Many had married new American money and were ignored for it by the old

Creole regime. They had to have someone of interest for their entertainments.

"They should have called it a riot instead of a rout," Giles said, surveying the company with wry amusement.

"If you don't like it we can always——"

"What is it?" Giles asked as Catherine stopped.

There was no time to tell him. Marcus, thin to emaciation, his chestnut hair lying flat and gray streaked across his skull, was bowing before them.

"An—unexpected pleasure," he murmured.

It would be impolitic to cut him directly in front of everyone. There was no point in lending free weight to his story. An impression of casual friendship might be best.

"I think not," Catherine said, gently smiling.

"Not unexpected?"

"Not a pleasure."

Watching the blood rush to his face was gratifying. That he was as vulnerable to insults as she had once been to his superior strength was disturbing, however. It seemed to argue that he was not indifferent to her; that his peculiar love-hate attitude still endured, was, perhaps, intensified by the punishment he had so obviously suffered.

"We have not seen you in town lately," Giles said, easing into the conversation.

"No. I make my home in the country."

"You don't miss the amusements of the season?"

"I keep myself busy," Marcus answered, an odd glitter at the back of his sunken hazel eyes. "In the swamps I have discovered a *contre-danse* I prefer. It features the beat of drums."

His voice bland, Giles asked, "Haitian, I presume."

"As it happens, yes," Marcus replied, his animation quenched.

"Take care. These primitive dances are very well on an island, but they can be dangerous when transferred to the mainland. They may spread beyond control, and will surely destroy the dancers."

A frown knitting her brow, Catherine stared from one man to the other. She could hear the undertone, catch the

331

sense of a warning given, but could not understand the meaning.

"Ah, well," Marcus said, his thin lips stretching thinner in the parody of a smile. "I am here, now, among the cultivated and the captivating." He bowed first to Giles and then to Catherine.

"It occurs to one to wonder why—" Giles said, musingly.

"For Catherine's sake, without doubt. To see such a beautiful corpse."

"We heard of your near demise also. Your second escape was from my husband's sword, was it not?" Catherine asked in cool tones. "Perhaps we should congratulate each other."

"Without doubt, and I will add felicitations for your good fortune in finding a new protector so quickly. You will not mind, I take it, if at my third meeting with Rafael destiny should guide my hand and make of you a widow?"

"That requires thought," she answered, one finger tapping her chin. "Or, perhaps not. Even with the help of destiny it seems unlikely. I *am* persuaded at a third meeting that one of you must die, however. Poor Marcus."

At the involuntary move of the other man, Giles shifted, blocking his path. Taking Catherine's arm, he inclined his head in the most spare of bows. "You must excuse us. Catherine's mother requires to be rescued from the clutches of the faro dealers. I gave her my most solemn oath that I would come and carry her off before she lost her last picayune."

A few minutes later, waiting for their carriage to be brought around, he leaned to whisper, "You are a witch."

"Thank you," Catherine said, and did not smile.

The days of early winter passed, fluctuating from cold to warmer again and again, followed in this repetitious cycle by the inevitable chill, depressing rain. The streets became quagmires impassable to carriages. Giles, Catherine, and her mother walked to the cathedral for the celebration of Midnight Mass on Christmas eve. It was cold in the church, and crowded, but Catherine knelt for a long time, the flames of the votive candles flickering in her eyes.

New Year's was a more festive occasion with the exchanging of gifts reserved for this day instead of the more solemn holiday of Christmas. There were a number of soirees planned for the evening before New Year's eve. Catherine had promised to drop in on at least two of them following a late dinner at home with Giles and her mother.

Due to the condition of the streets sedan chairs, relics of the last century, musty smelling, with peeling paint, were brought out for the ladies. They could be seen everywhere, lurching down the streets, swaying around corners, four slaves grasping the carrying poles. A few of the more sumptuously fitted out ones were the property of those who lived in town. It was one of these, upholstered and curtained in aqua velvet, its carving touched with gold leaf, that Giles had procured. He did not say so, but Catherine suspected it had come from the Navarro townhouse. She found the letter "N" embossed on the squabs. Riding in it, Catherine felt like a lady of the court of the Sun King. She had leaned to confide the observation to Giles, strolling beside the chair when it came to a halt that sent her flying off the seat onto her knees.

"What is it?" she called. She could hear whistles now, and cowbells ringing, and the beating of what sounded like pans and pots and kettles. Shouting grew into the roaring of a moving mob.

"It's a charivari," Giles shouted about the din. "They are turning down this street."

Catherine sighed, and righting herself, pulled aside the curtain and looked out. A rickety sedan chair was just passing. From behind its curtain peered the pale, frightened face of a young girl little more than a child. Tears glistened on her cheeks and her wedding veil was askew. The man racing at her side, his head twisted back over his shoulder, was middle-aged, with gray peppering his hair and a near white mustache. His small rounded belly was supported by thin legs, and his stockings were parting company with his old-fashioned formal knee-breeches.

Though understandable, there was no need for such

333

fright. Charivaris were always given to widows and to widowers, which the man undoubtedly was. The yowling and noise would stop as soon as the crowd was invited to partake of food and drink at the groom's expense. The flight was a mistake. It only made the gathering of high spirited men and boys more determined, and attracted the attention of others. They were capable of keeping up the racket for days, or until they were satisfied.

Step by step Catherine's chair was forced back against the wall as the narrow street filled with the surging mob. The noise was deafening.

And then the sound around Catherine's chair changed, taking a vicious tone. She felt one of the carriers stagger. The chair shuddered under an impact and was dropped with a teeth-rattling jar. There was a scrabbling grab at the handle, and without thinking, Catherine reached to hold it from the inside. A man screamed. The scrabbling stopped. Voices cursed and yelled. The chair was buffeted as in a strong wind with the scrape and slide of struggling men vibrating against its side.

Trapped on one side by a house wall, and the back of Giles's dark blue evening cloak on the other, Catherine could not get out. She could only crouch, waiting her chance.

"Navarro! For Navarro! To me! To me!"

The voice was Giles's. The words in the charging soldier's rallying cry made little sense. From what quarter did he hope, or, expect, succor?

Abruptly the clash of arms grew louder. The growl and grunt of hand to hand combat intensified. A hoarse yell broke. The wet thud of running feet in the mud slapped the air. Within seconds all that was left was the panting quiet of victory.

Drunkenly, the chair righted itself and moved off, turning back the way they had come. In a single glance, Catherine saw Giles, cleaning his sword on his handkerchief, his beaver hat gone, and blood dripping from a cut over one eye onto the snowy folds of his cravat. She sat back, clasping her hands tightly in her lap, thinking furiously.

At her mother's house Giles drew her from the chair with firm but gentle hands and half led, half carried her into the entrance hall. The long echoing space was lighted but empty since they were not expected back for some time.

In the soft glow of a girandole, Giles halted and gathering both her hands in his, stood inspecting the oval of her face minutely for sign of pain or injury.

His eyes darkened. A faint tremor ran through him. Slowly he drew her into his arms to rest her head against the broadness of his shoulder.

"Catherine," he said on a long sigh. "Beautiful, brave Catherine. It is more than a man can, or should, be asked to bear, to see you, and know you are set apart for friendship's sake. It is more than I can bear—for I do love you so."

"Touching," a voice drawled from the direction of the salon.

Giles stiffened, then slowly they drew apart, facing the man lounging at his ease in the doorway.

"Touching," he said again. "I find it so, and I am the wronged husband."

CHAPTER TWENTY-THREE

"Rafe," Catherine breathed because she could not help herself. The sound lingered in the air, to her ears a supplicating exposure.

"Madame, I give you joy of the day," he said, his bow wholly lacking in deference. "I had the traditional token gift about me to present to you in observance of the season, but I seem to have mislaid it." Rafael bowed, then turned the impact of his gaze on Giles.

"I will not fight you, Rafe," the big man said with emphasis.

"No?" was the soft reply. "I will agree that I might have some slight advantage since you appear to have just come from a fray."

"We were attacked by some of Marcus's paid ruffians."

"That explains the tender scene I so basely interrupted then, as an excess of the protective instinct."

"Not entirely, though I shudder to think of Catherine in that madman's hand," Giles answered. "I love her and I want her for my wife. I am not without influence in the territorial legislature. A civil divorce can be arranged, if you will let her go."

"And what makes you believe I will do that?"

"I think we all know the circumstances of your marriage," Giles said, steadfastly refusing to be intimidated by the man before him. "No one could say you have ever been devoted to Catherine, but I will give you credit for being concerned with her welfare."

"Will you? Thank you, Giles. And am I to take it she will fare better with you?"

"I believe she will."

"That's all very well, but how does Catherine feel about it?"

With a shake of her head, Catherine refused the question. "Tell me, Giles," she said, "just now when you raised the cry of Navarro, who came to your aid? Not Navarro himself?"

"No—"

"Was it, perhaps, Rafe's river boatmen?"

Giles nodded, his face pensive with lack of understanding.

"Men, you, my husband, had set to follow me, to spy on me?"

"I had a different word for it," Rafe said, tilting his head, "but I suppose the effect was the same."

She looked away from that bright and secret face sculptured in shadow. Giles was a secure bulwark behind her. "I am so tired," she said, "tired beyond telling, of standing a pawn in this game you and Marcus are playing."

"It has been an exciting game," Rafe suggested.

Listening carefully, she could hear no plea in his light tone. "Yes," she said, "but all I want now is peace."

"And love?" When she did not answer he added, "Courage, *ma lionne*."

"And love unbartered, freely given," she agreed carefully.

The spitting of a candle wick was loud in the quiet. "You see so much, chérie, that one expects your vision always to be clear. This time there is the chance that it is clouded by fear. Make your safe marriage, and welcome, if that is what you want. But be certain that is what you want."

Was he, in his cryptic fashion placing a choice before her? If so the allusion was too fragile to wager her heart upon.

And Giles, what of him? He had given her uncomplicated kindness and the unexpected boon of his love. What had she to give in return as the hours slipped away into the New Year? She felt, in very truth, empty-handed, empty-hearted.

"Since you leave it with me," she said as coolly as possible, "I will let you know what I decide when I have had longer to consider."

Derision leapt into her husband's eyes. His glance flicked to Giles and locked. "That answer, I think, is not worth the crossing of swords."

For him to mock her caution was insupportable. It touched off a slow burning anger that charged her thinking. A man with so small a regard for the cautious way would not cavil at speaking his love—if it was there. No, if a choice was being offered to her, it was between love and mere desire.

"My answer did not please you?" she asked. "Let me try again—"

The coldness of her tone was a warning. A guarded look appeared on Rafe's face. "Out of pique?"

"It may be as good a way as any, and at least it will be a marriage of my own choosing. If Giles does not object, how can you?"

"Easily. I could claim his life as forfeit."

Giles stirred as if he would confront Rafael, but Catherine lifted her hand, touching the back of it to his chest. Without taking her eyes from her husband's she parroted, "Out of pique?"

Caught in his own trap, a dull flush mounted to the angular planes of his face. He did not speak; certainly he did not give Catherine the better answer she waited for in hope and dread. Victorious, she watched him leave the field, crossing the hall with his lithe stride, and let himself out into the cold night. It was a pity, then, that his going left her with the hollowness of defeat.

"I am sorry," Giles said abruptly. "I would not have caused you this embarrassment if I could have prevented it."

"It doesn't matter." Reaching up, Catherine unfastened her cloak and let it fall from her shoulders. Giles caught it, tossed it with his split gloves onto a walnut side table, and followed her as she moved slowly into the salon.

"Would you like something to drink?" Catherine asked, pausing at a cabinet with her hand resting on the ornate knob. A moment after she had spoken she noticed that the brandy decanter had already been taken out. It sat near the most comfortable chair in the room, an empty glass beside it.

"Thank you, no."

Giles's voice sounded strained. She turned her head, her amber eyes wary.

"Catherine, you must realize what was said tonight was not as I planned it. But neither was it a sudden decision, something concocted from the need of the moment. I have discussed what I proposed with your mother—"

"But not with me?" she interrupted.

"Credit me with a little sensibility, please, Catherine. You weren't ready to trust another man."

"I—you are right. I'm sorry," she said, her gaze falling. "My acceptance was less than gracious, and I am sorry for that also. Consenting to marry one man with all due form and delicacy while freeing yourself of another requires, I find, more subtlety than I can manage."

"I have nothing to complain of," he replied and

338

paused. When she only smiled wryly without replying, he went on. "The process of setting you legally free may be disagreeable. There is, and always has been, a stigma attached to divorce. Is this what is troubling you?"

Catherine shook her head. "Hardly. I should, by now, be used to having my name bandied about. You do realize, don't you, that you are proposing to take to wife a woman who masqueraded as a quadroon and was mistaken for one in truth, one who was so thoroughly compromised in the process that she was forced to marry her abductor? A woman that then betrayed her marriage vows with another man and eloped with him only to fall into the hands of river boatmen—"

"Catherine, please, there is no need."

"A creature who seduced a rich merchant, and afterward, descending to her proper level, spent a number of weeks in a bawdy house; and when rescued from such degradation by her husband, was then, humiliatingly, returned home to her mother as unwanted?"

"You are too harsh with yourself."

"How can I be? I am the scandalous, the notorious Catherine Navarro, née, Mayfield, *La Lionne.*"

"And you are becoming overwrought," Giles said, moving to cup her elbows with his hands. "You can't discourage me with a list of your misdeeds. I know the truth."

"The truth is what the world believes to be the truth. Are you certain you want to jeopardize your future by marrying someone of my character and reputation?"

"Don't say that, don't ever say that." He gave her a slight shake. "You are a beautiful and courageous woman who was caught in events over which you had no control."

"And an innocent one?" she asked.

He did not hesitate. "As innocent as it pleases you to tell me you are."

"Dear fool," she whispered, her laugh shaky. She had to laugh. She could never explain tears to him.

"And if it does not please you to tell me," he continued, without objecting in the least to the odd endearment,

339

"I will never ask. I will try all my life to cherish you and keep you safe—and at peace."

"Why, Giles. Why me?" It was a cry that questioned the attraction she had seen in too many faces.

"There is about you, Catherine, the bright sweetness of a dream I have had all my life. When I first saw you it was as if I recognized you, and wanted there and then to hold and keep you for my own."

"Oh, Giles—" Compassion ran with the husky timbre of penitence through her voice. Pity was near to loving, but for this man it was not enough.

As if divining her thoughts, he lifted his head, his blue eyes clear. "I don't ask you to love me," he said, "only that you allow me to love you."

It was too much, a declaration too near stripping the soul to nakedness. That he was willing to do it for her sake was an obligation of unbearable weight.

Gently she freed herself, eyes on a level with the dark blue shimmer of the short cape overlying his evening cloak. "I will never forget the things you have said," she told him in her softest tone. "At this moment I am more grateful for them than I can say. But there is much time before us, much waiting before we come to pledges and plighting. I will promise this, if you will continue to be patient with me, I will try with all my heart to be what you deserve."

Giles inclined his head in acquiesence. If he was disappointed, he hid it well. Stepping aside, he threw his cloak behind his shoulders, then from an inside pocket, brought out a handful of small but gaily wrapped packages. "It is nearly 1811. Open your gifts, and I will go and let you rest. Perhaps in the new year you will find an answer which will gladden both of us."

She had for him a muffler of white silk which she had embroidered and fringed herself. His first gift to her was a small theatre fan of painted satin with mother-of-pearl sticks. His second was a slim volume in red morocco of *The Iliad*, translated by M. de Rochefort. The third was a box of ebony inlaid with ribbon streamers in mother-of-pearl.

340

"You have given me too much," Catherine protested as she lifted the cleverly hinged lid. She looked down. Her fingers grew numb. The small box fell from her hand, strewing pins in a gleaming arc. They scattered over the rug, golden hairpins among the wool garlands of pink roses and purple lilac, softly shining with remembrance.

"No!" Catherine cried in denial of the black wave of pain sweeping past her careful defenses. "No—"

Picking up her skirts, she evaded Giles's restraining hand and ran from the room. At the foot of the staircase she turned, and saw him, indistinct through her tears, in the doorway behind her.

"Forgive me," she said, "but I cannot marry you after all. The fault it not yours. It—is in me."

It was her old nursemaid, Dédé, blundering into her room in the middle of the morning who roused her. The Negro woman had aged tremendously in the months Catherine had been gone. Her hair had grown white, her hands trembled visibly, and she had developed a timidity of manner which hurt Catherine as much as it irritated her.

"Why, Madame Catherine, you still here?"

Catherine turned her head on her pillow, surveying the concerned surprise imprinted on that lined, brown face. "Shouldn't I be?"

"Your maman, she say your *mari*, M'sieur Navarro, came for you last night to take you away with him."

There was a pause. "Did she?" Catherine said when she could force words through her throat.

Dédé nodded. "She was upset, her, that you would go into danger, and sad that there was nothing she could do to stop you."

"I see. Then I must see if I can reassure her."

"It would be a kindness, ma chérie."

Catherine smiled. "I haven't wished you a Happy New Year, Dédé. Your gift is on the dressing table."

"Thank you, chérie—and a joyous New Year to you also."

"Yes. Thank you," Catherine replied without assurance.

She found her mother in bed almost lost among the letters, invitations, visiting cards, the foil wrappings of candy, bonbons, and dragées, and of New Year's gifts. All went flying as Madame Mayfield saw her daughter on the threshold and screamed her name.

Entering the room, Catherine knelt and began to retrieve the papers and candies, handing them up to her mother. "It's as Dédé said, then. You expected me to be gone. Why were you so certain?"

"You gave me such a start, child. But I can't tell you how relieved—well, never mind. Why was I certain? I suppose because Rafael Navarro is a most persuasive man, and you are, whether you admit it or not, susceptible to his form of persuasion."

"You knew he was here, waiting for me?"

"Oh yes. He came before I left the house. We had an interesting conversation before I had to be off. I was promised to M'sieur Marigny for whist, you know. I meant to warn you, truly I did, but I saw nothing of you anywhere, and the man is still your husband. I—hope nothing went wrong?"

"That depends on your point of view, Maman. Rafe discovered me in Giles's arms."

"*Mon Dieu!* And how does it go with the poor *Americain?*"

A smile curved Catherine's mouth. "He goes very well, all in one piece."

"Odd," was her mother's comment. "Does that mean, then, that you are to be free of Navarro?"

"By the civil divorce you discussed with Giles behind my back? I don't know. As you can imagine, it was not a—calm—meeting."

"No," Yvonne Mayfield agreed reflectively, and popped a bon-bon into her mouth.

Catherine reached for an almond dragée and began to unwrap it. "Dédé also said you were concerned that Rafe might be taking me into danger."

"Yes. I had not really considered it, but Rafael seemed to feel it so himself that I was alerted."

"What danger?"

"Why, from the slaves of course. They are still in ferment, more so even than when you were at Alhambra. They had been particularly upset by the recent freeing of all slaves of Indian extraction. It was folly to even think of involving you in that situation again, and I will concede that Navarro was reluctant to let you risk it, but his desire for your presence had, apparently, overcome his scruples."

"He said that?" Catherine asked, rolling the pink candy coated almond between her fingers.

"Not in so many words, but I am not a novice, ma chèrie, at discerning a man's motives."

"Do you think, perhaps, the reason Rafe brought me to New Orleans was because of this danger at Alhambra?"

Caution tempered her mother's agreement. "It is possible."

"He didn't say this was the reason?"

Madame Mayfield flung up her hands. "He spoke of his own stupidity and impatience and lack of faith. He questioned me about your attachment for him—as if I would know. Then he settled down with my best brandy to await your return."

"What, precisely, did he want to know about my attachment?"

"I don't remember his exact words. I think he wished in general to know your feelings about being abandoned here with me. Naturally I did my possible to have him believe you were enjoying a life of gay dissipation. I don't think he found that entirely to his liking."

"No?" Catherine said encouragingly.

"On the other hand, I gained the impression he was not as surprised as one might have expected. It occurred to me that he may have had prior warning of your activities."

Fanny, once, had given Rafe a warning. Could she, knowing the possible consequences for her brother, have

343

done so again? Was she that impulsive, or that bitter? Would she have risked so much on so desperate a gamble?

Three days later Catherine found cause to re-evaluate her opinion of Fanny. It was possible the girl had had no expectation of turning Rafe's affections in her own direction. Her purpose may have been to gain the precise results she effected; to detach Giles from Catherine and encourage him to return east with her. On the fourth day of January, Fanny Barton, accompanied by her brother, at last took ship for the port of Boston.

Fanny and Giles. They left behind them a residue of differing emotion. Catherine could not, despite knowing what would surely have happened if Rafe had not been sent after her, rid herself of the feeling that Fanny had deceived and betrayed her. Not withstanding her partisanship on that difficult trip upriver and afterward, Giles's sister had shown herself to be Rafe's friend, not Catherine's. The things she had done were for his sake. That Fanny's love for him had been unselfish, unreturned, did not make it more acceptable.

Guilt and self-reproach colored her feelings toward Giles. Hearing his brief but dignified good-bye was one of the most difficult things she had ever been called upon to endure. When he was gone she had sat for a long time alone. People cannot be held accountable for the love others give them unasked, she told herself. They cannot prevent it, cannot share or alleviate the pain it causes. They are only responsible for the love they themselves give. Such sophistry was not a satisfactory antidote to remorse.

It seemed possible that Rafe, learning of Giles's departure might pay her another visit. The days Catherine spent waiting at home were wasted. She learned quite by accident that he had returned to Alhambra, going straight from his meeting with her to his boat on the levee.

Having formed the habit of staying in, Catherine continued. When she had refused enough invitations, society, in its hectic forgetfulness, finally began to pass her by.

She was left in isolation, and in isolation she found a commodity she had almost forgotten existed. Time. Time to collect herself, time to examine what had gone before, time to remember.

Snatches of conversation, half-heard, ignored, came back to her. A woman's reciting a litany of her fears. A planter nervously planning to arm his home with a brass ship's cannon. Servants, good, trusted ones, who had unaccountably run away. Travelers set upon and left maimed, savaged. Fowling pieces, ammunition, stolen. Tools missing. A child from the country complaining of drums, drums deep in the swamp. An old lady, dressed in the bright silks of Santo Domingo, telling monotonously of the death of her children and grandchildren in the uprising there, and of the drums beating like great unceasing hearts, their sound rolling down the mountainsides of Haiti.

And Marcus. *"In the swamps I have discovered a contre-danse I prefer. It features the beat of drums."*

While Marcus was staying near Alhambra a group of blood mad slaves had nearly overrun the defenders of the house. Marcus, with much reason to hate Rafe, had spent a considerable amount of time in the swamps then. India had never named the leaders. It was assumed they were among the men killed but that need not be so. India had had plenty of opportunity to speak to Marcus. Indeed, once Catherine had seen a slave unrecognizable as belonging to Alhambra leaving the area where Marcus had been waiting, and India had explained the man's presence away.

Now Marcus was in the country, haunting the swamps again and the smell and taste of insurrection was in the air once more.

"Haitian, I presume?" Giles had asked, querying Marcus's flippant remark. He had continued with what had sounded like a warning. As a landowner, had he with Rafael, guessed at Marcus's activities? Was the possibility of another full-scale uprising the reason why Giles had brought his sister to town—and stayed himself? Equally, was that why Rafe, a different breed of man, was staying

near the plantation he had begun to bring back from the brink of ruin with his own sweat?

But if they knew Marcus was urging rebellion, why could he not be stopped? It followed that they were guessing only. It might have been Giles's part to push Marcus into admitting his guilt, or to discover, if he could, the date set for the beginning of the blood-letting.

You are deranged, she told herself. Men of good family, like Marcus, do not, even in madness, set in motion forces which could result in the slaughtering of hundreds, even thousands, of innocent women and children, forces which could even threaten New Orleans itself. Still, she could not stop the turning of her mind or erase the conclusion she reached each time she came full circle. Insurrection was like a contagious disease, spreading with deadly quickness over a wide area. And since those who, by contagion, would become the enemy were already among them, there was little defense against it. Of the twenty-four thousand people living in the city, more than half were slaves. The element of surprise would increase the odds in the favor of those in revolt. The free men and women of color, because they were property owners, could probably be counted among the defenders, but there was no guarantee.

There had never been a major slave uprising in the Louisiana territory, not in the near hundred years of its history as a colony under flags of both France and Spain. Credit for the comparative peace most likely was due to the French Governor Bienville, who laid down a Bill of Rights for slaves through the promulgation of his famous *Code Noir*. The code provided for the proper feeding and clothing of the slaves, for care in time of sickness and old age, and prohibited shackles and torturing. Stricter rules were put in force during the Spanish Regime, especially after the revolt in Santo Domingo, but there had been a sincere effort to make the condition of the slaves bearable.

That there were inequities in the system could not be denied. Catherine was as familiar with them as she was with the inequities practiced against her own sex. Still, though it might be morally reprehensible for a stronger,

346

more cultured society to enslave a weak and primitive one, that was the way of the world. That was the way it had been since the dawn of recorded history, that was the way it would continue until man discovered some other means of having his most backbreaking and monotonous tasks performed for him. Slaves were called hands—and that was their precise function. They were so many able hands to ease the labor and increase the productivity, and thereby the wealth, of a man. If they could also add to his comfort, so much the better. Until a substitute could be found for those extra hands, it was futile to revolt against the institution of slavery. Such a threat to the lives and livlihood of so many had only one answer. Death.

And India of Natchez Indian blood, plotting, dying in a rage of vengeful rebellion, while freedom for her people, her son, hovered so near. How many lives had turned in new directions because of that bitter irony? There was anguish in dwelling upon it, and yet, she could not stop.

"Catherine?"

"Yes, Maman?"

"Why are you lying here in the dark? Why haven't you called for a light?"

"I was just thinking."

"You have been so listless. Do you feel unwell?"

"Not particularly." Nor did she feel particularly well.

"I hope you aren't sickening with something."

"No, Maman. I don't think so."

"Dinner is almost ready. Perhaps you will feel better when you have bathed your face and changed. Shall I send Dédé to you?"

"I don't believe I will come down to dinner. Perhaps I could have a tray, something light."

Standing in the doorway of Catherine's room, Madame Mayfield's face was in shadow. She drew in her breath with an audible sound, as if she would put a further question, then let it out in a sigh.

"I'm sure Dédé will bring a tray, but you will miss your visitors."

"Visitors?"

347

"Yes. They are eating at the moment, but the eldest seemed anxious to speak to you as soon as possible."

"Eating? Now?"

"In the kitchen. It is a man, a child, and a woman I took to be the child's wet-nurse, some of Rafael's people from Alhambra."

Catherine raised herself on one elbow. "A man with the features of an Arabian, with a baby?"

"How did you know?"

"It could be no one else," Catherine explained, throwing back the covers, searching for her slippers. With hands that trembled a little, she smoothed her hair. Why would Ali come? Had he brought a message for her? Or was something amiss at Alhambra?

"Don't forget your shawl. You'll catch a chill," her mother said as she started from the room.

Catherine thanked her with an absent smile, flinging the triangle of Persian wool about her shoulders as she went.

Ali got to his feet as she hurried into the kitchen. On a pallet before the fireplace a child of about six months sat, solemnly trying to manuever a cookie into his mouth. He was plump, with bright round eyes and a mass of soft black ringlets on his head. His nurse sat just behind him, steadying his back with her hand, watching him with quiet devotion. Catherine could not quite remember her name, but she smiled in recognition. She had been a maid of the Bartons', and had lost a child, a blue baby, a week before India was brought to bed.

"Maîtresse. It is good to look upon you again."

The valet seemed grayer, but little changed otherwise. His bow was as deep, as respectful, as ever.

"And you, Ali. You have everything you need?"

"I have been treated most royally, Maîtresse, but I am done."

"*Très bien.* My mother says you were anxious to speak to me."

"If it pleases you."

Something in his stance conveyed the impression that
348

he would prefer privacy. Catherine nodded. "Come with me, then."

Gripping her hands together, she led the way to the petit salon. As he saw the room she intended, Ali stepped before her to open the door, then closed it gently behind them.

"You have a beautiful son, Ali."

"Thank you. He is the joy of my existence. I am happy that he finds favor in your eyes, Madame Catherine, for I have brought him to you."

The moon of my delight—

"What did you say?" Catherine asked in bewilderment. Her attention had wandered.

"I have brought my Rif to you. Give him shelter and the mantle of your gracious protection, and he is yours, to do with as you will."

"I don't understand, Ali. Where are you going?"

"I return to Alhambra and the Maître."

"But, you speak as though—as though you expect never to see your son again."

"Who can say, Maîtresse? These things are written, but only the eye of God can travel the page."

"You must know I will watch over your son—and India's—as I would my own, but you will have to explain to me why."

"My loyalty to M'sieur Rafe goes beyond my love as a father, Maîtresse. I cannot allow him to face the danger that waits alone."

"The danger from our people, as before."

He inclined his head. "As you say, only a greater force."

"So there will be two of you against them? Is that all? Can't you alert the constables, the militia?"

"The constabulary is responsible only for the city. The militia requires names, dates, proof, before they will move. They will not believe, Madame. They say there has never been trouble, and for this reason there will never be any."

"But you are certain they are wrong?"

"The signs are there for those who can see them. The

drums in the swamp spell killing, the hands leave their beds at night and return before dawn—if they return at all. The cook and the maids are sullen. The knives disappear from the kitchen, the hoes and scythes from the toolhouse. The dogs howl, the owls call, and the moon rises red."

"Then if you are sure, why must you stay? Why can't you—and your master—seek safety?"

"An Arab, Maîtresse, does not leave the desert to the jackals. More, there comes to men at times a stirring in the blood, the heart-singing glory of a necessary fight, well-fought. And last, there is the lust for the arms of death, if a man cannot have those of life."

Catherine took a deep breath, her mouth tightening in a straight line. "What do you mean?"

"I think you know, Maîtresse. Though men will deny it, they seek to touch life in the arms of the women they love."

"And for whom were you speaking?"

"For both, Maîtresse."

"I don't believe you. I've seen no proof that your M'sieur Rafe could not live well enough if he never saw me again."

"You did not see him the night he thought you were drowned—or the day he knew you lived."

—I caused to be raised a tomb in memory of my beloved wife—

"To speak of love is a difficult thing," she said slowly, her eyes darkening, "but not impossible."

"No, but first a man of pride must be able to hope for a return of his affection. Later there was danger here, and he knew your mettle. It was necessary to force you from him to keep you safe."

"If it is as you say, then—" But what was there to object to? The depth of his concern?

She found that what she resented most was being once more denied a choice.

No, that was not true. The choice had been there. She had known it, she could have made it, if she had not been afraid to trust her instinct. It was fear, as Rafe had said, which had betrayed her. The fear of loving without return. Now it was too late.

Or was it? Hadn't the choice been set before her again?

"When do you return to Alhambra?" she asked, her voice brisk with decision.

"The boat waits."

"Good. I regret, Ali, that I cannot stay and care for your son. My mother, I promise you, will see to his welfare with more competence than I, and as much sympathy."

Ali hesitated. "The boat, Maîtresse, is only a canoe hired for the journey. Swift, but not comfortable."

"No matter. My place is at Alhambra."

"M'sieur Rafe will not permit you to endanger yourself in such a way."

"I hardly see how he can stop me," she answered, eyes shining. "And, perhaps if I put him to the trouble of keeping me safe, he will also manage to save himself."

CHAPTER TWENTY-FOUR

The wind sweeping across the wide expanse of the river was cold. The boat breasting the current into it was drenched with blown spray. Bundled as she was with shawls, cloak, and woolen scarves, and covered to the eyes with robes of buffalo fur, Catherine could still feel the damp and penetrating chill. Ali and the two Indians, Choctaw in beaded buckskin and a variety of dolman made of buffalo wool, had her sincere commiseration. Tirelessly, endlessly, they leaned into their paddles, sending the long and fragile craft northward against all odds of wind and river and black night danger.

More distracting than being cold was the taste of nausea at the back of her throat. The movement of the boat, though she had never been troubled by such a thing before, was a torment. Worse still were the smells of long dead fish and rancid bear grease, odors so pervasive even the fresh wind could not subdue them.

The gray dust of a cloudy dawn was sifting down over them, etching the leafless trees in blackness, when they heard the first drums. Rolling toward them like a murmurous fog, the sound seemed to come from far away, deep in the forest. Gradually, it increased in volume and tempo as the day grew lighter, causing Ali to stare, frowning, at the close-packed trees. No birdsong greeted the day, not even a crow sent out his impudent caw. White cranes sat like wise old men on their perches, solemnly eyeing the passing canoe. But as they skimmed by the slough where Aunt Em's flatboat lay half-hidden they saw an updraft of buzzards, patiently wheeling.

There was smoke coming from the chimneys of the Tregpagnier house. All appeared orderly and normal, though quiet. Ten miles to go. Ali spoke, and the stroke of the paddles quickened. With daylight they could go faster since they would not have to be so wary of floating logs and other debris.

There was no smoke at Alhambra. The house sat cold and unwelcoming among the dank shadows. Its shutters were barred; its white paint looked as gray and mournful as the ragged strings of moss blowing in the wind moving among the trees.

Catherine, her legs cramped from sitting in one position, stumbled as she stepped from the boat. Ali reached to steady her, then turned back, extending payment to the two Indians. They accepted with satisfied nods, but, asked to wait, glanced toward the house then pushed without ceremony back out into the river, letting its swiftness carry them away.

For an unguarded instant Ali's rich brown eyes met Catherine's in a brooding concern that had little to do with personal danger. She smiled, rejecting what she sensed was a sudden onslaught of chivalry. Raising her skirts above the frost-wet grass, she began to march to the house. It was not a pleasant walk. Her knees trembled with an aching weakness not entirely due to sitting, and in

352

the center of her back a spot tingled as at the impact of hundreds of watching eyes.

Dry, brown leaves lay crushed upon the steps and moved in wind-blown drifts across the floor of the gallery. The sound of them underfoot, scratching along under the sweep of her skirts, was a sound to tauten the nerves, one nearly as grating as the abrupt screech of hinges when the front door was flung open.

"What in the sacred name of God is she doing here?" Rafael demanded of Ali.

"I think, my husband, that you are addressing the wrong person," Catherine said.

He seemed not to hear. "You will have to take her back, at once."

"How, Maître?" Ali asked, his gaze steady. "The boat is gone."

"There are horses, two of them, waiting behind the house."

"The swamp road is not safe, Maître, even if I could leave you."

"You may discuss this at length, if it pleases you," Catherine said distinctly, "but I still do not intend to go, especially not if it means taking away your means of escape. I would, however, like to come in. I am tired and cold."

Rafael looked as if he would refuse her, then he stepped back without grace, allowing them to enter.

A footed, brass brazier threw off smokeless heat in the entrance hall. Catherine went toward it, gratefully holding her hands to the warmth. For all her absorption, she was intensely aware of Rafe, closing the door, bolting it, turning to come toward her. He had the look of weary sleeplessness about his dark eyes, but other than that, he seemed fit. There was ready strength in the set of his shoulders, alertness in his manner. The anger narrowing his eyes could not quite conceal the fierce glow of anticipation for what lay ahead. His preparations had been made. On a table beside the door was an array of guns, pistols, fowling pieces, muskets, all loaded, with several powder horns and pouches of ball.

353

Inside the thick walls of the house, the silence was suddenly oppressive. It was a long moment before Catherine realized that it was also because the drums had stopped.

"Well?" Rafe's voice was harsh in the quiet.

During that interminable journey Catherine had planned what she would say. It was a pity she had not spent more time committing it to memory.

"You need not treat me like a trespasser," she said defensively. "I do have some right to be here."

"You chose an odd time to remember it."

"I might have done so earlier, given encouragement."

His lashes flickered and were still. "I rather thought your sights were set on Cypress Bend."

"I found I could not supplant Fanny as hostess there after all. Giles has gone. If he ever returns to Orleans territory, it will not be soon."

"It is well, then, that you have a husband to fall back upon."

Catherine, feeling that sneering shaft sink home, knew the return of her every doubt of the things Ali had asserted. A swift glance at the manservant's dark, secretive face revealed nothing. "Yes, isn't it?" she agreed, her voice constricted. "Now that I am here, perhaps you will tell me the situation."

A grim smile lit his face in the shuttered gloom. "Everyone is gone. The field hands and their families were gone yesterday morning, the house servants, even cook and her daughters, deserted last night. All were not rebellious, I think, just afraid not to join the others. The effect is the same."

"Where did they go? What are they doing?"

"They went deep into the swamp, joining the rebels. I am told their time is spent there shouting their grievances, dancing for unity and courage to the blood-beat of the drums—and forming themselves into companies in the manner of the Haitian armies."

"Dear God," Catherine whispered.

"Did you think it would be like the other time, a few desperate malcontents who would scatter at the first death? It won't be so easy—"

"M'sieur Rafe?"

Ali stood, an intent look on his fine features. A second later he moved with sinuous quiet to a window and drew aside the drape. Through the slim opening, Catherine could see a wave of black bodies on the far side of the grounds. Here and there above their heads the light of a torch shone. They were advancing toward the front gallery. The silence that had been imposed on their ranks was ominous. Had they been there among the trees that hedged the house all along? Had it been more than imagination, that itching between her shoulder blades? A shudder caught her unprepared. She suppressed it with determination, clasping her hands together tightly before her.

Rafe swung, and walked with a steady stride toward the front door.

Catherine opened her mouth, then shut it. She had forfeited the right to object. The taste of blood made her realize she had set her teeth in her lip.

The hinge shrieked as the door was drawn open. Unobtrusively, Ali moved to stand beside the table where the guns lay. Step by careful step Catherine eased into a position beside him. It had been hot the day she and Aunt Em and Jonathan had used the black lumps on the buzzard tree for target practice. Pray God she had not forgotten how and her hands were steady. She had knifed a man once, in the heat of the moment. Given provocation, shooting one should be easier. And while these thoughts scampered like mice across the surface of her mind, she never removed her eyes from the man striding out onto the gallery as if the mob below had gathered at his express command.

His voice, rising above the mutter, held the steady timbre of reason. "Who is your leader? Let him come forward."

One man stepped to the fore. He was big, a giant of a Negro man with a barrel chest and matted beard. He carried a musket in his left hand, for his right arm ended in a stump—the removal of the right hand was a not uncommon punishment for stealing in some parts of the world.

He did not speak, allowing the belligerence of his wide-legged stance to carry his message.

"What is your quarrel with me?" Rafe asked. "State it plainly, and we will talk about it like men."

"Oh, *oui*, now we be men, with a weapon in our fists," the big man cried. A traveling chorus of agreement backed him.

Rafe acknowledged both the truth and justice of that with a brief nod. "And as men," he said carefully, "what do you want?"

"Freedom!" the big man shouted. "Freedom for all!"

There was a moment when it seemed that if Rafe could find a logical, honorable answer to that request the day would be won. Then from the midst of the motley array a different voice screamed, "Revenge!"

A shot exploded in a burst of orange fire and black smoke. Rafe spun off balance, lurching against the door frame. A full-throated roar came from the crowd, a roar of triumph and frenzied blood-lust. They surged toward the curving steps, brandishing hoes and rakes and machetes, axes and pitchforks and staves, and clubs of tree limbs.

Snatching up a gun, Catherine raised it and fired into that seething mass. Ali aimed more carefully, and was repaid by a bubbling scream and a minor check as men stepped over or around the victim. In that brief moment of advantage, Catherine and the manservant dragged Rafe, stunned, blinded by the free-running blood from a head wound, into the house, slammed the heavy door, and dropped the bar across it.

The barricades were up, but for how long? The door and the shutters were stout, built to repell marauding Indians or white men as well as storms, but they could not hold for any length of time before such a force. There had been a hundred men, possibly more, in that swarm.

Whipping a scarf from a table, Catherine held it to Rafe's forehead. His hand came up, pressing it to his eyes.

A knot in Catherine's throat loosened. Her fingers trembling, she wiped away gouts of blood already growing sticky, the better to see the gory channel that angled across his temple. An inch more to the left, she found herself thinking fearfully, and snapped, "Now what?"

Blows thudded ineffectually on the door behind them and rattled against the shutters.

"Do something with this," Rafe said, gesturing with impatience at the flapping ends of the scarf.

Now was not the time for laughter. She obeyed, forming a competent turban with the ends tucked in securely. He leaped from under her hands.

"Smoke, Maître," Ali reported, breathing deep.

It was not unexpected in view of the torches, trailing black, pagan incense, so thoughtfully brought along.

Rafe looked from the guns to Catherine, his black eyes measuring. A sharp nod, and he scooped up a pistol to tuck in his waistband and one for each hand. "The horses, then, and hope the dogs prefer to drag the foxes out the front door of the den."

Ali grabbed up a gun, fired it into the door as incentive, then taking three more, pushed one of them into Catherine's hand as they ran.

Rafe went first out the back door, first down the endlessly spiralling staircase. He paused at the foot until Catherine was close behind him, then he moved out, crossing the court with swift caution.

To the right lay the curving road to Cypress Bend. Straight ahead was the quarters, wrapped in stillness. Their direction lay to the left, past the cold bulk of the kitchen, the leafless fig trees and pears, and under the clothes line to the woods.

Of what use was stealth? Speed, the cunning use of cover, however spare, was more essential. They were running under the wide branches of transplanted wild pecans when a shout rang out.

"There they go! Don't let them get away!"

Catherine stumbled. That voice. Strident, cracking with strain, it was still the voice of Marcus Fitzgerald. She had been right.

The yelling, like human hounds baying at their heels, increased. A quick glance over her shoulder gave Cather-

357

ine a view of the howling mob sweeping around the end of the house, emerging from a pall of low-hanging smoke.

In the distance a clanging began. It was the plantation bell hanging in the quarters. Its clear tone carried for miles. Not for waking, not for resting, but for death. Death to the masters.

Ali dropped to one knee, firing his pistols one after the other at the blur of a white form to one side. They had no visible effect except to make Marcus duck out of sight. Rafe was only slightly more fortunate, dropping two of the horde before tossing his pistols away as useless. The marksmanship made no difference. The fallen were pounded under foot before the onslaught. Rafe did not wait for Catherine to fire. Grasping her wrist, he dragged her into step with his long stride, heading for the trees.

The horses, excited by the noise and smell of burning, could be heard before they were seen. Sidling, rearing, white-eyed, they would be difficult to mount. Rafael stripped the reins from the tree branch and swung into the saddle. Controlling the frantic gelding under him with his weight and iron muscles, he reached down to clasp Catherine's forearm, heaving her up behind him the instant her foot touched the stirrup.

Ali was not so adroit. His mount backed, rearing, plunging among the trees and saplings, preventing Ali from approaching his side or Rafael from catching the bridle. The vicious screaming grew louder. Catherine could see the contorted faces, some painted in hideous splotches of white and orange. Leading was the man with one hand, and in that hand he hefted a homemade spear.

To fire her pistol might destroy Ali's last chance of controlling his mount, and would be unlikely to be effective from the back of the jockeying gelding. For an instant Catherine leveled her gun, then brought it down.

Abruptly Rafael was in position. He grabbed the bridle near the bit and dragged the horse's head down. Ali reached for the pommel.

In that instant the leader launched his spear. It arched high, rolling with its warped shape, then began its whistling fall.

358

"Ali!" Catherine screamed a warning. With one foot in the stirrup, the manservant looked back over his shoulder. The spear's metal-sheathed point sped to strike, quivering, through his upper thigh and lodged with half its length protruding, glistening evilly with warm blood.

Ali grunted. The leg buckled, spouting blood as he fell. The horse reared in wild terror. With a violent oath, Rafael released his hold on the bridle to prevent Ali from being trampled. Tossing its head, the horse wheeled and broke away through the trees.

"Give me your hand!" Rafael called. "Now!"

Ali had taken the spear at an awkward angle. He would not be able to straddle the horse. Standing, even, would be difficult. Face contorted, he shook his head.

"Obey me!" Rafe grated.

Never had Catherine heard Rafe use those words, that tone, to his manservant. Nor had Ali. The habit of obedience was strong. He lifted his hand.

Rafe leaned down, and with an effort that seemed to wrench the muscles of his back into knots, dragged Ali up and over the withers of his horse. There was no time for care. The first hailstorm of rocks and sticks was falling around them. Rafe kicked the horse into a run. Catherine, twisting back, discharged her pistol. What effect it had, she did not see. Holding on was more important than knowing.

The gelding was game, but so heavily loaded and unbalanced that he could not quite reach his stride. Still, they began to pull away. The voices faded. The figures faltered, dropped back, drawn, perhaps, by the spoils at Alhambra being destroyed in the fire-shot clouds of smoke rising now above the treetops. A few came on, but then they too were lost to sight among the trees as the horse's hooves struck the easier going in the soft ruts of the river road.

Ali, hanging limp, stirred, trying to push himself up. "Maître—M'sieur Rafe. Let me go. Leave me."

Rafe did not reply, nor did he slacken the pace.

"Madame, tell him. The horse can carry two, perhaps,

359

not three, even if I could bear the pain of it. You must leave me."

"They will kill you," Catherine said, her heart torn by the gray cast of Ali's features where he hung face down over the saddlebow. Perspiration shone on his face. His lips were drawn back over his clenched teeth.

"Not now," he panted. "I have the color of my skin for protection. I can, if I must, become—one of them. The river is there. It has a smoother ride. You cannot take it, not yet, but I can. Hurry—before we—meet—other gangs brought—by the signal bell."

Still Rafe did not stop. How could he?

Catherine saw the tightening about Ali's eyes, then tensing of his muscles as he pushed with his hands bracing against the bellows-like chest of the horse. She thought he meant to shift in an attempt to find a less painful position. Instead he suddenly kicked out, levering himself up with unexpected force. He teetered for an instant, long enough to grab the pistol at Rafe's waist, then he hurtled backward, falling with a helpless, cracking thud.

Dirt flew in clods as Rafe drew up. He swung the horse around in time to see Ali pulling the broken spear on through his leg with both hands. At the sound of returning hooves, the manservant looked up and grabbed for the pistol.

"No," he said with finality, staring up at them. "I will not be dragged along, a helpless burden. I am a man, no slave of yours, no responsibility of yours, Rafael Navarro, and I will be my own saviour."

"And it you are not, how will I forgive myself?" Rafe asked.

"I forgive you, here, now."

"It isn't enough."

"Then think of Madame Catherine and of how little rest I shall have in paradise if I have brought her here to die, as we all surely will if we go on in this way."

Their calm voices touched off a spark of irritation. "But your leg," Catherine cried, "you'll bleed to death."

"That may be. But not now. I have my turban to wrap it in. And better, I have a reason for surviving. I have

360

seen the face of the man who caused my India's death. He is here—and will stay until he realizes the thing he has started. Then he will run—or perhaps he will not, if I play nemesis well enough."

"Ali—"

But the man would not be swayed by an undertone of pleading.

"I have my mission, M'sieur Rafe, and you have yours. Someone must go for the militia to contain the jackals. Don't! Don't get down. I could not shoot you, you know that, and I would be most reluctant to kill myself before I taste vengence, but I will. Would you trouble to save my corpse?"

In the waiting quiet the horse snorted his impatience. The wind swept down the open road. She felt the dampness of misting rain on lips and lashes. In the back of her mind a question echoed. Why? Why must these things be? But she knew there was no answer.

Rafael squared his shoulders. "I will wish you good hunting then—mon ami."

Swinging his horse around he rode away. Catherine, clearing her eyes with the back of first one hand and then the other, looked behind them before the road curved. The dirt track with its middle of dry grass and broom sedge was empty.

They could not keep to the road; they knew that, but every mile closer to New Orleans was important. Eventually they must return to the river, but not yet. It was too soon, too near Alhambra.

Under the double weight, the gelding flagged quickly. So did Catherine. Her gown, thick and serviceable, was still not made for riding astride. It was rucked up well above her knees. The wide cloak spread around her preserved modesty, but it did nothing for the insides of her legs. Encased only in silk stockings, they were chafed by horsehair, the back of the saddle, and a pair of bulging saddle pouches. Her husband gave no sign that he was aware of her behind him, still she did not like to cling too closely. The effort to sit erect and stay firmly in place slowly exhausted what strength she possessed. Her main concern became to keep the trembling of her strained muscles from him. She thought she had succeeded, until he swerved into the bordering woods behind a tangled bank of blackberry vines and feather brown heads of frost-killed goldenrod.

Rafe dismounted, then led the horse deeper into a thicket of magenta sumac, sassafras, and young oaks. The taller trees among them were black about their bases as if the area had burned not too many years before. The scorched earth had been covered again by a deep carpet of blowing leaves. Black walnuts and hickory nuts lay underfoot, but where they stopped an ancient hickory towered, stubbornly holding the last of its nuts, tiny black balls, against the darkening gray of the sky. The damp air was heavy with the mustiness of decaying leaves and the sour reek of the swamp which began a half mile's distance away through the trees.

Catherine allowed herself to be swung down without protest. They had come a good distance, but there was still far to go and it was better to slow their progress than to hinder it altogether. Besides, until Rafe said otherwise she could always pretend it was the horse who was in need of rest.

"When did you eat last?" Rafe asked abruptly.

"When? I—yesterday, at luncheon, I think."

"I expected as much." With economic movements, her husband unbuckled a saddle pouch and handed her a piece of smoked beef and a thick chunk of bread wrapped in a napkin.

Catherine accepted it in wordless gratitude. From the saliva released at the smell of the food, she realized a good portion of her weakness was from hunger. Scrupulously fair, she waited until Rafe had taken out his own packet before she began. She caught a glimpse of sardonic humor in his dark eyes as she bit into the meat with sharp teeth, but she was too hungry to care.

"You must have left New Orleans in a hurry."

"Yes," Catherine answered. "It seems I'm not as good at planning for sudden departures as you."

"Practice should remedy that," he commented, a bleak look flitting across his face. "What puzzles me is your reasons for coming—and the diabolical logic you used to persuade Ali to bring you."

Catherine swallowed with difficulty. "You regret both, I suppose, since without my interference Ali might be with you now, sharing this meal as he was meant to do?"

"It pleases you to be an enigma," he answered slowly.

"While you, of course, may be understood with ease?"

"I thought so. It may be I was wrong. But I will contract to answer clearly all you wish to know, if you will do the same."

It sounded simple. It was. And yet, the truth could be a trap. Might it not also be a shield?

Before she could answer a frown drew his black brows together. Thunder rumbled overhead, soft winter thunder without the harsh power of a spring storm. As if glad of the distraction, Rafe swept the sky with a narrow gaze. Then he went still.

Following the direction of his eyes, Catherine saw the flicker of torchlight through the trees. In that instant of time while fear was suspended, she recognized in the brightness of the brands an indication of how unnaturally dark it was growing.

Rafe moved quickly to the horses's head, ready to prevent it from neighing a greeting. Catherine barely breathed, following the progress of the laughing, talking band with eyes and ears. There was an exultant, uncontrolled sound to their voices that reminded Catherine of the yodeling of drunken river boatmen, but whether these slaves were drunk on rebellion or the contents of some planter's wine cellar, she could not tell.

Rafe, after long minutes of waiting, began to make his way deeper into the forest skirting the swamp. Catherine did not question; she only followed.

It had not been a wet winter. The swamp therefore was not the endless mosquito-ridden bog it could become. It was a place of meandering bayous whose black stained waters had to be crossed time and time again, a place of flat, dank land where only cypresses towered above the dense mat of tree branches that choked out the sun. Alligators rested sluggishly, buried in mud, along the bayous. Opossums and raccoons and squirrels made their homes in the tops of the trees, while the open floor beneath was left to wildcats, panthers, and bears.

Treading its primeval sanctity in this eerie half light was bad enough, Catherine thought. What would it be like at night? Would the sound of drums have drowned the panther's scream, the bear's growl, or alligator's hoarse bellow?

Southward. How Rafe kept the direction, she could not have said, but he made no more of it than finding his way about the *Vieux Carré*. For the most part, their path was the middle ground, that narrow stretch of wood between the river, and the river road, on the left, and the swamp on the right. They rode, rested, walked in a constant cycle, though after a time Rafe refused to allow Catherine to go on foot.

The rain, constantly threatening, held off until mid-afternoon when the fine, vaporous mist grew heavier, then, without warning, turned into a deluge. The wind swept the steel-gray mantle of rain toward them, enveloping them in its wet, sightless folds that had the sting of sleet.

Catherine closed her eyes against the drops pelting into her face. When she opened them the horse was moving beneath the thick spreading branches of an enormous magnolia. The sound of the rain turned to a clattering clash against the hard evergreen surface of the broad leaves above her. The undersides of the leaves were rust-colored. Looking up at them was looking at the inside of a lined umbrella. It was not completely dry, the rain penetrated in spatters and unexpected drops, but the improvement was great.

Without waiting for help, Catherine slid from the horse. She landed ankle deep in a litter of dry, rust-brown leaves and old, blackened seed pods. Clinging to the pods were the pulpy red seeds which shone like drops of blood in the dimness.

Rafe unsaddled the gelding and set saddle and blanket near the base of the tree where it was driest. From the saddle pouch he took one of their napkins and began to rub down the horse. Catherine watched for a moment, watched the rainwater, tinted red, running from the clumsy bandage slipping over his brow. She tossed back the hood of her cloak and went to kneel beside the saddle where she busied herself tearing the other napkin into strips and knotting them together.

She did not speak until he was done, and then she made her voice flat, emotionless. "Come," she said, indicating the length of white in her hand. "Let me see to your head."

His stance was wary as he stared at her. Catherine wondered for an instant if he had understood her above the rattling of the driven rain. Then he gave a last firm pat to the horse and came toward her.

He dropped to one knee on the saddle blanket, resting his forearm on the other. Panic flared along her nerves at his nearness. She wanted to draw away, and at the same time, to move closer, to feel the warm strength of his arms about her. She did neither. Schooling her features to unconcern, she removed the scarf, using it to wipe away the trickling of rain-diluted blood before throwing the soggy cloth aside.

The wound was not pretty, but it was not as bad as she had expected. The ball had torn a gloove along his scalp that would, no doubt, always be an extra part. The bleeding had stopped, however, except for a slow ooze at the deepest point near the temple, and she thought that was probably from being wet.

"Does your head ache?" she asked, taking up the strip of bandaging and pad she had made. He was so long in answering that she glanced up, and found his gaze resting on her face, speculation hovering in its black depths.

"No," he said hurriedly, "at least, not enough to worry about."

That was good, the skull was not damaged.

"Do you remember the night you embroidered my side?"

Catherine's chin tilted, but she kept her attention on the task in hand, placing the pad over his temple, care-

365

fully winding the cloth about his head so it would stay. The soft black wave of his hair persisted in falling over the strip and she pushed it gently out of the way.

"Do you?" he insisted.

"Yes." She was proud of the steadiness of her voice.

"You wore that same look of determined concentration. I think—"

It was her turn to insist. "You think what?"

He shook his head, dislodging her handiwork, and she frowned.

"Why did you send Giles away?"

"Does it matter?" she asked, tying a flat knot over his ear with tremendous care.

"I'm not sure."

"Then why did you ask?"

"Let us say—curiosity," he answered, his eyes intent on her flushed face as she settled back on her heels.

"I would have thought my reasons were obvious."

"But then," he said quietly, "I have grown to mistrust the obvious."

Catherine stared past his shoulder at the rain battering the ground, forming muddy runnels, miniature cataracts, among the fallen leaves. The wind shook the topmost branches of the magnolia. A large drop spattered down upon Rafael's shoulder, but he did not notice.

"I—sent him away because—I had no wish for a divorce," she said at last, forcing the words through a throat constricted by the high beating of her heart.

With mesmerizing slowness, his hand moved to the fastening of her cloak. It fell away behind her, and his fingers cupped her neck, drawing her toward him. She could see the dancing brightness of desire in his eyes, feel the leap of yearning within herself to meet it, still she put her hand on his chest, an unspoken question in her eyes.

"My—curiosity," he whispered against her mouth, "is not—satisfied."

Catherine abandoned pretense, pride, resistance. That it left her vulnerable could not be helped. She needed Rafael Navarro with a tearful and steadily rising desperation, needed the touch of his lips, the enclosing haven of his arms, the merging sensation of lying close against him. No one else could soothe this pain of loving, no one else give her the release from mental anguish that she thought of as heart's case.

"Catherine—sweet Catherine." His voice caught on the words. He laid her down upon the stinging wool of the horse blanket, covering their nakedness with her cloak. Softness, hardness, they sought each other, pressing close, their blood running warm and wild. The rain and the madness of the world were things apart, as nothing compared to this encompassing ecstasy. Bodies fitted, mingling, they strove soaring into the crystalline gray sky, mounting higher until they crashed against the glass dome and fell back among endless shards of softly sparkling mica.

In the shuddering aftermath Catherine turned her face blindly into the hollow of his throat. Close held, she could feel beneath the palm of her hand the smooth working muscles under the scarred skin of his back as he stroked her hair back from the dampness of her neck. His lips brushed the top of her head. His hand moved, smoothing down her shoulder, tracing the indention of her waist, and back up to gently cup her breast. Catherine was dimly conscious of the tickle of the hairs on his chest, and of the burning where his beard had scoured her face. Neither required comment, even if she had been able to summon the effort. This, then, was the peace she had been seeking. There was no other.

The rain slackened to a drizzle. The horse was saddled. Rafe clasped Catherine's cloak about her, kissed the tremulous corner of her mouth, and lifted her to the back of the gelding. Mounting behind, he encircled her with his arms, drawing her back to rest against his chest.

Later in the afternoon they left the woods and paralleled the river, cantering along a grassy trace, all that remained, in this section, of the river road. Rounding a curve, a watery sun broke through the leaden clouds. Its pale yellow light outlined in stark clarity the low shape of a weathered flatboat. Smoke rose in lazy curls from the chimney and the smell of frying fish lay upon the heavy, damp air.

It was the flatboat of Aunt Em and Jonathan. Tied to its front railing, gently bobbing with the current, was a snub-nosed keelboat.

CHAPTER TWENTY-FIVE

The essentials are few when survival is threatened. The fire was doused, food, bedding, clothing loaded, and the boat manuevered into the mainstream of the river almost before the echoes of Rafe's hallo had died away.

Aunt Em was persuaded to abandon her floating home, for what she persisted in calling an undersized Noah's Ark, with more difficulty than the others. She might not have agreed at all but for her new granddaughter-in-law who refused to leave without her. The old woman could not bear the thought of endangering her prospective great-grandchild. Jonathan, without too much delay, had married the buxom daughter of the keelboatman who had ferried them all to Natchez. He was to become a father in the late spring or early summer, and in token of the event, had joined his wife's family in their freighting business. His in-laws were, of course, aboard. In addition there was the crew of twenty men, who, once they were started downstream, had little to do except take their ease, lying about the deck or on top the cargo box. Despite Ali's confident words earlier, it did not look to be a comfortable trip, though Catherine was ready to admit its advantages over a horse.

It was Rafe who took the tiller. Jonathan, after a long, considering look from Catherine to his wife, joined him there. From the scraps of conversation that drifted to her, Catherine thought they were discussing the possibilities for freight in the new steam powered boat Fulton was building in Pittsburgh. There were rumors it would be churning the waters of the Mississippi by fall.

Setting aside her weariness, she made an effort to engaie Jonathan's wife in conversation. The girl was in an odd humor, however. She had sought Catherine out where she stood in the bow, but she replied to all ploys with monosyllables. She made much of her discomforts although her waistline had only just begun to thicken, and, when Aunt Em joined them, she insisted on sighing after first one item and then another that had been left behind in their hurried departure. Committed to the trip downriver, she began to wonder aloud if it was really necessary, if they might not have been left alone in their isolation, if the danger had not been exaggerated. Aunt Em's frowns did not deter her; it took a sharp set-down from the old woman to do that. It also relieved them of her presence. The girl flounced off in search of her husband whom she took to one side in order to confide her treatment.

"Don't think too hard of her," Aunt Em said, watching the pair. "She's always been jealous, I expect because my fool of a boy never made a secret of the feeling he had for you. It doesn't help to have you turn up looking blooming just when she's feeling, if not looking, her worst."

A frown between her eyes, Catherine looked at the older woman. "I'm sorry."

"Why should you be? It's not your fault. Jonathan loves his wife in a way that's sound, long lasting. It's real, not a young man's dream of what love and a woman should be. They'll be all right."

Catherine, hearing the confidence in the soft tones, wished someone could say as much for herself. It had not been an idle whim which had taken her to the front of the boat. The air was fresher there, untainted by the smell of fried fish and raw wild onion being laid out for supper. It was not that she scorned such simple fare, the odors simply made her ill, as did the pervasive smell of horse clinging to her clothes. With the example of Jonathan's wife before her, the cause was not hard to find. Thinking back, she realized she had been troubled by her monthly

369

courses since leaving Natchez. In addition to her recurring nausea, her breasts were swollen and tender. She was, in a word, *enceinte*. Her child would be born in the autumn, perhaps six to eight weeks after Aunt Em's great grandchild.

Why now? Why could it not have occurred before she ran away from Alhambra—or perhaps two or three months hence? At either of those times it might have brought her closer to Rafe. Now it could only drive them apart. Her husband could hardly be blamed if he refused to believe the child was his. It would not be surprising if he concluded it was her sole reason for returning to his protection. To see either accusation written upon his face would be insupportable. There was only one thing to be done. Shivering a little, Catherine drew her cloak closer around her, staring with bleak, unseeing eyes at the wide gray river. Loneliness stretched, like the river ahead of her, moving toward a limitless gulf.

"Why aren't you eating?"

"I'm not hungry," Catherine said, summoning an uneasy smile as Rafe came to stand beside her. Jonathan had taken his place at the stern while Rafe went to supper.

"I'm not surprised. You're frozen," he said, touching the backs of his fingers to her numb cheek. "What is the matter? Why are you out here?"

"Nothing is the matter," she answered, allowing a trace of her tight-held distress to escape into irritability.

"No complaints? That is a novelty, after listening to your friend's wife. You would think breeding was an ailment visited on her alone."

Did she, in her sensitive state, read more into his regard than was there? She must have. "I suppose most women share a little of that feeling."

Rafe shifted so that his body blocked the wind. "Not all of them feel they must put it into words. That is one of your most endearing charms, Catherine. When you speak, what you say has meaning."

"I thought I was enigmatic," Catherine fenced.

"Only in self-protection, I think."

370

"Then let me protect my blushes by asking what you intend to do when we arrive in New Orleans," she said with brittle composure.

For a moment it seemed doubtful that he would follow her lead, then he gave an abrupt nod. "General Wade Hampton must be contacted. There is little doubt that he will put a detachment of troops in the field. I intend to join them."

"But your head—"

"Your concern is flattering," he said quizzically, "but I know these people, and the country, as no other. I must go."

"Yes—yes, of course," Catherine agreed. "It was not such a desperate wound after all."

"The merest graze."

"Yes," she said dully.

"Nothing to vex yourself over."

"No." Frowning, she missed the laughter that sprang like the devil's imp into his black eyes.

The barracks, then, was their first stop when they reached the city. For all Rafe's haste to reach the city others were before him. Several of his neighbors, alerted by the smoke at Alhambra and the ringing of the plantation bell, had been able to escape to the river ahead of the insurrectionists. The news had also been carried up-river to Baton Rouge.

According to reports, the number of Negroes in revolt was steadily increasing as plantations were looted and burned and the slaves drawn into the swarming columns. They were moving downriver at a ragged quick-march, spreading destruction as they came. It was feared their objective was to overrun New Orleans. From that stronghold they could find the men and the means, the money, arms, and ammunition, to launch a new offensive. It had been done in Haiti, it could be done in the territory of Orleans. Instead of admitting a new state, the congress convened in Washington might be called upon to recognize a new Black Republic. This was not a mere slave revolt. It was war.

The militia, under General Hampton, would pull out at

371

dawn. It was only a short while till that time. Catherine tried to persuade Rafe to allow her to find her way to her mother's house alone. But there was already a stirring in the streets as rumors of the rebellion began to fly. Crowds of gesticulating men were gathered around the doors of the coffeehouses and barrooms. Carriages and wagons rattled up and down the streets and there was considerable activity around the levee as people searched for some means of getting out of the city. Her husband declined to let her make her way unaided through this climate of growing panic.

Catherine did not appreciate such solicitude. It made it much harder to do what she knew she must. The sooner the break was made, the better. She did not feel, however, that it would be fair to force the issue now. Was it cowardice that urged her to postpone it? She did not like to think so—and yet she would infinitely prefer to leave him by stealth, without bitterness. She would like the taste of a kiss of trust to remember.

Torchlight flared before an arch wide enough to admit a carriage, grilled with intricately patterned wrought iron. The haired hackney drew up beside it.

"This isn't my mother's house," Catherine protested as Rafe reached across her to open the door.

"It's my townhouse," he answered.

"But—I thought—"

"The servants here are elderly. They are more concerned with a full belly and a warm fire than the dubious joys of rebellion. Most of them were born in the service of the Navarros. I trust them much more than your mother's people—if your old nurse is any example."

This was not the time to argue. He was waiting to help her step down. In any case, she would not be remaining long once he was gone.

With a hand beneath her elbow, he escorted her across the banquette to a small door of wrought iron set into the grillwork arch. Hanging to one side was a bell, but the door creaked open at a touch. A frown drew Rafe's brows together, still they passed through it and moved down the dark tunnel of a *porte-cochere* which led to the courtyard.

In the center of the ballast stone-paved court a small fountain stood, its bowl filled with sour, wet leaves. Around the edges were planted ferns, roses, and palmetto palms untouched by frost, all overshadowed by the spreading arms of a young live oak tree. A spiral staircase much like the one at Alhambra reached toward the upper gallery and the main rooms on the second floor. The rooms above were in darkness. The only light beneath the gallery was the faint orange glow of a banked kitchen fire.

The hesitant light of a pale, cold moon cast the shadow of the oak toward them across the court. From this shadow stepped the figure of a man. The moonlight gleamed auburn across the waves of his hair and slid with a silver streak down the barrel of the pistol in his hand.

"My dear Rafe—and Catherine," Marcus Fitzgerald said with deadly affability. "This is a double pleasure. Do come in."

A sudden stillness was the only outward expression of Rafe's surprise, though he caught Catherine's arm as if he would place her behind him. The rapier at his side was useless against the greater reach and quickness of the gun. He confronted his enemy, his face showing none of the tense watchfulness hidden in the depths of his eyes. "So kind of you to play the host in my absence, Marcus, but then you have always had a penchant for usurping my place."

Marcus frowned. "You took what was mine first," he replied, his reasoning frighteningly childish.

"Did I? I was under the impression you threw Alhambra away, tossed it carelessly upon a baize table. Do you deny it?"

"I didn't know what I was doing. I was foxed, and you took advantage of it."

"Men who can't drink should not mix cards with liquor."

"So superior. See how much good that high tone does where you are going."

The pistol in Marcus's hand leveled. Catherine made an abrupt movement with her hand. "Why, Marcus? Why are you doing this? Isn't it enough that you have destroyed his home? That you caused the death of the child-mistress, Lulu, and helped me dishonor his name?"

"No, never! I'll not be satisfied until he lies dead at my feet!" His eyes glittered with a savage light. Flecks of spittle appeared on his lips, gleaming wetly in the moonlight. He was mad, quite mad.

"Why?" she asked again.

"Everything I ever loved, everything I ever wanted, has been his. He put his mark on them and ruined them for me. But if I can't have them, neither can he. Even you—I have plans for you when Navarro is dead. I was enraged when those stupid animals with their craze for freedom got out of hand. I think now that, before they are all killed, their idiotic revolution will have its uses. It shouldn't be hard to make it appear they murdered your husband, then violated you. I will have to stop your tongue afterward, but you must have expected that."

Her arm felt paralyzed by her husband's grip upon it. All she possessed or ever hoped to possess Catherine would have given for the feel of her knife against her thigh; a moment's inattention, a flip of the wrist, and she might have evened the odds. It was gone, gone since Rafe had taken it from her while she lay in a drugged sleep aboard the keelboat. She must try the effect of an insolent smile as a defense, insolent words as a distraction. If his anger could be diverted to her it was possible Rafe could discover an opportunity to disarm him.

"How?" she asked. "You have only one charge in that pistol. I can promise you that if you touch me you will have no time for reloading."

"There are other ways," Marcus said, his lips stretching back over his teeth in a humorless smile.

Rafe, watching for an opening, made an involuntary movement. The barrel of the the pistol swung, centered on his heart.

"That disturbs you, does it? You don't like the idea of our Catherine thrashing under me?"

Catherine, afraid Rafe might be goaded into action, said quickly, "I am not your Catherine, I have never been, nor ever will be. You are a destroyer, Marcus.

Lulu, India, Alhambra, the men, women, and children who will die in this holocaust you have begun. Even me, in your devious way. Now you intend to add killing an unarmed man, defiling a woman, to your list. Do you think you will never pay for your crimes? A fool's wager, Marcus. Those who sow destruction will themselves be destroyed."

"Eloquent indeed, Catherine. You failed only to appeal to my sense of honor to stay my hand."

"Because I doubt you ever had any," came the biting retort.

Senseless rage contorted his pallid features. "You will pay for that," he breathed.

His gaze flicked to Rafe. The pistol trembled as his grip tightened, his finger curling lovingly around the trigger. Catherine could feel the coiled strength in the man beside her as he made ready to whip his sword out and launch himself forward at Marcus.

In that instant a ringing cry shattered the night, vibrating around the courtyard. From the dark opening of the *porte-cochere* a man appeared, running with a swift but lopsided gait that gave him an inhuman appearance. A white turban shone about his head, a cloak of white and black stripes streamed from his shoulders. Held with both hands before his face, the blade pointed skyward Berber fashion, was the curving silver blade of a sword. It was Ali, looking neither to right or left, glaring with black avenging eyes as he bore down on his quarry, Marcus Fitzgerald.

Marcus started at the yell, the gun in his hand wavering.

Rafe lunged, then stopped short at a shout from Ali.

"Mine! He is mine!" was the cry.

With a visible effort Marcus braced himself, raised the pistol, and fired.

The ball struck Ali. Catherine saw the sudden dark blossom appear on his tunic. He did not slow, he gave no sign he felt the jarring hit. He raised the sword high above his head, and as he reached Marcus, brought it straight down in a blow that cleaved the skull.

A strangled gasp caught in Catherine's throat. Wide-eyed, she watched blood splatter wide from the open wedge in Marcus's face, saw him topple backward, his eyes bulging in disbelief. Ali dragged his blade free, then drawing it back stabbed down into the heart of the fallen man.

Blooded sword in hand, Ali turned slowly to face Catherine and the man beside her. He inclined his head in a bow, but the weight of his turban seemed too heavy to allow him to raise it again. He leaned toward them, then as Rafe moved to catch him, crumpled, falling full length on the gray ballast stones.

Rafe turned him on his back. As Catherine knelt beside him, his eyelids fluttered.

"India—" he sighed.

Catherine felt the burning of salt tears behind her eyes. There was a gaping hole in Ali's chest filling like a well with the pulsing fluid of his life. Her voice was no more than a whisper as she answered.

"India will be proud and will rest easy beside you tonight in paradise."

A smile touched his mouth and was gone. "My—son?"

Rafe answered. "He shall receive the sword of his father and be raised as my own, free, in possession of no one other than himself and the hands of destiny."

"You, Madame, will teach him love—by loving him?"

"I will try," Catherine said.

"I ask—no more."

His gaze seemed to find and hold the silver disk of the moon, and for the space of a dozen heartbeats it was reflected in his dark eyes. Then their surface clouded like steam on a mirror, hazing over the image.

Ali was dead.

There were certain disadvantages to being a strong woman. At the time one most wanted to weep and be comforted, pride required an unbowed head, a show of competence. Blankets to wrap the bodies, a table to lay them on, these things were found as the servants, awakened by the shouting, came creeping from their rooms.

376

And then it was time to turn to her husband, give him her hand, and send him away to where duty and inclination demanded his presence. There was something in him, she thought, which, after his passive participation in the scene of danger, required violent action. He did not tarry long.

"You will be all right?" he asked, taking both her hands in his, holding them against his chest.

"Yes," she replied. It was a lie, but if she could keep the tears from rising to her eyes it might pass for the truth.

"You won't be frightened, here, alone?"

She shook her head, producing a small smile. That at least could have an honest answer.

"If there is danger to the town, you know I will come for you?"

Her smile wavered, but she managed to nod. If he came she would not be there.

Staring down at her, he frowned. "Something is wrong," he began.

"No, no," she said hastily. "Only—take care."

He caught her close, satisfied it was anxiety for his safety he saw in her amber eyes. His lips were warm and firm against hers, and then she was forced to let him go.

She watched, hands tightly clasped, as he strode across the court and was swallowed up by the dark entrance way.

Ladies in New Orleans were spared the ordeal of attending funerals. Defying convention had become commonplace to Catherine, however; she made a point of seeing Ali placed in the Navarro family vault. With her went the child, Rif, staring solemn-eyed from the arms of his nurse. He would not remember, of course, but it was possible that he would absorb something of the moment, something that in later years would help him understand the manner of man his father had been.

Following the funeral she returned home to finish packing her trunks. She had booked passage aboard a ship which was leaving for France via Cuba with the dawn. She would have liked an earlier departure, but the hordes

377

of people fleeing the city had made it impossible. Now that the danger had passed, there had been a number of cancellations.

Discreet inquiries among her mother's friends brought news of a free stateroom well before it was known at the booking office. She had hastened to engage it. Arranging burials, procuring staterooms were only two more things expected of a woman of strength.

The revolting slaves on their rampage had fired five plantations other than Alhambra, and recruited a rabble army of more than five hundred. They had laid waste an area ten miles below where they had started, and were thought to have killed at least thirty people, though an accurate count could not yet be made. At one point, however, the entire force had been held at bay by a single man. M'sicur Trepagnier had sent his wife and children to safety, but he himself refused to flee before the swarming columns. He had set in place a brass bound ship's cannon on his front gallery and dared any man to come within reach of his fire. None had.

It was a mile below the Trepagnier estate, some twenty-five miles above the city, that the militia under General Hampton, reinforced by men under Major Hilton from Baton Rouge, met the insurrectionists. The engagement was brief, but decisive. The slaves attacked in a dark and sweeping tide. The troops fired a single volley into the mass. Sixty-six fell dead on the field while scores of wounded broke ranks and ran for the protection of the swamp. Several companies of the militia, who had received no injuries, were sent in after them. At last account they were still recovering bodies. This was one reason the militia had not returned to the city. Another concerned the sixteen men who were taken prisoner. They were being escorted back to the city by slow stages, exhibited as an example at each landing. Among them was the one armed mulatto who had challenged Rafael at Alhambra, a Santo Domingan who had entered the territory illegally by way of Barataria.

It was said the captives would be publicly executed in the Place d'Armes. Their heads would be struck off and placed at intervals on poles along the river. Already Catherine had heard some of her mother's friends discussing the ensembles they would wear to view the spectacle.

The time for vigilance was past, now was the time for rebuilding. Despite fear and smoke, sweat and carnage, men must always rebuild. The great estates would rise again. The wounds would heal. The lot of some slaves would be worse for what had happened; for some, those owned by men of insight like her husband, it would be better. The land along the river would return to something approaching normality, except she would not be there.

Catherine had returned to the house of her mother. Because the older woman would not understand otherwise, Catherine told her of her dilemma. Madame Mayfield was not in sympathy with her daughter's scruples. She hinted, delicately, that since Catherine knew the child was Rafe's there could be no harm in living with him a time before she informed him of its advent, then claiming an eight-month baby. Failing to persuade Catherine, she made plans to join her as soon as she was settled, perhaps in a village near the Mediterranean. She would remain with her until after the birth.

Money was not a factor in this move. Rafe's arrangements for her to draw on his bank were still in effect, and because she knew she was carrying his child, Catherine felt no compunction in taking an amount large enough to assure the comfort and well-being of them both for some time. She had no idea that her husband would ever deny her access to funds, but she could not afford to take chances at this juncture.

The sun set, dropping below a mass of white braided ripples. Slowly the interlacing of clouds was tinted pink, darkening to gray-streaked rose that washed the dark roofs of the houses with dusky carmine. By imperceptible degrees, the color dissolved into a broad band of salmon smudged into the gray night sky. Against it, the houses formed sharp, black angles. Catherine, watching from her bedchamber window, did not move until it grew dark.

Behind her stood her trunks, strapped and waiting. Her traveling gown of pale green muslin with its matching high-waisted pelisse of emerald green velvet banded in fur was laid out. Fur bonnet, corded reticule, slippers, money, papers, were all in readiness. She had bathed and donned her lawn nightgown in expectation of making an early night. Now she wished she had not. Company might have been an antidote to the doubts that plagued her mind.

Had she the right to keep the knowledge of his child from Rafe? Was she being fair to him?

It was not that she expected Rafe to repudiate her, to refuse to accept the child she carried or give it the Navarro name. He was not so petty. But though she went over and over the circumstances in her mind, she could find no way to convince her husband the child had a right to bear his name. He believed she had played the whore's part in Natchez. How could he help doubting? She could explain, of course. Still, if he only pretended to believe her, or if he extended once again the chill comfort of his tolerance, how could she endure it?

Added to this was a niggling feeling that there was some justice in his suspicions. If she had married a lesser man, one who could not inspire love, she might, in desperation, have accepted the position planned for her by Betsy Harrelson. For a woman, selling herself was a last resort, but the possibility was always there, buried with varying degrees of success, at the back of her mind.

Her decision to go was made; there was little chance of her reversing it. She could not calm herself to sleep, however, until long after the moon invaded the room. She shut her eyes then against the bright torment of old memories, and was vanquished at last by the tired aftermath of tears.

She awoke with a mind-jarring suddenness. With every nerve and muscle, she knew there was someone in the room, someone standing beside her bed, staring down at her. She wanted to open her eyes, but with the paralyzing certainty of a nightmare, knew if she did they would strike.

A whisper of sound released her. Her eyelids flew open in time to see the flaring folds of an eiderdown as it descended over her. She screamed, but the sound was smothered in the soft, padded coverlet. Strong arms rolled her over, encasing her in a cocoon of bedclothes, then she was lifted, struggling, into the air. Her arms were confined, she could not see, yet she knew when she was carried from the room and down the stairs. The fresh night air penetrated to her, there was an instant when she was held close against a hard body and manuevered through a small opening, then she heard the sound of carriage wheels.

She lay in a man's arms, a single man; she had heard, felt, no other. How had it been possible for him to enter her mother's house and take her away? Were the servants deaf? Or had they, perhaps, been bribed? Neither explanation could account for her mother's lack of intervention.

There was another explanation. No one, least of all Madame Mayfield, would question the right of Rafael Navarro to remove her. Resignation drained her strength, and she lay still.

The carriage halted. By sound she could trace their progress across the banquette, along the echoing passage of the *porte-cochere,* over the stones of the court and step by ringing step up the spiral staircase. They crossed a carpeted floor. The man paused. Catherine braced herself for a fall. Then she was laid gently upon the soft mattress of a bed and the eiderdown stripped away.

She drew a deep breath, trying to find within herself some anger, some indignation to use as protection. There was nothing except the mute fear of self-betrayal. Slowly she lifted her eyes to brave the jet black mockery of her husband's.

He seated himself on the edge of the bed and leaned over her. "Tiresome," he said, taking up the lock of honey-gold hair that lay across her breasts. "When will you learn to stay where you belong, in my bed?"

Her voice was a thread of sound. "Is that where I belong?"

"There, and at my left hand, near my heart, always."

"You don't understand—" she said, turning her face away.

381

"Nor do you, sweet Catherine. *Je t'aime*, I love you. You are my life, my soul. Nothing, not even death itself, can take you from me, for I will hold you enshrined in my heart for all time."

Her eyes were melting amber pools of desolation. The ache in her throat was a sharp and cutting thing. She could not have spoken, even if she could discover the words that would effect her release.

"Nor," he continued, his voice hardening, "will I permit you to leave me. If you wanted freedom you should never have come to Alhambra, never given yourself beneath a magnolia tree. I thought then you felt something for me. If I was wrong you may tell me so, but I warn you, it will make no difference."

Moistening her lips, she began, "I—don't love—"

"Take care. Will you perjure yourself for the sake of an old grudge?"

The warning with its hint of censure undermined her resolution. Her chin came up. "I bear you no grudge," she replied carefully.

"Nor love?" he said.

All she had to do was confirm it. The moments ticked by. Caught by the compelling darkness of his eyes, she could not force the words past her lips.

Abruptly his face cleared. "I should be flogged for a dolt," he said quietly. "It is the child."

"Rif? No—"

"No indeed, my precious idiot. Your child—and mine!"

"How—how can you know? she whispered, the color draining from her face then returning in burning spots to her cheekbones.

"Did you really expect me not to see, and feel, the change? Your body, chérie, is as known to me as my own, perhaps more so. I have an intimate interest in the slightest alteration."

Which meant he had guessed almost before she was aware of it herself. "I might have gained weight," she said in unreasoning obstinance.

"Not, I think, under the circumstances. Besides," he said gently, "your mother confirmed it."

382

Her lashes veiled her eyes. "She had no right to interfere."

"She only answered my questions. You will understand I was at something of a loss when I returned to find you gone."

"And did one of the questions you asked deal with whether you were in fact responsible for my condition?"

He covered her hands where she was pleating the bedsheet. "No, it did not, but she informed me that you were afraid to tell me I was to be a father. Why, Catherine?"

"You must know why. I tried once to tell you there had never been another man but you. You wouldn't listen. You—you forgave me!"

Angry tears sparkled in her eyes as she accused him. Seeing them, he smiled. "Does that still rankle? I'm sorry. Allow me, please, the weakness of jealous pride and anxiety. You had dared to leave me. I had searched for you so long with fading hope that when I found you I wanted to punish you—or make violent love to you—I couldn't decide which. I forgot that in hurting you I also hurt myself."

"You knew what I wanted to say, you were convinced it was the truth?"

He inclined his head in a slow assent. "I knew in my heart, if not in my mind. I knew your idealism, the integrity and sensibility that would ultimately reject such a life. And I needed convincing, there was evidence in your favor. Dan, who had seen you in the Harrelson house, led the ladies there to talk of you. Were you aware they called you 'the nun'? Some were malicious, most gave you an envious respect, a few held you in affection. All were agreed you were pining for a man believed to be your husband."

"How romantic of them," she said in a voice like breaking glass.

"Doubtless," he answered, "but was it true?"

She looked away, the candlelight moving with an ivory sheen across her face. He should be forced to pay recompense for the wound he had inflicted. Yet, wasn't the fullness of his confession enough? Wasn't it all she had ever wanted? "It was," she replied.

"And now?"

His voice was inplacable, the question impossible to ignore or evade. Her voice reduced to a whisper, she said, "It still is."

He dragged her into his arms and set his mouth to hers.

When she was permitted to draw breath at last, her smile was tremulous and there was a drowsy languor in her gold-flecked gaze. "I do love you, Rafael Navarro."

The embers of the fire burned on the hearth in the darkened room. Their light glowed orange-red in the black of her husband's eyes as he came to her. She did not hesitate. Throwing back the coverlet, she reached out to him, unafraid.